TIME FLYZ

TIME TRAP

ZONDERVAN

Time Trap
Copyright © 2009 by Ben Avery
Illustrations © 2009 by Brethren Entertainment Studios

Requests for information should be addressed to:

Zondervan, *Grand Rapids, Michigan* 49530

Library of Congress Cataloging-in-Publication Data

Avery, Ben, 1974-
  Time trap / story by Ben Avery ; art by Scott Wong and Brethren Entertainment Studios.
    p. cm. — (TimeFlyz)
  Summary: Trapped by a menacing Venus fly trap, Laurel is left alone to rescue the other
TimeFlyz, while also trying to keep famous astronomer Galileo out of prison and away from
the evil Darchon.
  ISBN 978-0-310-71366-1 (softcover)
  1. Graphic novels. [1. Graphic novels. 2. Time travel — Fiction. 3. Galileo, 1564-1642 — Fiction.
4. Christian life — Fiction. 5. Italy — History — 1559-1789 — Fiction.] I. Wong, Scott, ill. II. Brethren Entertainment. III. Title.
  PZ7.7.A94Ti 2009
  741.5'945 — dc22
                                                          2008045625

Series Editor: Bud Rogers
Managing Art Director: Merit Kathan

Printed in the United States of America

09 10 11 12 13 14 • 22 21 20 19 18 17 16 15 14 13 12 11 10 9 8 7 6 5 4 3 2 1

GRAPHIC NOVELS

TIMEFLYZ

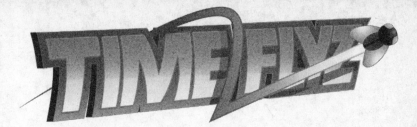

TIME TRAP

SERIES EDITOR: BUD ROGERS

STORY BY BEN AVERY

ART BY SCOTT WONG
AND BRETHREN ENTERTAINMENT STUDIOS

LETTERING AND PRODUCTION: NOLEN LEE

STUDIO MANAGEMENT: MASATAKA IHARA

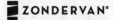

ZONDERVAN®

ZONDERVAN.com/
AUTHORTRACKER
follow your favorite authors

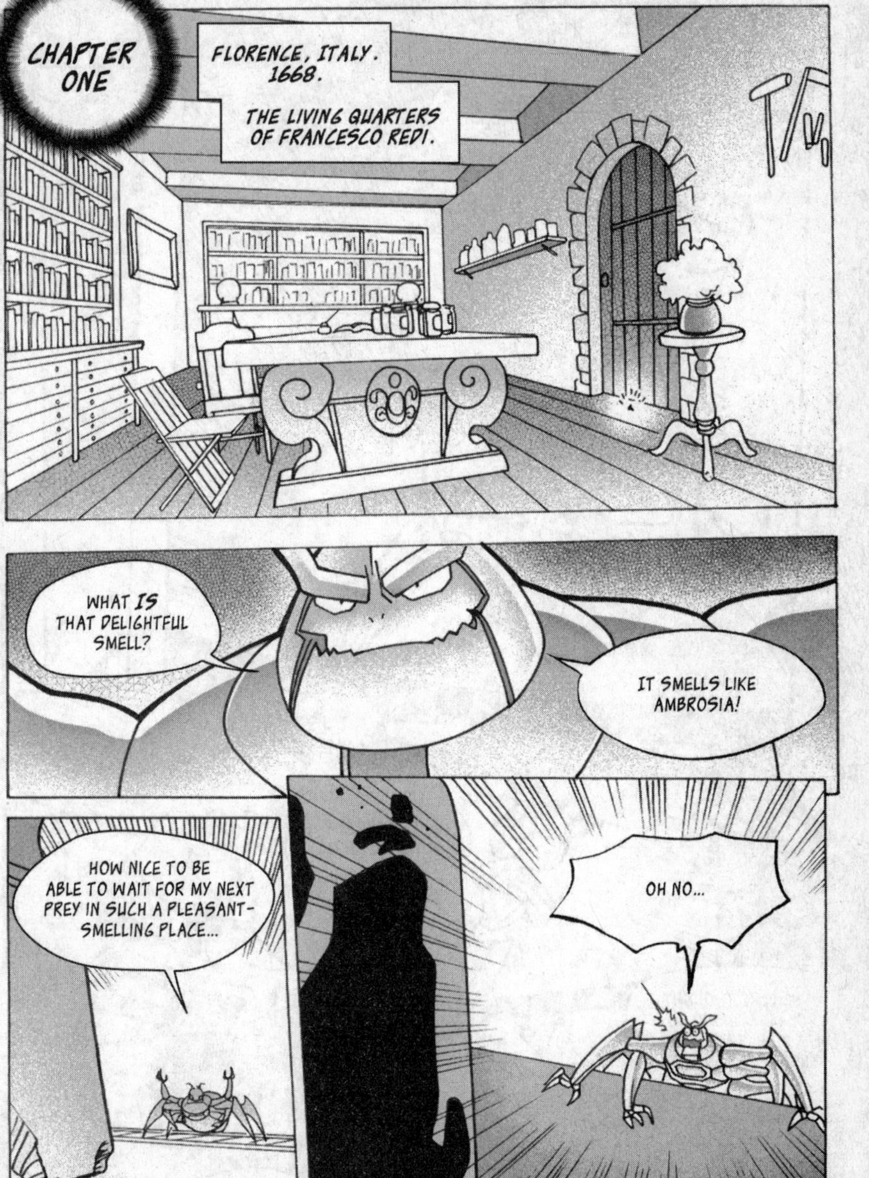
CHAPTER ONE
FLORENCE, ITALY. 1668.
THE LIVING QUARTERS OF FRANCESCO REDI.
WHAT IS THAT DELIGHTFUL SMELL?
IT SMELLS LIKE AMBROSIA!
HOW NICE TO BE ABLE TO WAIT FOR MY NEXT PREY IN SUCH A PLEASANT-SMELLING PLACE...
OH NO...

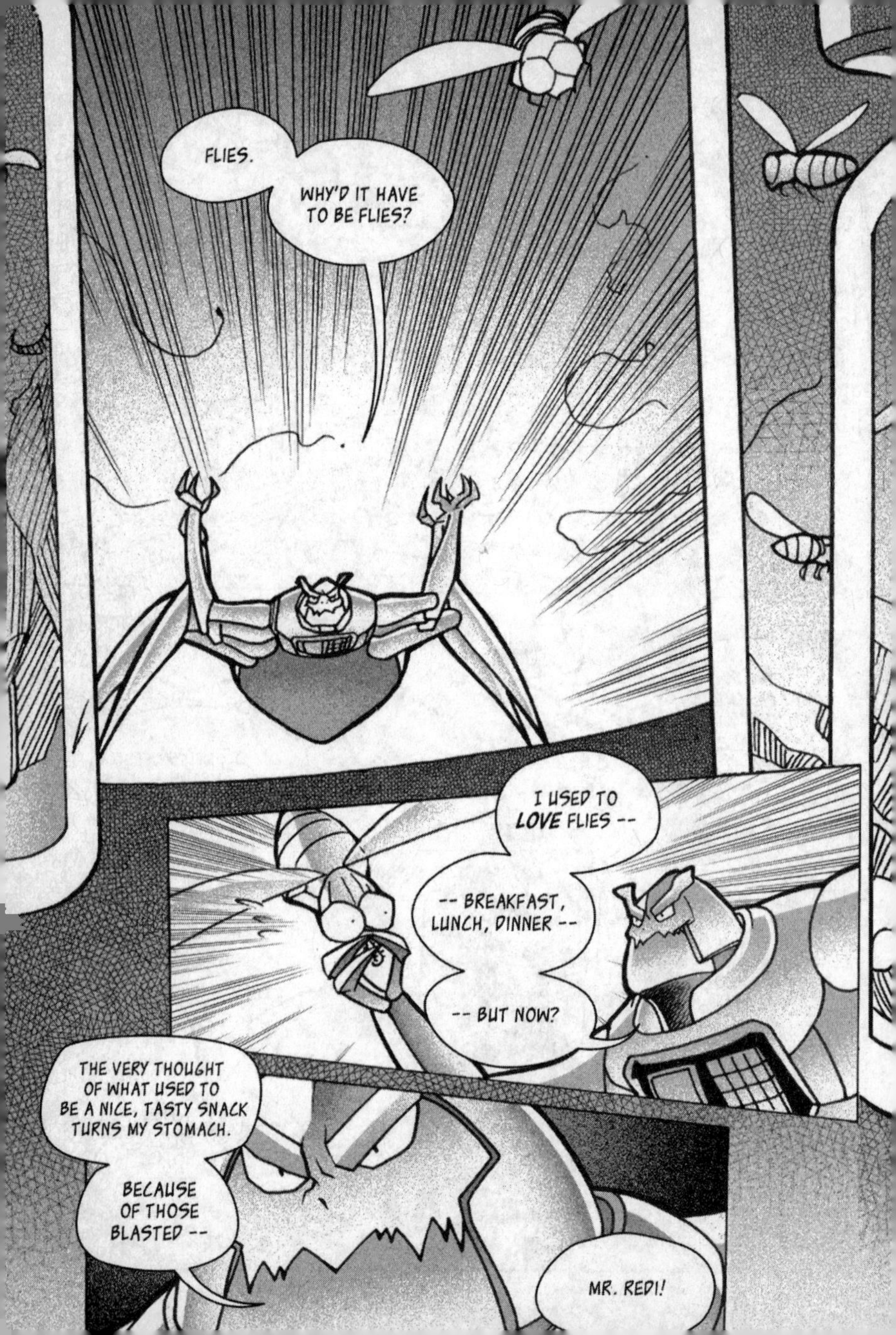
FLIES.
WHY'D IT HAVE TO BE FLIES?
I USED TO *LOVE* FLIES --
-- BREAKFAST, LUNCH, DINNER --
-- BUT NOW?
THE VERY THOUGHT OF WHAT USED TO BE A NICE, TASTY SNACK TURNS MY STOMACH.
BECAUSE OF THOSE BLASTED --
MR. REDI!

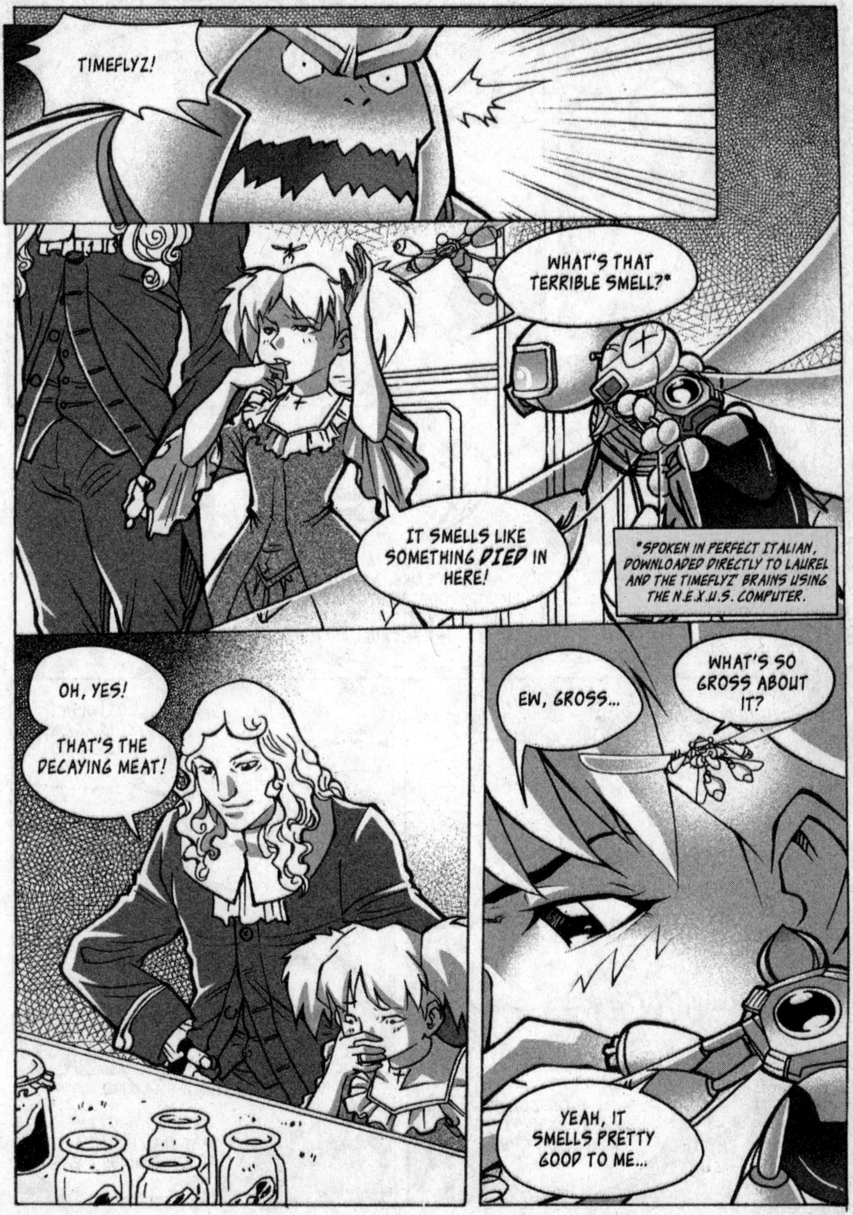
TIMEFLYZ!
WHAT'S THAT TERRIBLE SMELL?*
IT SMELLS LIKE SOMETHING DIED IN HERE!
*SPOKEN IN PERFECT ITALIAN, DOWNLOADED DIRECTLY TO LAUREL AND THE TIMEFLYZ' BRAINS USING THE N.E.X.U.S. COMPUTER.
OH, YES!
THAT'S THE DECAYING MEAT!
EW, GROSS...
WHAT'S SO GROSS ABOUT IT?
YEAH, IT SMELLS PRETTY GOOD TO ME...

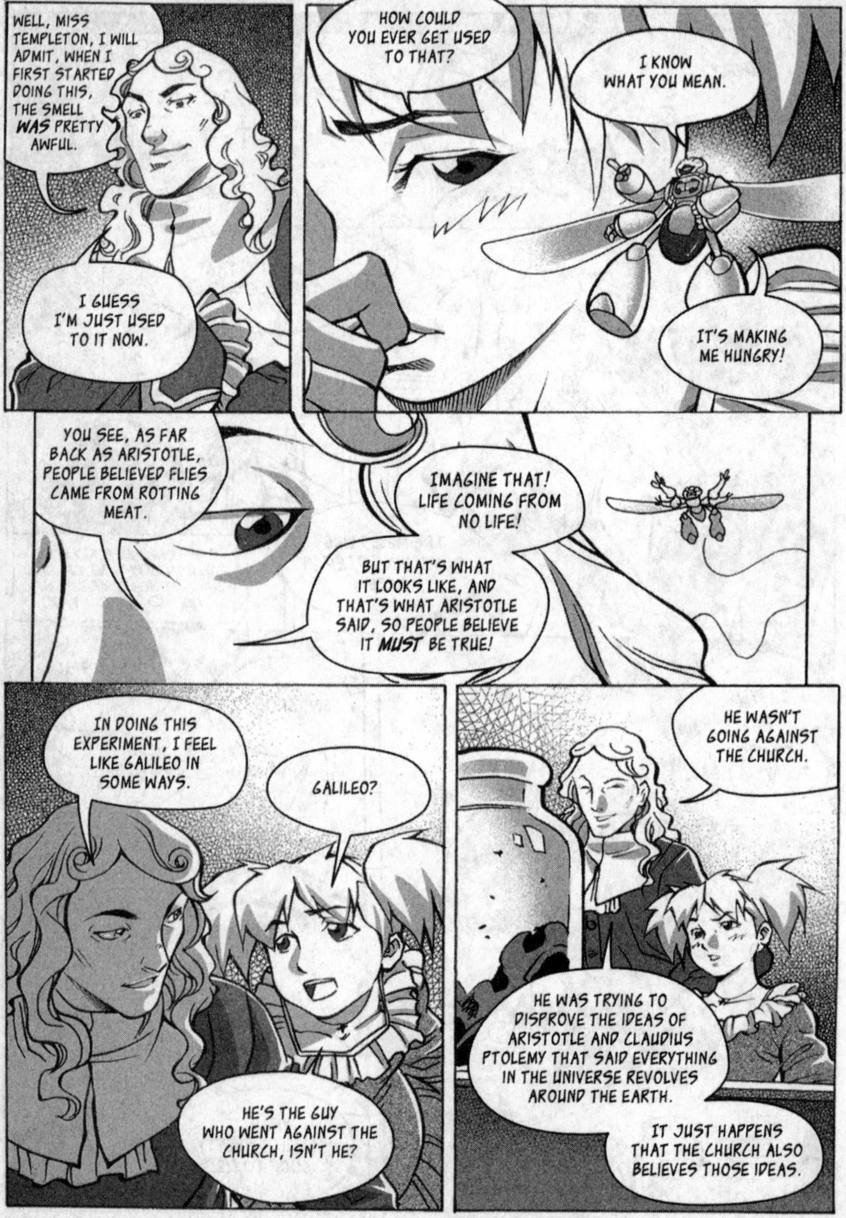
WELL, MISS TEMPLETON, I WILL ADMIT, WHEN I FIRST STARTED DOING THIS, THE SMELL *WAS* PRETTY AWFUL.
I GUESS I'M JUST USED TO IT NOW.
HOW COULD YOU EVER GET USED TO THAT?
I KNOW WHAT YOU MEAN.
IT'S MAKING ME HUNGRY!
YOU SEE, AS FAR BACK AS ARISTOTLE, PEOPLE BELIEVED FLIES CAME FROM ROTTING MEAT.
IMAGINE THAT! LIFE COMING FROM NO LIFE!
BUT THAT'S WHAT IT LOOKS LIKE, AND THAT'S WHAT ARISTOTLE SAID, SO PEOPLE BELIEVE IT *MUST* BE TRUE!
IN DOING THIS EXPERIMENT, I FEEL LIKE GALILEO IN SOME WAYS.
GALILEO?
HE'S THE GUY WHO WENT AGAINST THE CHURCH, ISN'T HE?
HE WASN'T GOING AGAINST THE CHURCH.
HE WAS TRYING TO DISPROVE THE IDEAS OF ARISTOTLE AND CLAUDIUS PTOLEMY THAT SAID EVERYTHING IN THE UNIVERSE REVOLVES AROUND THE EARTH.
IT JUST HAPPENS THAT THE CHURCH ALSO BELIEVES THOSE IDEAS.

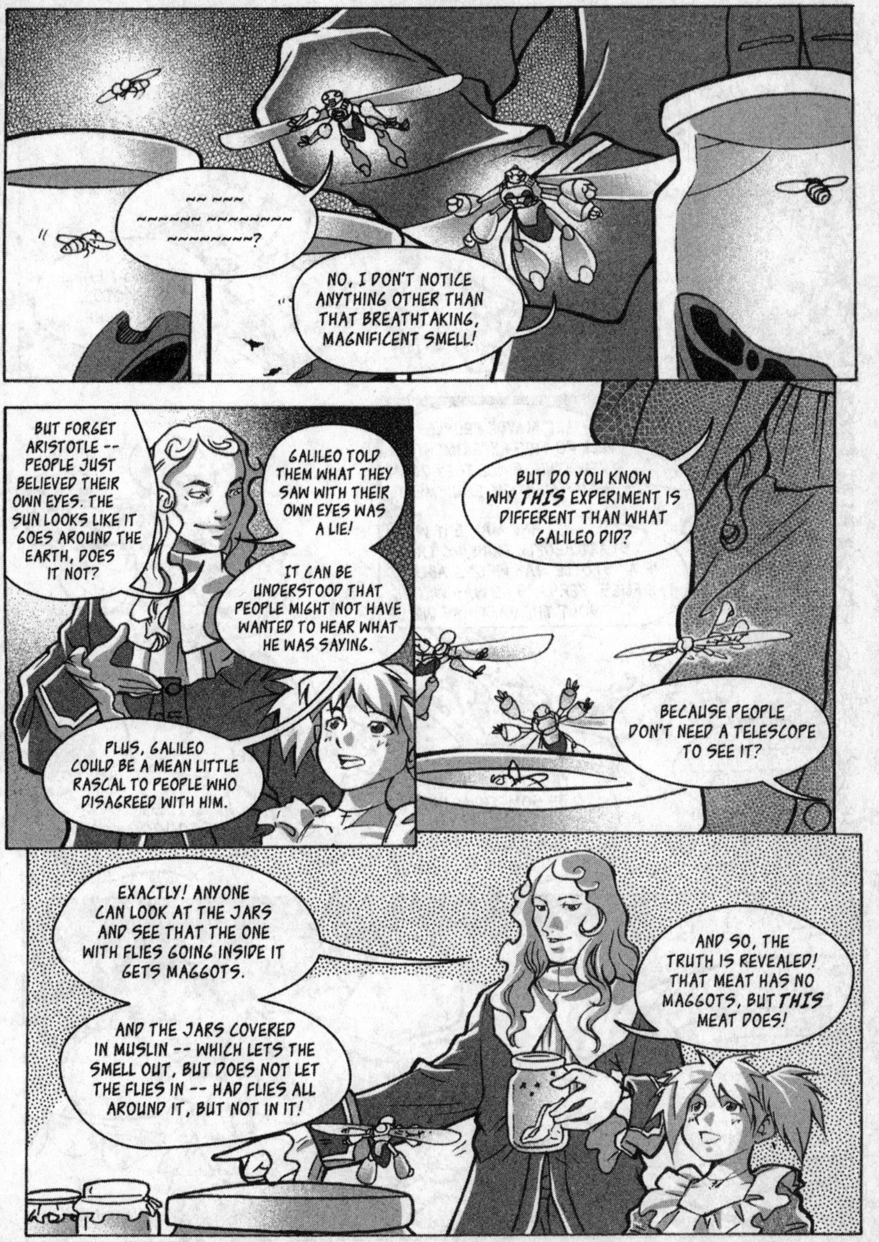
~~ ~~~ ~~~~~~ ~~~~~~~~ ~~~~~~~~?
NO, I DON'T NOTICE ANYTHING OTHER THAN THAT BREATHTAKING, MAGNIFICENT SMELL!
BUT FORGET ARISTOTLE -- PEOPLE JUST BELIEVED THEIR OWN EYES. THE SUN LOOKS LIKE IT GOES AROUND THE EARTH, DOES IT NOT?
GALILEO TOLD THEM WHAT THEY SAW WITH THEIR OWN EYES WAS A LIE!
IT CAN BE UNDERSTOOD THAT PEOPLE MIGHT NOT HAVE WANTED TO HEAR WHAT HE WAS SAYING.
PLUS, GALILEO COULD BE A MEAN LITTLE RASCAL TO PEOPLE WHO DISAGREED WITH HIM.
BUT DO YOU KNOW WHY *THIS* EXPERIMENT IS DIFFERENT THAN WHAT GALILEO DID?
BECAUSE PEOPLE DON'T NEED A TELESCOPE TO SEE IT?
EXACTLY! ANYONE CAN LOOK AT THE JARS AND SEE THAT THE ONE WITH FLIES GOING INSIDE IT GETS MAGGOTS.
AND THE JARS COVERED IN MUSLIN -- WHICH LETS THE SMELL OUT, BUT DOES NOT LET THE FLIES IN -- HAD FLIES ALL AROUND IT, BUT NOT IN IT!
AND SO, THE TRUTH IS REVEALED! THAT MEAT HAS NO MAGGOTS, BUT *THIS* MEAT DOES!

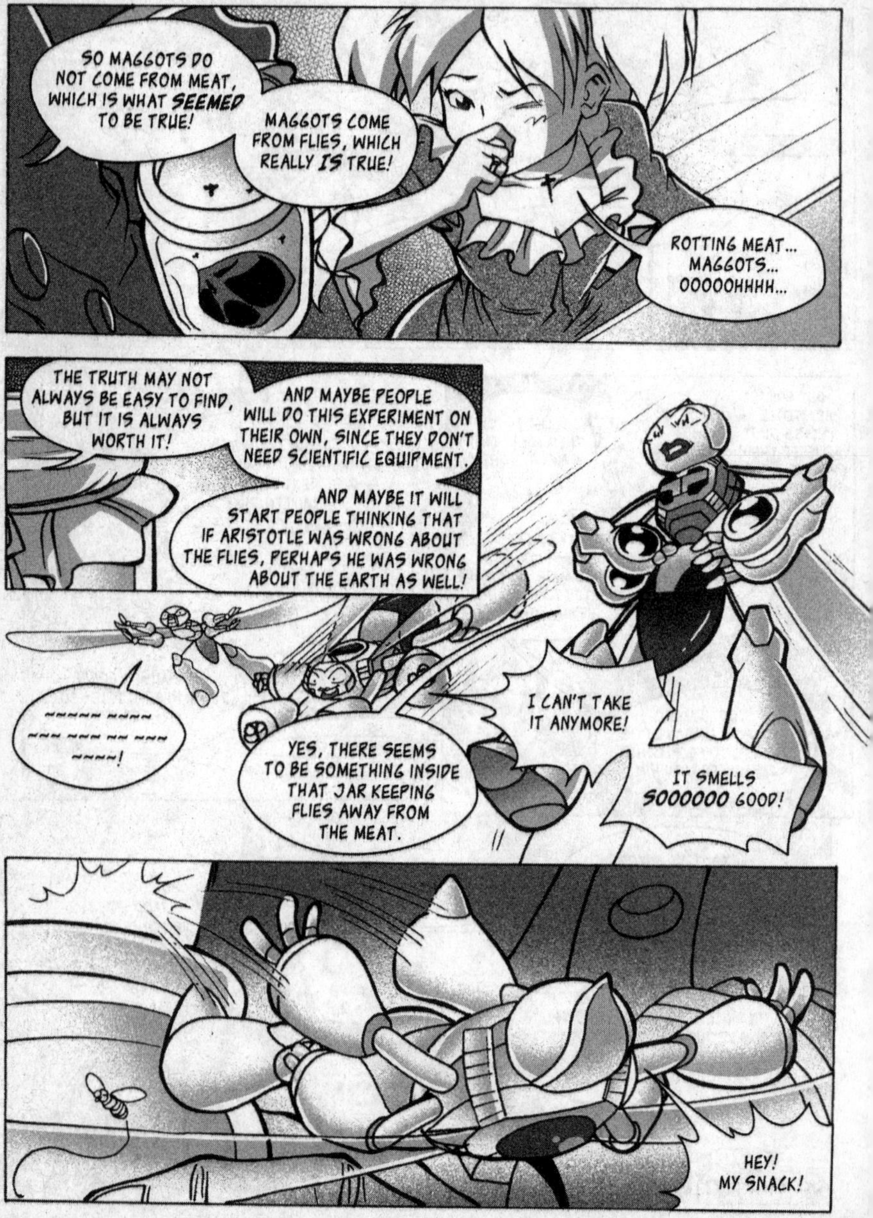
SO MAGGOTS DO NOT COME FROM MEAT, WHICH IS WHAT *SEEMED* TO BE TRUE!
MAGGOTS COME FROM FLIES, WHICH REALLY *IS* TRUE!
ROTTING MEAT... MAGGOTS... OOOOOHHHH...
THE TRUTH MAY NOT ALWAYS BE EASY TO FIND, BUT IT IS ALWAYS WORTH IT!
AND MAYBE PEOPLE WILL DO THIS EXPERIMENT ON THEIR OWN, SINCE THEY DON'T NEED SCIENTIFIC EQUIPMENT.
AND MAYBE IT WILL START PEOPLE THINKING THAT IF ARISTOTLE WAS WRONG ABOUT THE FLIES, PERHAPS HE WAS WRONG ABOUT THE EARTH AS WELL!
YES, THERE SEEMS TO BE SOMETHING INSIDE THAT JAR KEEPING FLIES AWAY FROM THE MEAT.
I CAN'T TAKE IT ANYMORE!
IT SMELLS **SOOOOOO** GOOD!
HEY! MY SNACK!

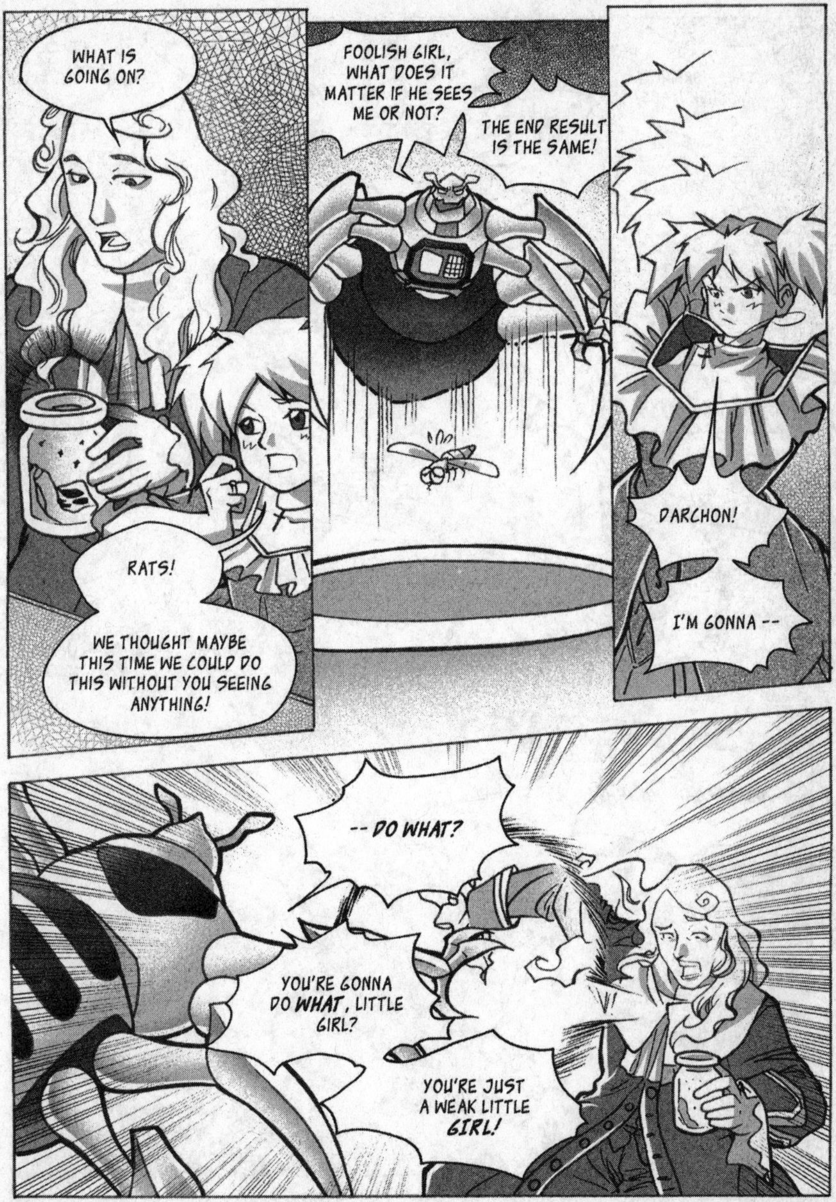
WHAT IS GOING ON?
RATS!
WE THOUGHT MAYBE THIS TIME WE COULD DO THIS WITHOUT YOU SEEING ANYTHING!
FOOLISH GIRL, WHAT DOES IT MATTER IF HE SEES ME OR NOT?
THE END RESULT IS THE SAME!
DARCHON!
I'M GONNA --
-- DO WHAT?
YOU'RE GONNA DO WHAT, LITTLE GIRL?
YOU'RE JUST A WEAK LITTLE GIRL!

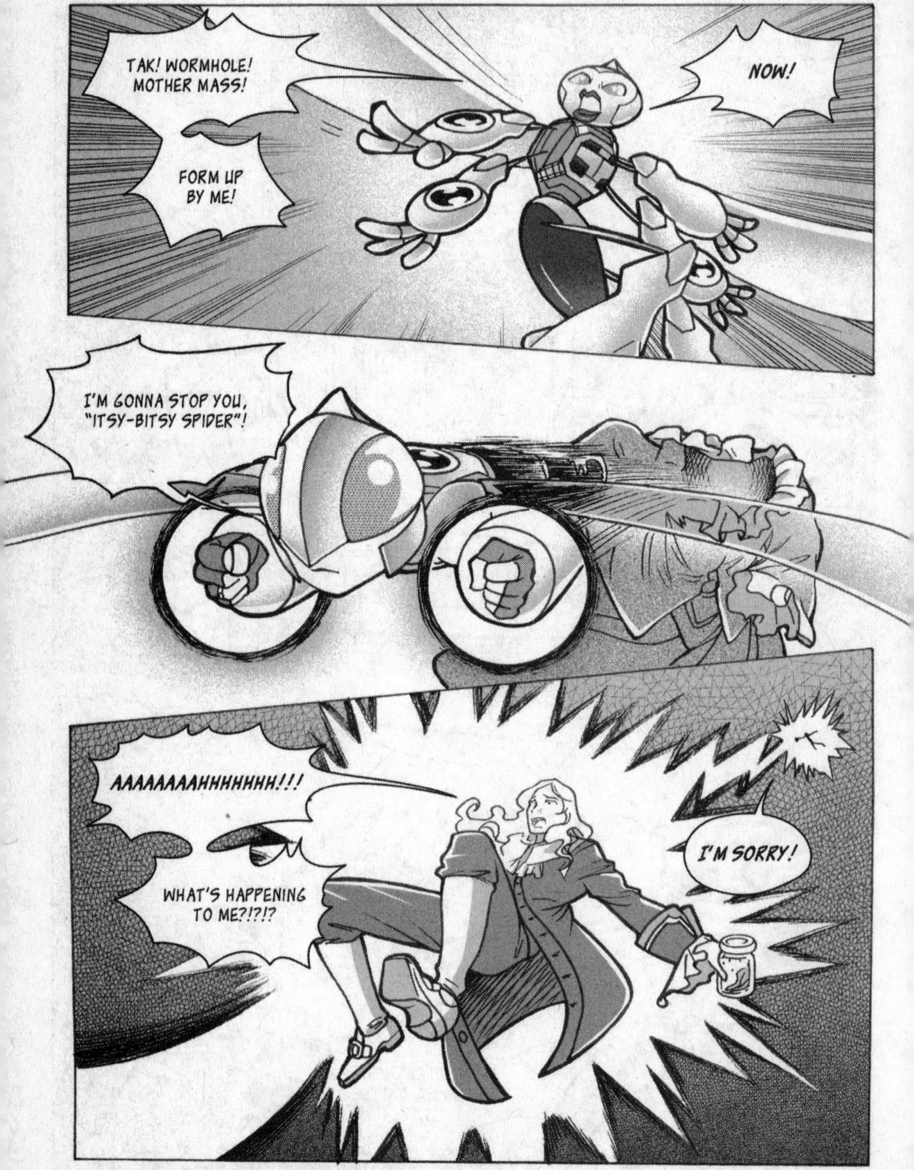
TAK! WORMHOLE! MOTHER MASS!
FORM UP BY ME!
NOW!
I'M GONNA STOP YOU, "ITSY-BITSY SPIDER"!
AAAAAAAAHHHHHHH!!!
WHAT'S HAPPENING TO ME?!?!?
I'M SORRY!

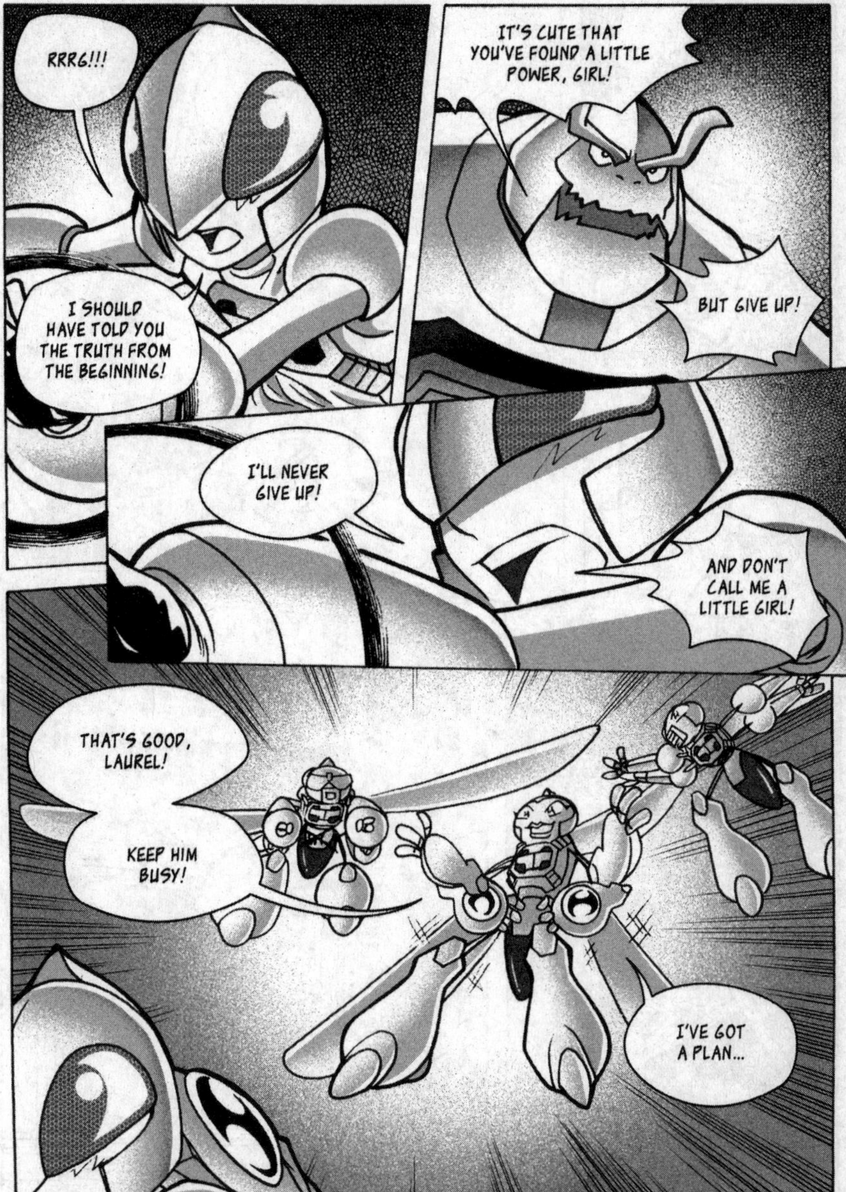
RRRG!!!
I SHOULD HAVE TOLD YOU THE TRUTH FROM THE BEGINNING!
IT'S CUTE THAT YOU'VE FOUND A LITTLE POWER, GIRL!
BUT GIVE UP!
I'LL NEVER GIVE UP!
AND DON'T CALL ME A LITTLE GIRL!
THAT'S GOOD, LAUREL!
KEEP HIM BUSY!
I'VE GOT A PLAN...

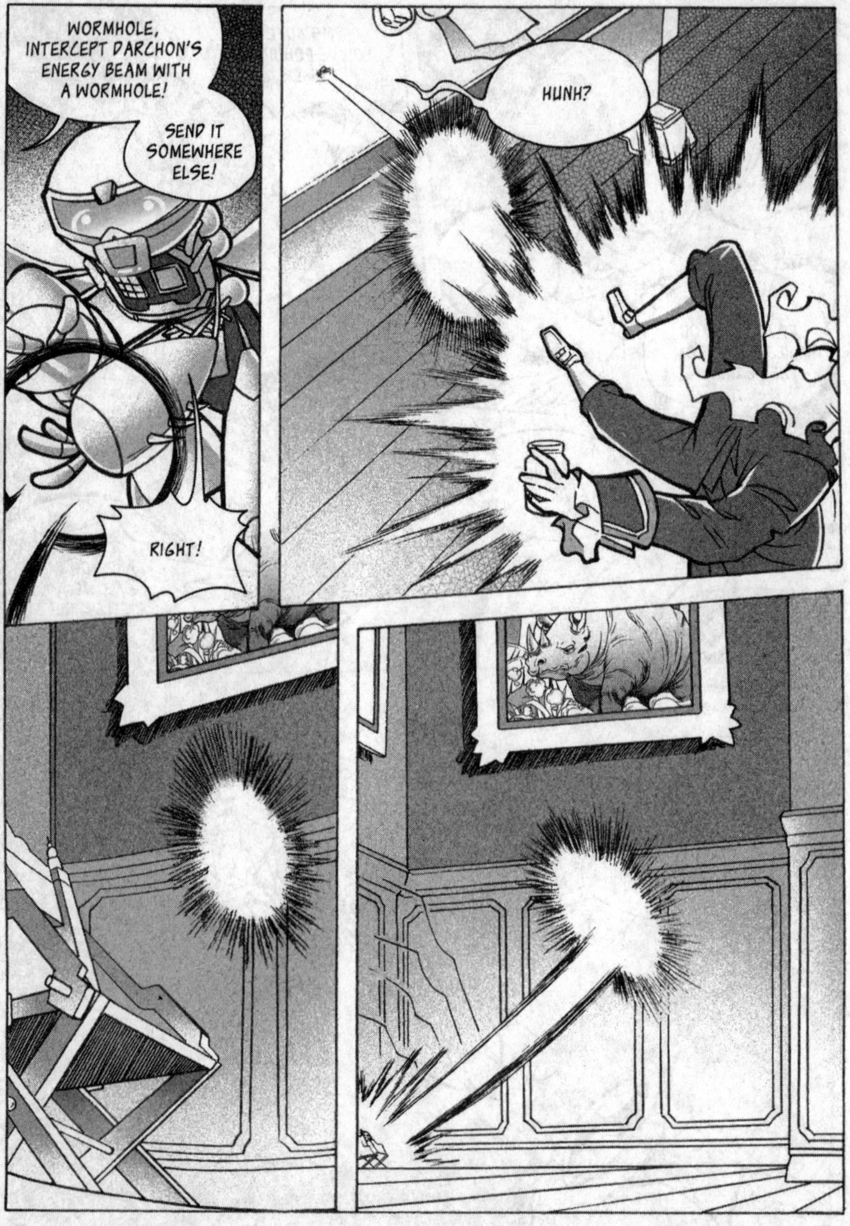
WORMHOLE, INTERCEPT DARCHON'S ENERGY BEAM WITH A WORMHOLE!
SEND IT SOMEWHERE ELSE!
RIGHT!
HUNH?

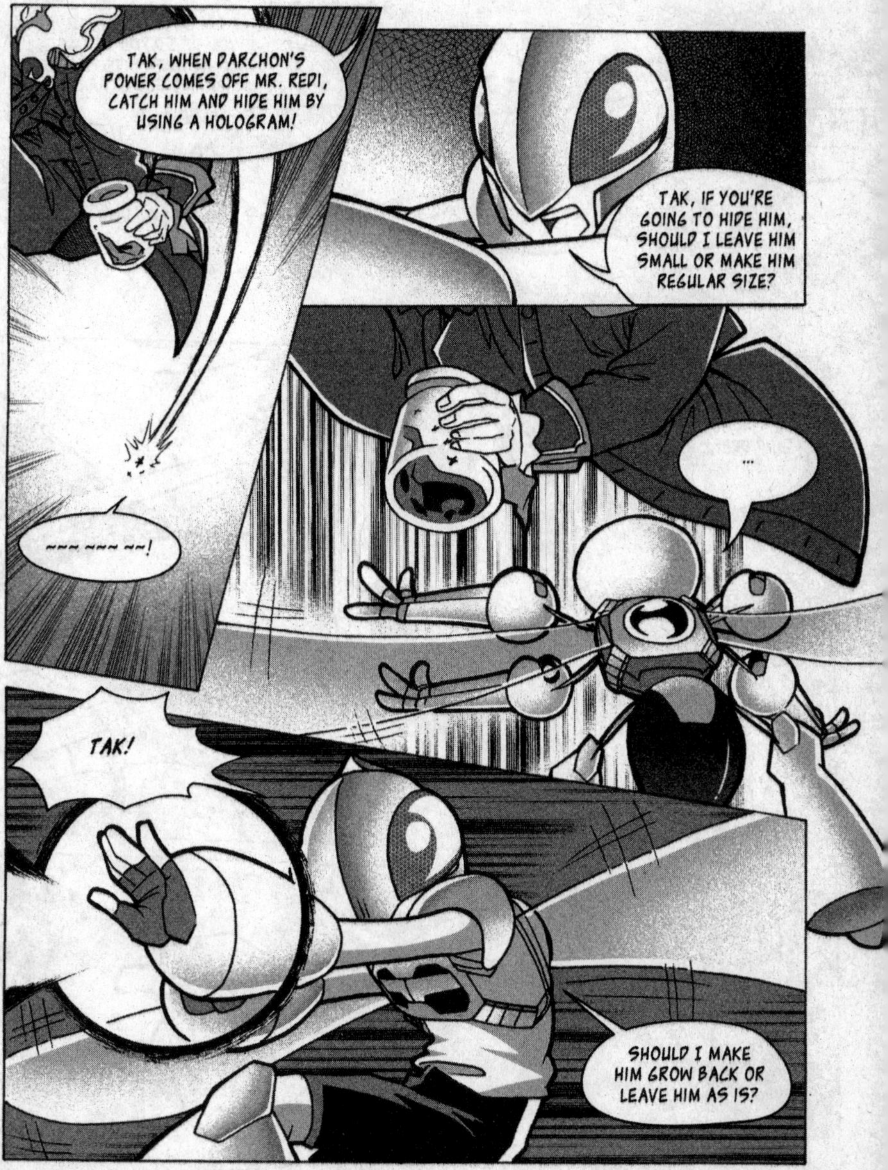
TAK, WHEN DARCHON'S POWER COMES OFF MR. REDI, CATCH HIM AND HIDE HIM BY USING A HOLOGRAM!
TAK, IF YOU'RE GOING TO HIDE HIM, SHOULD I LEAVE HIM SMALL OR MAKE HIM REGULAR SIZE?
~~~ ~~~ ~~!
...
TAK!
SHOULD I MAKE HIM GROW BACK OR LEAVE HIM AS IS?
~~~

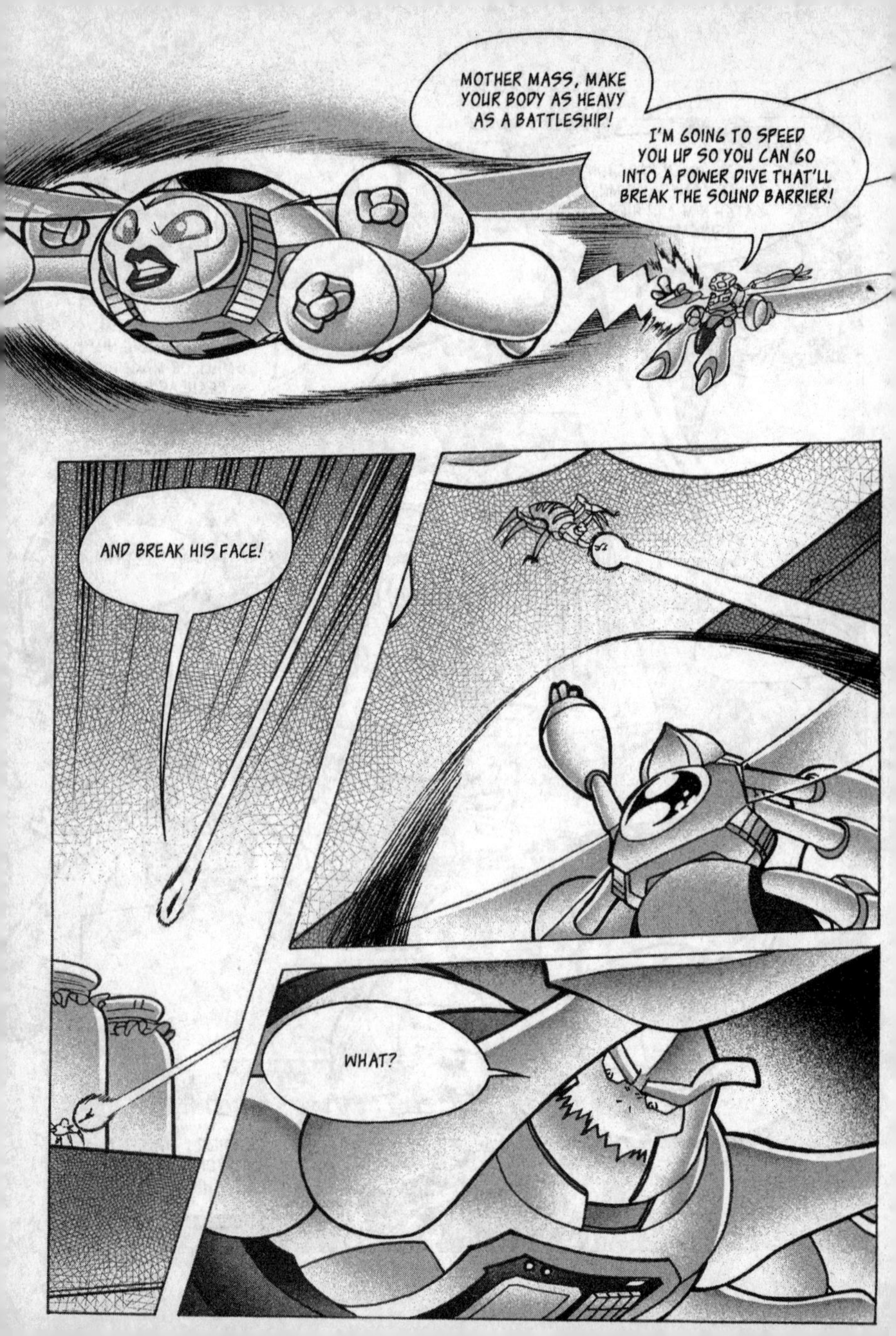
MOTHER MASS, MAKE YOUR BODY AS HEAVY AS A BATTLESHIP!
I'M GOING TO SPEED YOU UP SO YOU CAN GO INTO A POWER DIVE THAT'LL BREAK THE SOUND BARRIER!
AND BREAK HIS FACE!
WHAT?

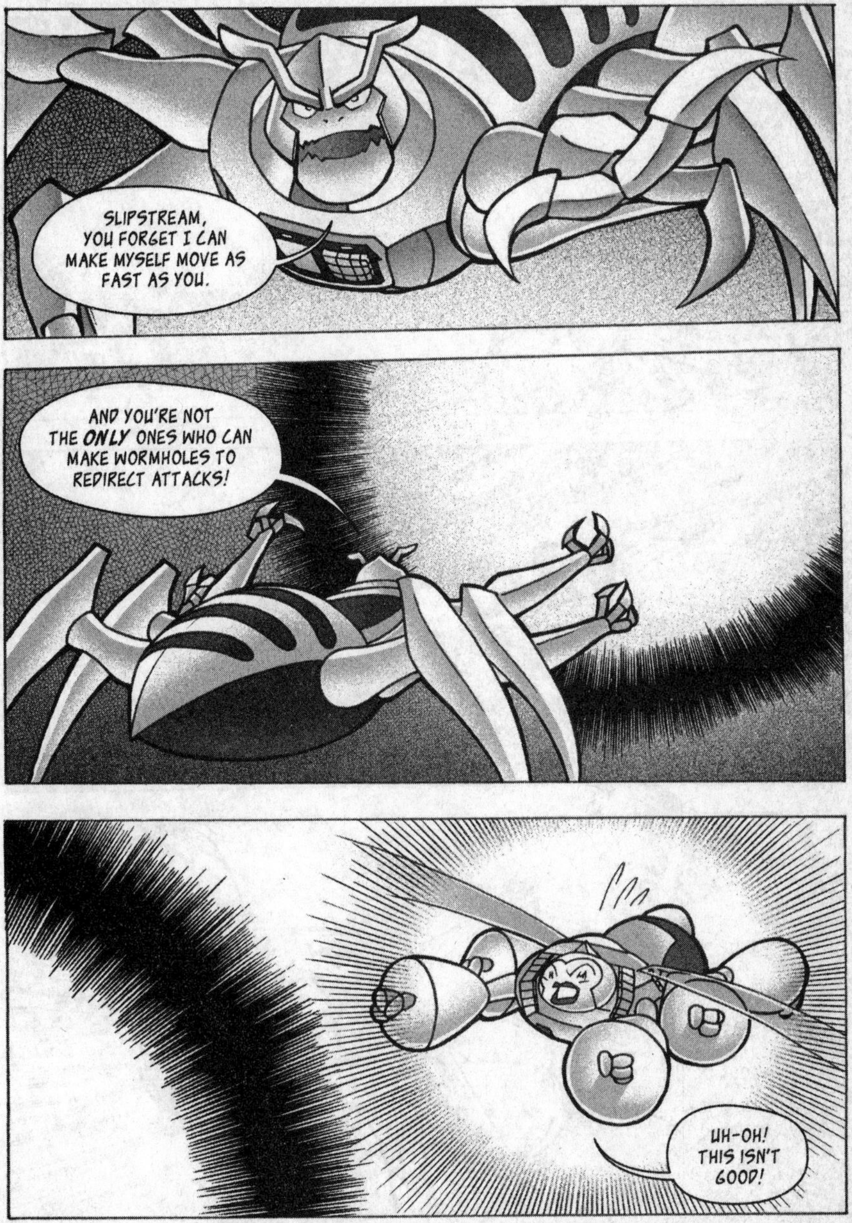
SLIPSTREAM, YOU FORGET I CAN MAKE MYSELF MOVE AS FAST AS YOU.
AND YOU'RE NOT THE ONLY ONES WHO CAN MAKE WORMHOLES TO REDIRECT ATTACKS!
UH-OH! THIS ISN'T GOOD!

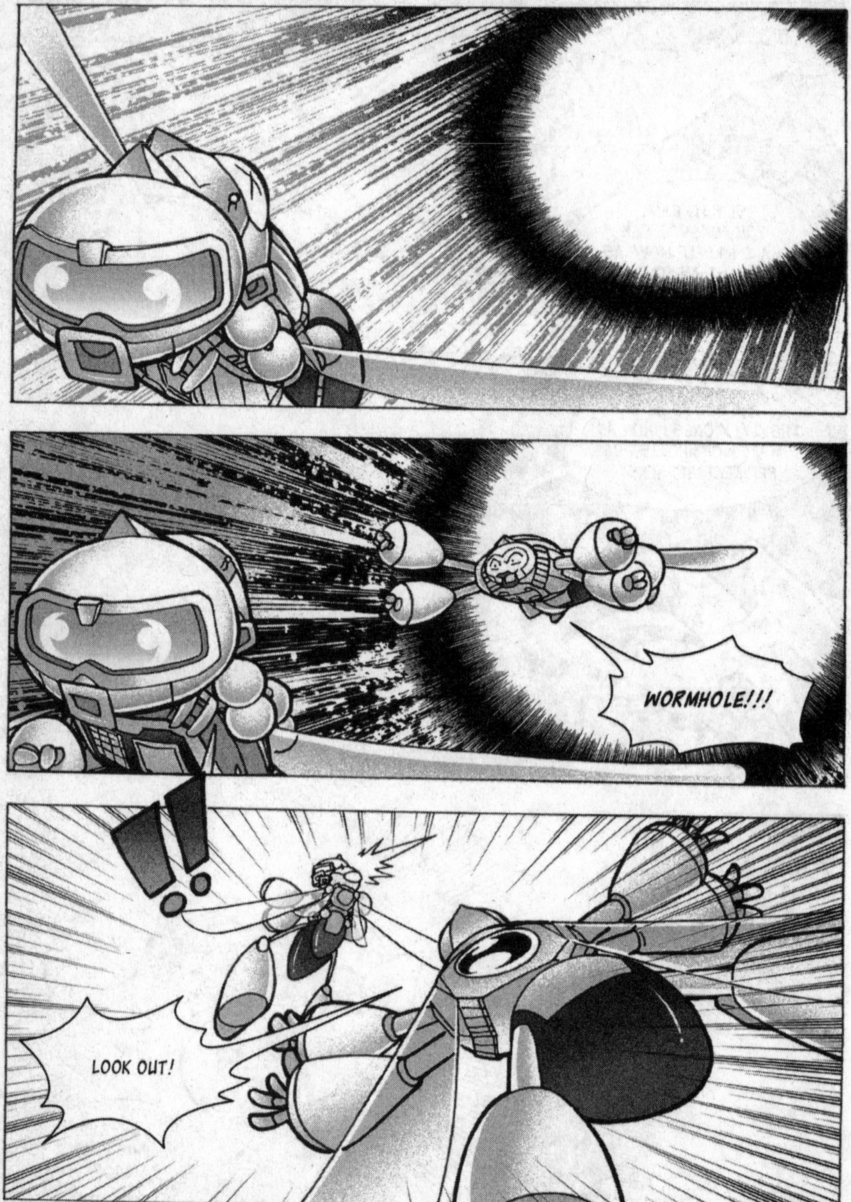
WORMHOLE!!!
LOOK OUT!

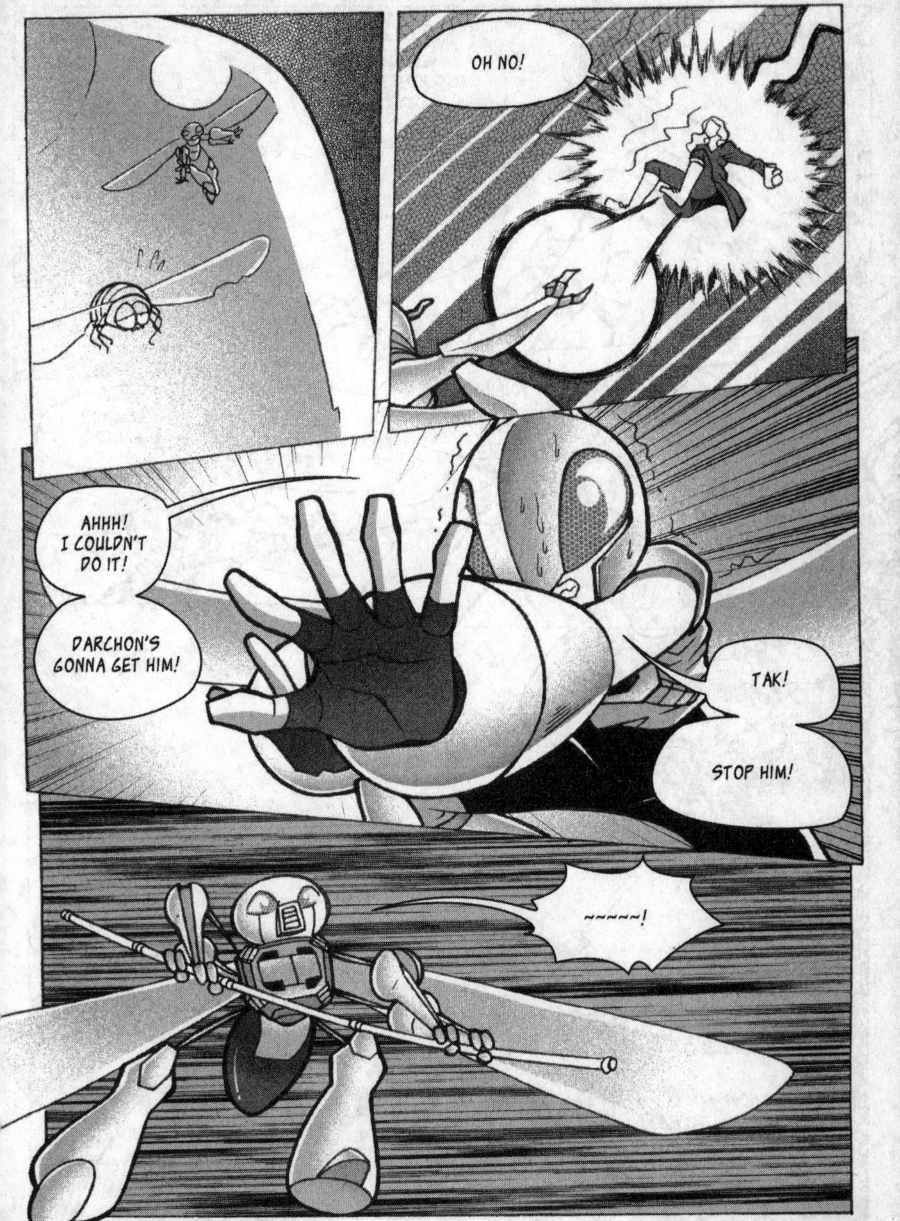
OH NO!
AHHH! I COULDN'T DO IT!
DARCHON'S GONNA GET HIM!
TAK!
STOP HIM!
~~~~~!
~~~~~

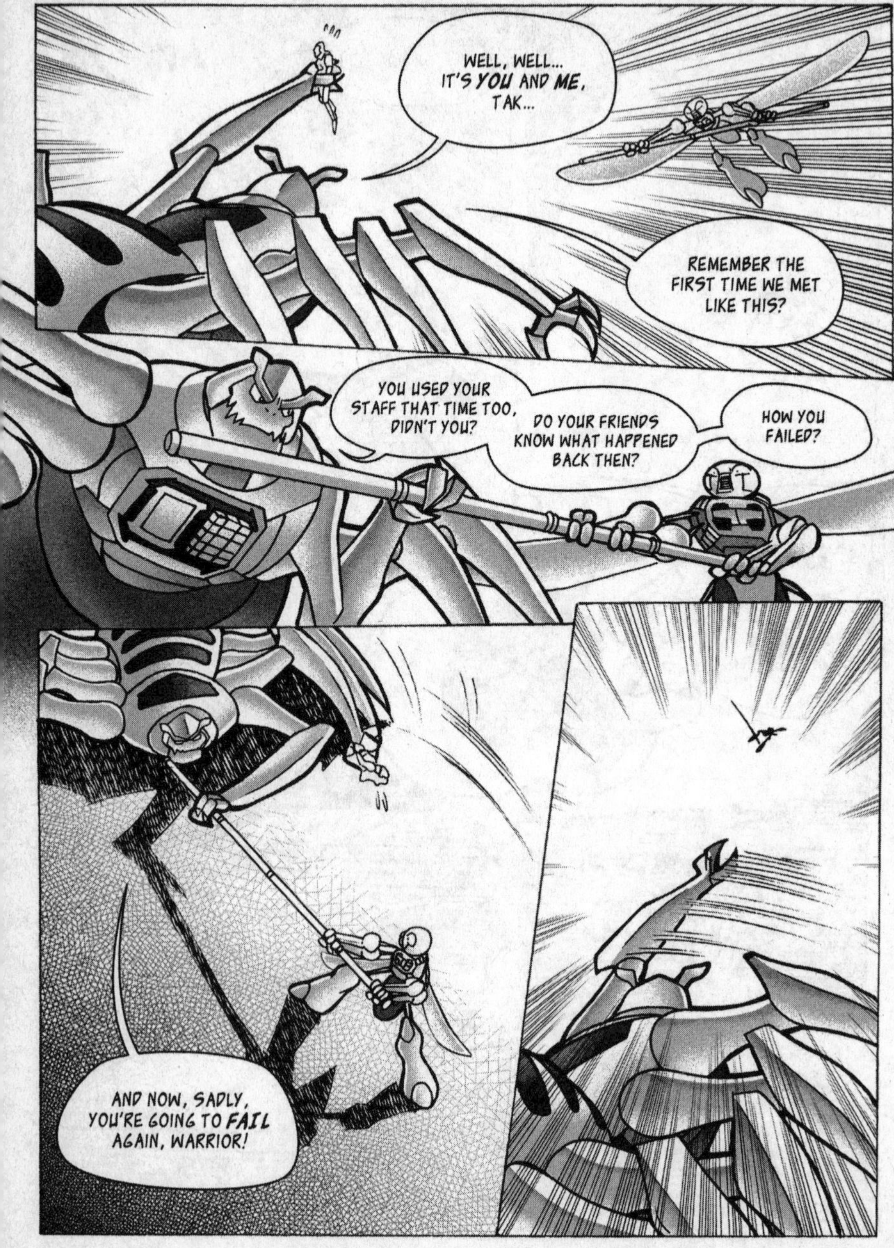
WELL, WELL...
IT'S *YOU* AND *ME*, TAK...
REMEMBER THE FIRST TIME WE MET LIKE THIS?
YOU USED YOUR STAFF THAT TIME TOO, DIDN'T YOU?
DO YOUR FRIENDS KNOW WHAT HAPPENED BACK THEN?
HOW YOU FAILED?
AND NOW, SADLY, YOU'RE GOING TO *FAIL* AGAIN, WARRIOR!

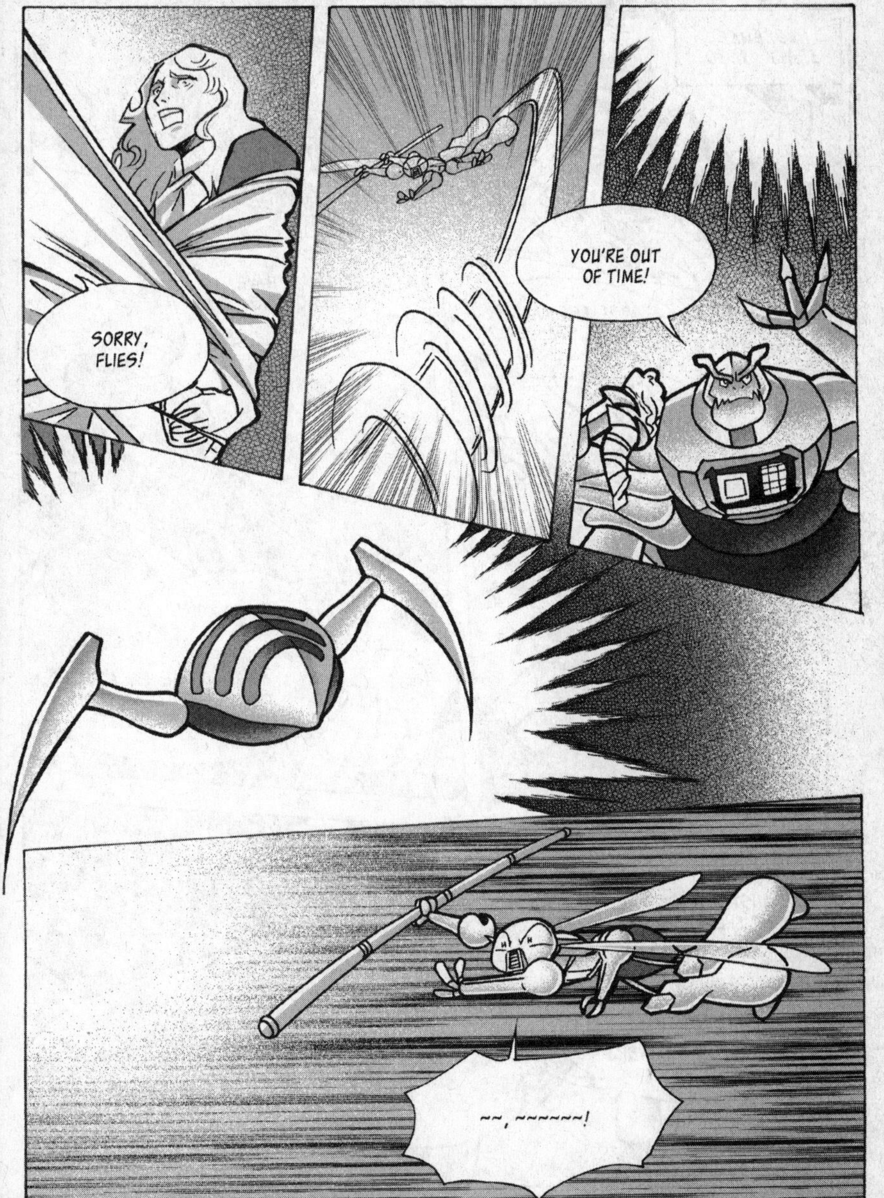
SORRY, FLIES!
YOU'RE OUT OF TIME!
~~, ~~~~~~!

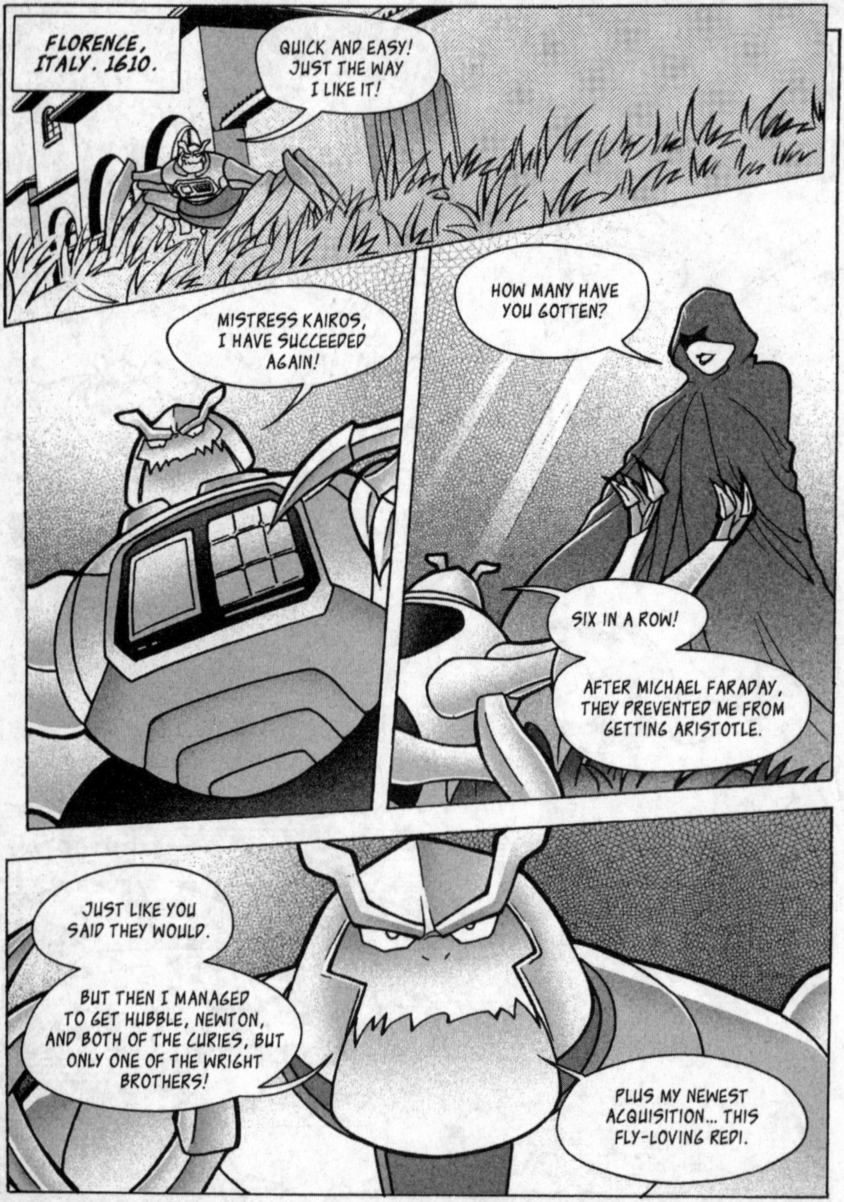
FLORENCE, ITALY. 1610.
QUICK AND EASY! JUST THE WAY I LIKE IT!
MISTRESS KAIROS, I HAVE SUCCEEDED AGAIN!
HOW MANY HAVE YOU GOTTEN?
SIX IN A ROW!
AFTER MICHAEL FARADAY, THEY PREVENTED ME FROM GETTING ARISTOTLE.
JUST LIKE YOU SAID THEY WOULD.
BUT THEN I MANAGED TO GET HUBBLE, NEWTON, AND BOTH OF THE CURIES, BUT ONLY ONE OF THE WRIGHT BROTHERS!
PLUS MY NEWEST ACQUISITION... THIS FLY-LOVING REDI.

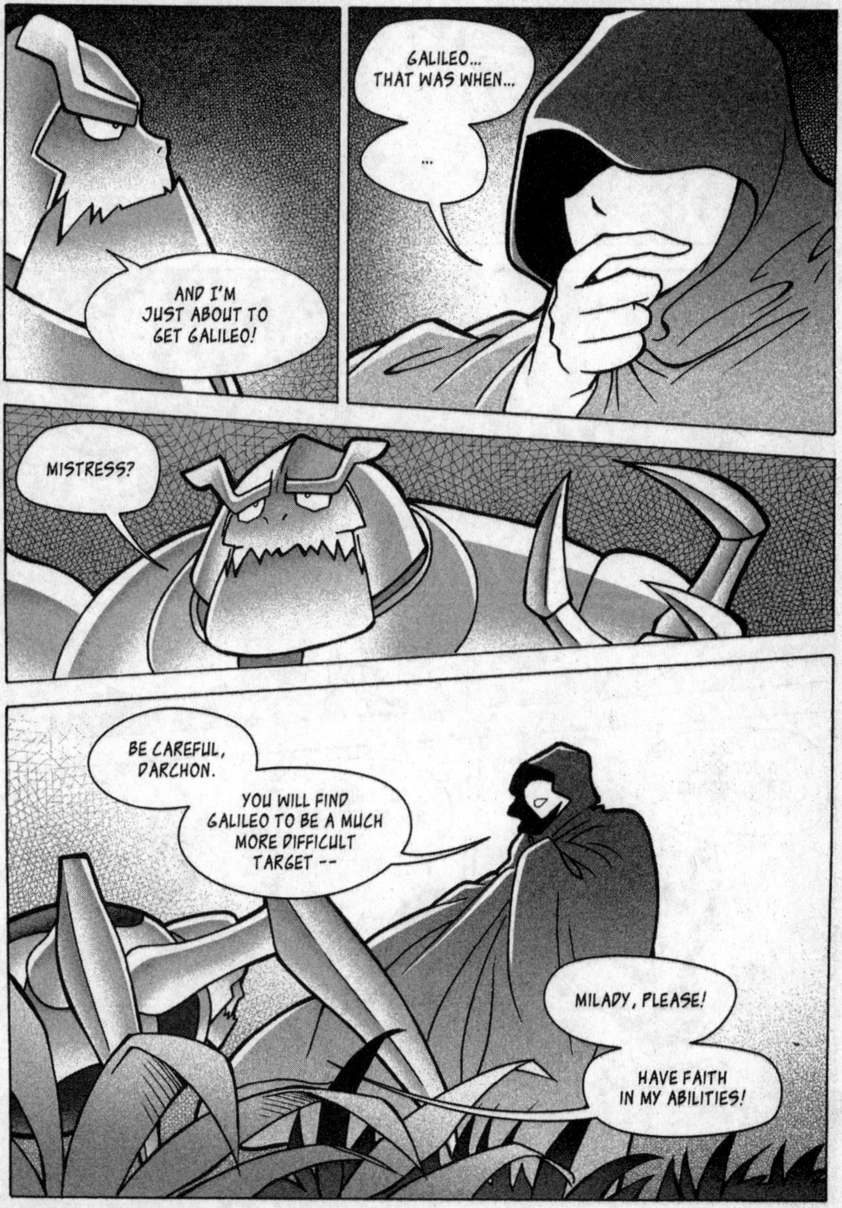
AND I'M JUST ABOUT TO GET GALILEO!
GALILEO... THAT WAS WHEN...
...
MISTRESS?
BE CAREFUL, DARCHON.
YOU WILL FIND GALILEO TO BE A MUCH MORE DIFFICULT TARGET --
MILADY, PLEASE!
HAVE FAITH IN MY ABILITIES!

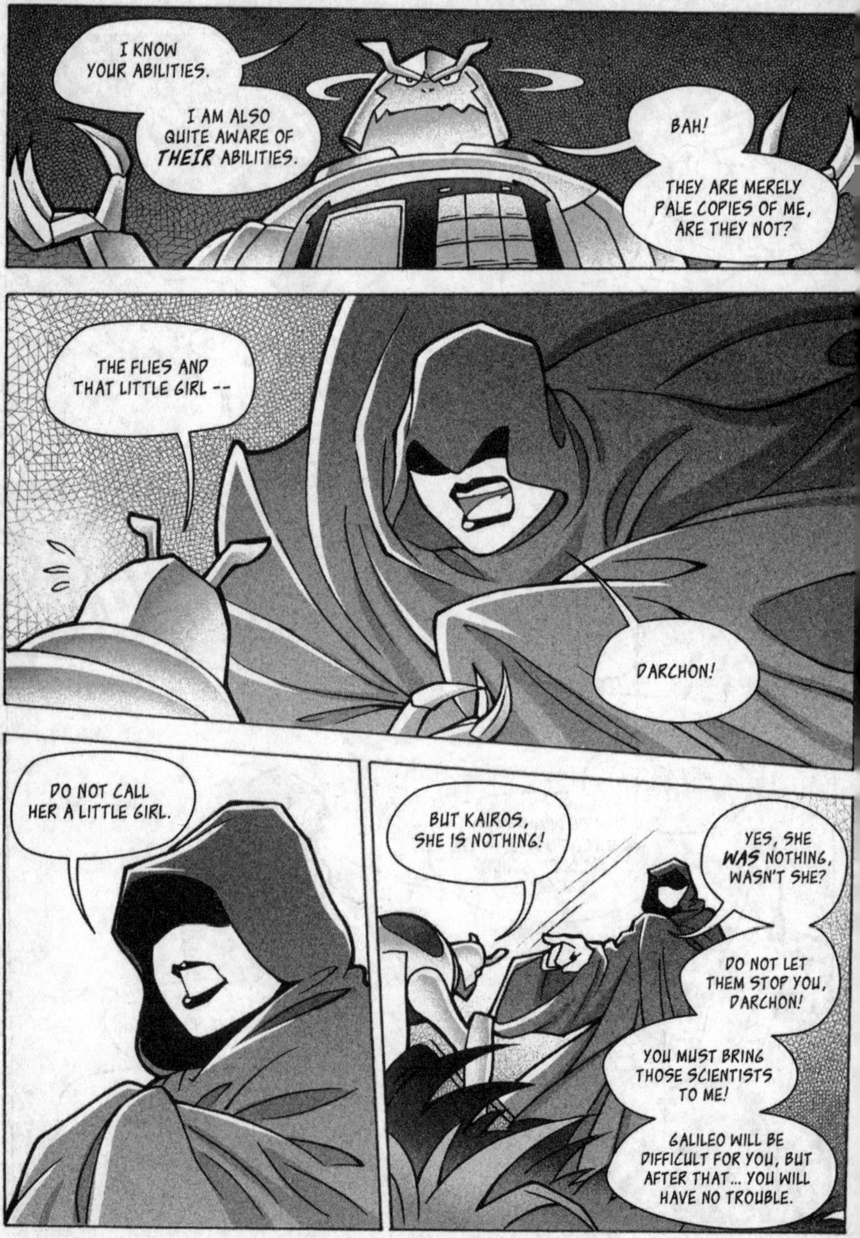
I KNOW YOUR ABILITIES.
I AM ALSO QUITE AWARE OF *THEIR* ABILITIES.
BAH!
THEY ARE MERELY PALE COPIES OF ME, ARE THEY NOT?
THE FLIES AND THAT LITTLE GIRL --
DARCHON!
DO NOT CALL HER A LITTLE GIRL.
BUT KAIROS, SHE IS NOTHING!
YES, SHE *WAS* NOTHING, WASN'T SHE?
DO NOT LET THEM STOP YOU, DARCHON!
YOU MUST BRING THOSE SCIENTISTS TO ME!
GALILEO WILL BE DIFFICULT FOR YOU, BUT AFTER THAT... YOU WILL HAVE NO TROUBLE.

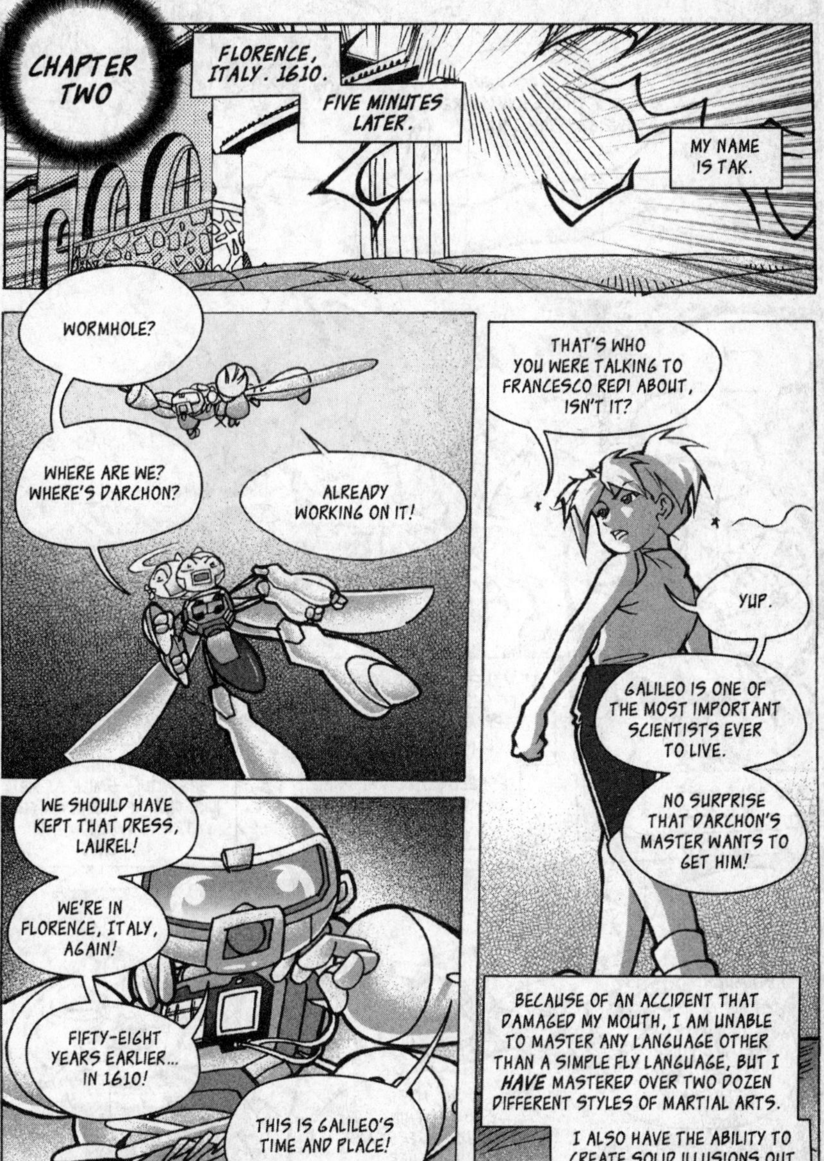

CHAPTER TWO
FLORENCE, ITALY. 1610.
FIVE MINUTES LATER.
MY NAME IS TAK.
WORMHOLE?
WHERE ARE WE? WHERE'S DARCHON?
ALREADY WORKING ON IT!
WE SHOULD HAVE KEPT THAT DRESS, LAUREL!
WE'RE IN FLORENCE, ITALY, AGAIN!
FIFTY-EIGHT YEARS EARLIER... IN 1610!
THIS IS GALILEO'S TIME AND PLACE!
THAT'S WHO YOU WERE TALKING TO FRANCESCO REDI ABOUT, ISN'T IT?
YUP.
GALILEO IS ONE OF THE MOST IMPORTANT SCIENTISTS EVER TO LIVE.
NO SURPRISE THAT DARCHON'S MASTER WANTS TO GET HIM!
BECAUSE OF AN ACCIDENT THAT DAMAGED MY MOUTH, I AM UNABLE TO MASTER ANY LANGUAGE OTHER THAN A SIMPLE FLY LANGUAGE, BUT I ***HAVE*** MASTERED OVER TWO DOZEN DIFFERENT STYLES OF MARTIAL ARTS.
I ALSO HAVE THE ABILITY TO CREATE SOLID ILLUSIONS OUT OF LIGHT PARTICLES.

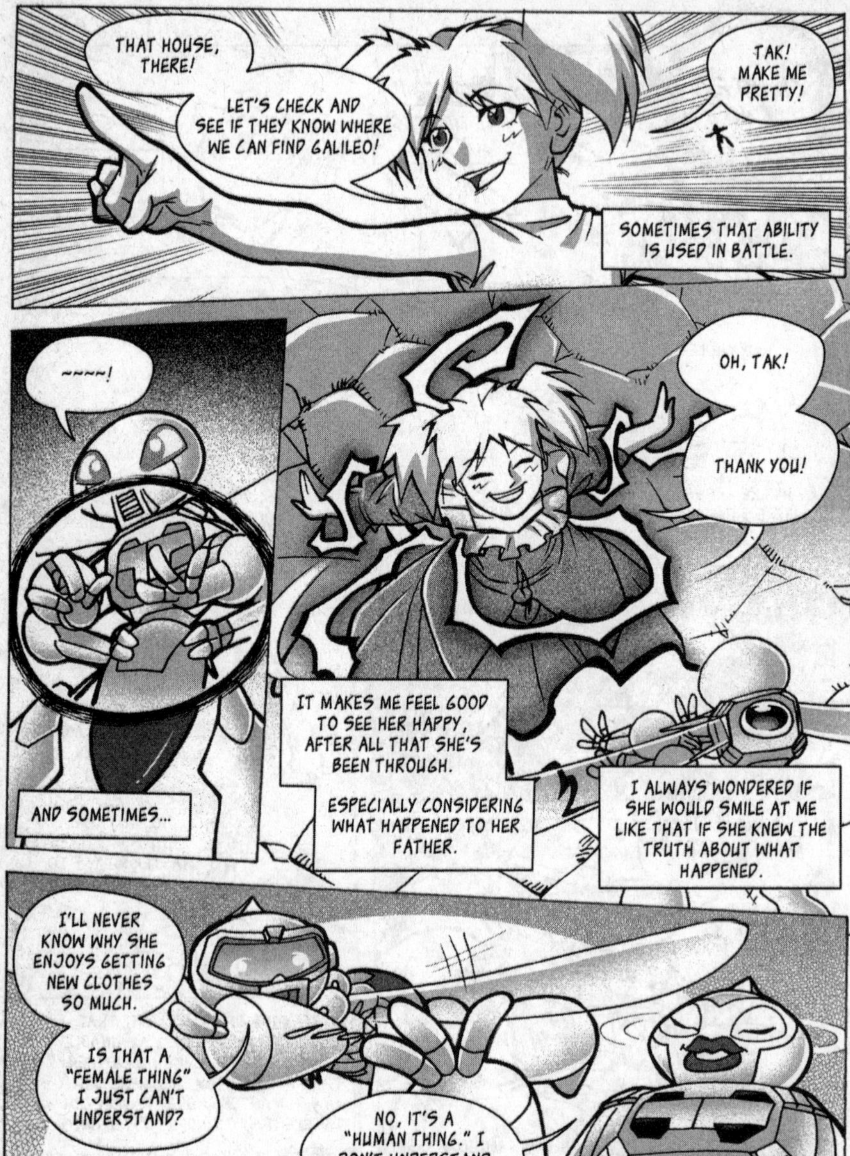
THAT HOUSE, THERE!
LET'S CHECK AND SEE IF THEY KNOW WHERE WE CAN FIND GALILEO!
TAK! MAKE ME PRETTY!
SOMETIMES THAT ABILITY IS USED IN BATTLE.
~~~~!
AND SOMETIMES...
OH, TAK!
THANK YOU!
IT MAKES ME FEEL GOOD TO SEE HER HAPPY, AFTER ALL THAT SHE'S BEEN THROUGH.
ESPECIALLY CONSIDERING WHAT HAPPENED TO HER FATHER.
I ALWAYS WONDERED IF SHE WOULD SMILE AT ME LIKE THAT IF SHE KNEW THE TRUTH ABOUT WHAT HAPPENED.
I'LL NEVER KNOW WHY SHE ENJOYS GETTING NEW CLOTHES SO MUCH.
IS THAT A "FEMALE THING" I JUST CAN'T UNDERSTAND?
NO, IT'S A "HUMAN THING." I DON'T UNDERSTAND IT EITHER.
~~~~

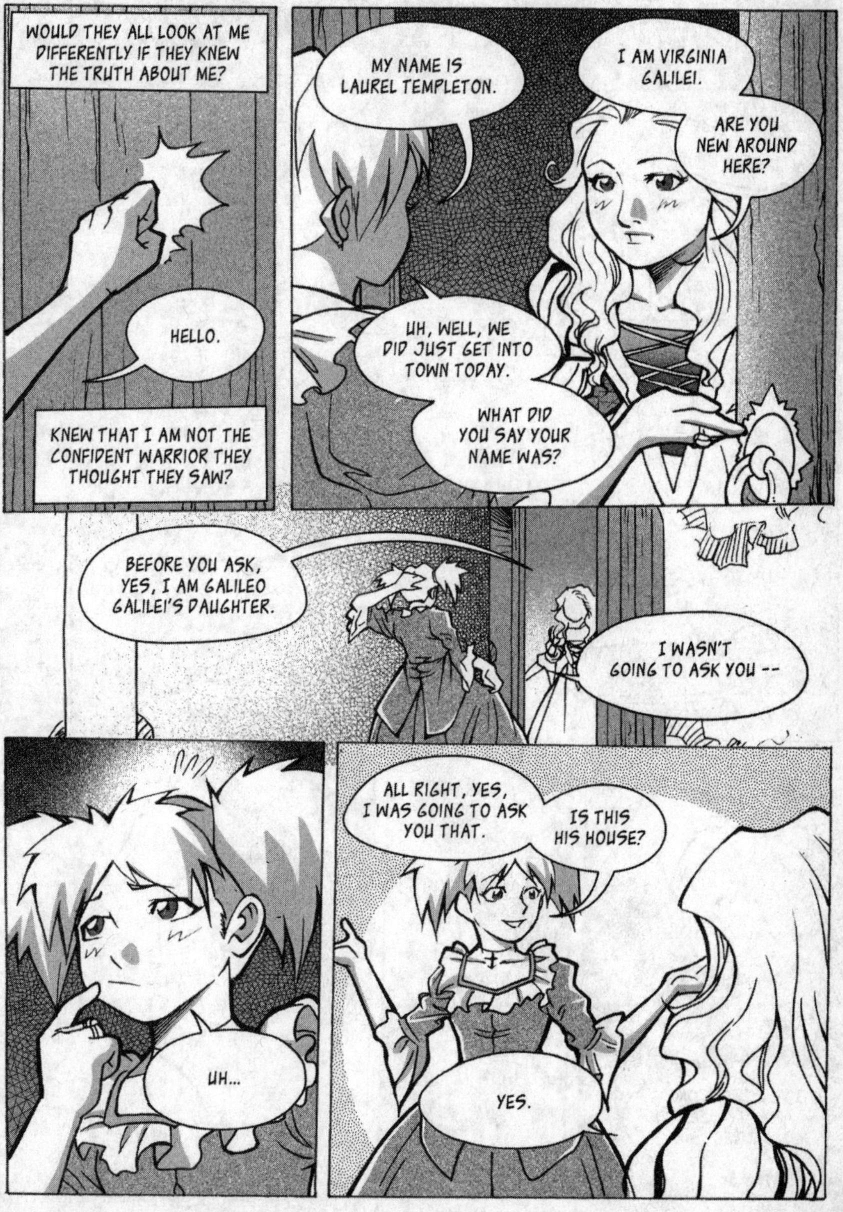

WOULD THEY ALL LOOK AT ME DIFFERENTLY IF THEY KNEW THE TRUTH ABOUT ME?
HELLO.
KNEW THAT I AM NOT THE CONFIDENT WARRIOR THEY THOUGHT THEY SAW?
MY NAME IS LAUREL TEMPLETON.
I AM VIRGINIA GALILEI.
ARE YOU NEW AROUND HERE?
UH, WELL, WE DID JUST GET INTO TOWN TODAY.
WHAT DID YOU SAY YOUR NAME WAS?
BEFORE YOU ASK, YES, I AM GALILEO GALILEI'S DAUGHTER.
I WASN'T GOING TO ASK YOU --
UH...
ALL RIGHT, YES, I WAS GOING TO ASK YOU THAT.
IS THIS HIS HOUSE?
YES.

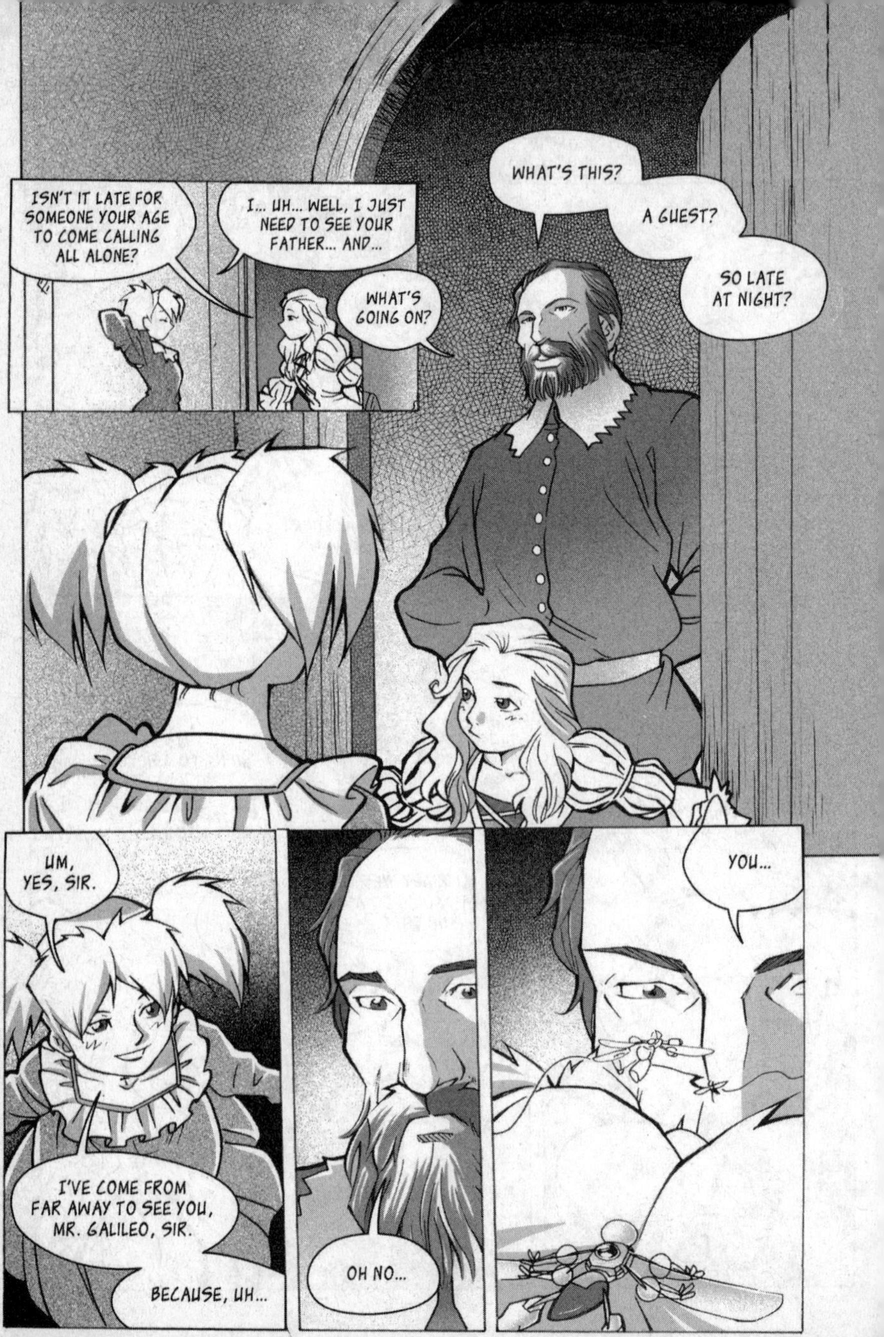
ISN'T IT LATE FOR SOMEONE YOUR AGE TO COME CALLING ALL ALONE?
I... UH... WELL, I JUST NEED TO SEE YOUR FATHER... AND...
WHAT'S GOING ON?
WHAT'S THIS?
A GUEST?
SO LATE AT NIGHT?
UM, YES, SIR.
I'VE COME FROM FAR AWAY TO SEE YOU, MR. GALILEO, SIR.
BECAUSE, UH...
OH NO...
YOU...

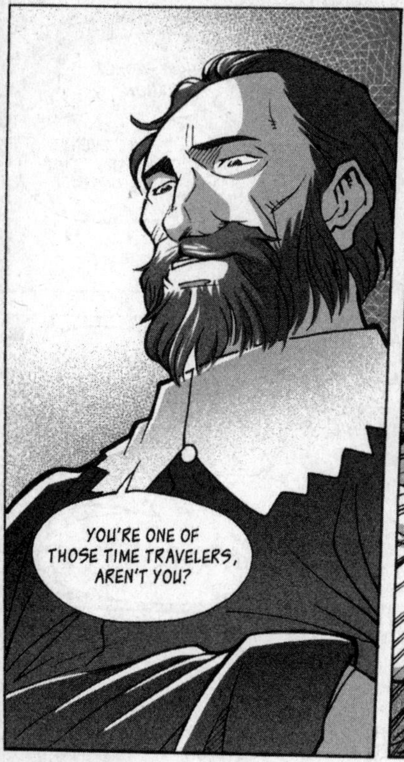
YOU'RE ONE OF THOSE TIME TRAVELERS, AREN'T YOU?
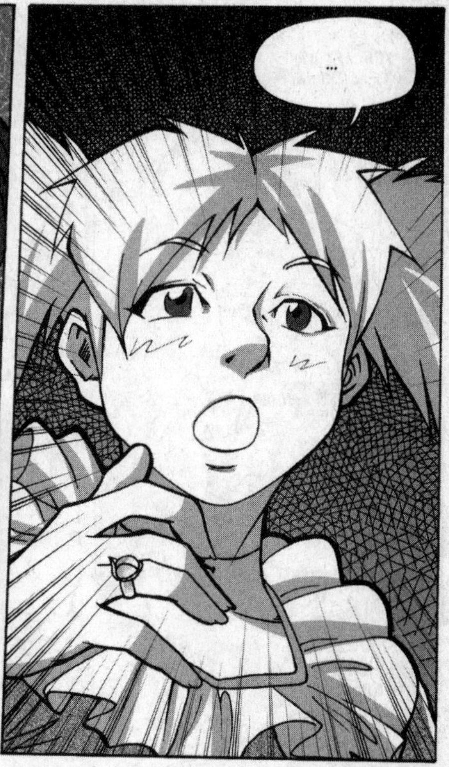
...
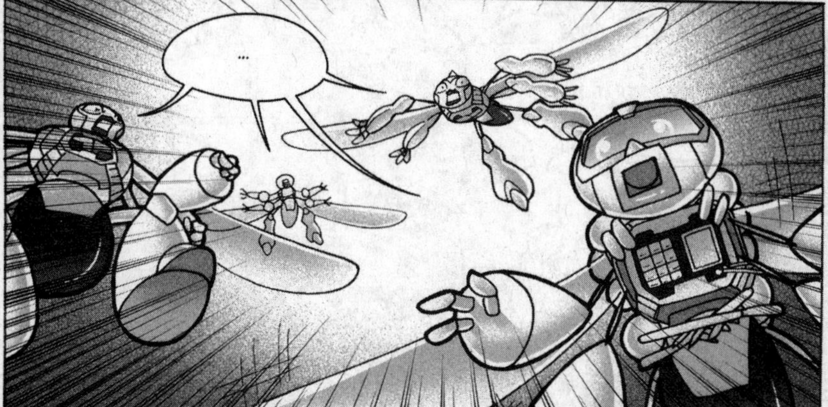
...

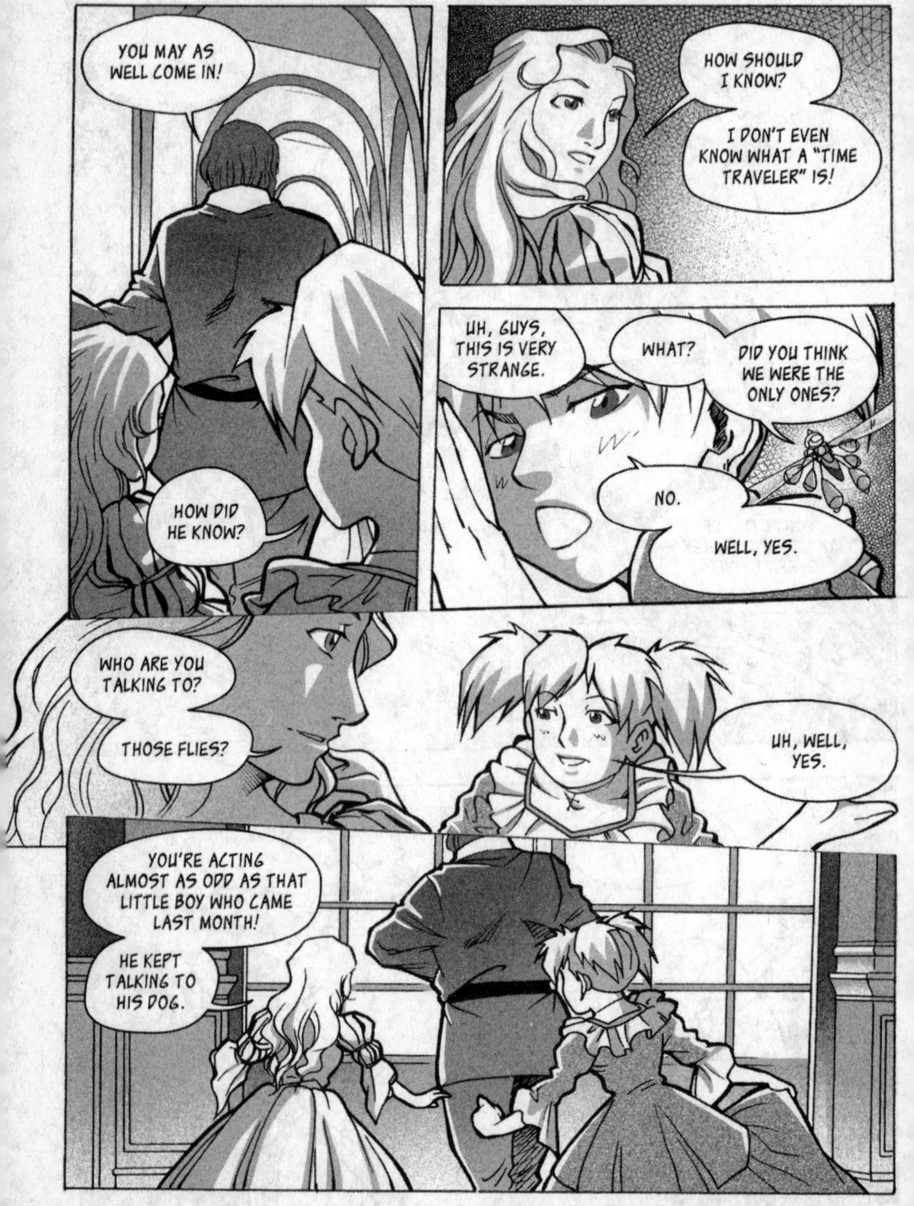
YOU MAY AS WELL COME IN!
HOW DID HE KNOW?
HOW SHOULD I KNOW?
I DON'T EVEN KNOW WHAT A "TIME TRAVELER" IS!
UH, GUYS, THIS IS VERY STRANGE.
WHAT?
DID YOU THINK WE WERE THE ONLY ONES?
NO.
WELL, YES.
WHO ARE YOU TALKING TO?
THOSE FLIES?
UH, WELL, YES.
YOU'RE ACTING ALMOST AS ODD AS THAT LITTLE BOY WHO CAME LAST MONTH!
HE KEPT TALKING TO HIS DOG.

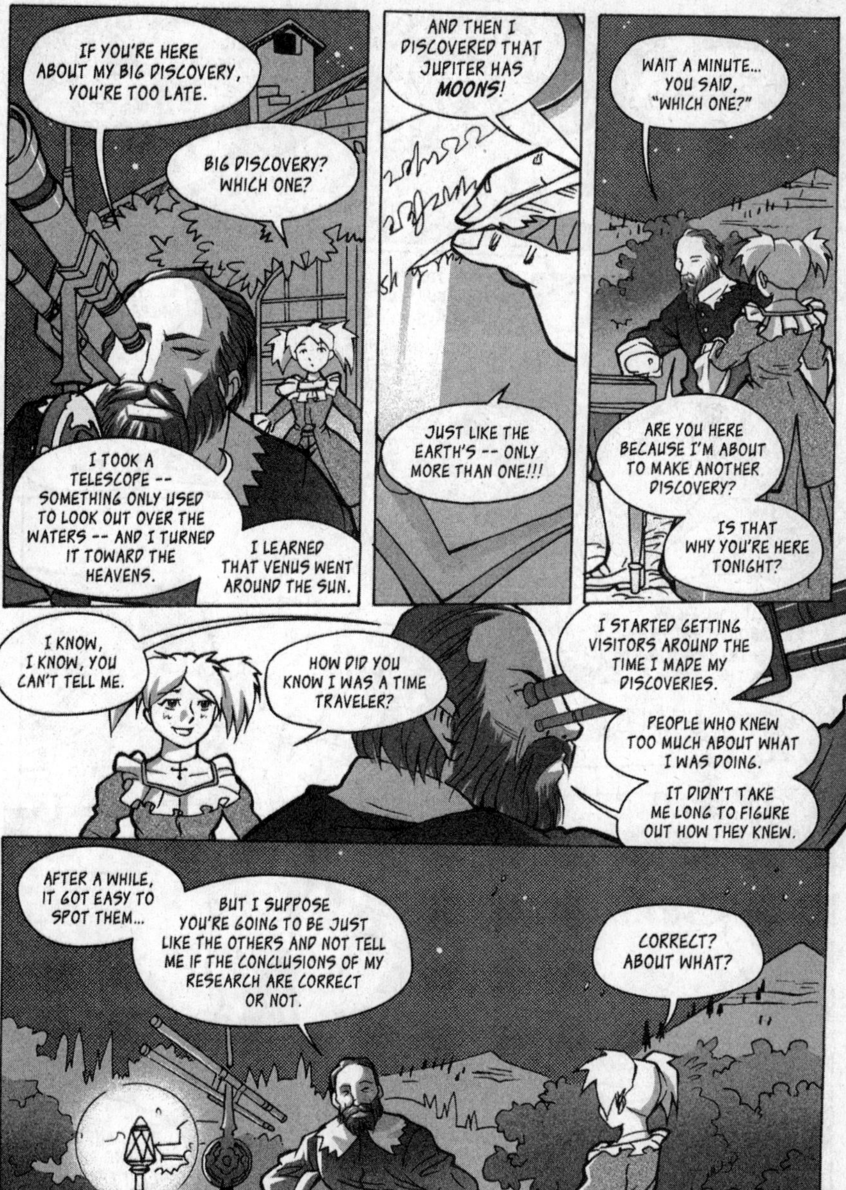

IF YOU'RE HERE ABOUT MY BIG DISCOVERY, YOU'RE TOO LATE.
BIG DISCOVERY? WHICH ONE?
I TOOK A TELESCOPE -- SOMETHING ONLY USED TO LOOK OUT OVER THE WATERS -- AND I TURNED IT TOWARD THE HEAVENS.
I LEARNED THAT VENUS WENT AROUND THE SUN.
AND THEN I DISCOVERED THAT JUPITER HAS MOONS!
JUST LIKE THE EARTH'S -- ONLY MORE THAN ONE!!!
WAIT A MINUTE... YOU SAID, "WHICH ONE?"
ARE YOU HERE BECAUSE I'M ABOUT TO MAKE ANOTHER DISCOVERY?
IS THAT WHY YOU'RE HERE TONIGHT?
I KNOW, I KNOW, YOU CAN'T TELL ME.
HOW DID YOU KNOW I WAS A TIME TRAVELER?
I STARTED GETTING VISITORS AROUND THE TIME I MADE MY DISCOVERIES.
PEOPLE WHO KNEW TOO MUCH ABOUT WHAT I WAS DOING.
IT DIDN'T TAKE ME LONG TO FIGURE OUT HOW THEY KNEW.
AFTER A WHILE, IT GOT EASY TO SPOT THEM...
BUT I SUPPOSE YOU'RE GOING TO BE JUST LIKE THE OTHERS AND NOT TELL ME IF THE CONCLUSIONS OF MY RESEARCH ARE CORRECT OR NOT.
CORRECT? ABOUT WHAT?

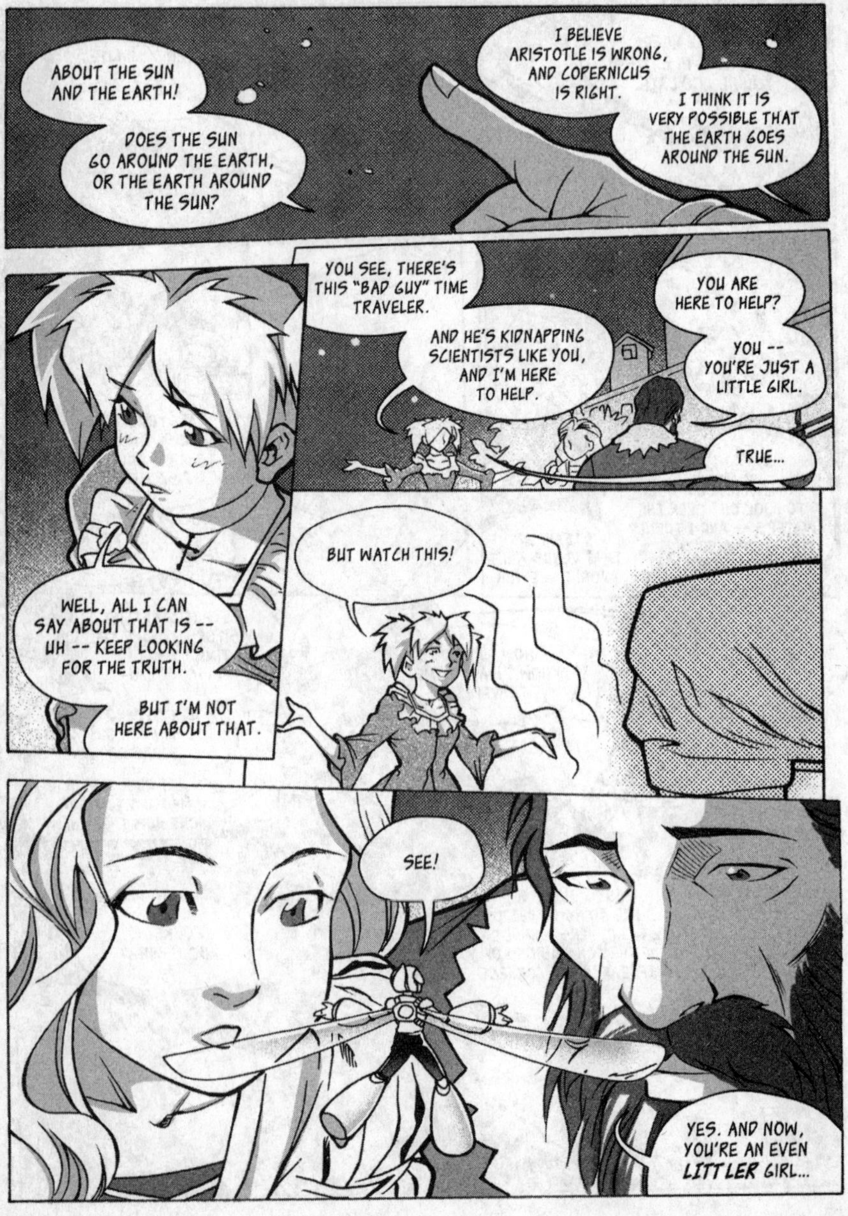
ABOUT THE SUN AND THE EARTH!
DOES THE SUN GO AROUND THE EARTH, OR THE EARTH AROUND THE SUN?
I BELIEVE ARISTOTLE IS WRONG, AND COPERNICUS IS RIGHT.
I THINK IT IS VERY POSSIBLE THAT THE EARTH GOES AROUND THE SUN.
WELL, ALL I CAN SAY ABOUT THAT IS -- UH -- KEEP LOOKING FOR THE TRUTH.
BUT I'M NOT HERE ABOUT THAT.
YOU SEE, THERE'S THIS "BAD GUY" TIME TRAVELER.
AND HE'S KIDNAPPING SCIENTISTS LIKE YOU, AND I'M HERE TO HELP.
YOU ARE HERE TO HELP?
YOU -- YOU'RE JUST A LITTLE GIRL.
TRUE...
BUT WATCH THIS!
SEE!
YES. AND NOW, YOU'RE AN EVEN ***LITTLER*** GIRL...

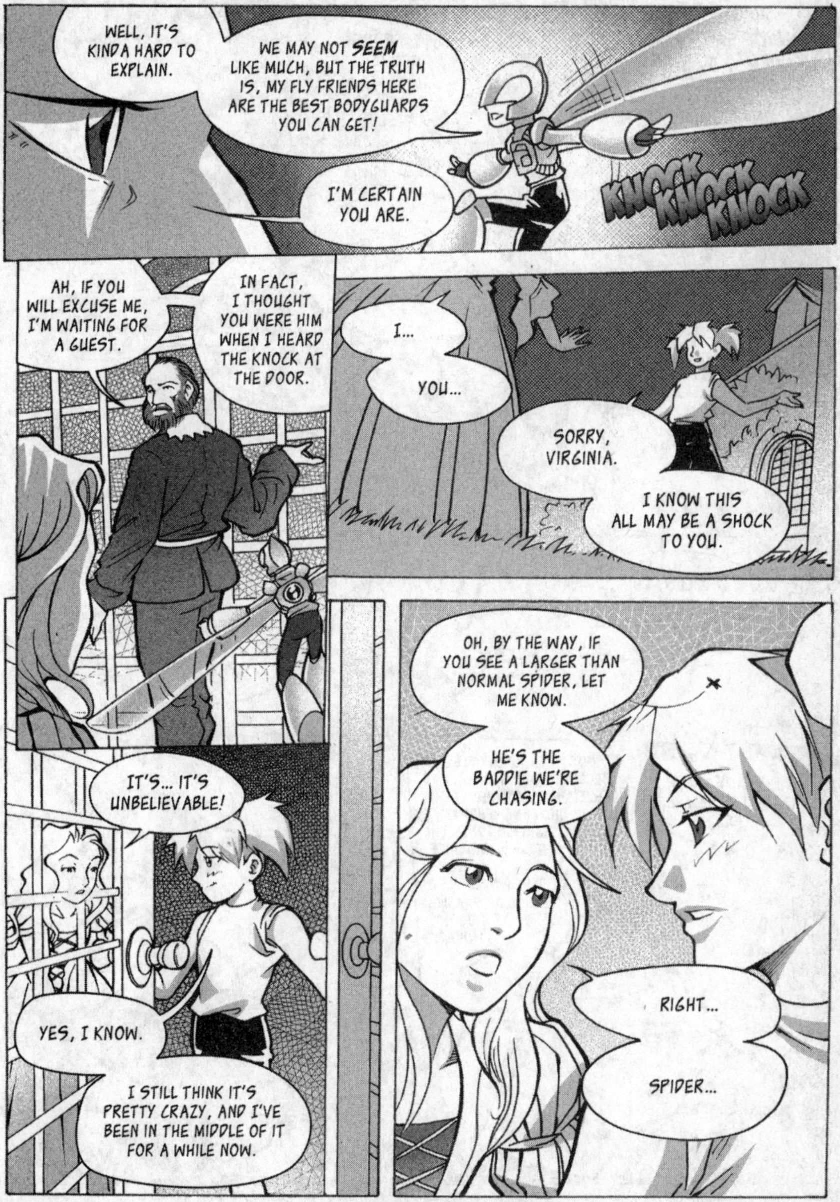
WELL, IT'S KINDA HARD TO EXPLAIN.
WE MAY NOT SEEM LIKE MUCH, BUT THE TRUTH IS, MY FLY FRIENDS HERE ARE THE BEST BODYGUARDS YOU CAN GET!
I'M CERTAIN YOU ARE.
KNOCK KNOCK KNOCK
AH, IF YOU WILL EXCUSE ME, I'M WAITING FOR A GUEST.
IN FACT, I THOUGHT YOU WERE HIM WHEN I HEARD THE KNOCK AT THE DOOR.
I...
YOU...
SORRY, VIRGINIA.
I KNOW THIS ALL MAY BE A SHOCK TO YOU.
IT'S... IT'S UNBELIEVABLE!
YES, I KNOW.
I STILL THINK IT'S PRETTY CRAZY, AND I'VE BEEN IN THE MIDDLE OF IT FOR A WHILE NOW.
OH, BY THE WAY, IF YOU SEE A LARGER THAN NORMAL SPIDER, LET ME KNOW.
HE'S THE BADDIE WE'RE CHASING.
RIGHT...
SPIDER...

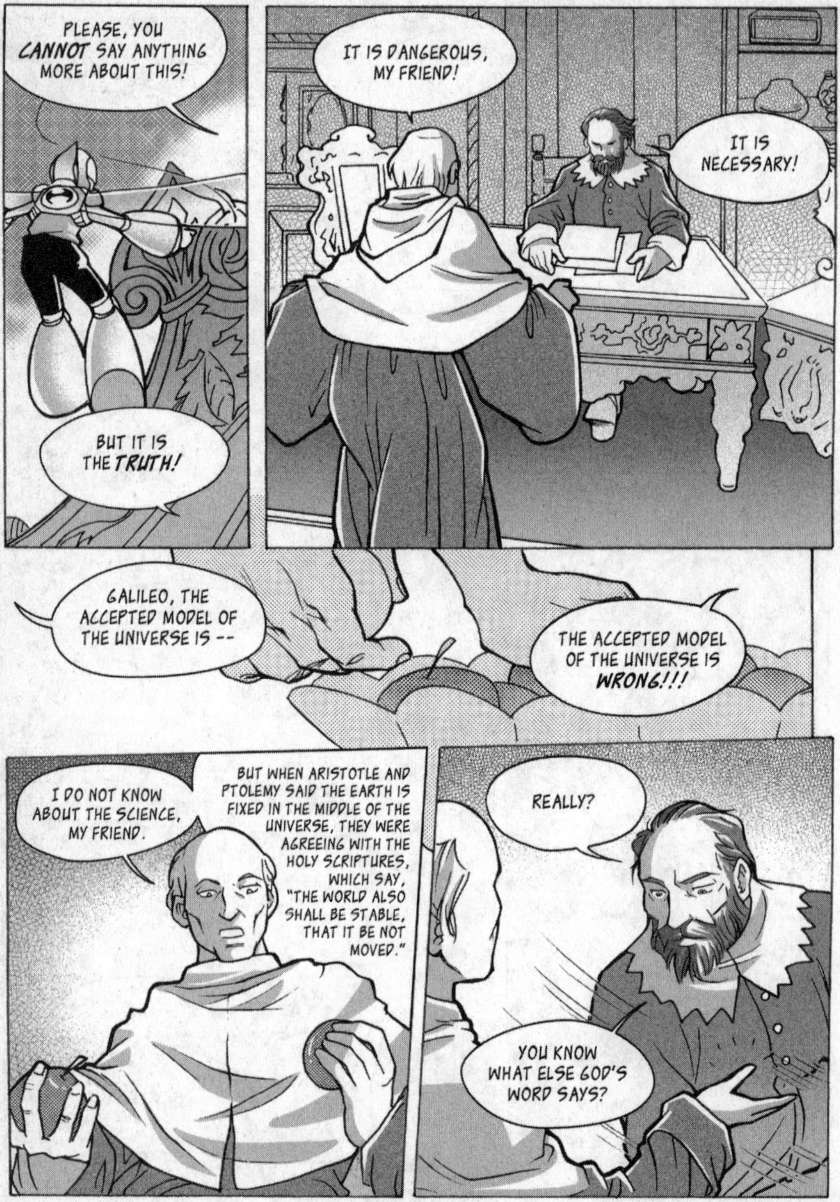

PLEASE, YOU *CANNOT* SAY ANYTHING MORE ABOUT THIS!
BUT IT IS THE *TRUTH!*
IT IS DANGEROUS, MY FRIEND!
IT IS NECESSARY!
GALILEO, THE ACCEPTED MODEL OF THE UNIVERSE IS --
THE ACCEPTED MODEL OF THE UNIVERSE IS *WRONG!!!*
I DO NOT KNOW ABOUT THE SCIENCE, MY FRIEND.
BUT WHEN ARISTOTLE AND PTOLEMY SAID THE EARTH IS FIXED IN THE MIDDLE OF THE UNIVERSE, THEY WERE AGREEING WITH THE HOLY SCRIPTURES, WHICH SAY, "THE WORLD ALSO SHALL BE STABLE, THAT IT BE NOT MOVED."
REALLY?
YOU KNOW WHAT ELSE GOD'S WORD SAYS?

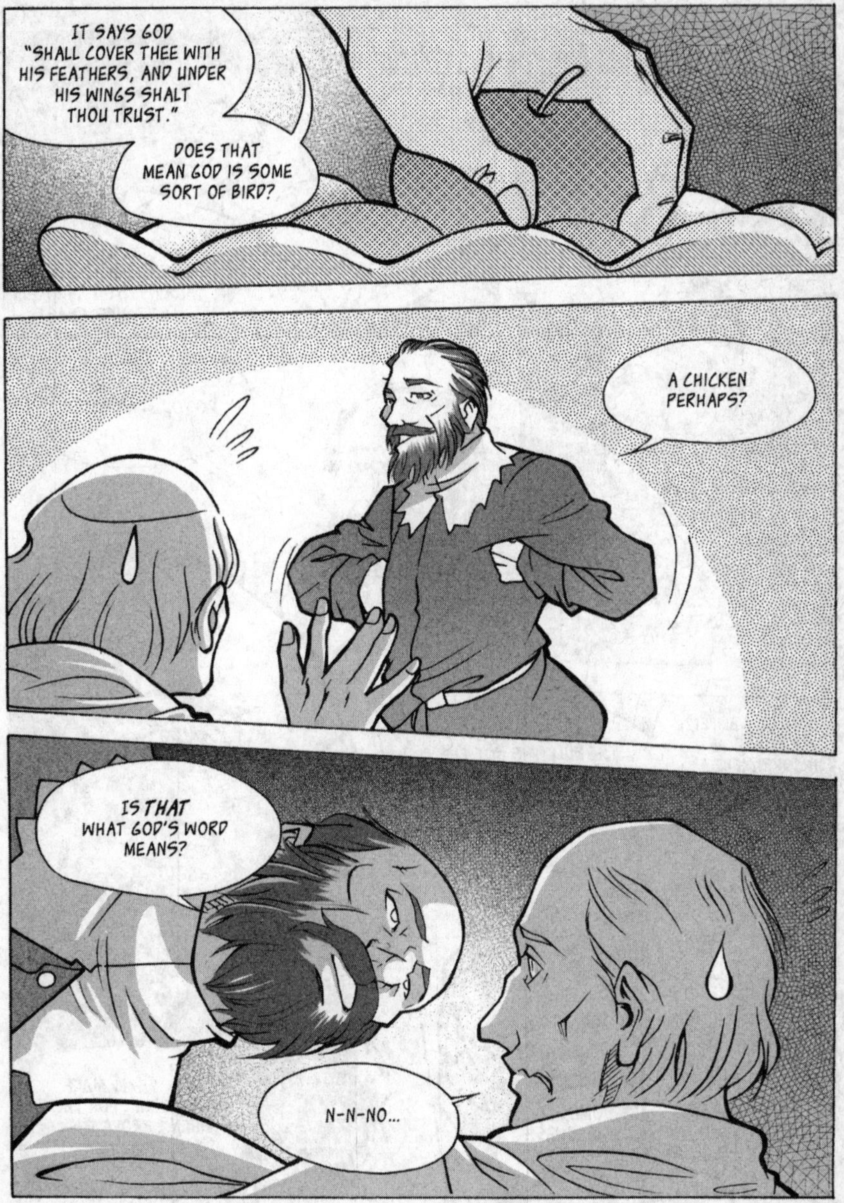
IT SAYS GOD "SHALL COVER THEE WITH HIS FEATHERS, AND UNDER HIS WINGS SHALT THOU TRUST."
DOES THAT MEAN GOD IS SOME SORT OF BIRD?
A CHICKEN PERHAPS?
IS *THAT* WHAT GOD'S WORD MEANS?
N-N-NO...

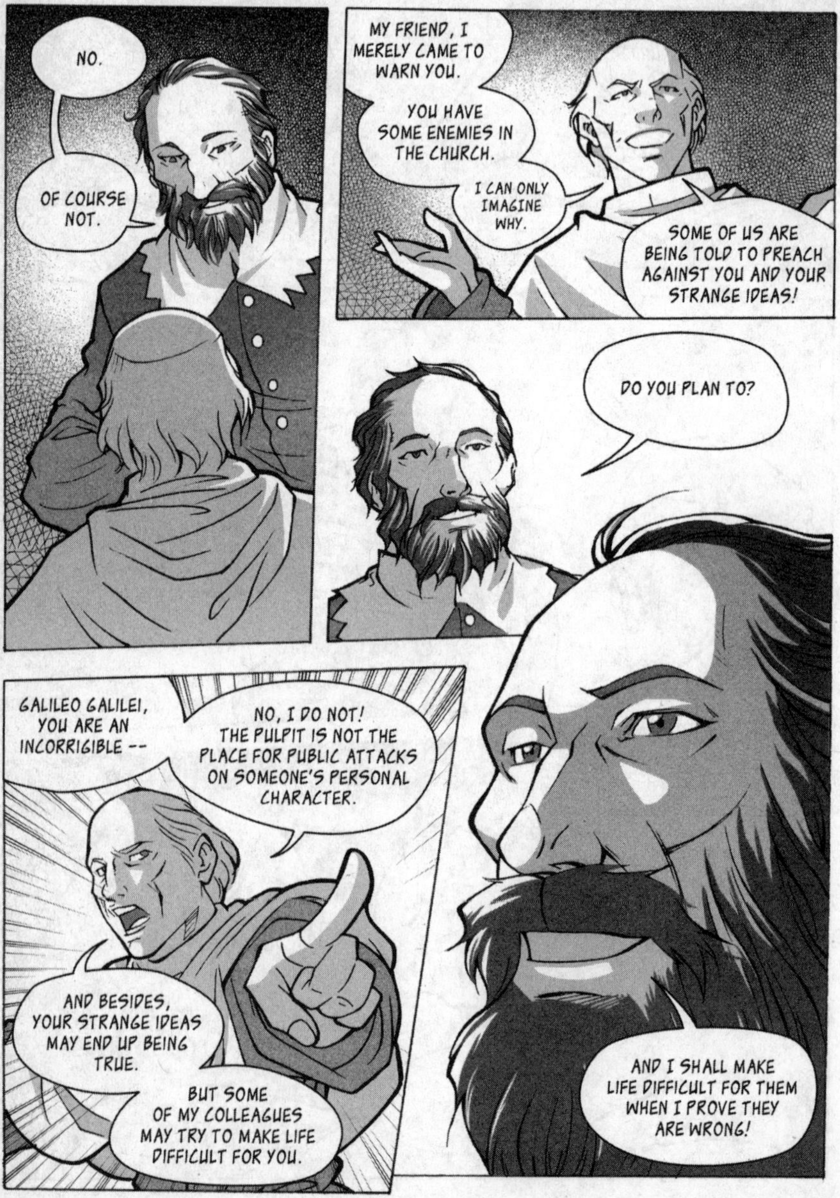
NO.
OF COURSE NOT.
MY FRIEND, I MERELY CAME TO WARN YOU.
YOU HAVE SOME ENEMIES IN THE CHURCH.
I CAN ONLY IMAGINE WHY.
SOME OF US ARE BEING TOLD TO PREACH AGAINST YOU AND YOUR STRANGE IDEAS!
DO YOU PLAN TO?
GALILEO GALILEI, YOU ARE AN INCORRIGIBLE --
NO, I DO NOT! THE PULPIT IS NOT THE PLACE FOR PUBLIC ATTACKS ON SOMEONE'S PERSONAL CHARACTER.
AND BESIDES, YOUR STRANGE IDEAS MAY END UP BEING TRUE.
BUT SOME OF MY COLLEAGUES MAY TRY TO MAKE LIFE DIFFICULT FOR YOU.
AND I SHALL MAKE LIFE DIFFICULT FOR THEM WHEN I PROVE THEY ARE WRONG!

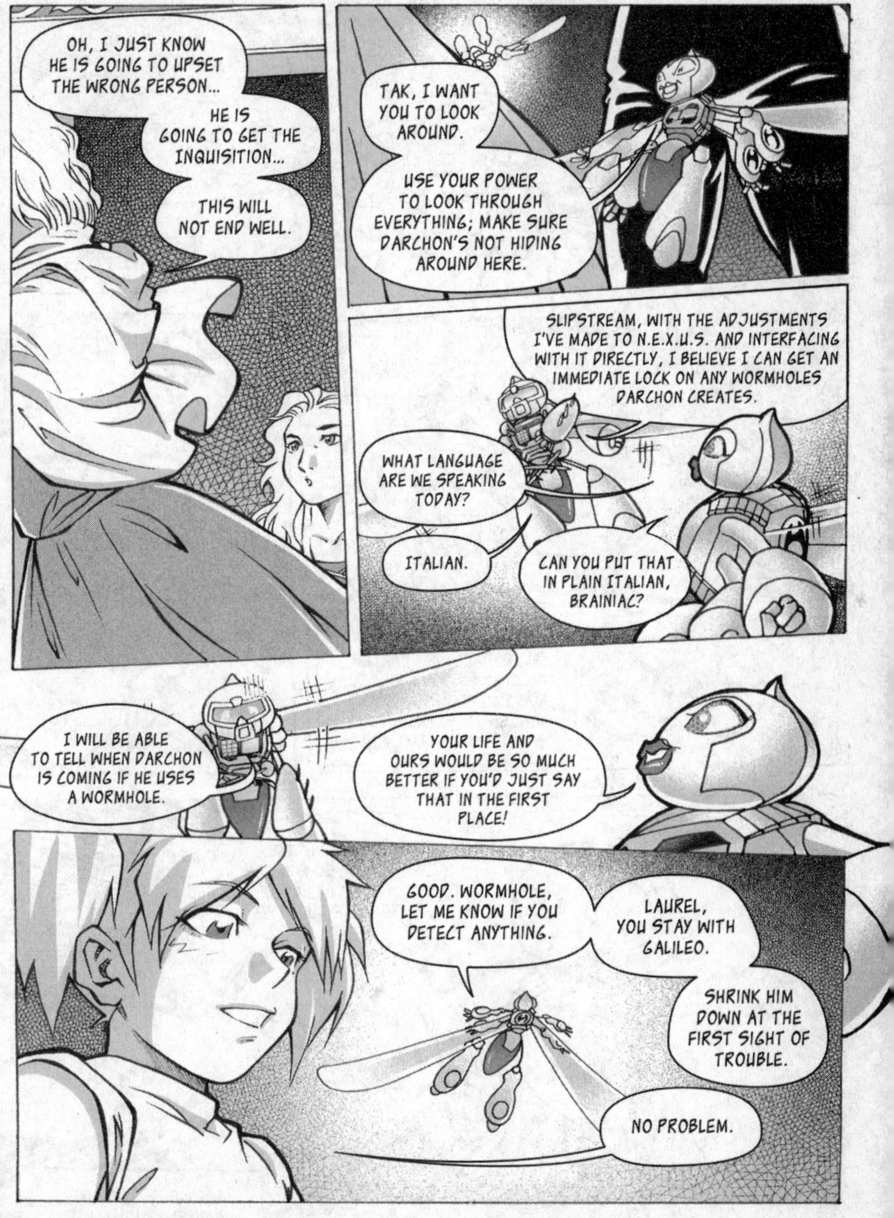
OH, I JUST KNOW HE IS GOING TO UPSET THE WRONG PERSON...
HE IS GOING TO GET THE INQUISITION...
THIS WILL NOT END WELL.
TAK, I WANT YOU TO LOOK AROUND.
USE YOUR POWER TO LOOK THROUGH EVERYTHING; MAKE SURE DARCHON'S NOT HIDING AROUND HERE.
SLIPSTREAM, WITH THE ADJUSTMENTS I'VE MADE TO N.E.X.U.S. AND INTERFACING WITH IT DIRECTLY, I BELIEVE I CAN GET AN IMMEDIATE LOCK ON ANY WORMHOLES DARCHON CREATES.
WHAT LANGUAGE ARE WE SPEAKING TODAY?
ITALIAN.
CAN YOU PUT THAT IN PLAIN ITALIAN, BRAINIAC?
I WILL BE ABLE TO TELL WHEN DARCHON IS COMING IF HE USES A WORMHOLE.
YOUR LIFE AND OURS WOULD BE SO MUCH BETTER IF YOU'D JUST SAY THAT IN THE FIRST PLACE!
GOOD. WORMHOLE, LET ME KNOW IF YOU DETECT ANYTHING.
LAUREL, YOU STAY WITH GALILEO.
SHRINK HIM DOWN AT THE FIRST SIGHT OF TROUBLE.
NO PROBLEM.

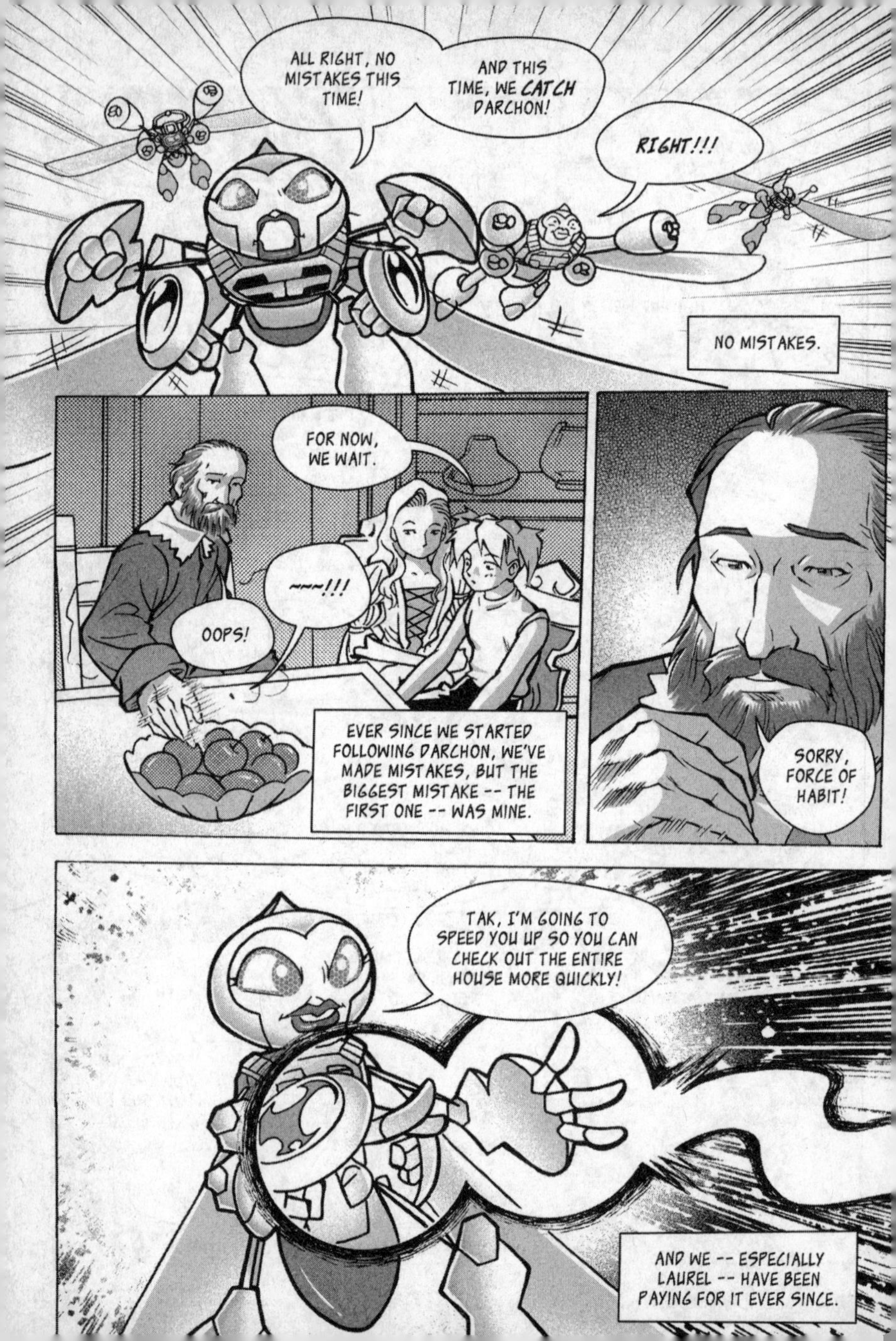
ALL RIGHT, NO MISTAKES THIS TIME!
AND THIS TIME, WE CATCH DARCHON!
RIGHT!!!
NO MISTAKES.
FOR NOW, WE WAIT.
~~~!!!
OOPS!
EVER SINCE WE STARTED FOLLOWING DARCHON, WE'VE MADE MISTAKES, BUT THE BIGGEST MISTAKE -- THE FIRST ONE -- WAS MINE.
SORRY, FORCE OF HABIT!
TAK, I'M GOING TO SPEED YOU UP SO YOU CAN CHECK OUT THE ENTIRE HOUSE MORE QUICKLY!
AND WE -- ESPECIALLY LAUREL -- HAVE BEEN PAYING FOR IT EVER SINCE.
~~~

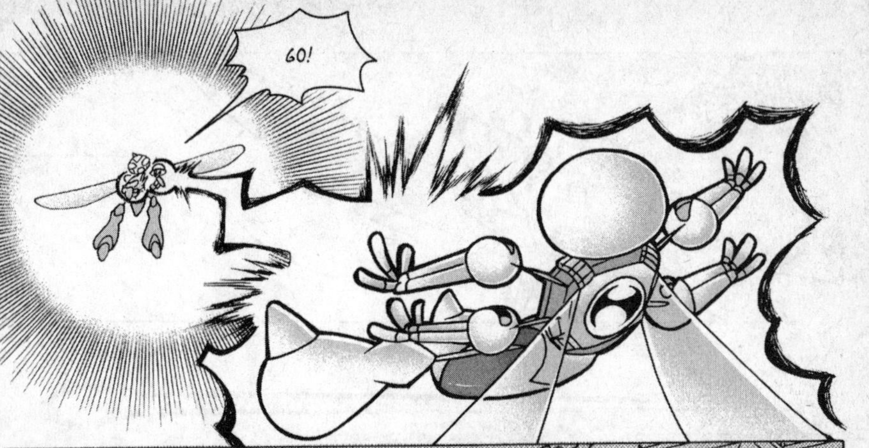
GO!

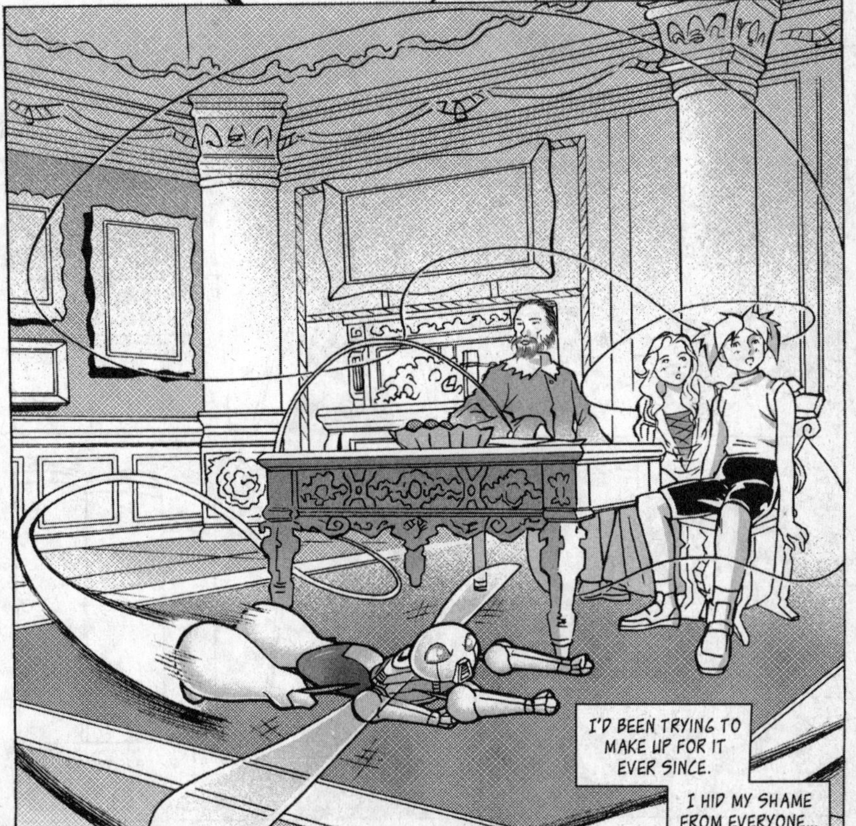
I'D BEEN TRYING TO MAKE UP FOR IT EVER SINCE.
I HID MY SHAME FROM EVERYONE...

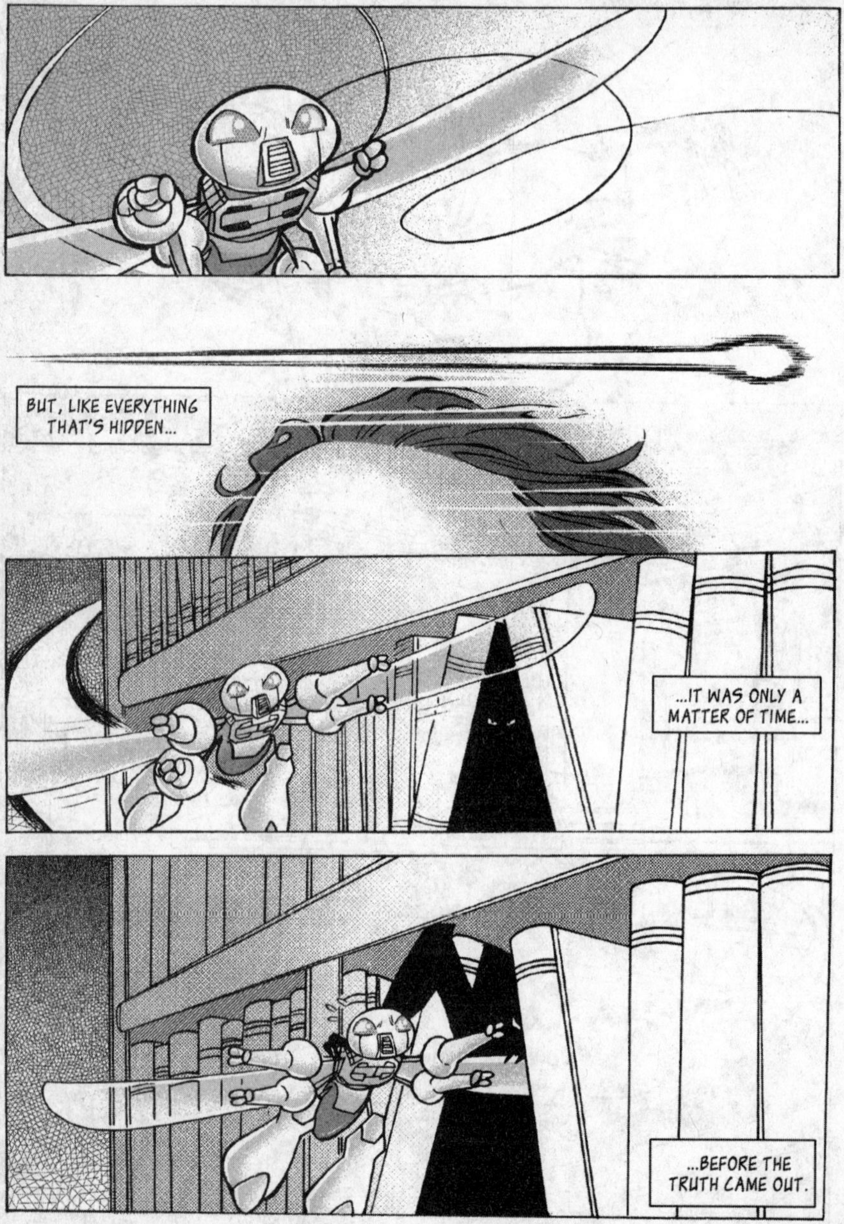
BUT, LIKE EVERYTHING THAT'S HIDDEN...
...IT WAS ONLY A MATTER OF TIME...
...BEFORE THE TRUTH CAME OUT.

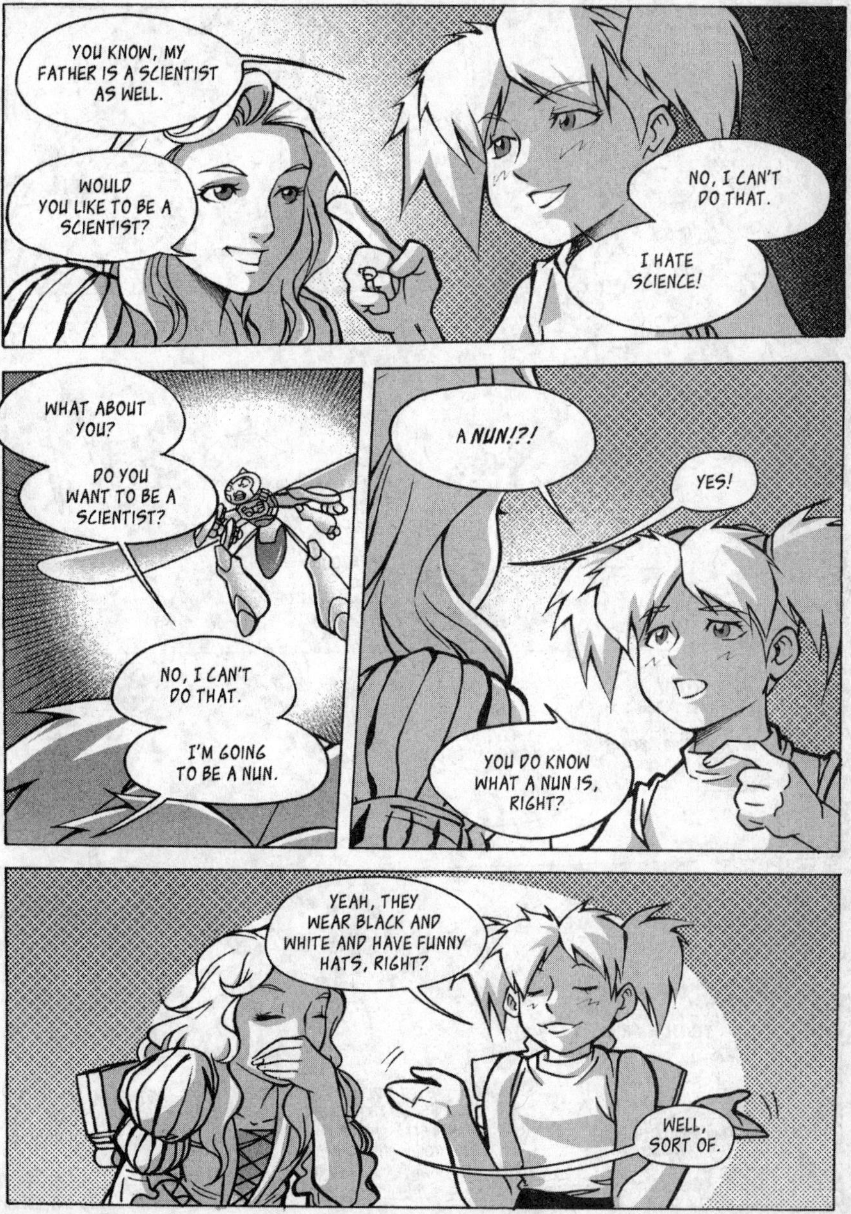
YOU KNOW, MY FATHER IS A SCIENTIST AS WELL.
WOULD YOU LIKE TO BE A SCIENTIST?
NO, I CAN'T DO THAT.
I HATE SCIENCE!
WHAT ABOUT YOU?
DO YOU WANT TO BE A SCIENTIST?
NO, I CAN'T DO THAT.
I'M GOING TO BE A NUN.
A *NUN!?!*
YES!
YOU DO KNOW WHAT A NUN IS, RIGHT?
YEAH, THEY WEAR BLACK AND WHITE AND HAVE FUNNY HATS, RIGHT?
WELL, SORT OF.

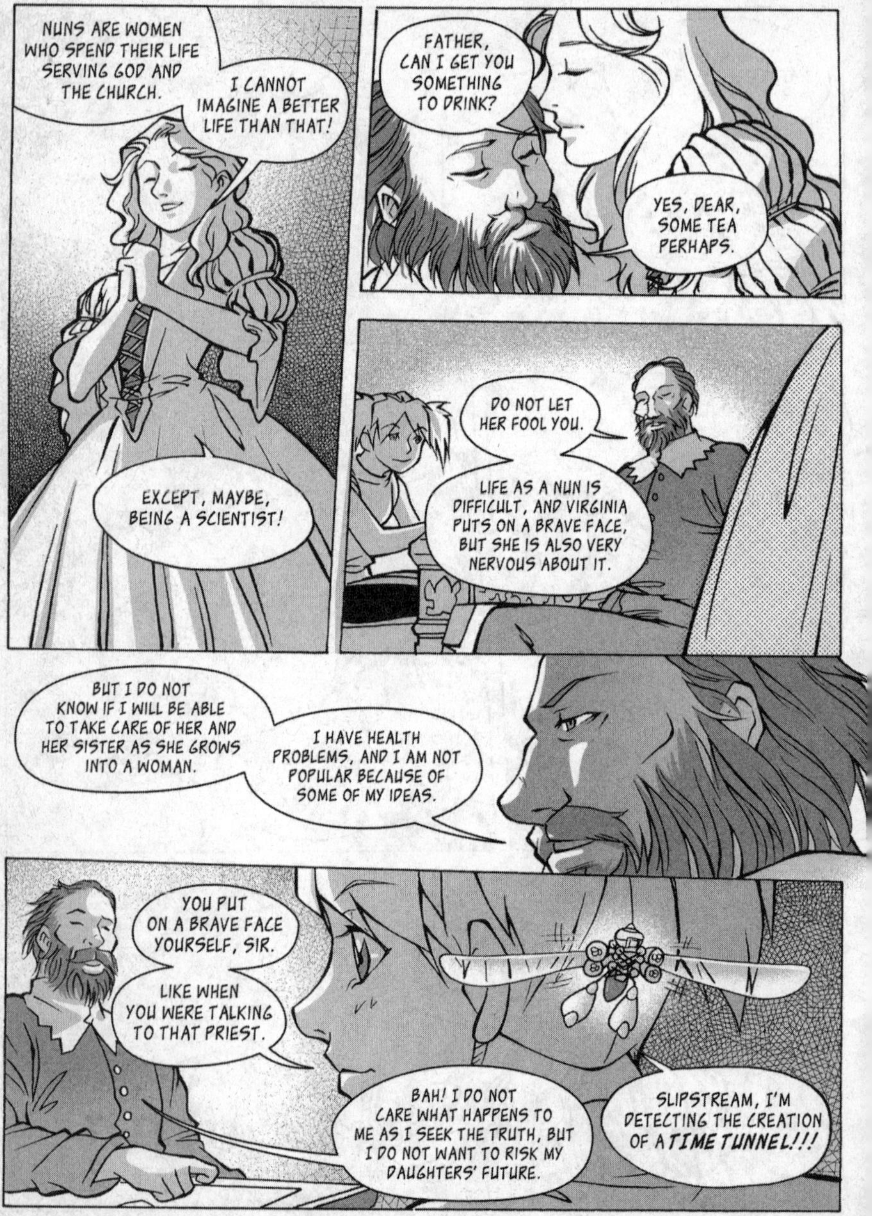
NUNS ARE WOMEN WHO SPEND THEIR LIFE SERVING GOD AND THE CHURCH.
I CANNOT IMAGINE A BETTER LIFE THAN THAT!
EXCEPT, MAYBE, BEING A SCIENTIST!
FATHER, CAN I GET YOU SOMETHING TO DRINK?
YES, DEAR, SOME TEA PERHAPS.
DO NOT LET HER FOOL YOU.
LIFE AS A NUN IS DIFFICULT, AND VIRGINIA PUTS ON A BRAVE FACE, BUT SHE IS ALSO VERY NERVOUS ABOUT IT.
BUT I DO NOT KNOW IF I WILL BE ABLE TO TAKE CARE OF HER AND HER SISTER AS SHE GROWS INTO A WOMAN.
I HAVE HEALTH PROBLEMS, AND I AM NOT POPULAR BECAUSE OF SOME OF MY IDEAS.
YOU PUT ON A BRAVE FACE YOURSELF, SIR.
LIKE WHEN YOU WERE TALKING TO THAT PRIEST.
BAH! I DO NOT CARE WHAT HAPPENS TO ME AS I SEEK THE TRUTH, BUT I DO NOT WANT TO RISK MY DAUGHTERS' FUTURE.
SLIPSTREAM, I'M DETECTING THE CREATION OF A ***TIME TUNNEL!!!***

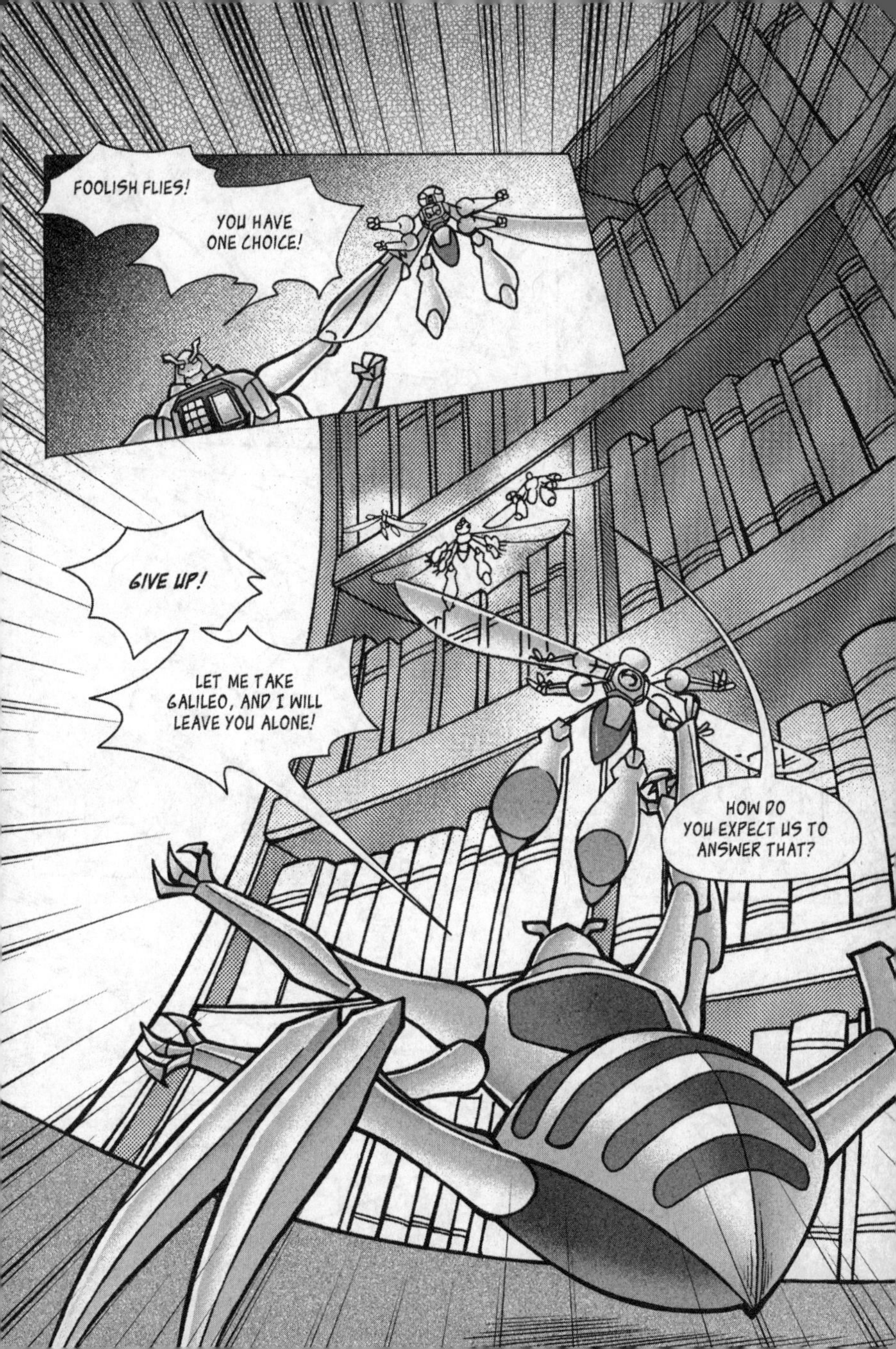
FOOLISH FLIES!
YOU HAVE ONE CHOICE!
GIVE UP!
LET ME TAKE GALILEO, AND I WILL LEAVE YOU ALONE!
HOW DO YOU EXPECT US TO ANSWER THAT?

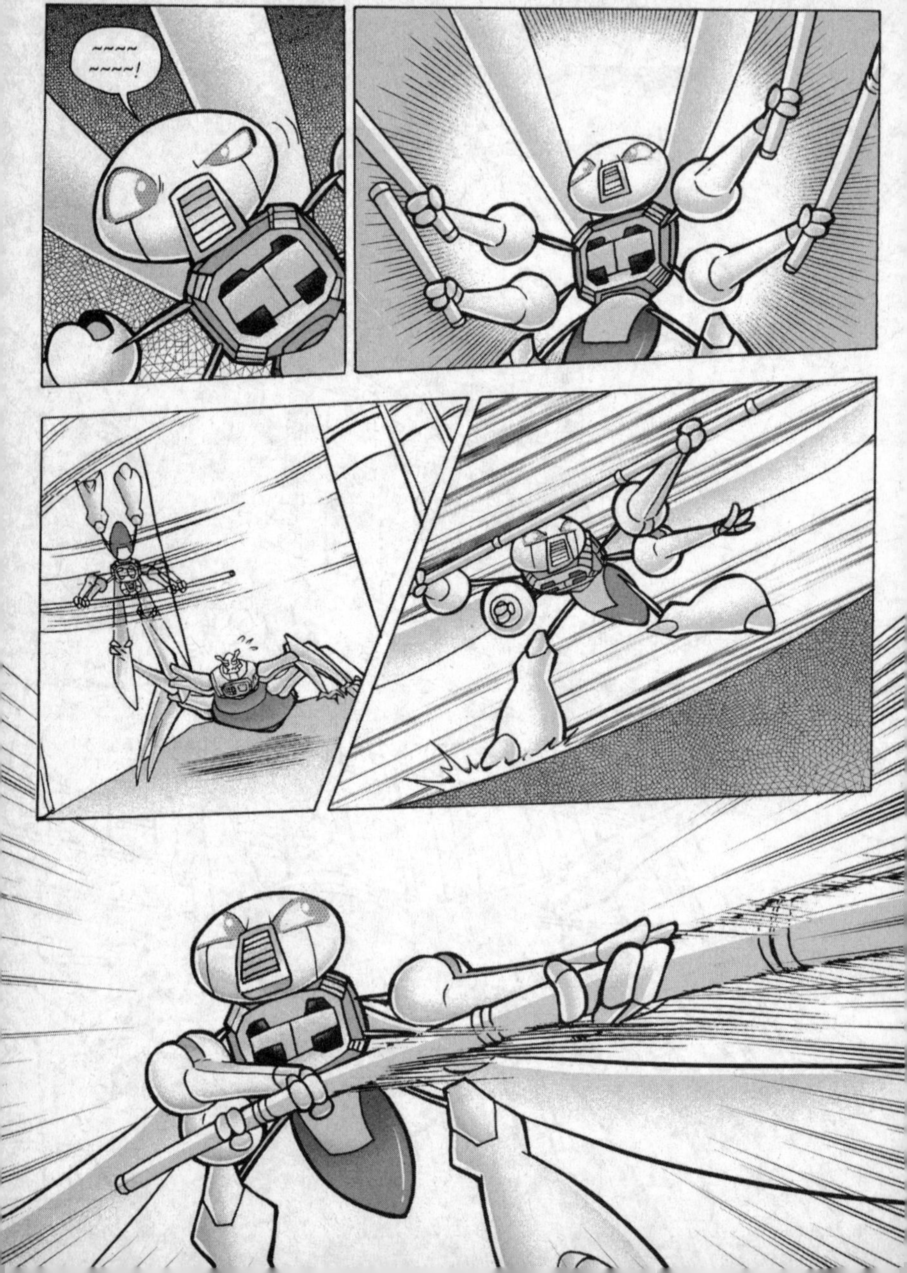

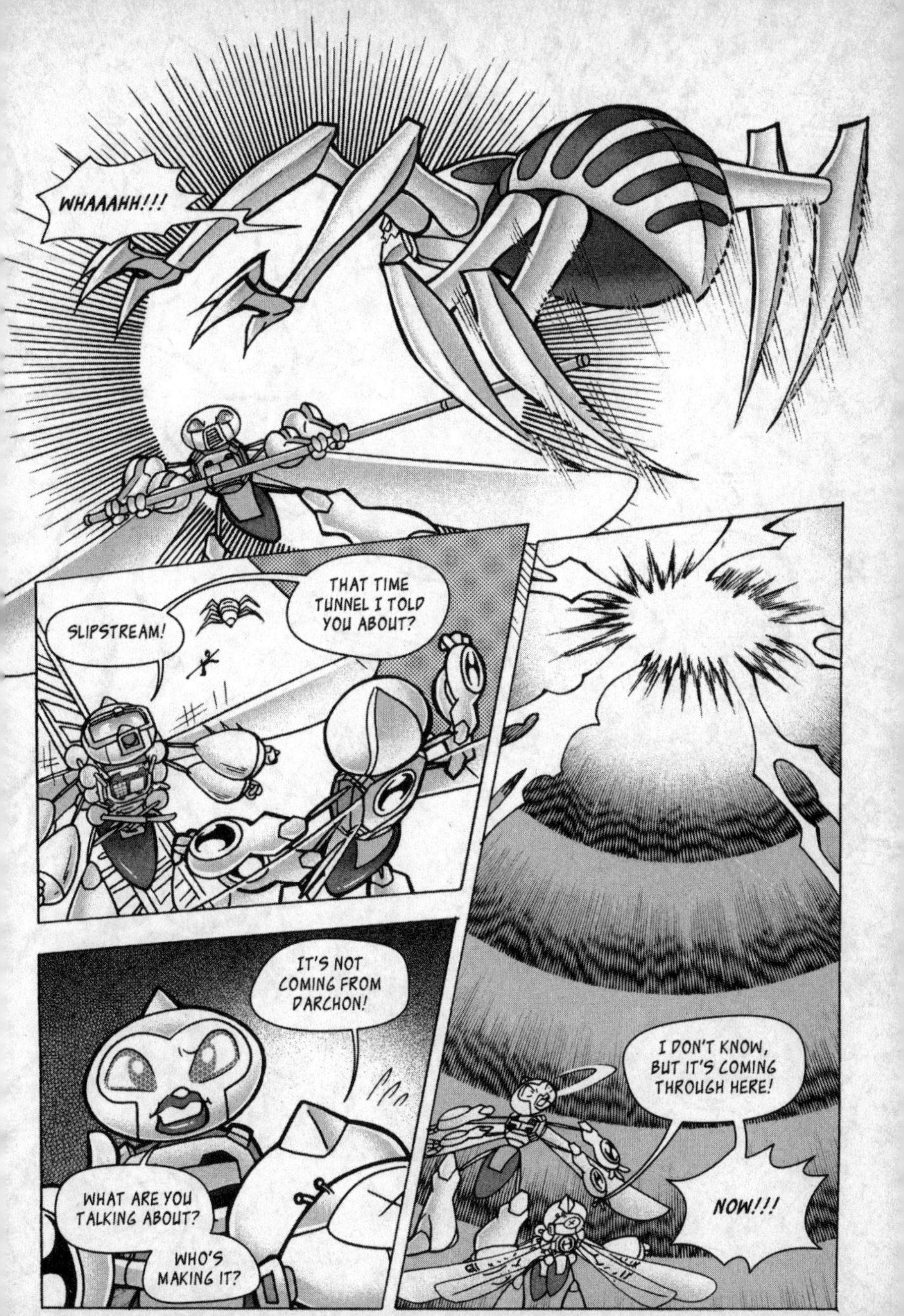
WHAAAHH!!!
SLIPSTREAM!
THAT TIME TUNNEL I TOLD YOU ABOUT?
IT'S NOT COMING FROM DARCHON!
WHAT ARE YOU TALKING ABOUT?
WHO'S MAKING IT?
I DON'T KNOW, BUT IT'S COMING THROUGH HERE!
NOW!!!

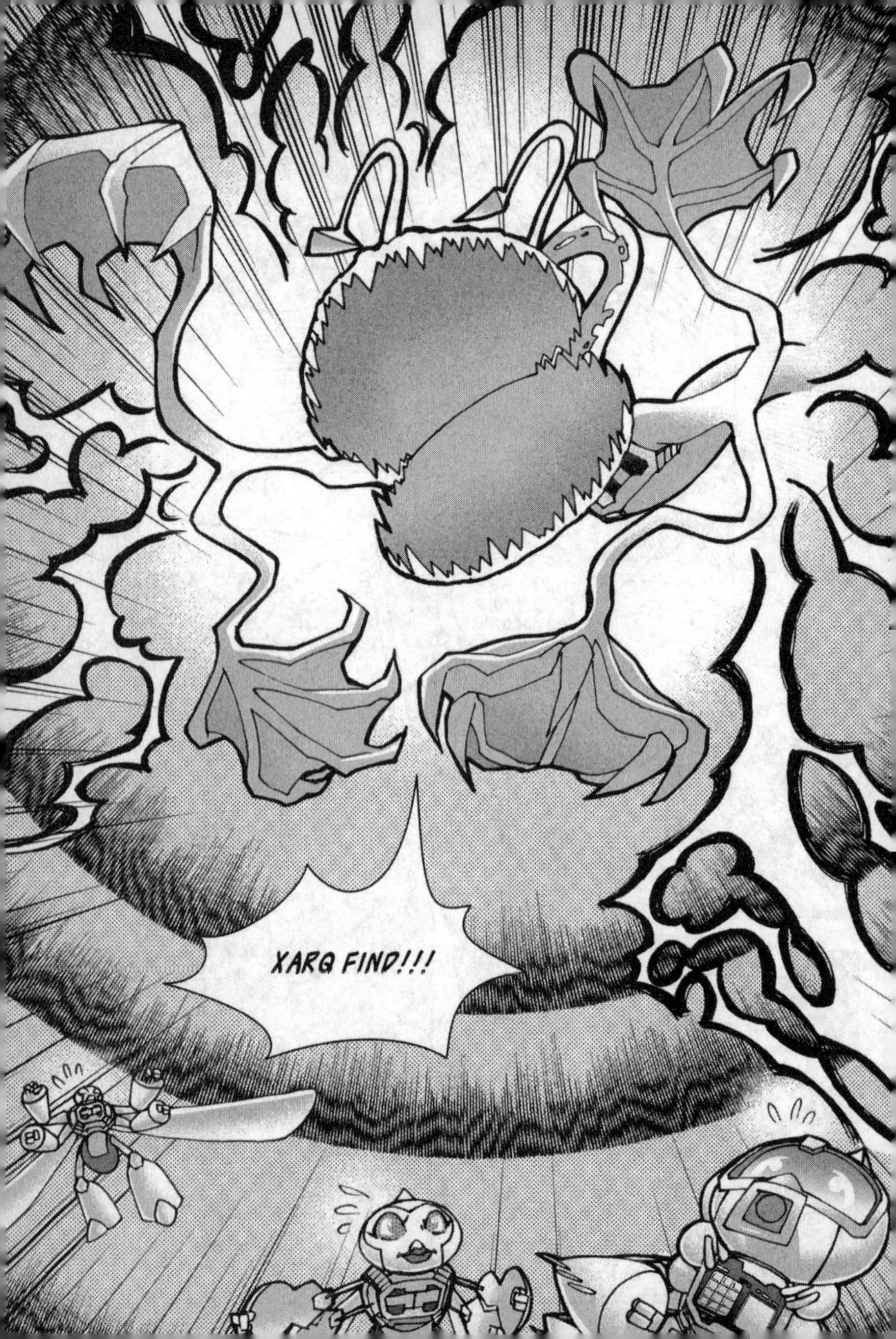
XARQ FIND!!!

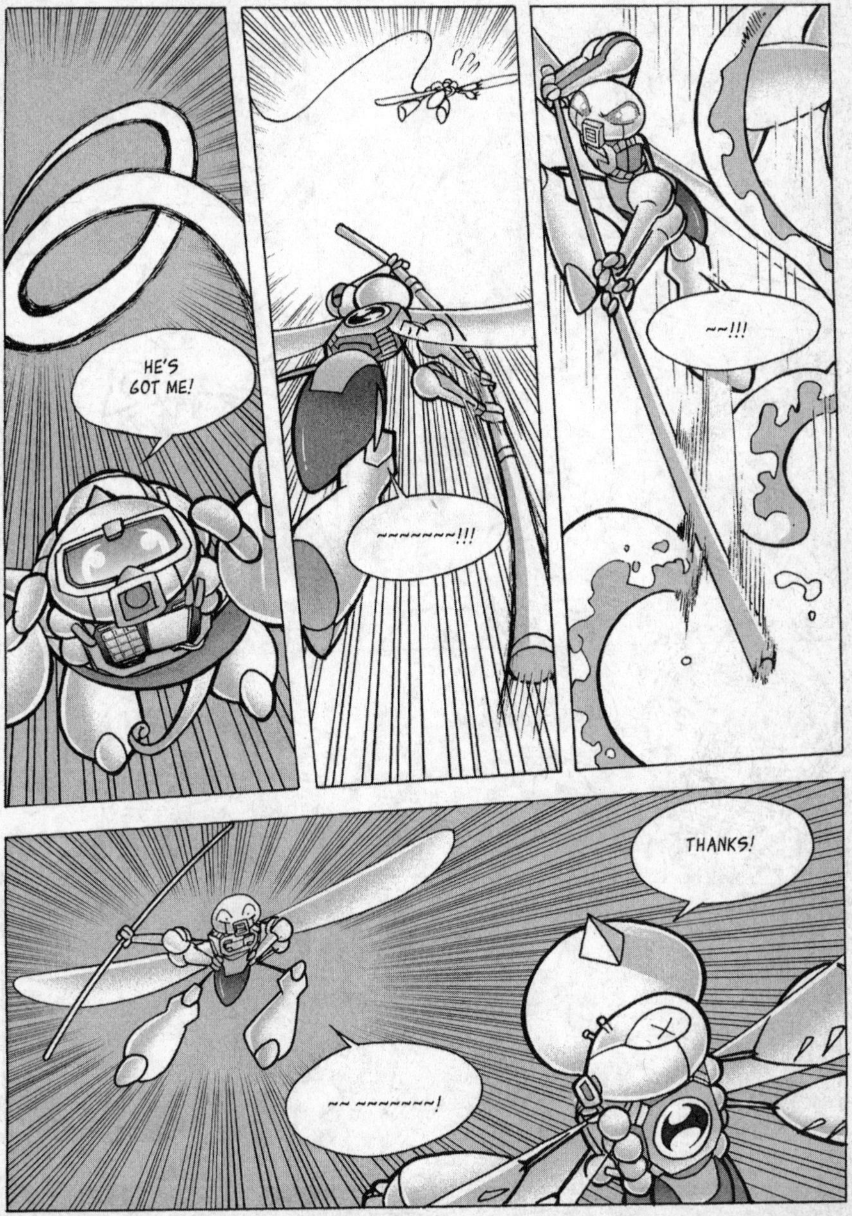
HE'S GOT ME!
~~~~~~~~!!!
~~!!!
THANKS!
~~ ~~~~~~~!
~~~~~~~~

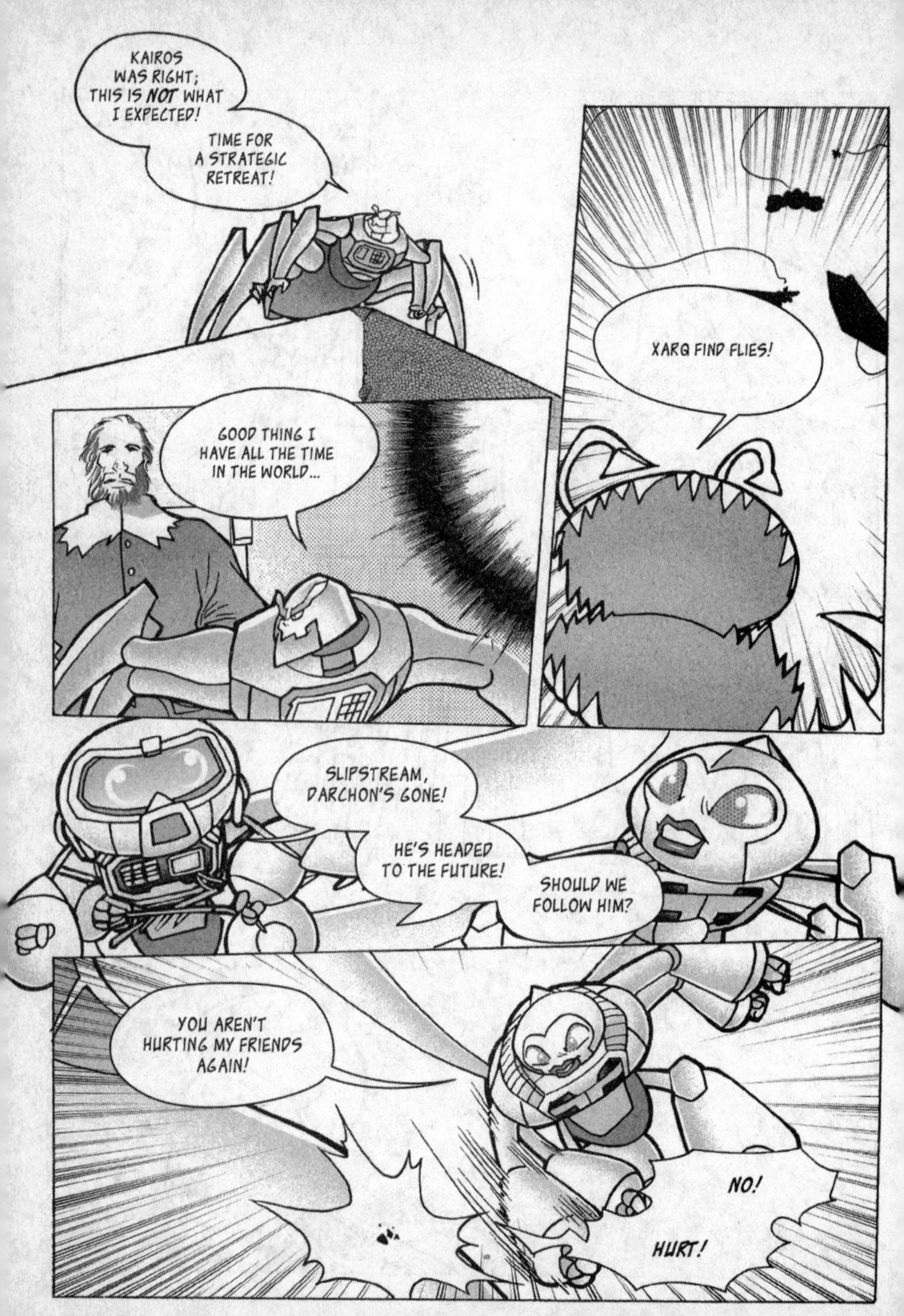
KAIROS WAS RIGHT; THIS IS **NOT** WHAT I EXPECTED!
TIME FOR A STRATEGIC RETREAT!
XARQ FIND FLIES!
GOOD THING I HAVE ALL THE TIME IN THE WORLD...
SLIPSTREAM, DARCHON'S GONE!
HE'S HEADED TO THE FUTURE!
SHOULD WE FOLLOW HIM?
YOU AREN'T HURTING MY FRIENDS AGAIN!
NO!
HURT!

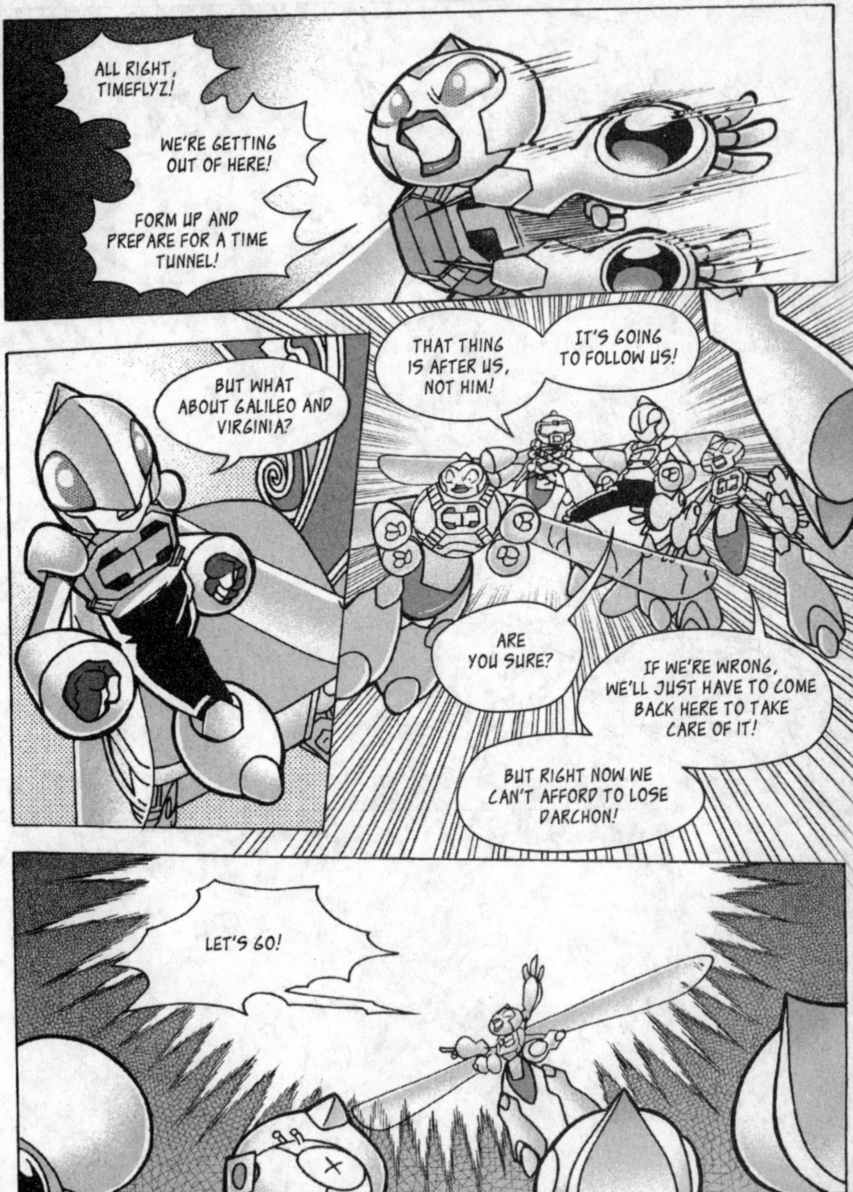
ALL RIGHT, TIMEFLYZ!
WE'RE GETTING OUT OF HERE!
FORM UP AND PREPARE FOR A TIME TUNNEL!
BUT WHAT ABOUT GALILEO AND VIRGINIA?
THAT THING IS AFTER US, NOT HIM!
IT'S GOING TO FOLLOW US!
ARE YOU SURE?
IF WE'RE WRONG, WE'LL JUST HAVE TO COME BACK HERE TO TAKE CARE OF IT!
BUT RIGHT NOW WE CAN'T AFFORD TO LOSE DARCHON!
LET'S GO!

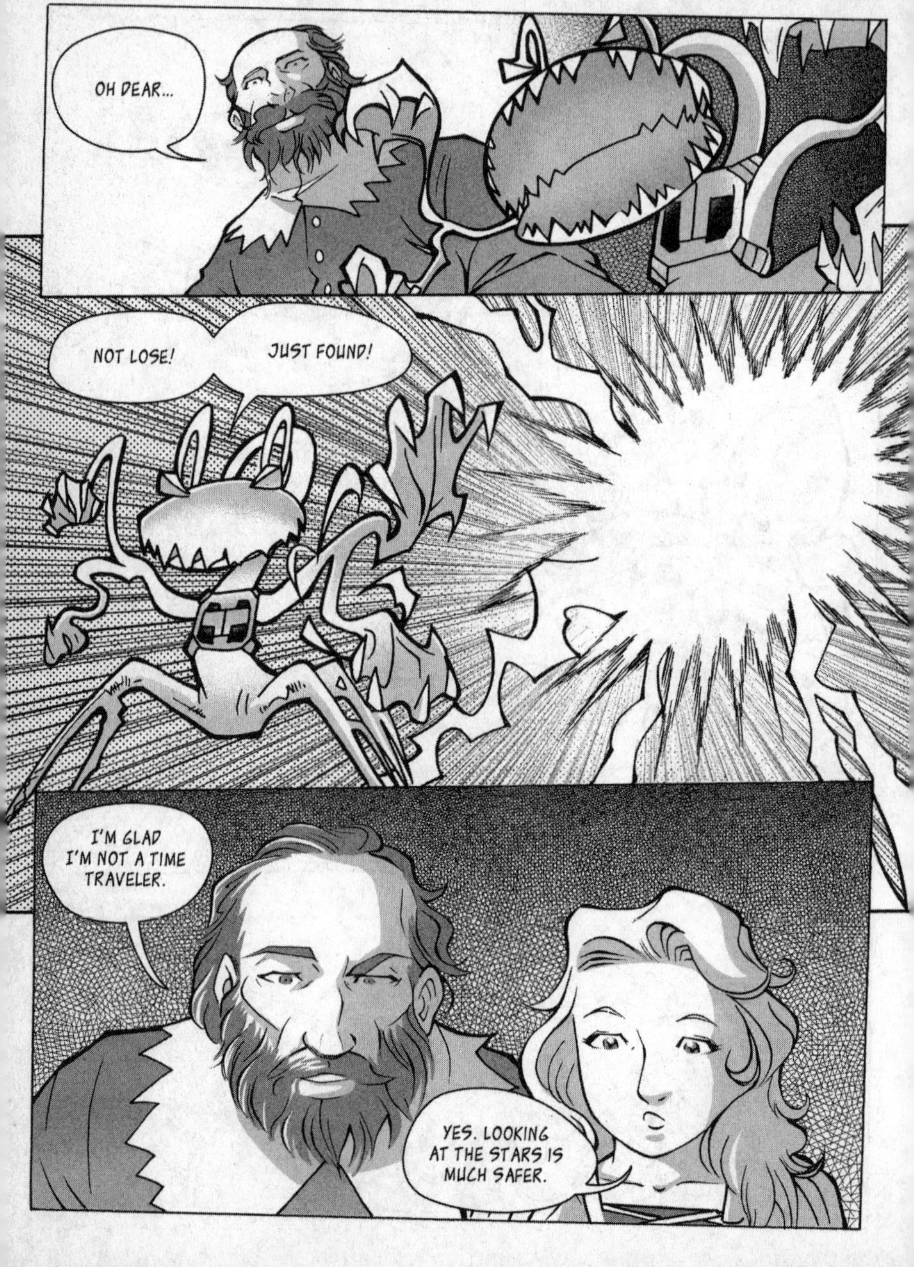
OH DEAR...
NOT LOSE!
JUST FOUND!
I'M GLAD I'M NOT A TIME TRAVELER.
YES. LOOKING AT THE STARS IS MUCH SAFER.

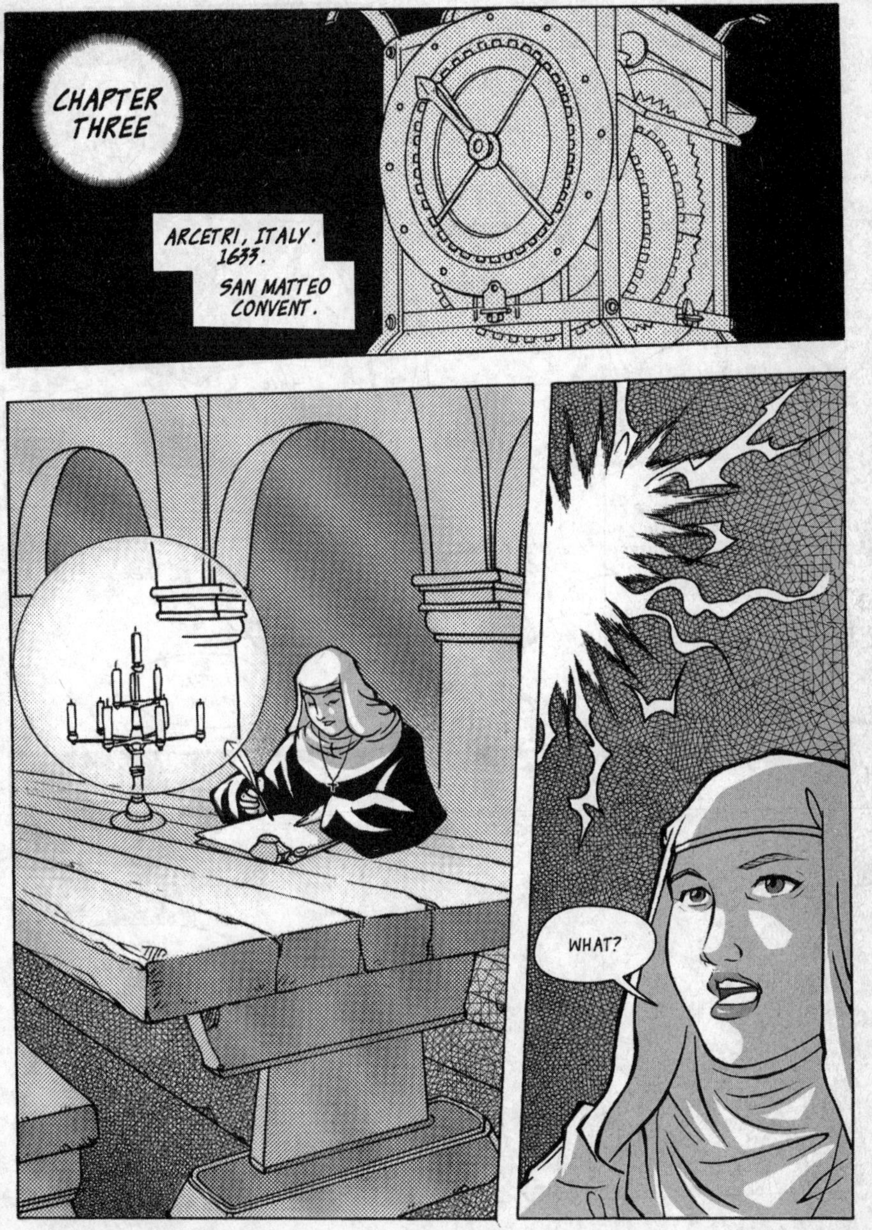
CHAPTER THREE
ARCETRI, ITALY. 1633.
SAN MATTEO CONVENT.
WHAT?

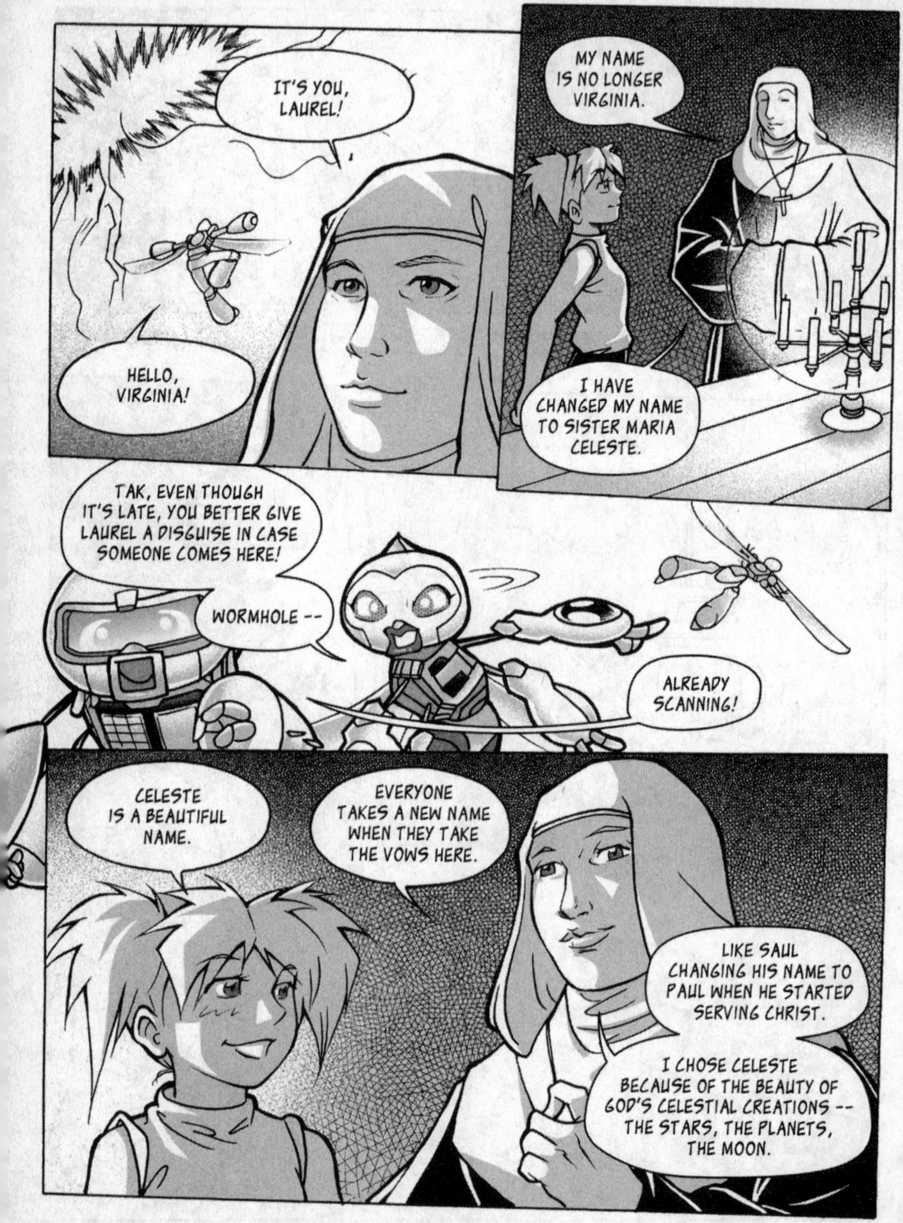

IT'S YOU, LAUREL!
HELLO, VIRGINIA!
MY NAME IS NO LONGER VIRGINIA.
I HAVE CHANGED MY NAME TO SISTER MARIA CELESTE.
TAK, EVEN THOUGH IT'S LATE, YOU BETTER GIVE LAUREL A DISGUISE IN CASE SOMEONE COMES HERE!
WORMHOLE --
ALREADY SCANNING!
CELESTE IS A BEAUTIFUL NAME.
EVERYONE TAKES A NEW NAME WHEN THEY TAKE THE VOWS HERE.
LIKE SAUL CHANGING HIS NAME TO PAUL WHEN HE STARTED SERVING CHRIST.
I CHOSE CELESTE BECAUSE OF THE BEAUTY OF GOD'S CELESTIAL CREATIONS -- THE STARS, THE PLANETS, THE MOON.

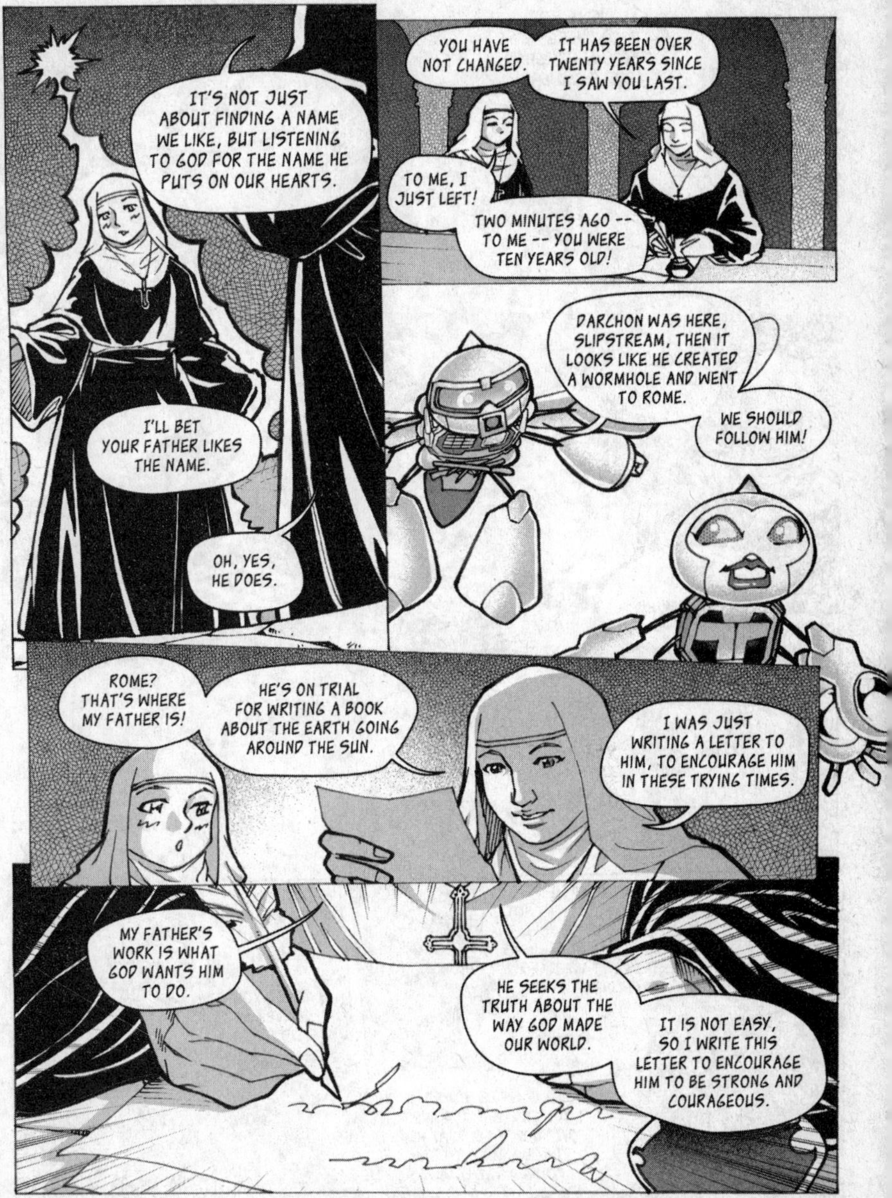

IT'S NOT JUST ABOUT FINDING A NAME WE LIKE, BUT LISTENING TO GOD FOR THE NAME HE PUTS ON OUR HEARTS.
I'LL BET YOUR FATHER LIKES THE NAME.
OH, YES, HE DOES.
YOU HAVE NOT CHANGED.
IT HAS BEEN OVER TWENTY YEARS SINCE I SAW YOU LAST.
TO ME, I JUST LEFT!
TWO MINUTES AGO -- TO ME -- YOU WERE TEN YEARS OLD!
DARCHON WAS HERE, SLIPSTREAM, THEN IT LOOKS LIKE HE CREATED A WORMHOLE AND WENT TO ROME.
WE SHOULD FOLLOW HIM!
ROME? THAT'S WHERE MY FATHER IS!
HE'S ON TRIAL FOR WRITING A BOOK ABOUT THE EARTH GOING AROUND THE SUN.
I WAS JUST WRITING A LETTER TO HIM, TO ENCOURAGE HIM IN THESE TRYING TIMES.
MY FATHER'S WORK IS WHAT GOD WANTS HIM TO DO.
HE SEEKS THE TRUTH ABOUT THE WAY GOD MADE OUR WORLD.
IT IS NOT EASY, SO I WRITE THIS LETTER TO ENCOURAGE HIM TO BE STRONG AND COURAGEOUS.

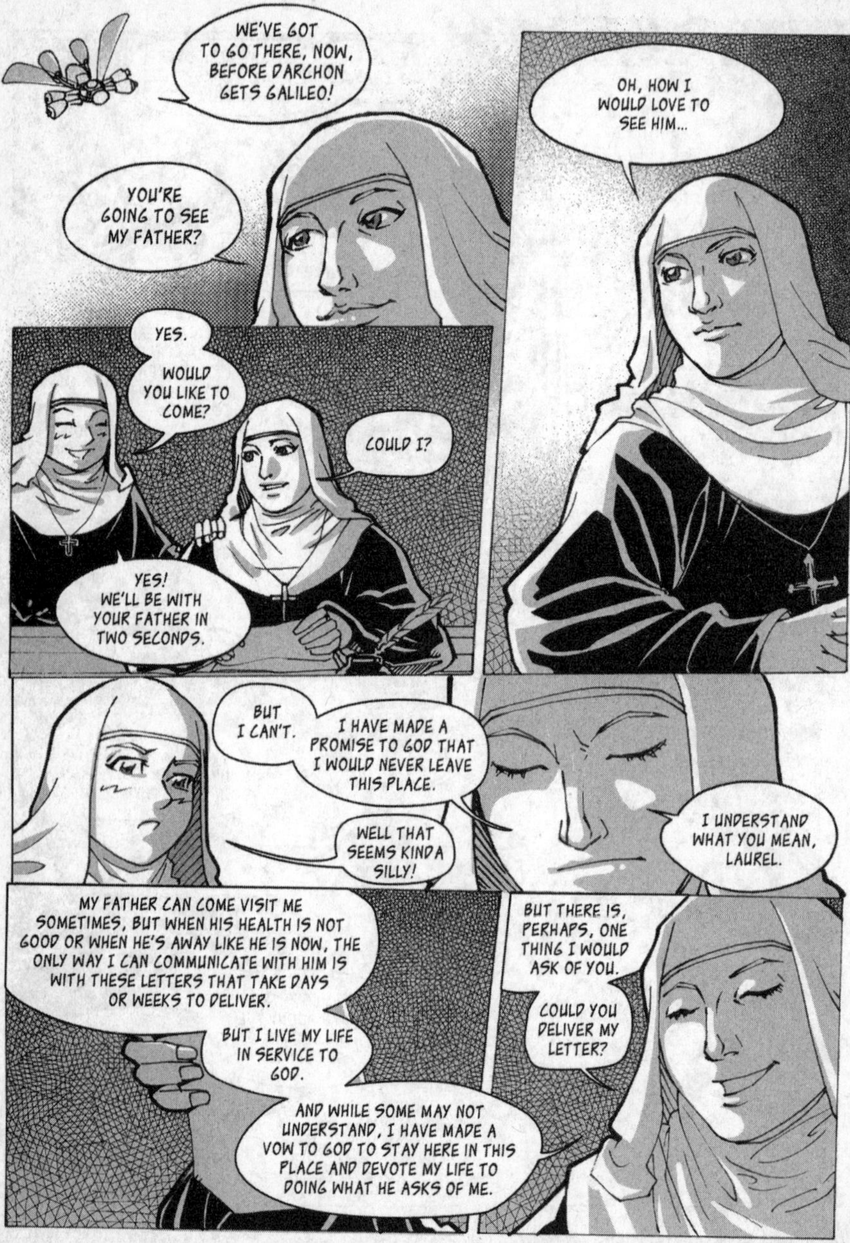
WE'VE GOT TO GO THERE, NOW, BEFORE DARCHON GETS GALILEO!
YOU'RE GOING TO SEE MY FATHER?
YES.
WOULD YOU LIKE TO COME?
COULD I?
YES! WE'LL BE WITH YOUR FATHER IN TWO SECONDS.
OH, HOW I WOULD LOVE TO SEE HIM...
BUT I CAN'T.
I HAVE MADE A PROMISE TO GOD THAT I WOULD NEVER LEAVE THIS PLACE.
WELL THAT SEEMS KINDA SILLY!
I UNDERSTAND WHAT YOU MEAN, LAUREL.
MY FATHER CAN COME VISIT ME SOMETIMES, BUT WHEN HIS HEALTH IS NOT GOOD OR WHEN HE'S AWAY LIKE HE IS NOW, THE ONLY WAY I CAN COMMUNICATE WITH HIM IS WITH THESE LETTERS THAT TAKE DAYS OR WEEKS TO DELIVER.
BUT I LIVE MY LIFE IN SERVICE TO GOD.
AND WHILE SOME MAY NOT UNDERSTAND, I HAVE MADE A VOW TO GOD TO STAY HERE IN THIS PLACE AND DEVOTE MY LIFE TO DOING WHAT HE ASKS OF ME.
BUT THERE IS, PERHAPS, ONE THING I WOULD ASK OF YOU.
COULD YOU DELIVER MY LETTER?

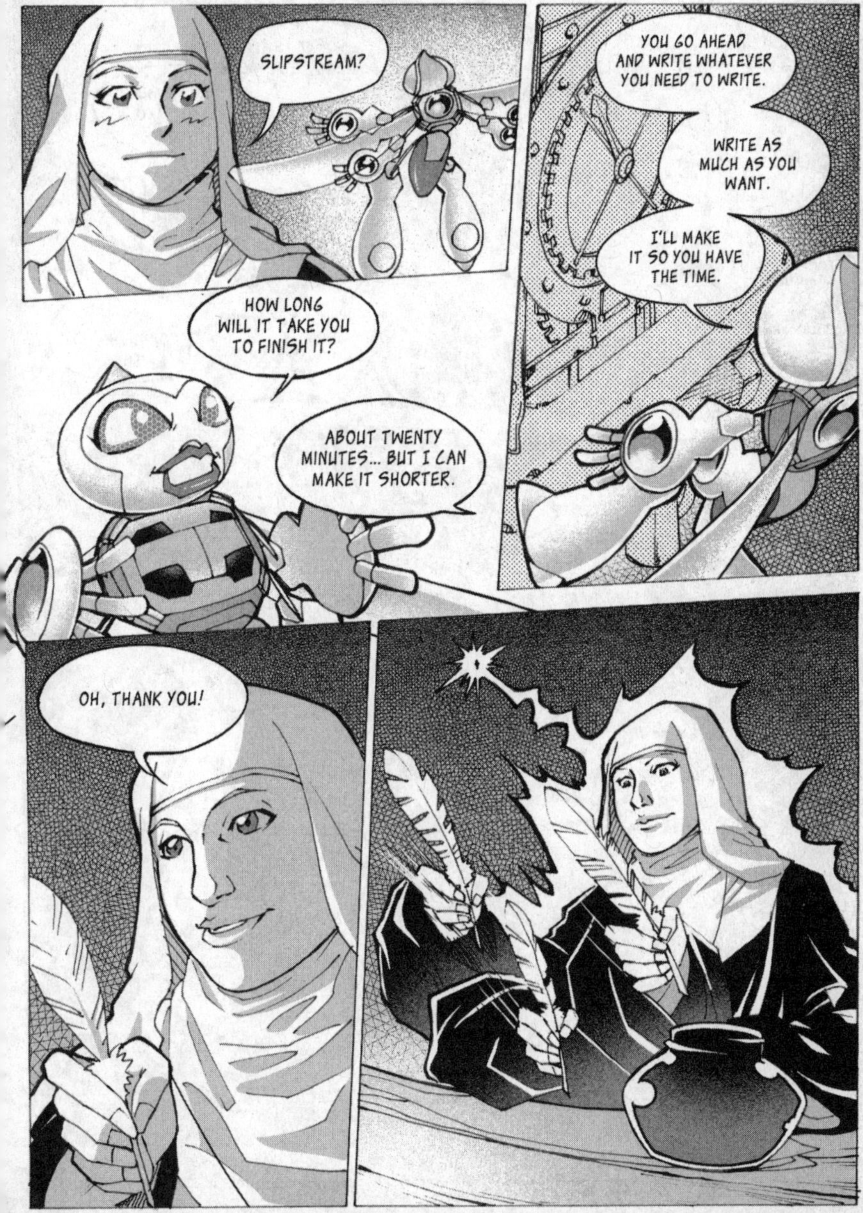
SLIPSTREAM?
YOU GO AHEAD AND WRITE WHATEVER YOU NEED TO WRITE.
WRITE AS MUCH AS YOU WANT.
I'LL MAKE IT SO YOU HAVE THE TIME.
HOW LONG WILL IT TAKE YOU TO FINISH IT?
ABOUT TWENTY MINUTES... BUT I CAN MAKE IT SHORTER.
OH, THANK YOU!

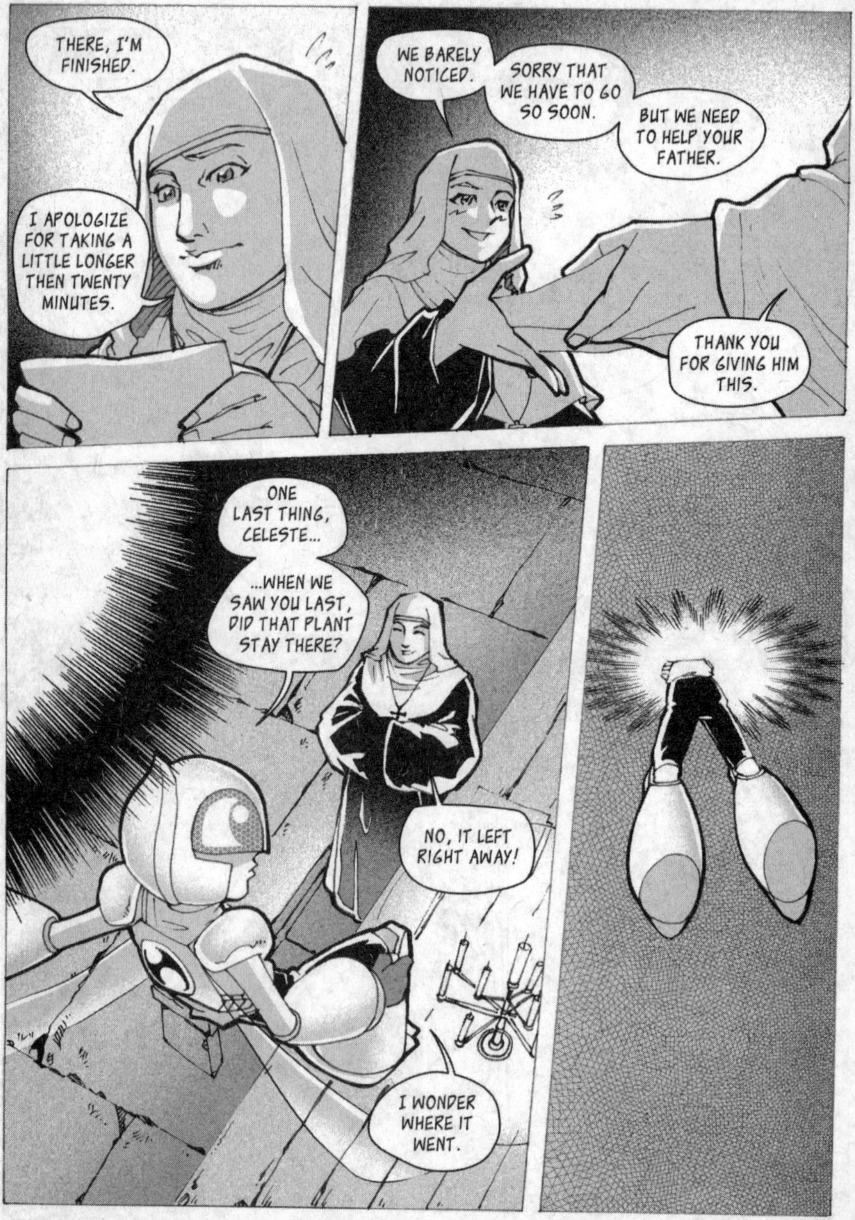
THERE, I'M FINISHED.
I APOLOGIZE FOR TAKING A LITTLE LONGER THEN TWENTY MINUTES.
WE BARELY NOTICED.
SORRY THAT WE HAVE TO GO SO SOON.
BUT WE NEED TO HELP YOUR FATHER.
THANK YOU FOR GIVING HIM THIS.
ONE LAST THING, CELESTE...
...WHEN WE SAW YOU LAST, DID THAT PLANT STAY THERE?
NO, IT LEFT RIGHT AWAY!
I WONDER WHERE IT WENT.

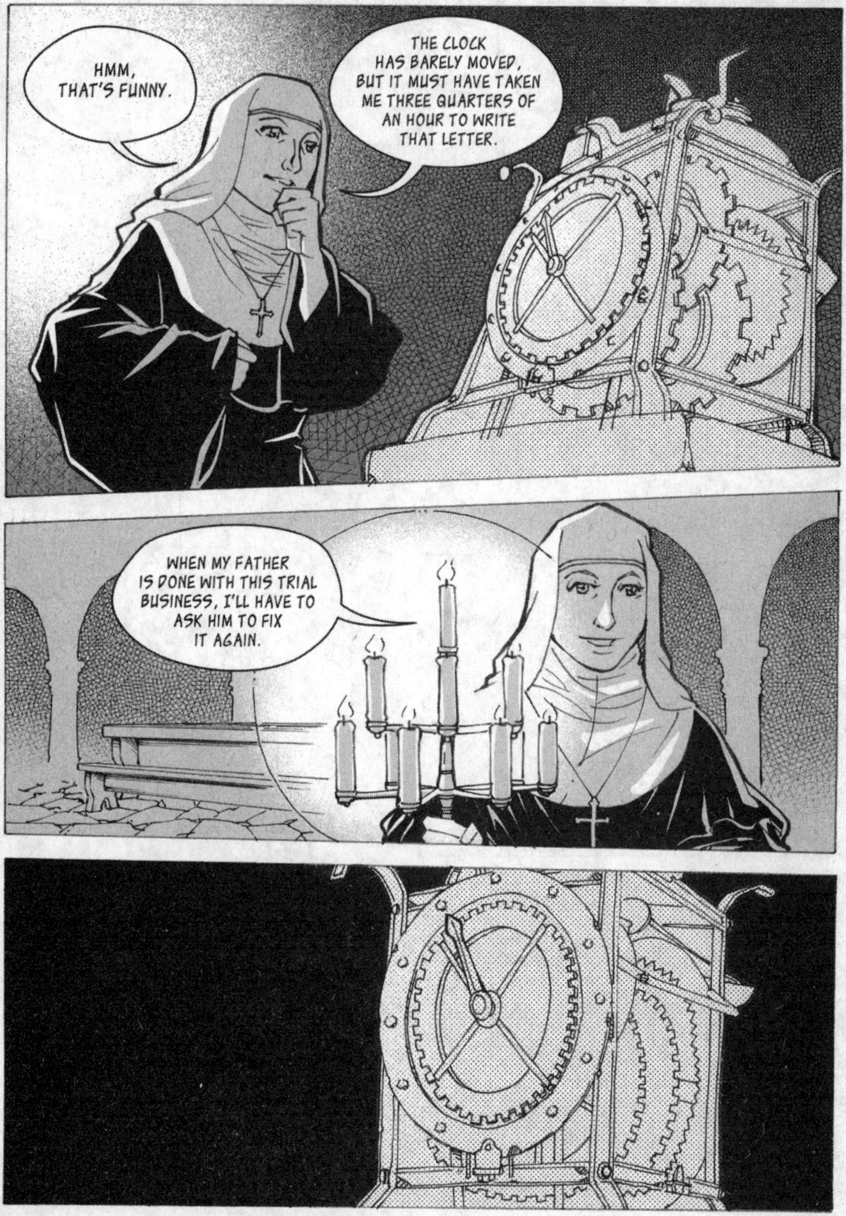
HMM, THAT'S FUNNY.
THE CLOCK HAS BARELY MOVED, BUT IT MUST HAVE TAKEN ME THREE QUARTERS OF AN HOUR TO WRITE THAT LETTER.
WHEN MY FATHER IS DONE WITH THIS TRIAL BUSINESS, I'LL HAVE TO ASK HIM TO FIX IT AGAIN.

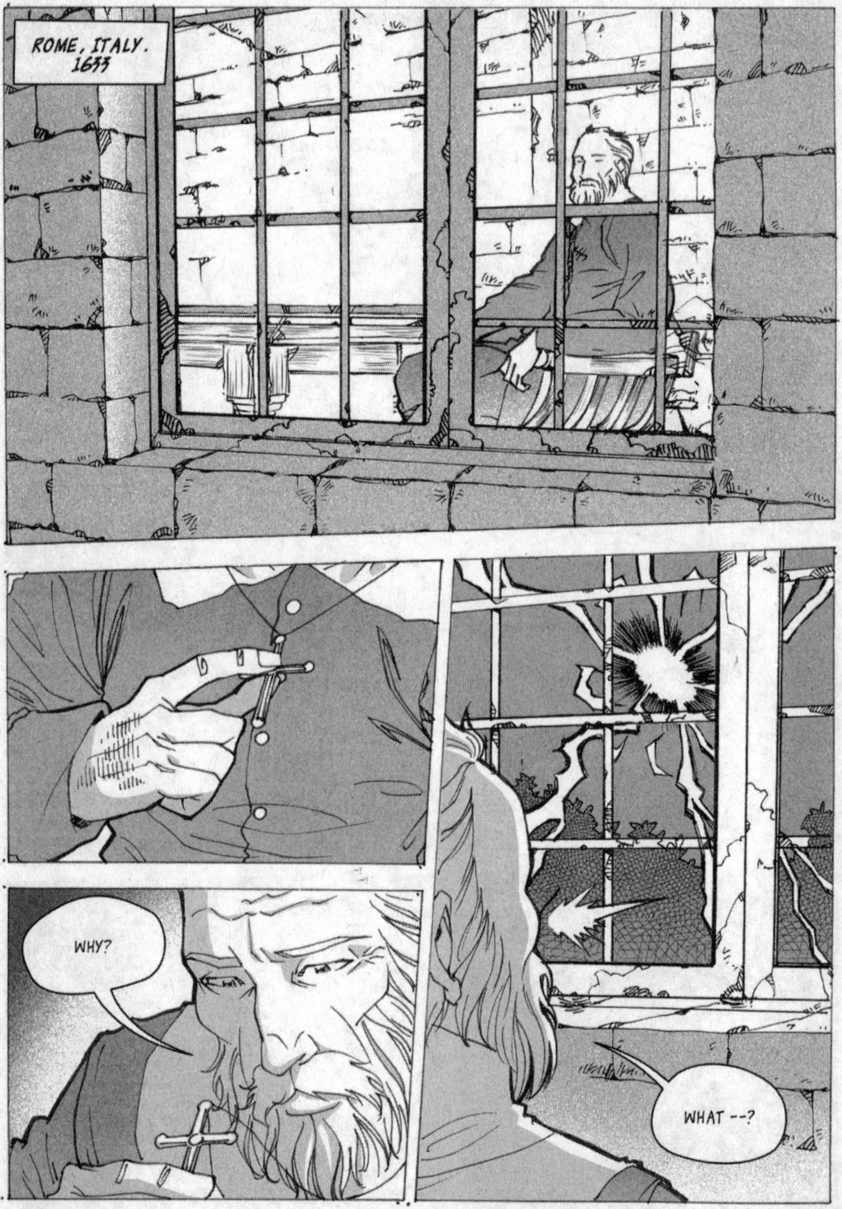
ROME, ITALY.
1633
WHY?
WHAT --?

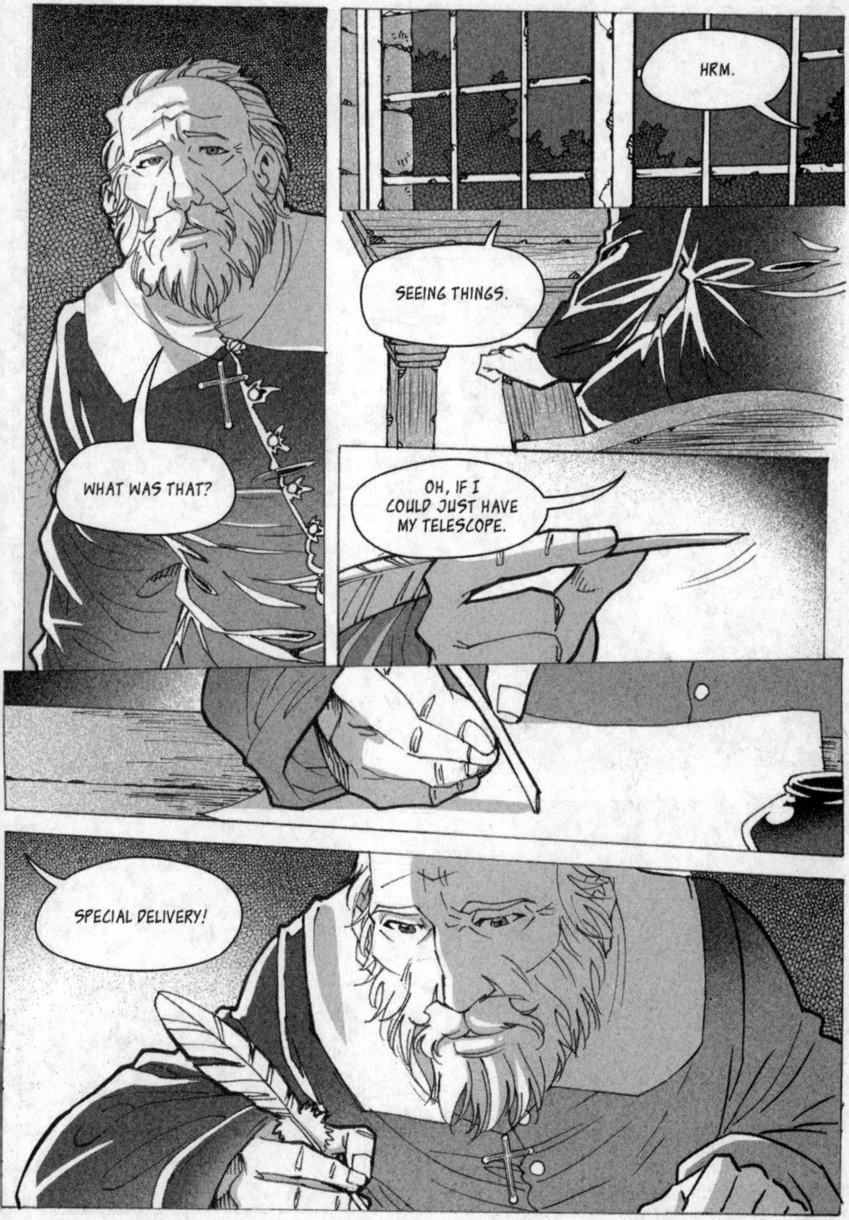
HRM.
SEEING THINGS.
WHAT WAS THAT?
OH, IF I COULD JUST HAVE MY TELESCOPE.
SPECIAL DELIVERY!

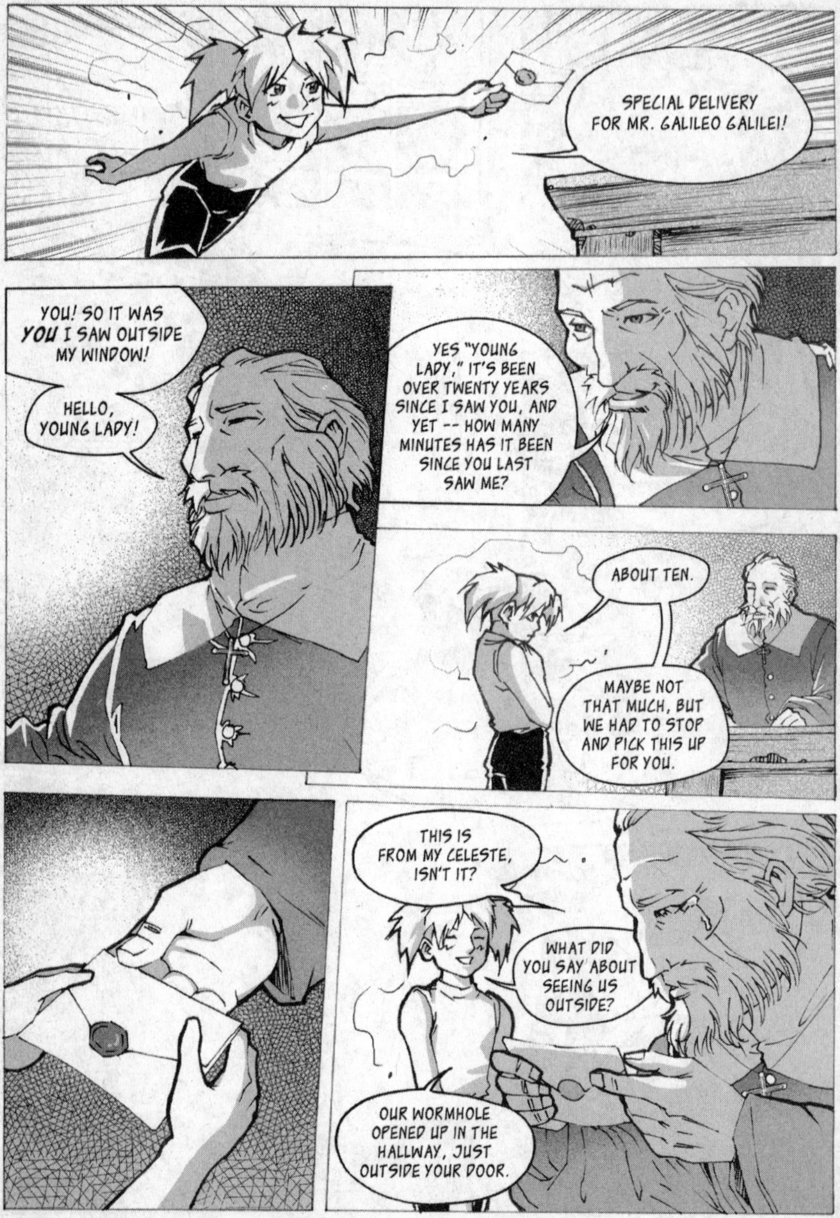
SPECIAL DELIVERY FOR MR. GALILEO GALILEI!
YOU! SO IT WAS YOU I SAW OUTSIDE MY WINDOW!
HELLO, YOUNG LADY!
YES "YOUNG LADY," IT'S BEEN OVER TWENTY YEARS SINCE I SAW YOU, AND YET -- HOW MANY MINUTES HAS IT BEEN SINCE YOU LAST SAW ME?
ABOUT TEN.
MAYBE NOT THAT MUCH, BUT WE HAD TO STOP AND PICK THIS UP FOR YOU.
THIS IS FROM MY CELESTE, ISN'T IT?
WHAT DID YOU SAY ABOUT SEEING US OUTSIDE?
OUR WORMHOLE OPENED UP IN THE HALLWAY, JUST OUTSIDE YOUR DOOR.

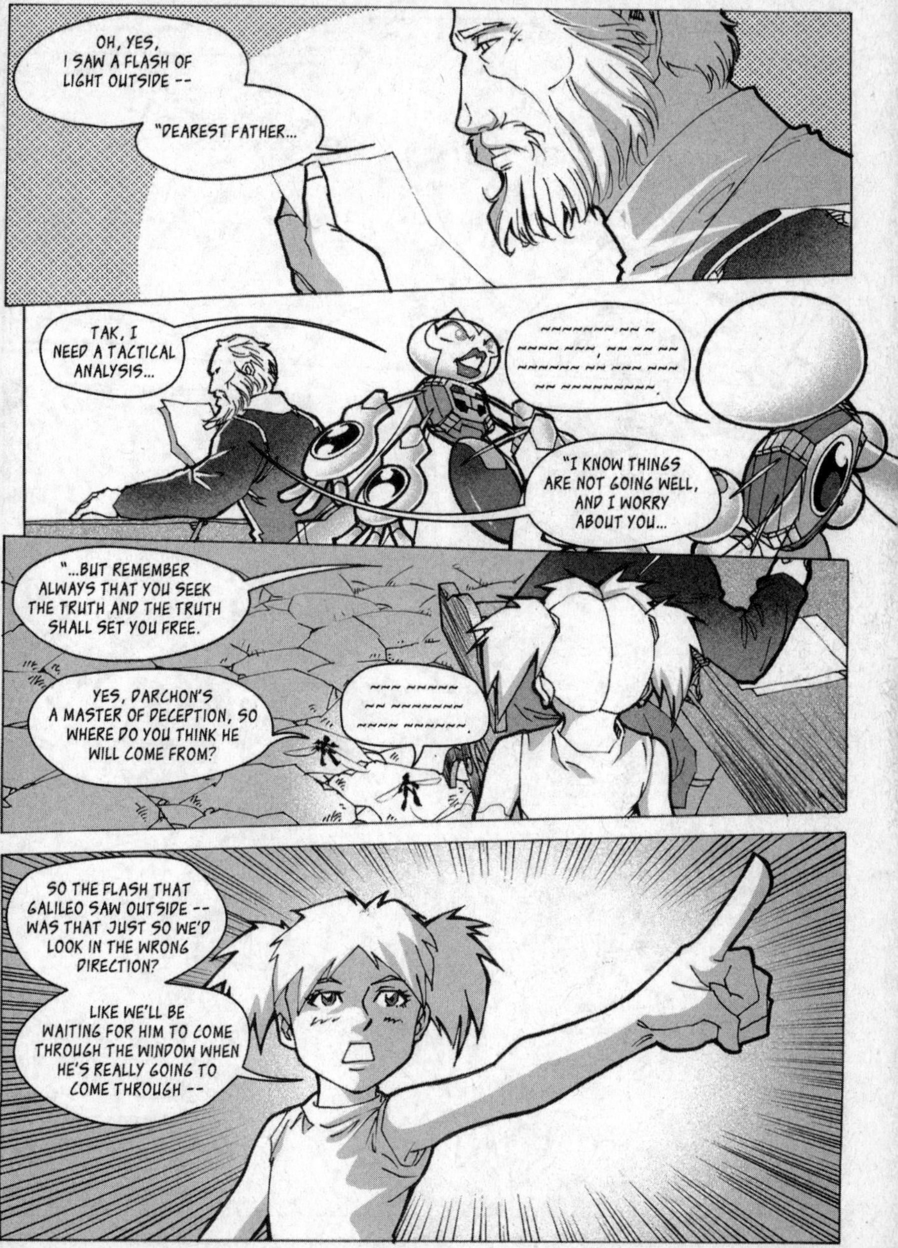
OH, YES, I SAW A FLASH OF LIGHT OUTSIDE --
"DEAREST FATHER...
TAK, I NEED A TACTICAL ANALYSIS...
"I KNOW THINGS ARE NOT GOING WELL, AND I WORRY ABOUT YOU...
"...BUT REMEMBER ALWAYS THAT YOU SEEK THE TRUTH AND THE TRUTH SHALL SET YOU FREE.
YES, DARCHON'S A MASTER OF DECEPTION, SO WHERE DO YOU THINK HE WILL COME FROM?
SO THE FLASH THAT GALILEO SAW OUTSIDE -- WAS THAT JUST SO WE'D LOOK IN THE WRONG DIRECTION?
LIKE WE'LL BE WAITING FOR HIM TO COME THROUGH THE WINDOW WHEN HE'S REALLY GOING TO COME THROUGH --

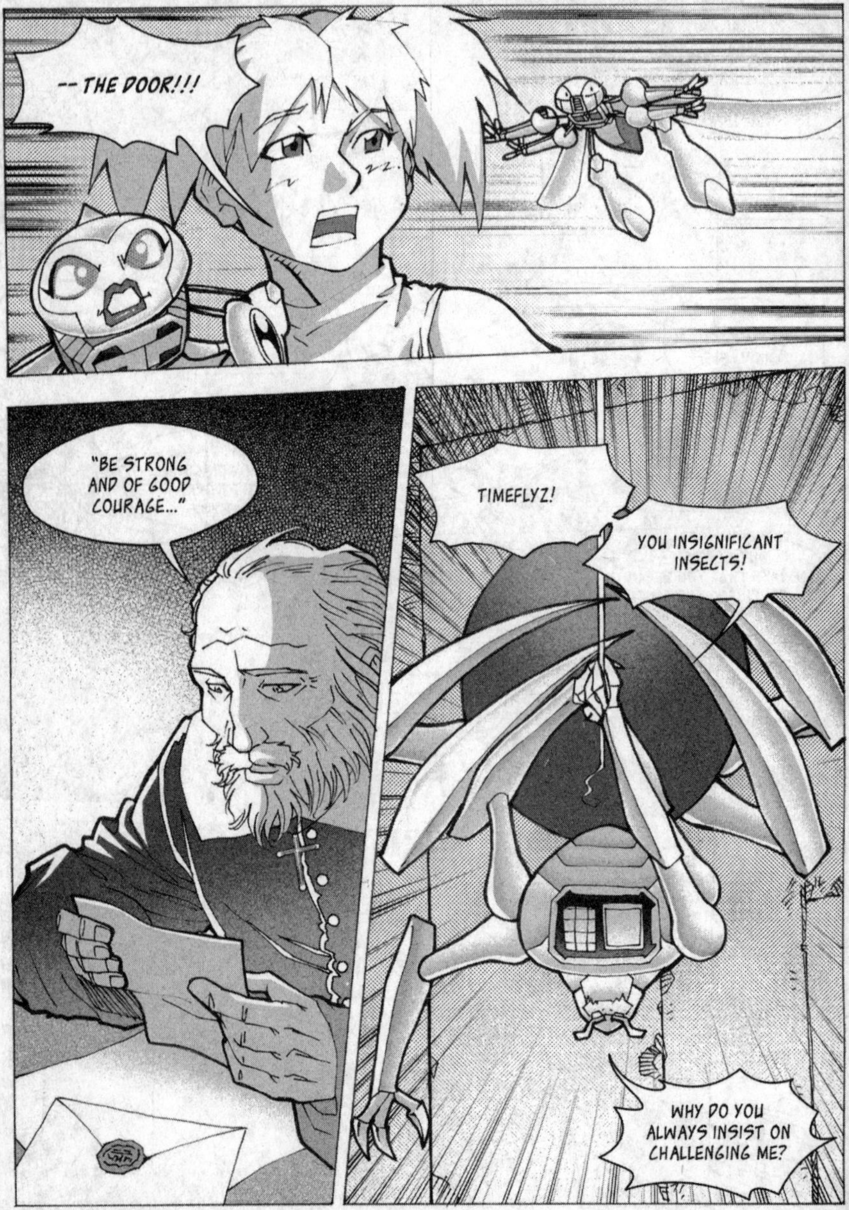
--THE DOOR!!!
"BE STRONG AND OF GOOD COURAGE..."
TIMEFLYZ!
YOU INSIGNIFICANT INSECTS!
WHY DO YOU ALWAYS INSIST ON CHALLENGING ME?

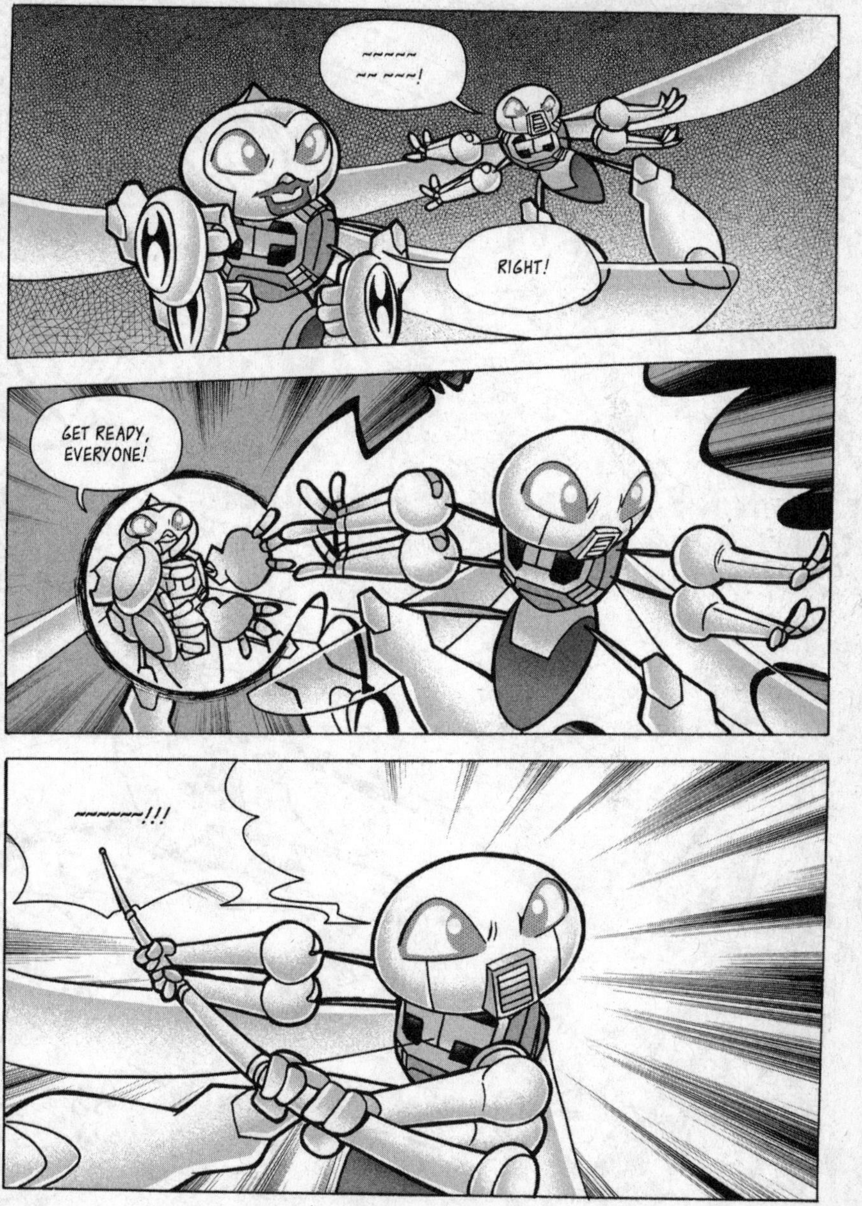
~~~~~
~~ ~~~!
RIGHT!
GET READY, EVERYONE!
~~~~~~!!!

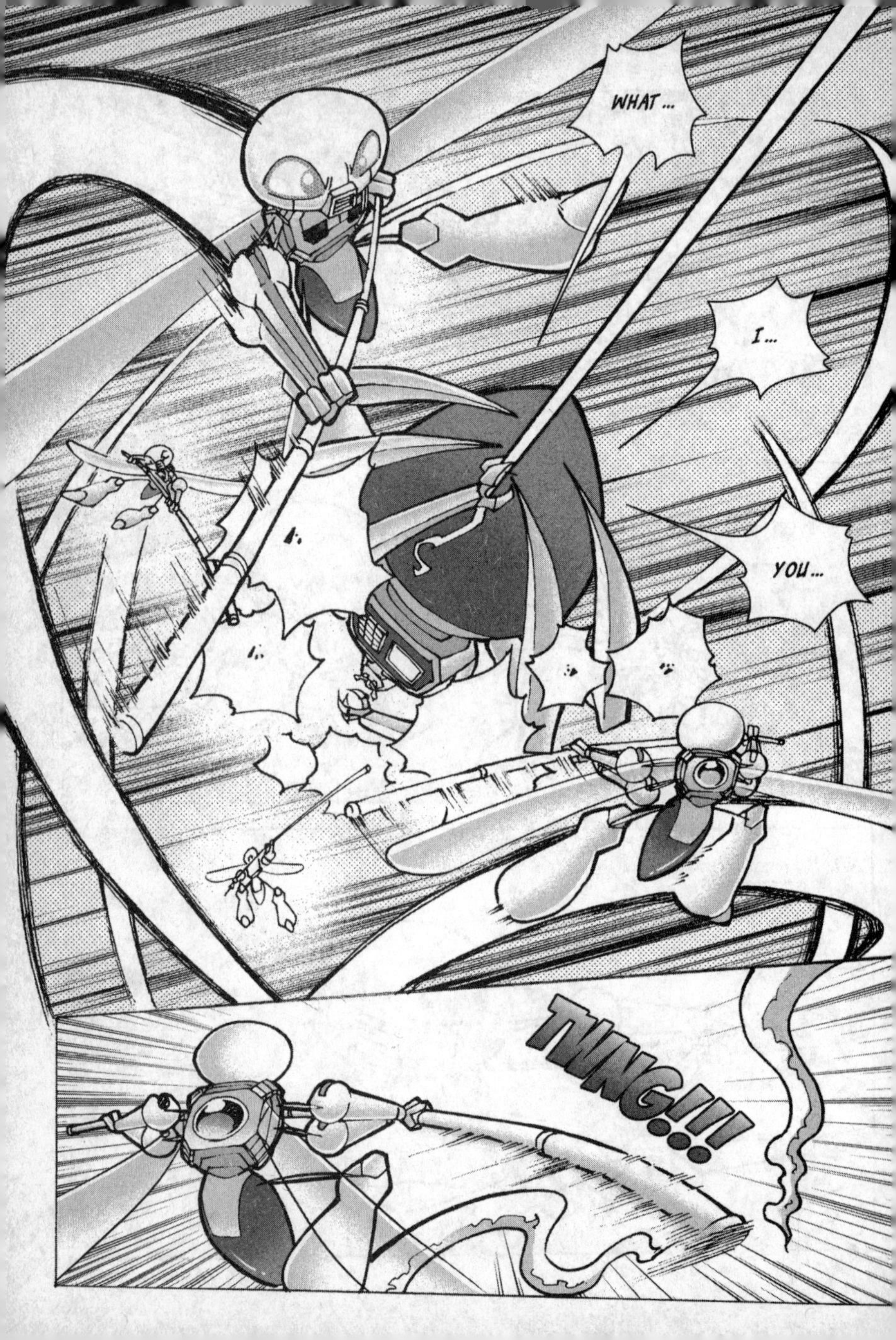
WHAT...
I...
YOU...
TWING!!!

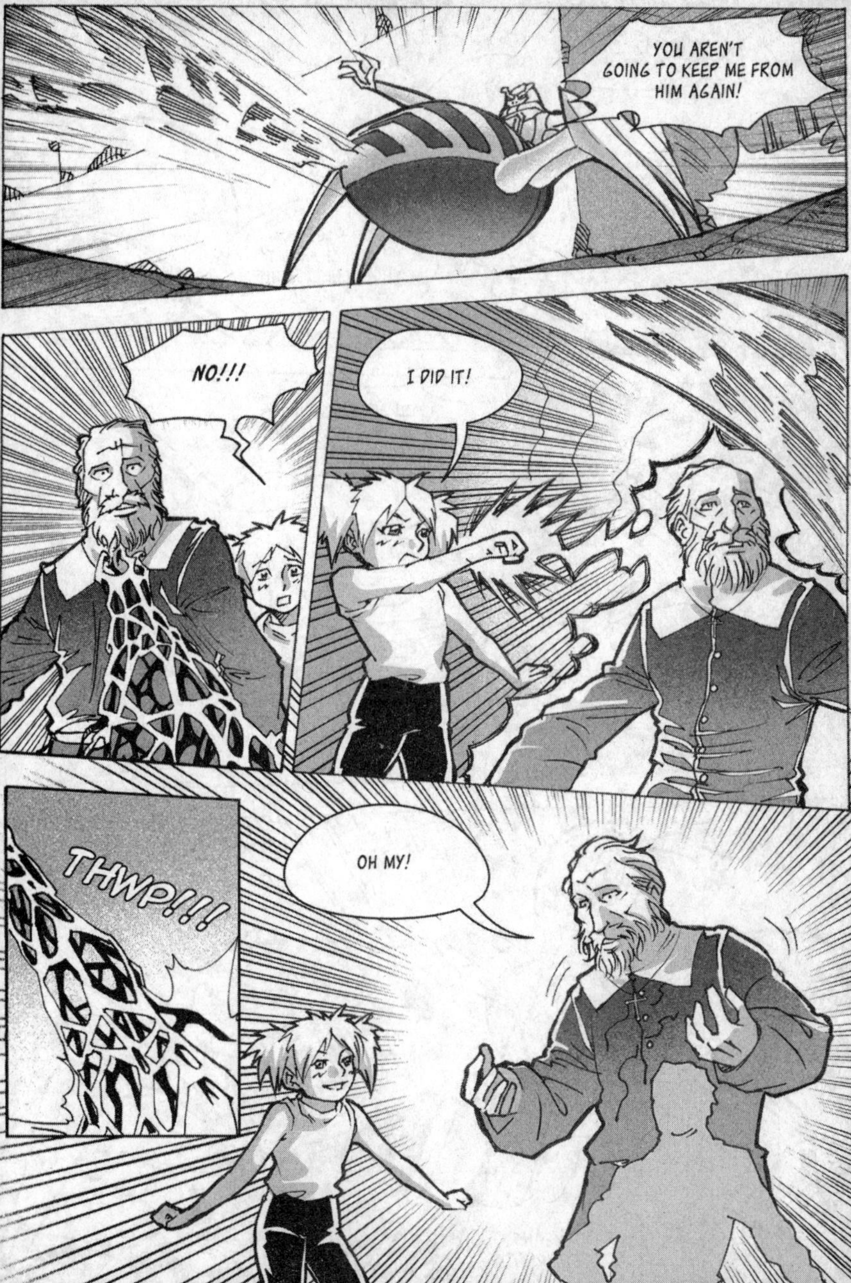
YOU AREN'T GOING TO KEEP ME FROM HIM AGAIN!
NO!!!
I DID IT!
THWP!!!
OH MY!

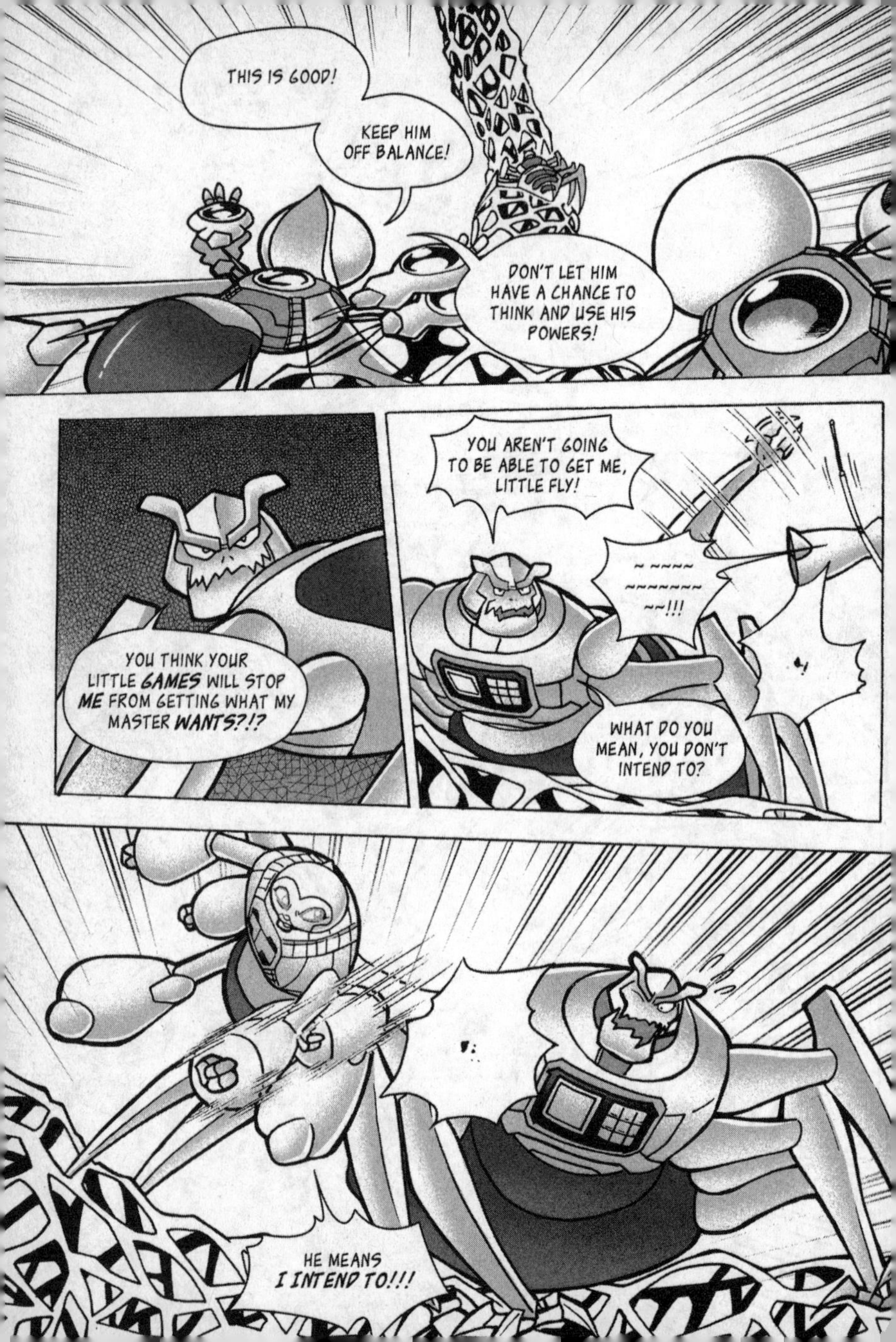
THIS IS GOOD!
KEEP HIM OFF BALANCE!
DON'T LET HIM HAVE A CHANCE TO THINK AND USE HIS POWERS!
YOU THINK YOUR LITTLE GAMES WILL STOP ME FROM GETTING WHAT MY MASTER WANTS?!?
YOU AREN'T GOING TO BE ABLE TO GET ME, LITTLE FLY!
~ ~~~~ ~~~~~~~ ~~!!!
WHAT DO YOU MEAN, YOU DON'T INTEND TO?
HE MEANS I INTEND TO!!!

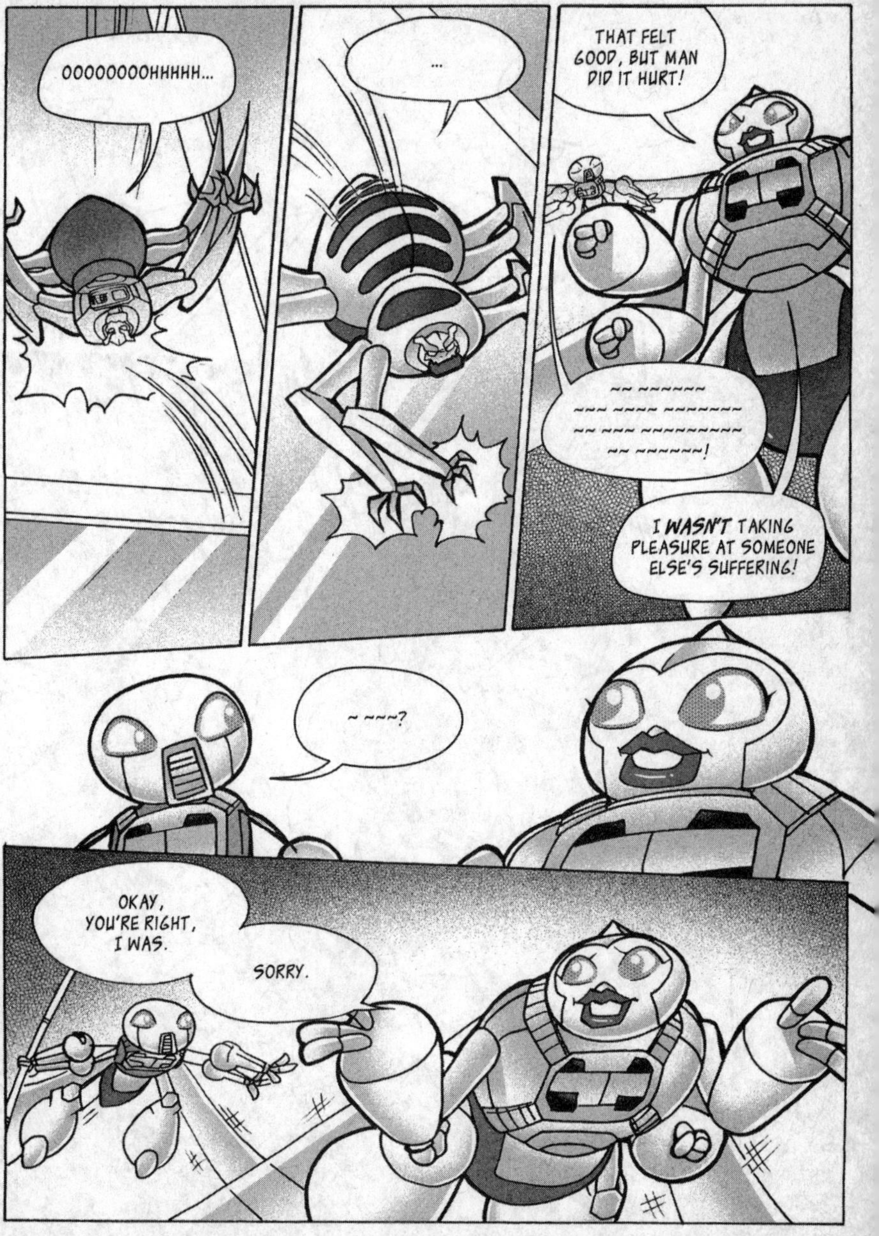
OOOOOOOOHHHHH...
...
THAT FELT GOOD, BUT MAN DID IT HURT!
I WASN'T TAKING PLEASURE AT SOMEONE ELSE'S SUFFERING!
OKAY, YOU'RE RIGHT, I WAS.
SORRY.

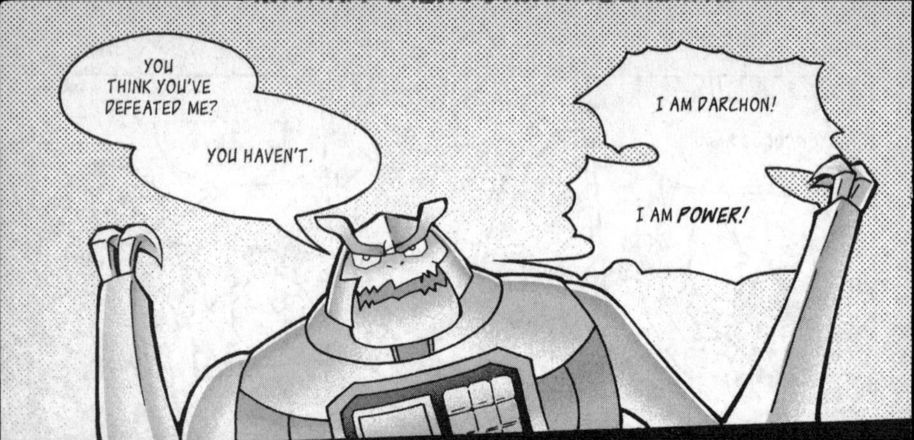
YOU THINK YOU'VE DEFEATED ME?
YOU HAVEN'T.
I AM DARCHON!
I AM *POWER!*
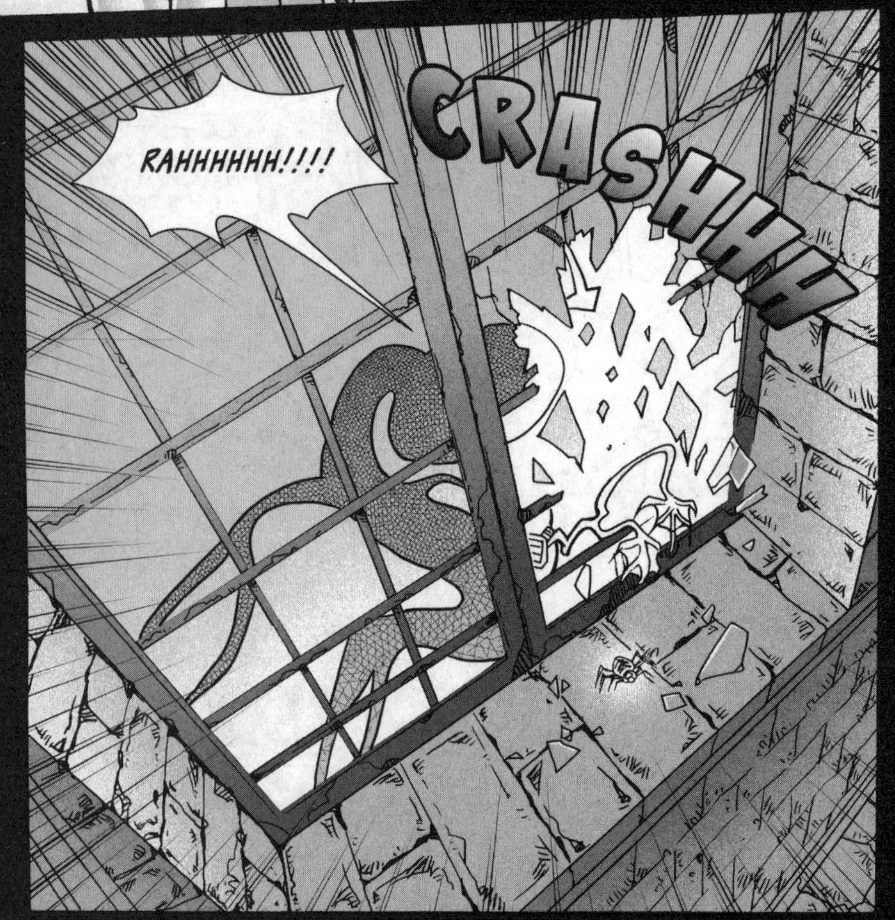
RAHHHHHH!!!!
CRASHHHH

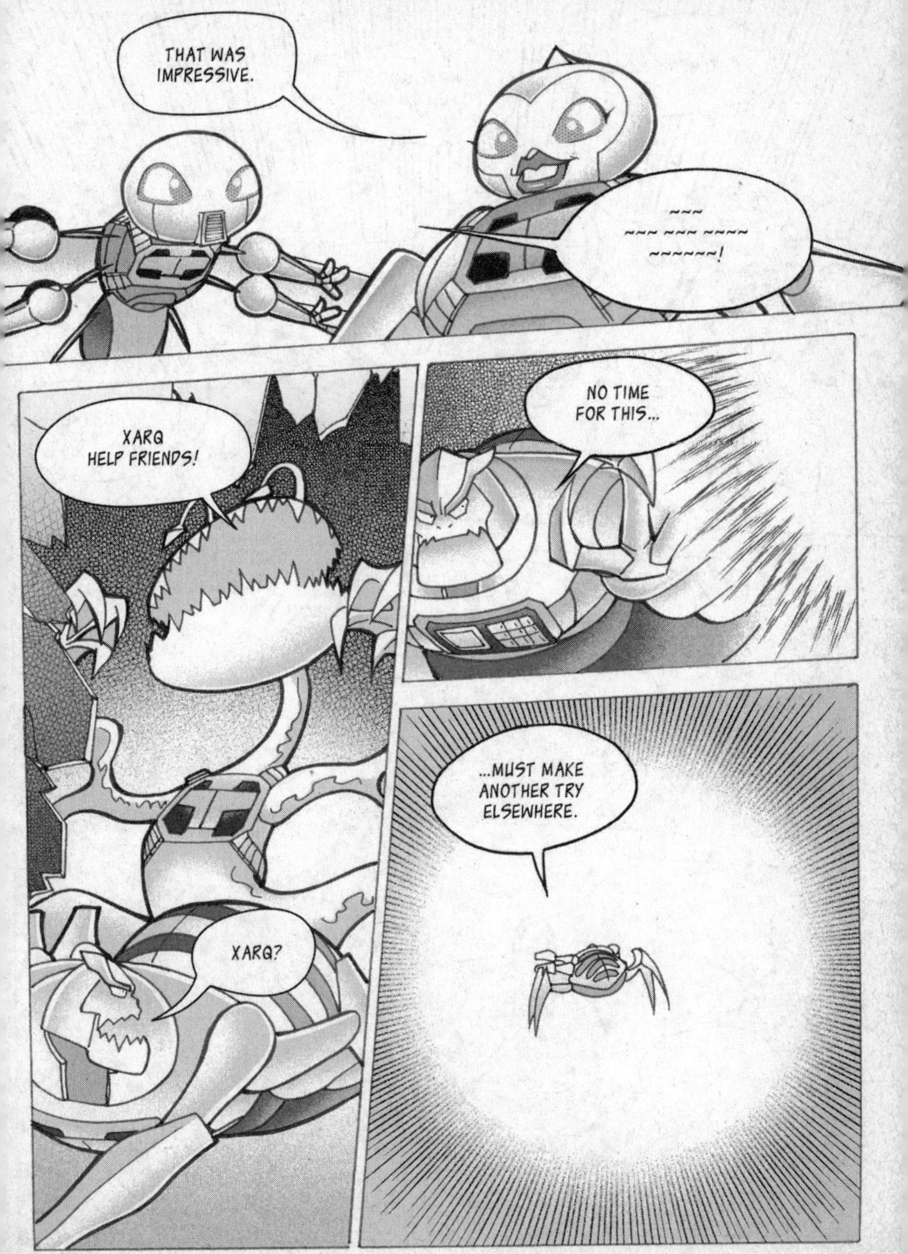
THAT WAS IMPRESSIVE.
~~~ ~~~ ~~~ ~~~~ ~~~~~~~!
XARQ HELP FRIENDS!
XARQ?
NO TIME FOR THIS...
...MUST MAKE ANOTHER TRY ELSEWHERE.
~~~

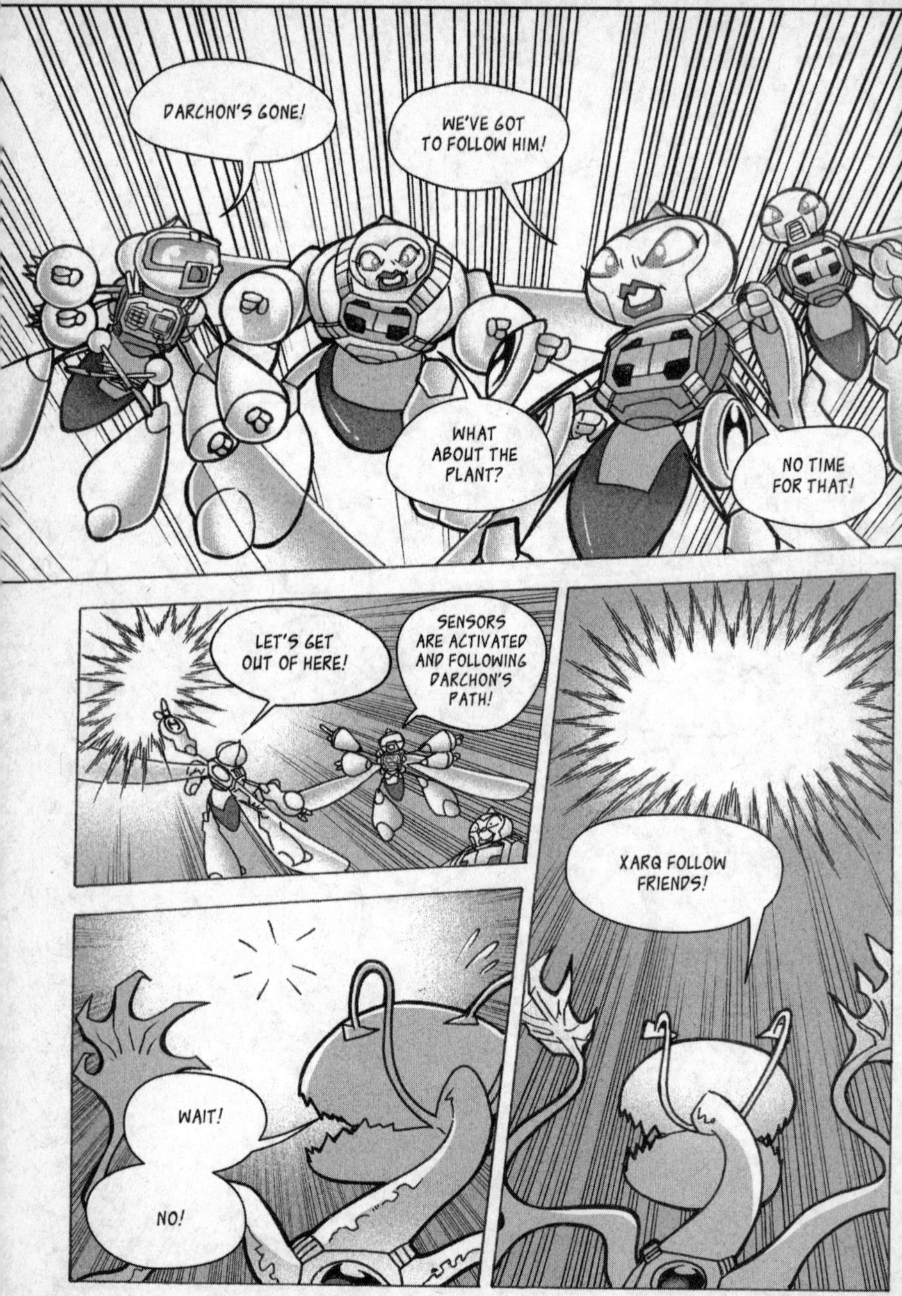
DARCHON'S GONE!
WE'VE GOT TO FOLLOW HIM!
WHAT ABOUT THE PLANT?
NO TIME FOR THAT!
LET'S GET OUT OF HERE!
SENSORS ARE ACTIVATED AND FOLLOWING DARCHON'S PATH!
XARQ FOLLOW FRIENDS!
WAIT!
NO!

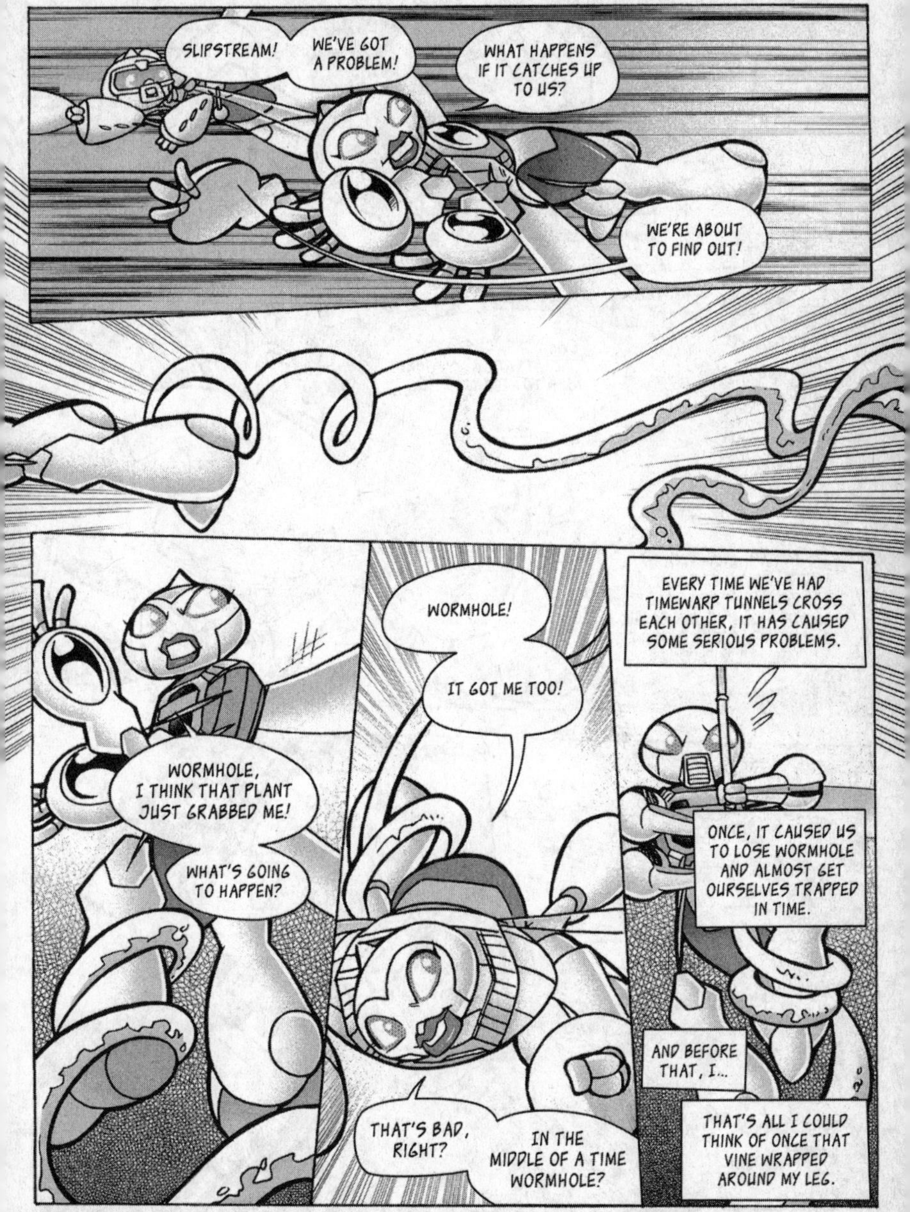
SLIPSTREAM!
WE'VE GOT A PROBLEM!
WHAT HAPPENS IF IT CATCHES UP TO US?
WE'RE ABOUT TO FIND OUT!
WORMHOLE, I THINK THAT PLANT JUST GRABBED ME!
WHAT'S GOING TO HAPPEN?
WORMHOLE!
IT GOT ME TOO!
THAT'S BAD, RIGHT?
IN THE MIDDLE OF A TIME WORMHOLE?
EVERY TIME WE'VE HAD TIMEWARP TUNNELS CROSS EACH OTHER, IT HAS CAUSED SOME SERIOUS PROBLEMS.
ONCE, IT CAUSED US TO LOSE WORMHOLE AND ALMOST GET OURSELVES TRAPPED IN TIME.
AND BEFORE THAT, I...
THAT'S ALL I COULD THINK OF ONCE THAT VINE WRAPPED AROUND MY LEG.

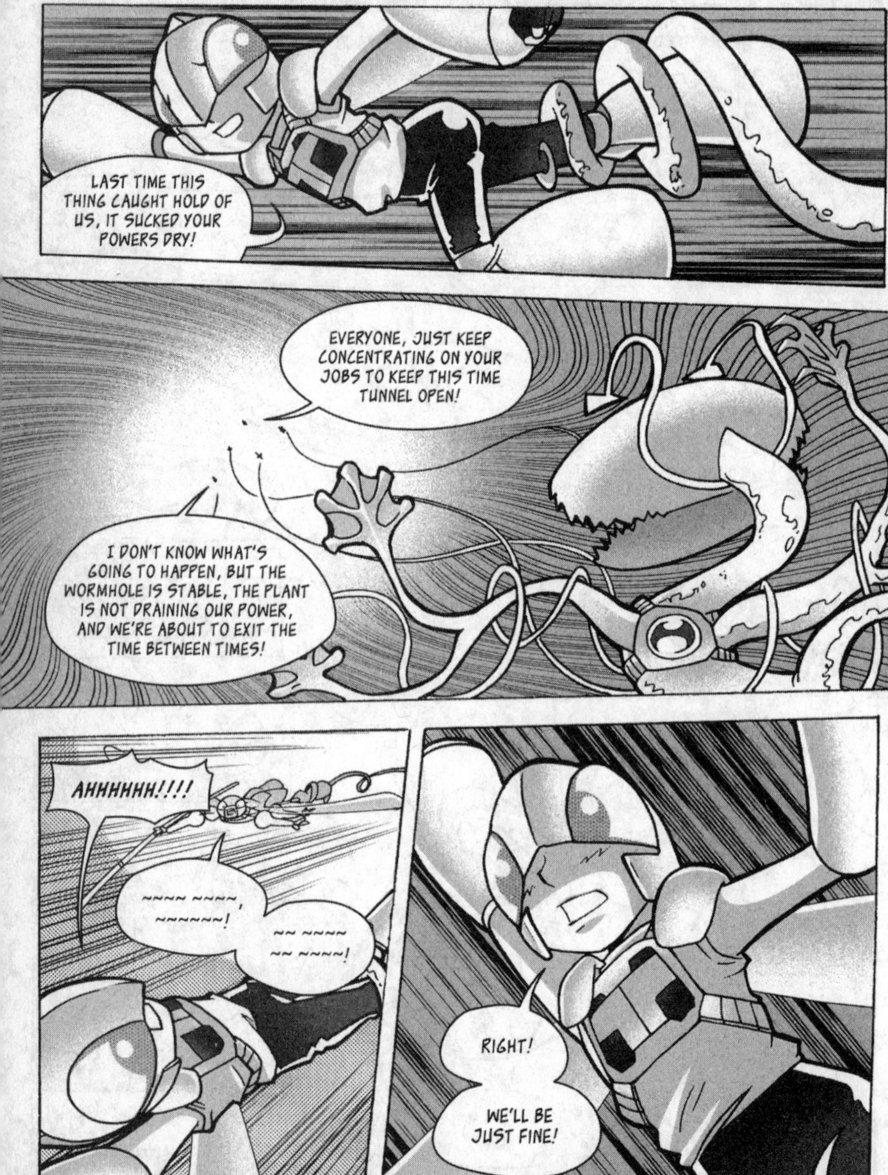
LAST TIME THIS THING CAUGHT HOLD OF US, IT SUCKED YOUR POWERS DRY!
EVERYONE, JUST KEEP CONCENTRATING ON YOUR JOBS TO KEEP THIS TIME TUNNEL OPEN!
I DON'T KNOW WHAT'S GOING TO HAPPEN, BUT THE WORMHOLE IS STABLE, THE PLANT IS NOT DRAINING OUR POWER, AND WE'RE ABOUT TO EXIT THE TIME BETWEEN TIMES!
AHHHHHH!!!!
~~~~ ~~~~, ~~~~~~!
~~ ~~~~ ~~ ~~~~!
RIGHT!
WE'LL BE JUST FINE!
~~~~

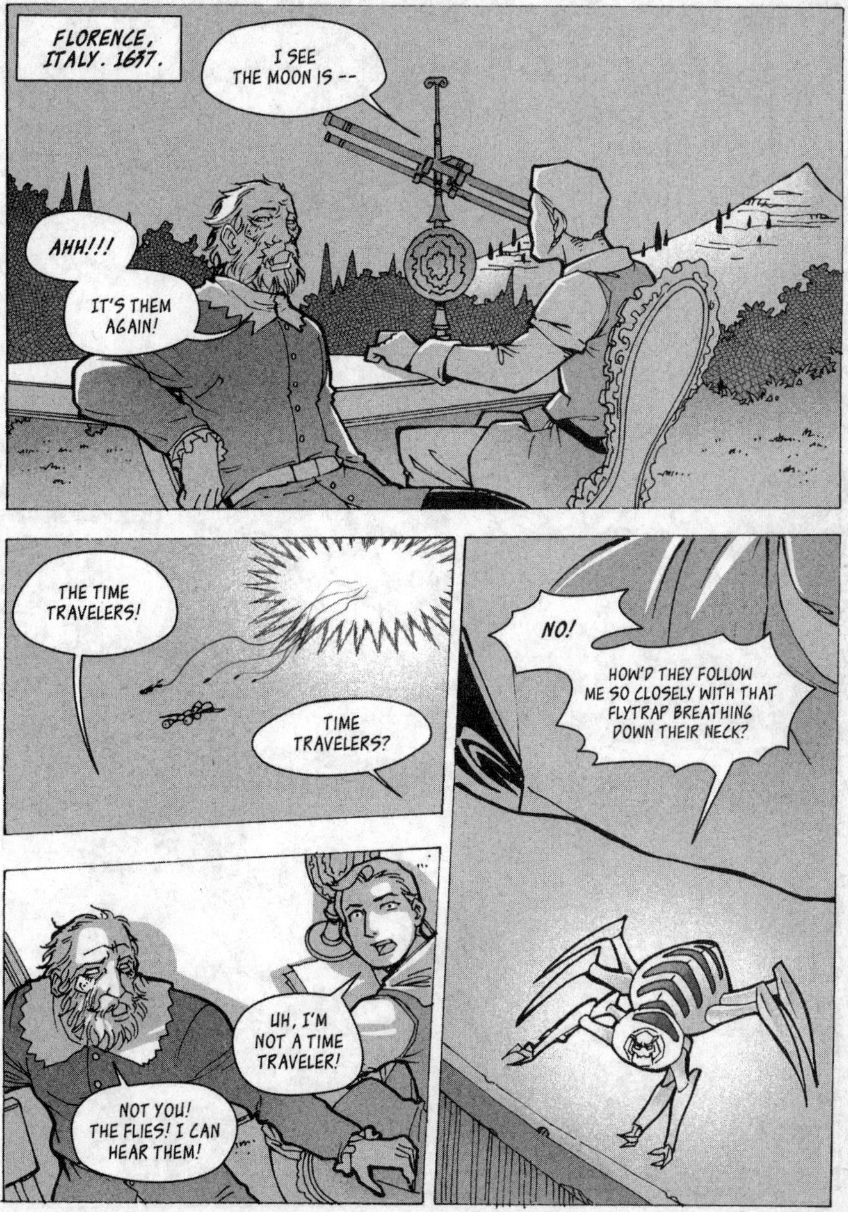
FLORENCE, ITALY. 1637.
I SEE THE MOON IS --
AHH!!!
IT'S THEM AGAIN!
THE TIME TRAVELERS!
TIME TRAVELERS?
UH, I'M NOT A TIME TRAVELER!
NOT YOU! THE FLIES! I CAN HEAR THEM!
NO!
HOW'D THEY FOLLOW ME SO CLOSELY WITH THAT FLYTRAP BREATHING DOWN THEIR NECK?

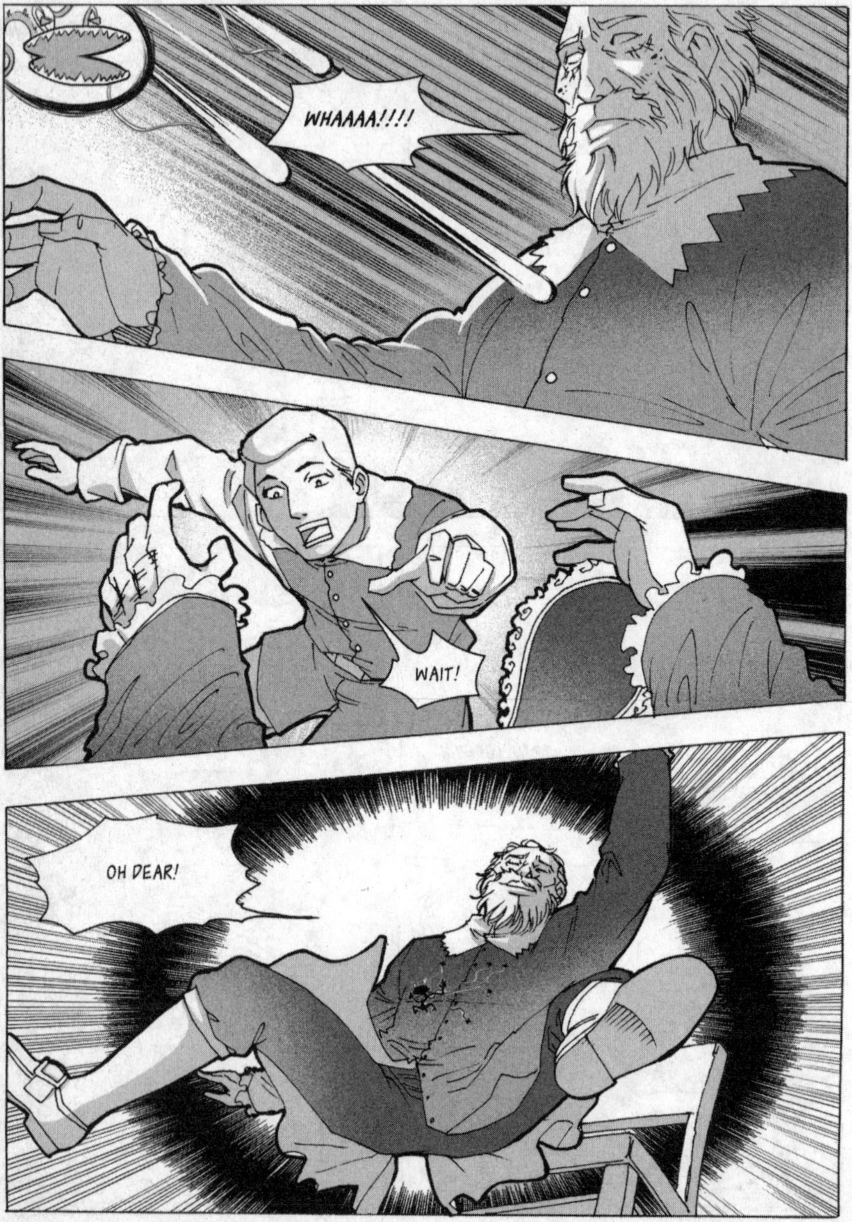
WHAAAA!!!!
WAIT!
OH DEAR!

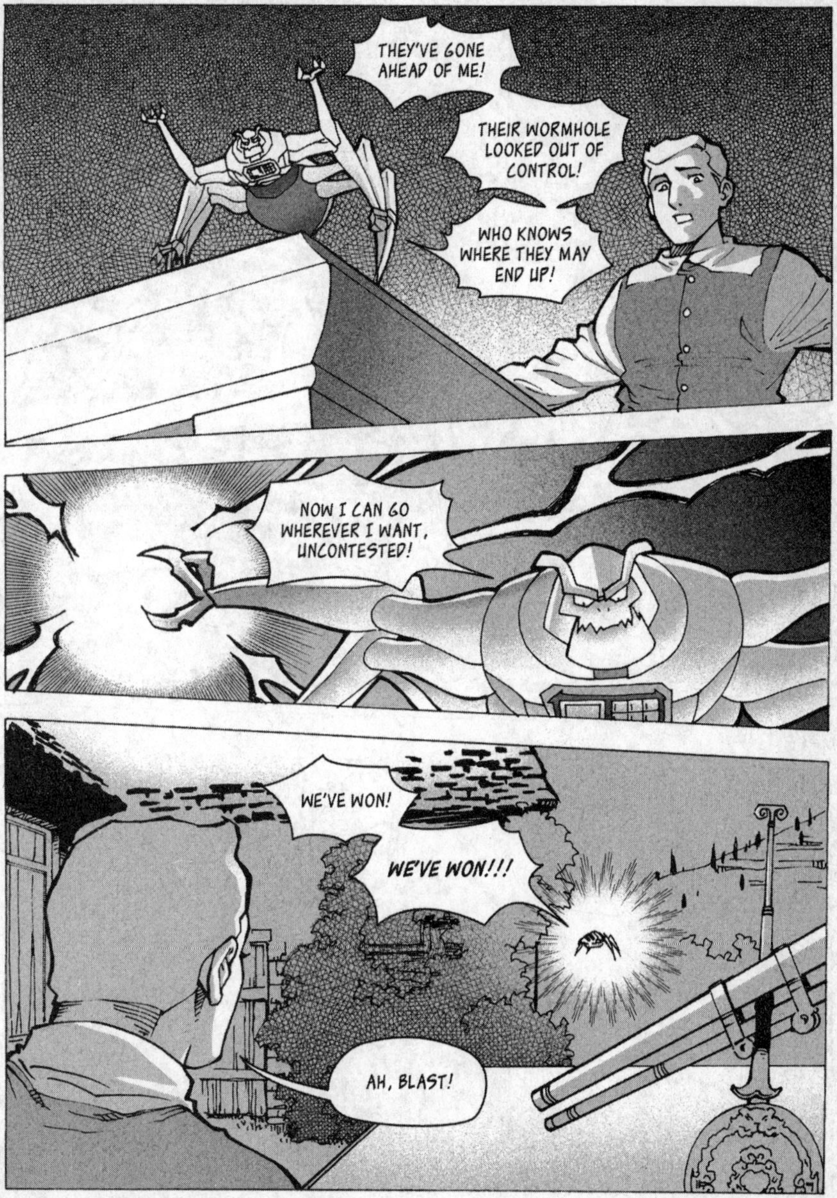
THEY'VE GONE AHEAD OF ME!
THEIR WORMHOLE LOOKED OUT OF CONTROL!
WHO KNOWS WHERE THEY MAY END UP!
NOW I CAN GO WHEREVER I WANT, UNCONTESTED!
WE'VE WON!
WE'VE WON!!!
AH, BLAST!

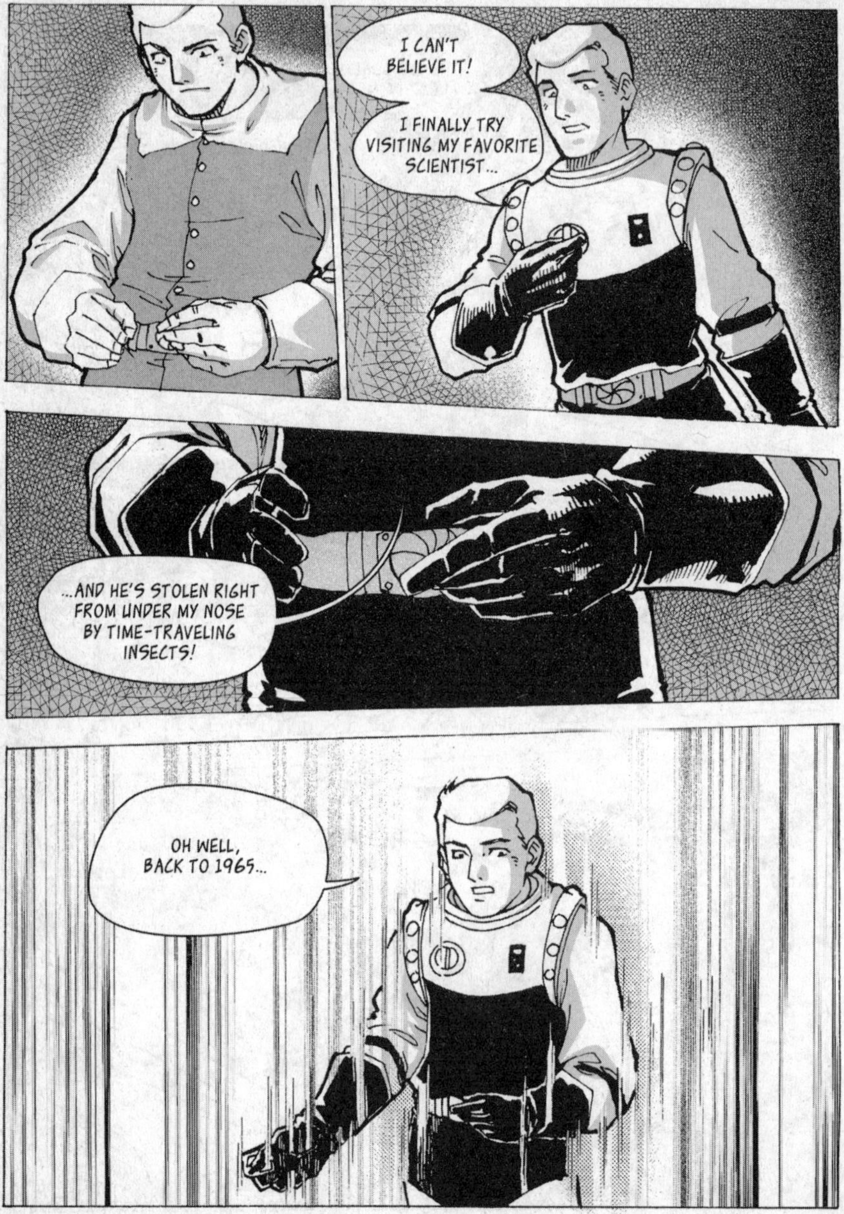
I CAN'T BELIEVE IT!
I FINALLY TRY VISITING MY FAVORITE SCIENTIST...
...AND HE'S STOLEN RIGHT FROM UNDER MY NOSE BY TIME-TRAVELING INSECTS!
OH WELL, BACK TO 1965...

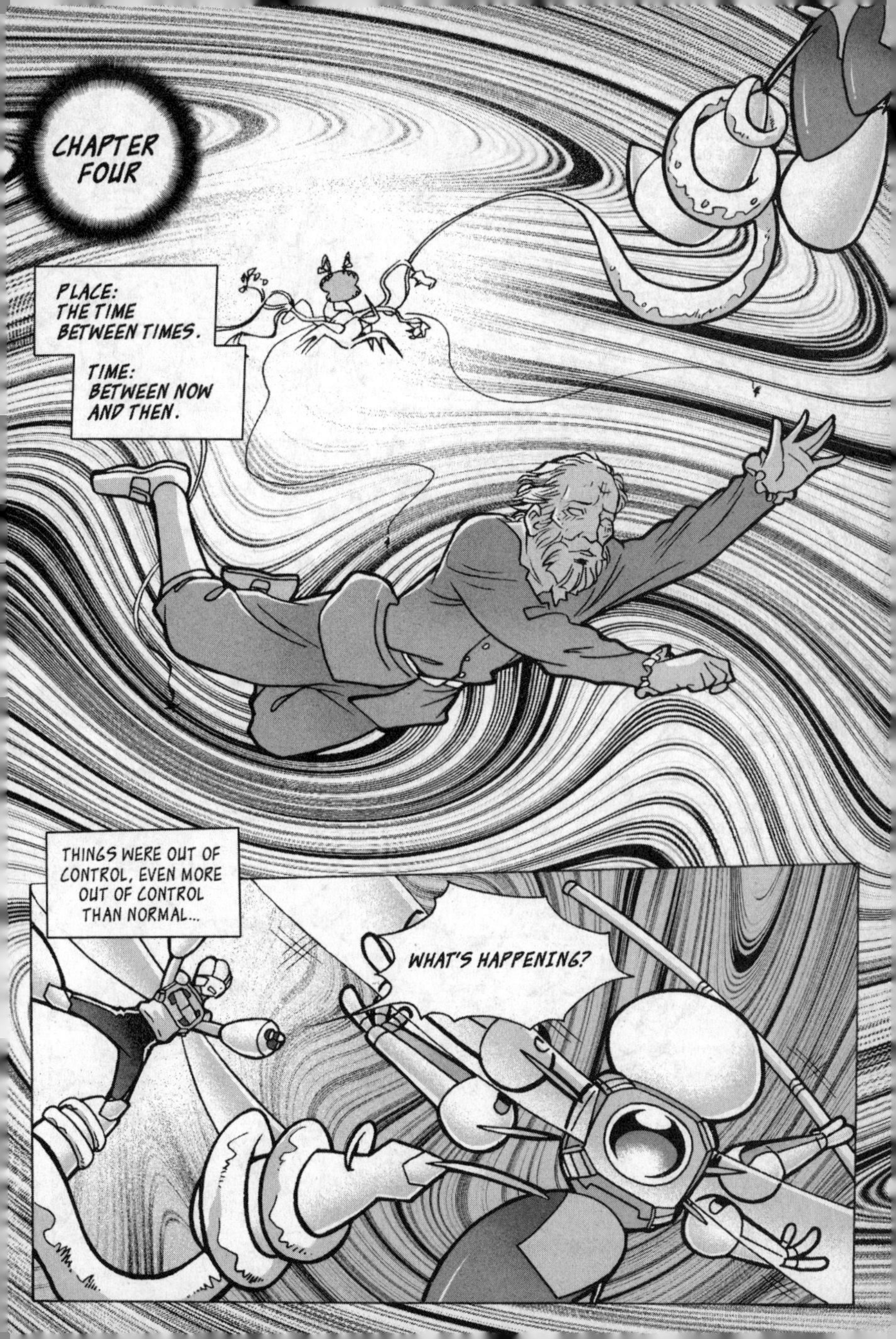
CHAPTER FOUR
PLACE: THE TIME BETWEEN TIMES.
TIME: BETWEEN NOW AND THEN.
THINGS WERE OUT OF CONTROL, EVEN MORE OUT OF CONTROL THAN NORMAL...
WHAT'S HAPPENING?

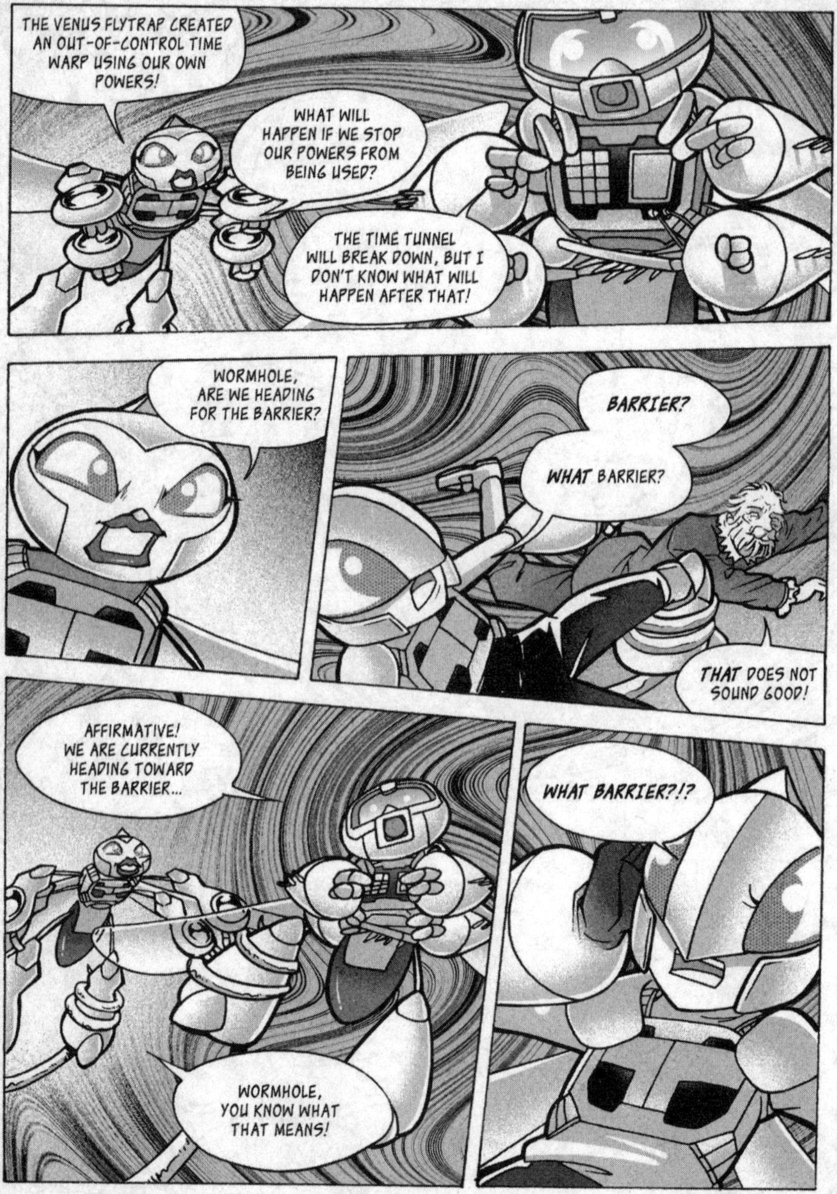
THE VENUS FLYTRAP CREATED AN OUT-OF-CONTROL TIME WARP USING OUR OWN POWERS!
WHAT WILL HAPPEN IF WE STOP OUR POWERS FROM BEING USED?
THE TIME TUNNEL WILL BREAK DOWN, BUT I DON'T KNOW WHAT WILL HAPPEN AFTER THAT!
WORMHOLE, ARE WE HEADING FOR THE BARRIER?
BARRIER?
WHAT BARRIER?
THAT DOES NOT SOUND GOOD!
AFFIRMATIVE! WE ARE CURRENTLY HEADING TOWARD THE BARRIER...
WORMHOLE, YOU KNOW WHAT THAT MEANS!
WHAT BARRIER?!?

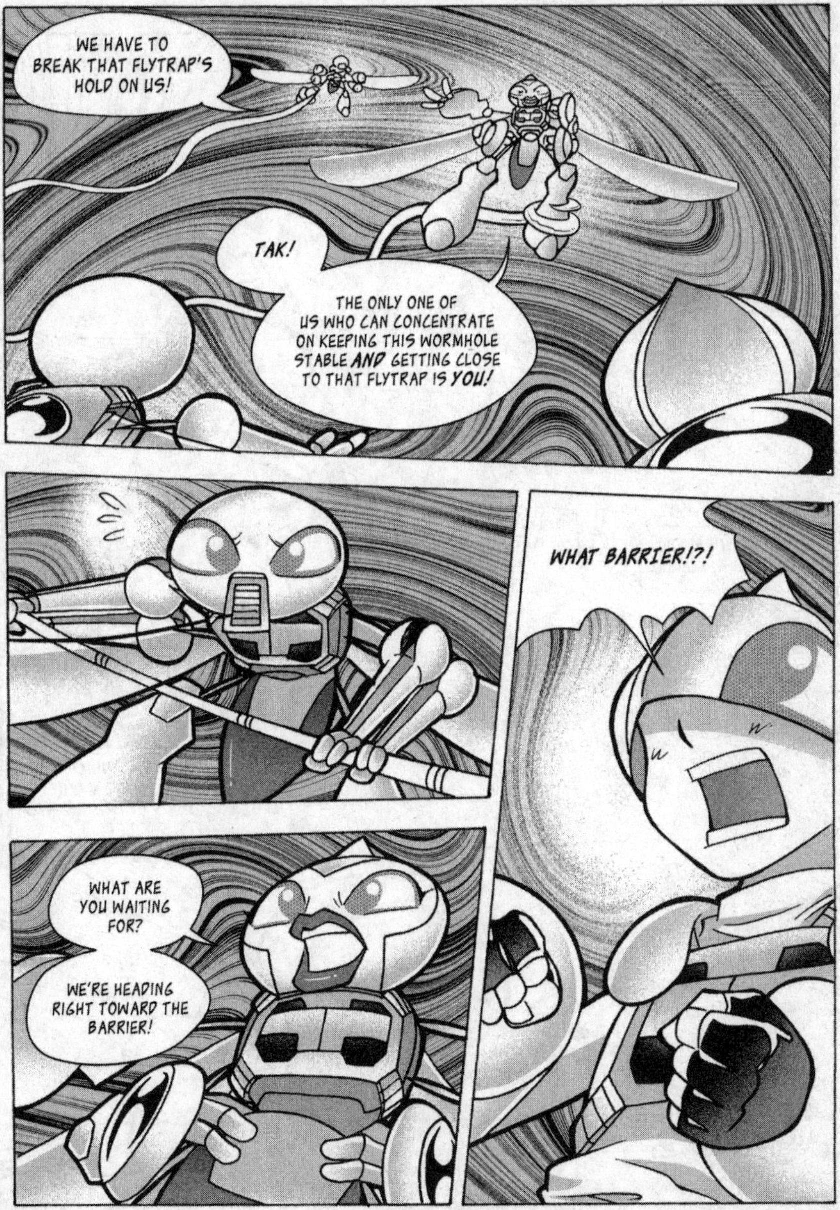
WE HAVE TO BREAK THAT FLYTRAP'S HOLD ON US!
TAK!
THE ONLY ONE OF US WHO CAN CONCENTRATE ON KEEPING THIS WORMHOLE STABLE *AND* GETTING CLOSE TO THAT FLYTRAP IS *YOU!*
WHAT BARRIER!?!
WHAT ARE YOU WAITING FOR?
WE'RE HEADING RIGHT TOWARD THE BARRIER!

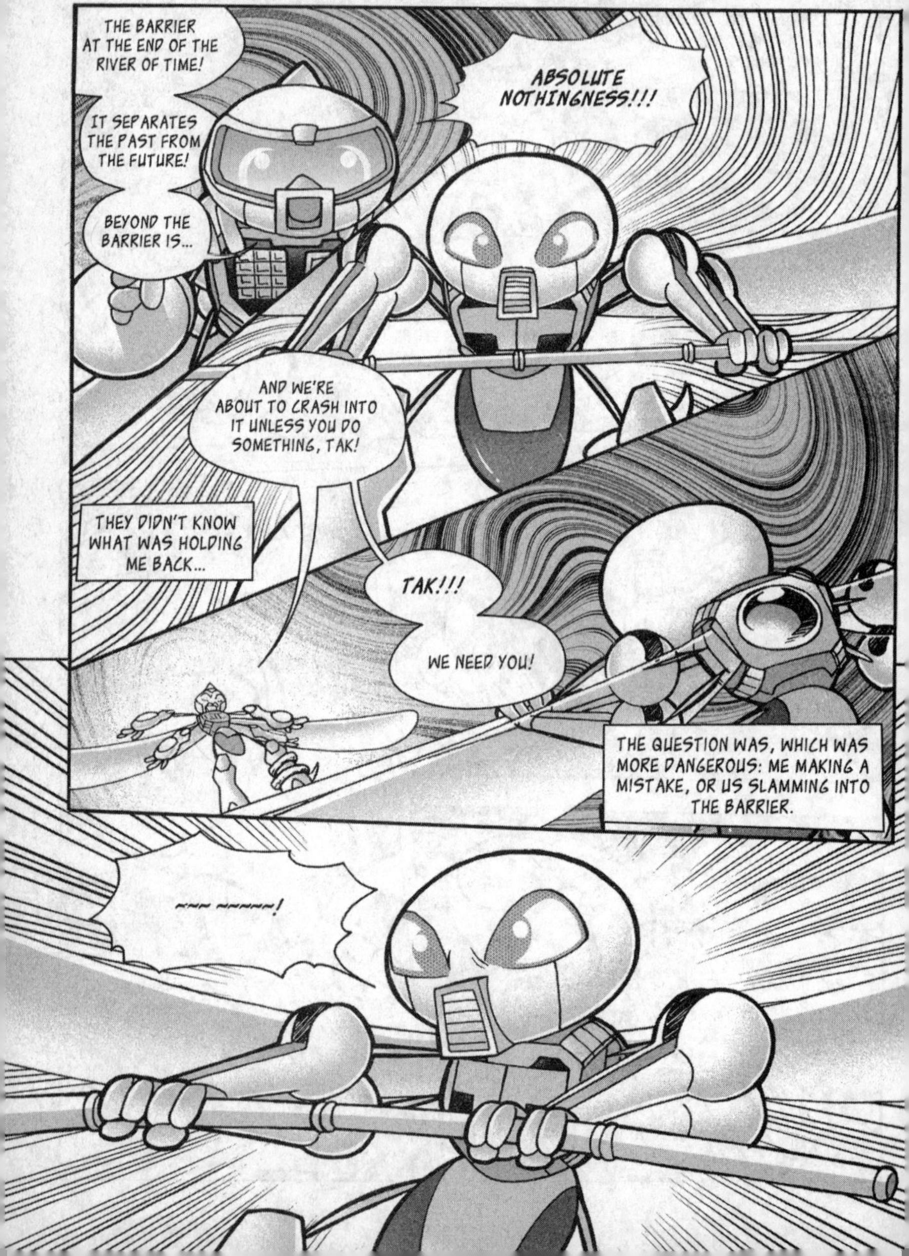
THE BARRIER AT THE END OF THE RIVER OF TIME!
IT SEPARATES THE PAST FROM THE FUTURE!
BEYOND THE BARRIER IS...
ABSOLUTE NOTHINGNESS!!!
AND WE'RE ABOUT TO CRASH INTO IT UNLESS YOU DO SOMETHING, TAK!
THEY DIDN'T KNOW WHAT WAS HOLDING ME BACK...
TAK!!!
WE NEED YOU!
THE QUESTION WAS, WHICH WAS MORE DANGEROUS: ME MAKING A MISTAKE, OR US SLAMMING INTO THE BARRIER.
~~~ ~~~~~!
~~~

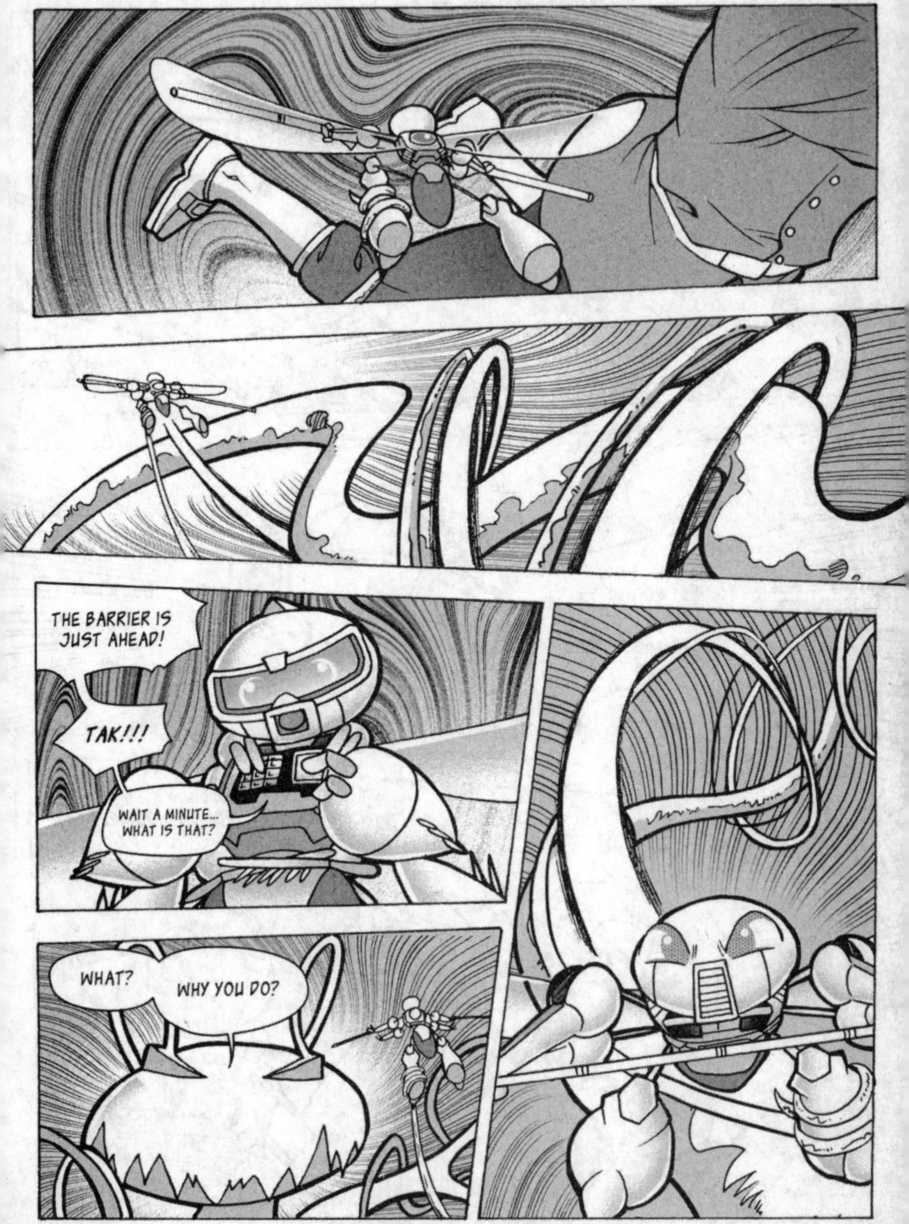
THE BARRIER IS JUST AHEAD!
TAK!!!
WAIT A MINUTE... WHAT IS THAT?
WHAT?
WHY YOU DO?

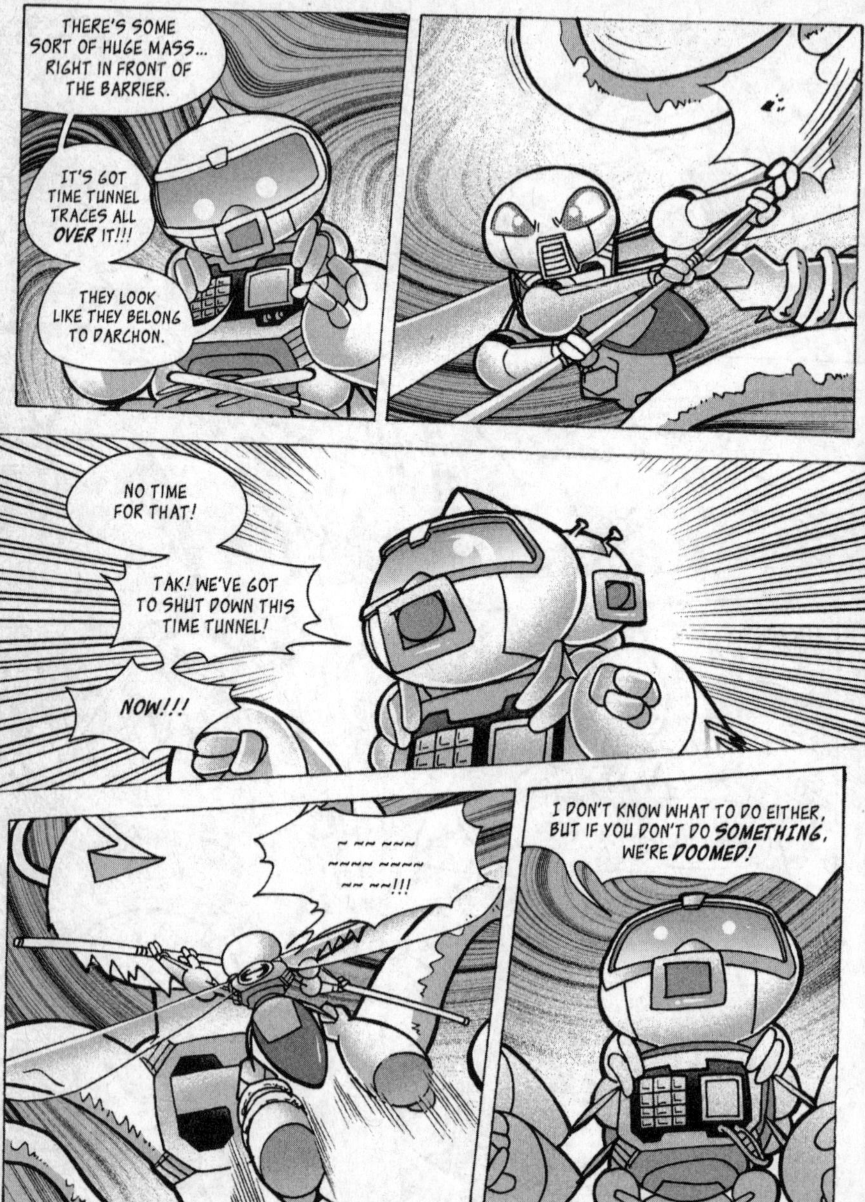
THERE'S SOME SORT OF HUGE MASS... RIGHT IN FRONT OF THE BARRIER.
IT'S GOT TIME TUNNEL TRACES ALL **OVER** IT!!!
THEY LOOK LIKE THEY BELONG TO DARCHON.
NO TIME FOR THAT!
TAK! WE'VE GOT TO SHUT DOWN THIS TIME TUNNEL!
NOW!!!
~ ~~ ~~~ ~~~~ ~~~~ ~~ ~~!!!
I DON'T KNOW WHAT TO DO EITHER, BUT IF YOU DON'T DO **SOMETHING**, WE'RE **DOOMED**!

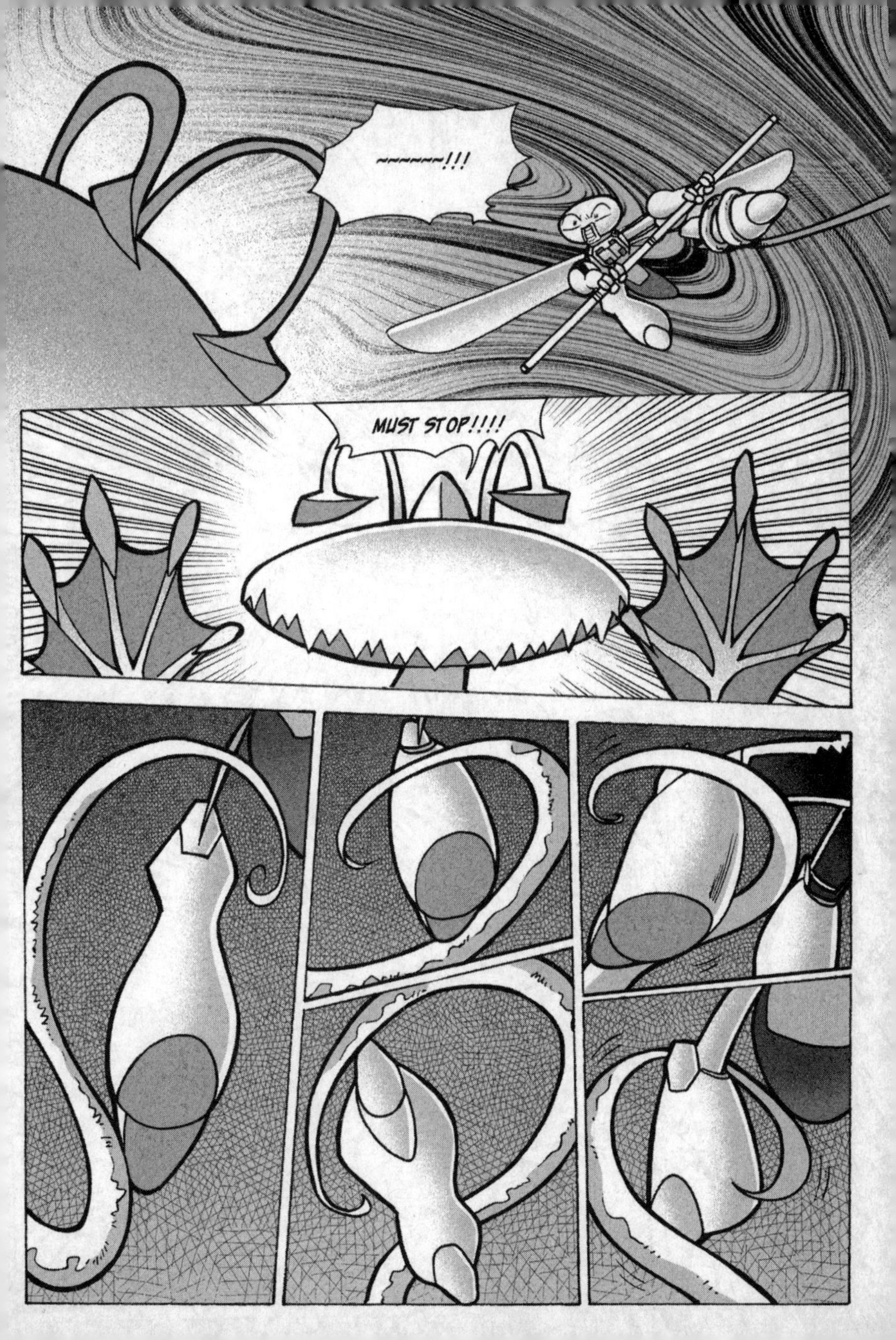

MUST STOP!!!!!

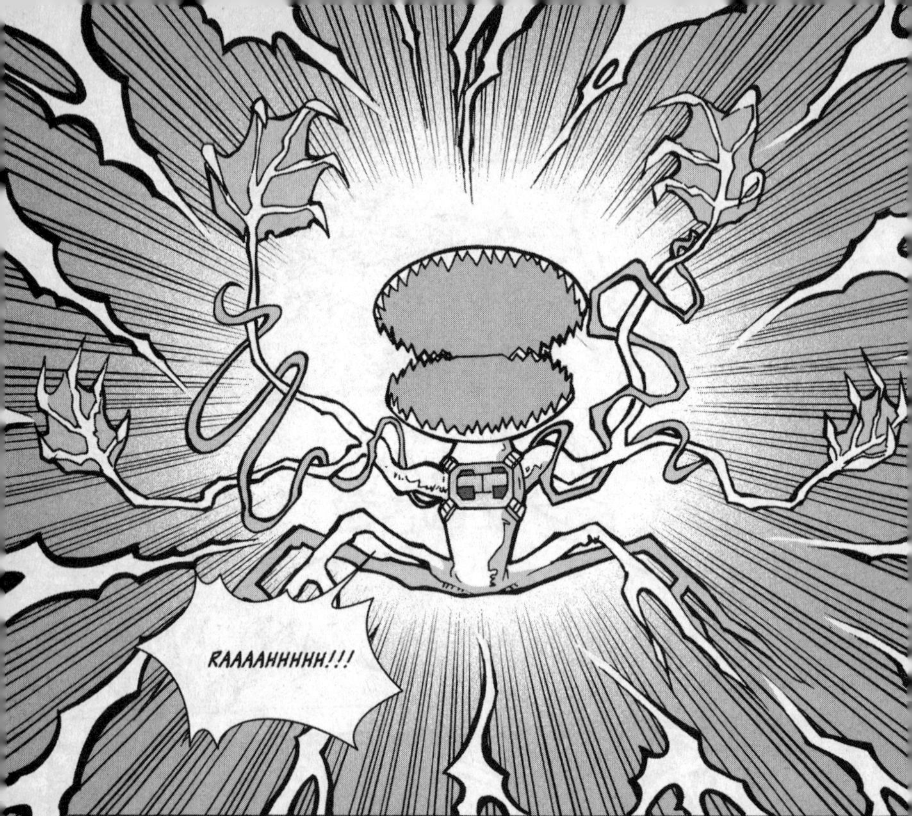
RAAAAHHHHH!!!
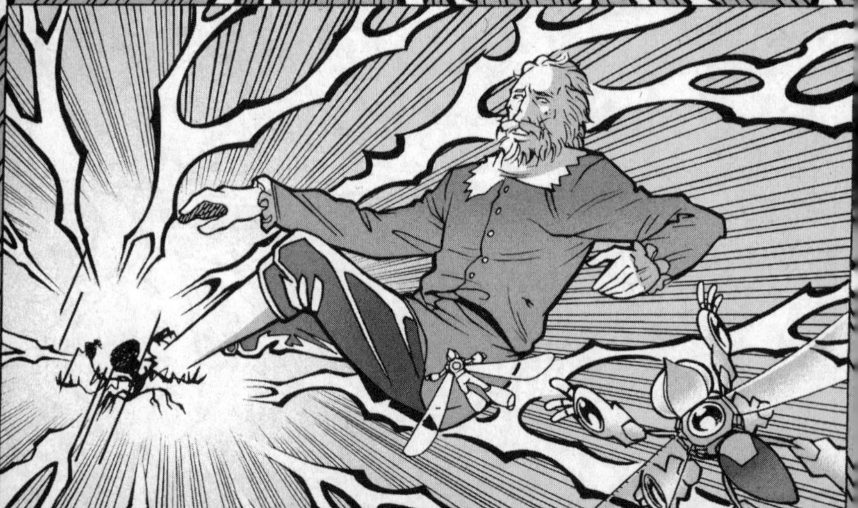

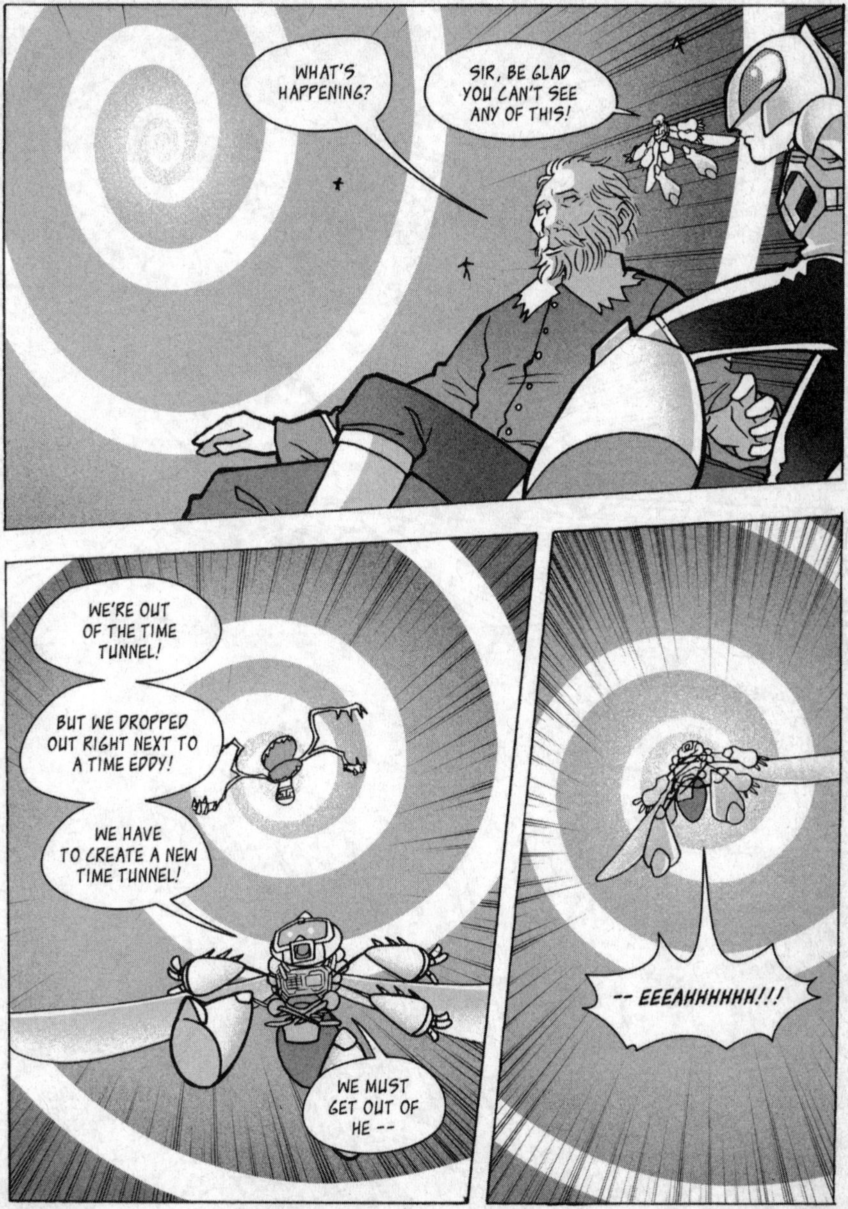
WHAT'S HAPPENING?
SIR, BE GLAD YOU CAN'T SEE ANY OF THIS!
WE'RE OUT OF THE TIME TUNNEL!
BUT WE DROPPED OUT RIGHT NEXT TO A TIME EDDY!
WE HAVE TO CREATE A NEW TIME TUNNEL!
WE MUST GET OUT OF HE --
-- EEEAHHHHHH!!!

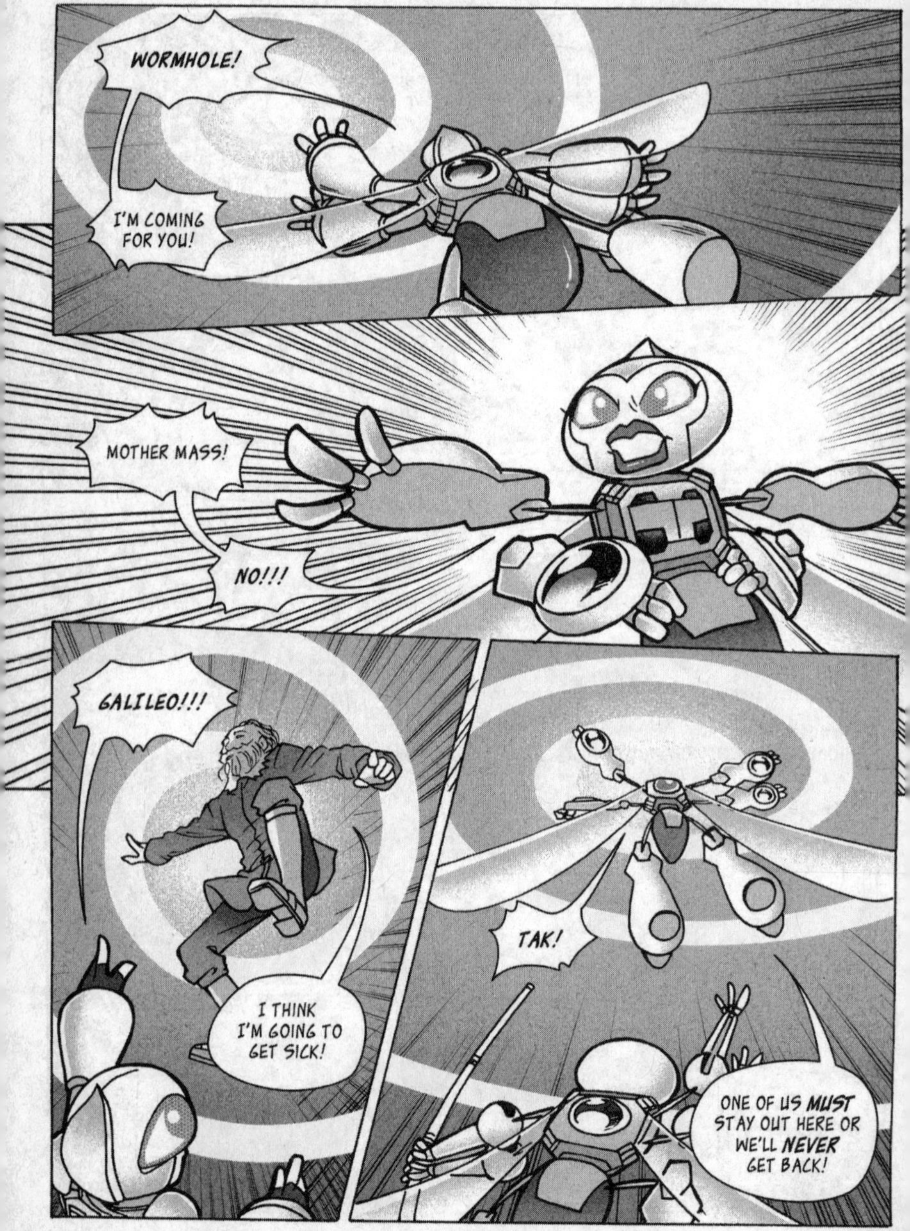
WORMHOLE!
I'M COMING FOR YOU!
MOTHER MASS!
NO!!!
GALILEO!!!
I THINK I'M GOING TO GET SICK!
TAK!
ONE OF US MUST STAY OUT HERE OR WE'LL NEVER GET BACK!

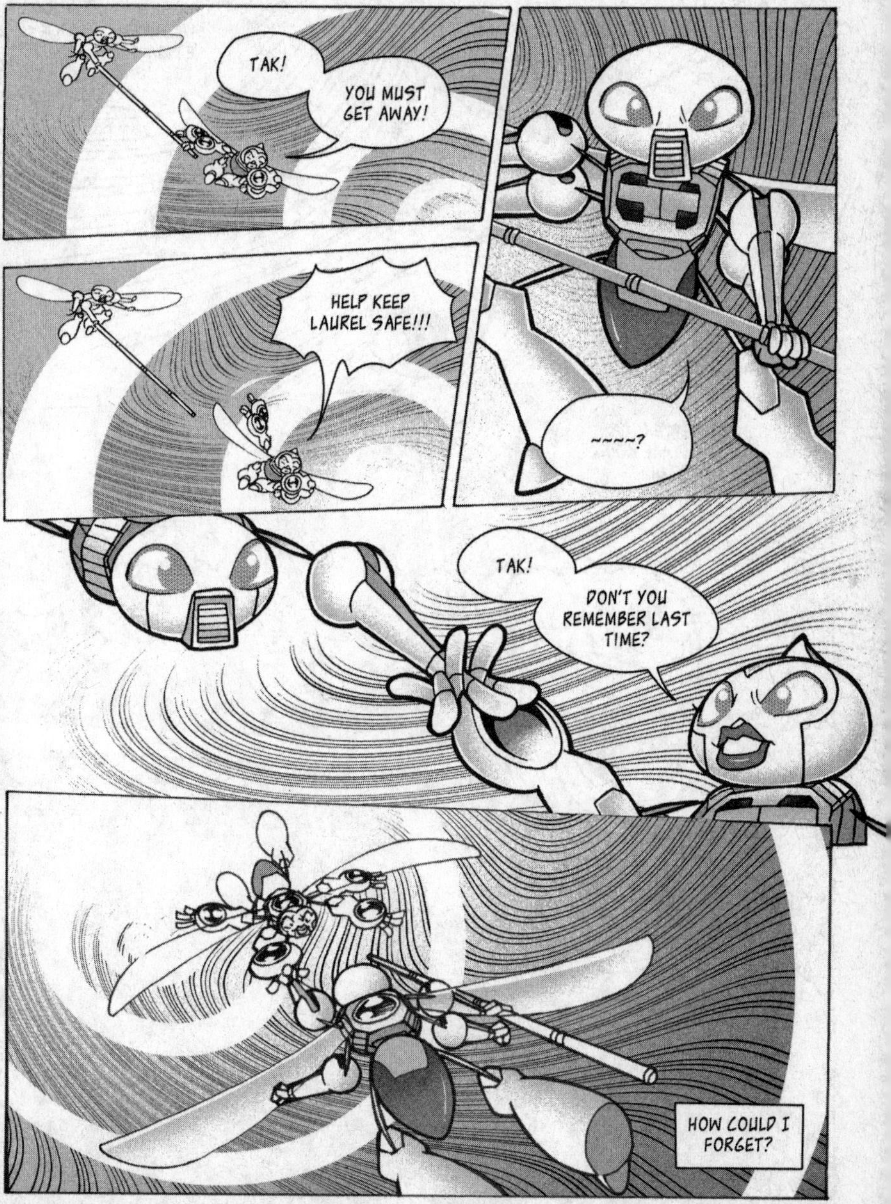
TAK!
YOU MUST GET AWAY!
HELP KEEP LAUREL SAFE!!!
~~~~?
TAK!
DON'T YOU REMEMBER LAST TIME?
HOW COULD I FORGET?
~~~~

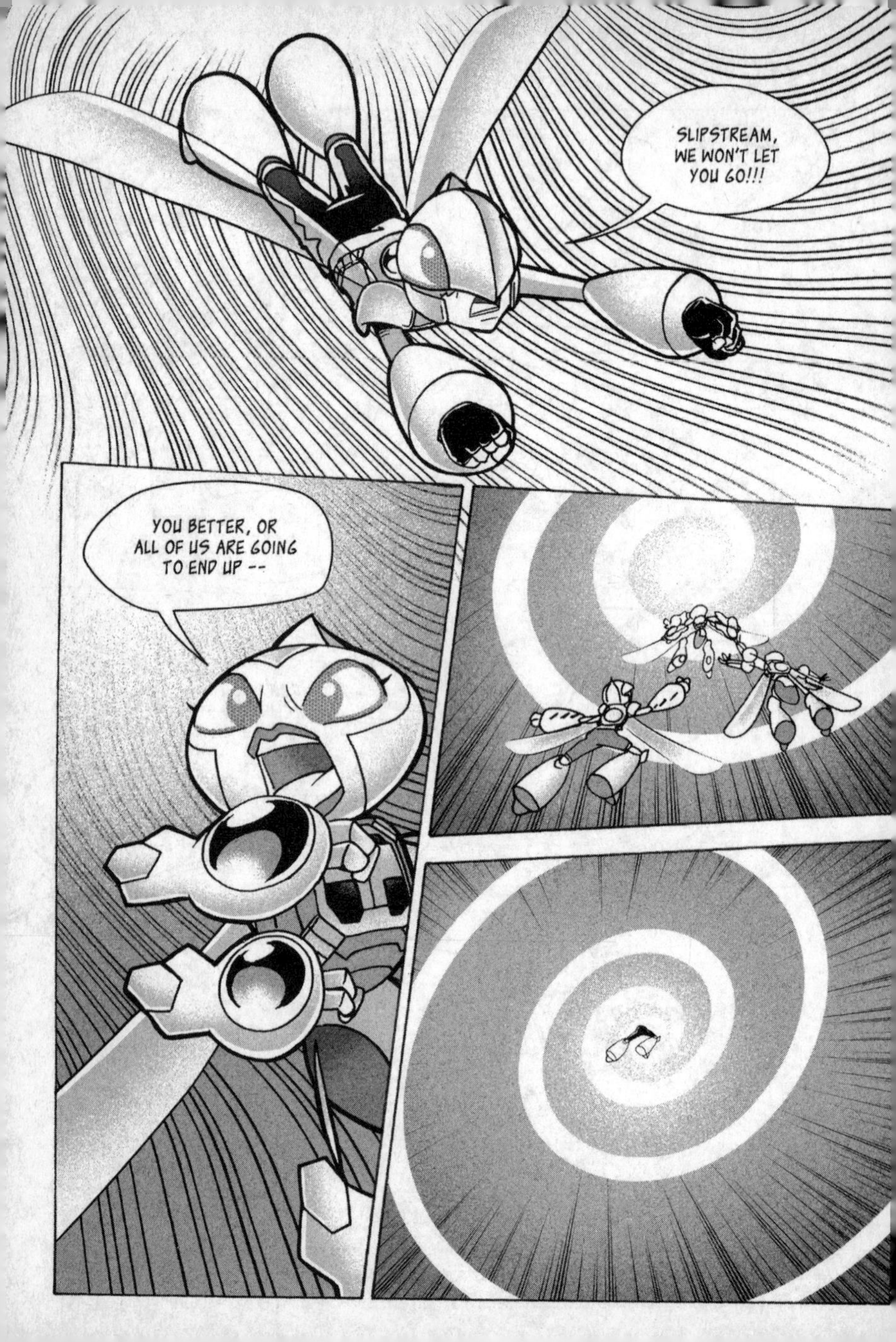
SLIPSTREAM, WE WON'T LET YOU GO!!!
YOU BETTER, OR ALL OF US ARE GOING TO END UP --

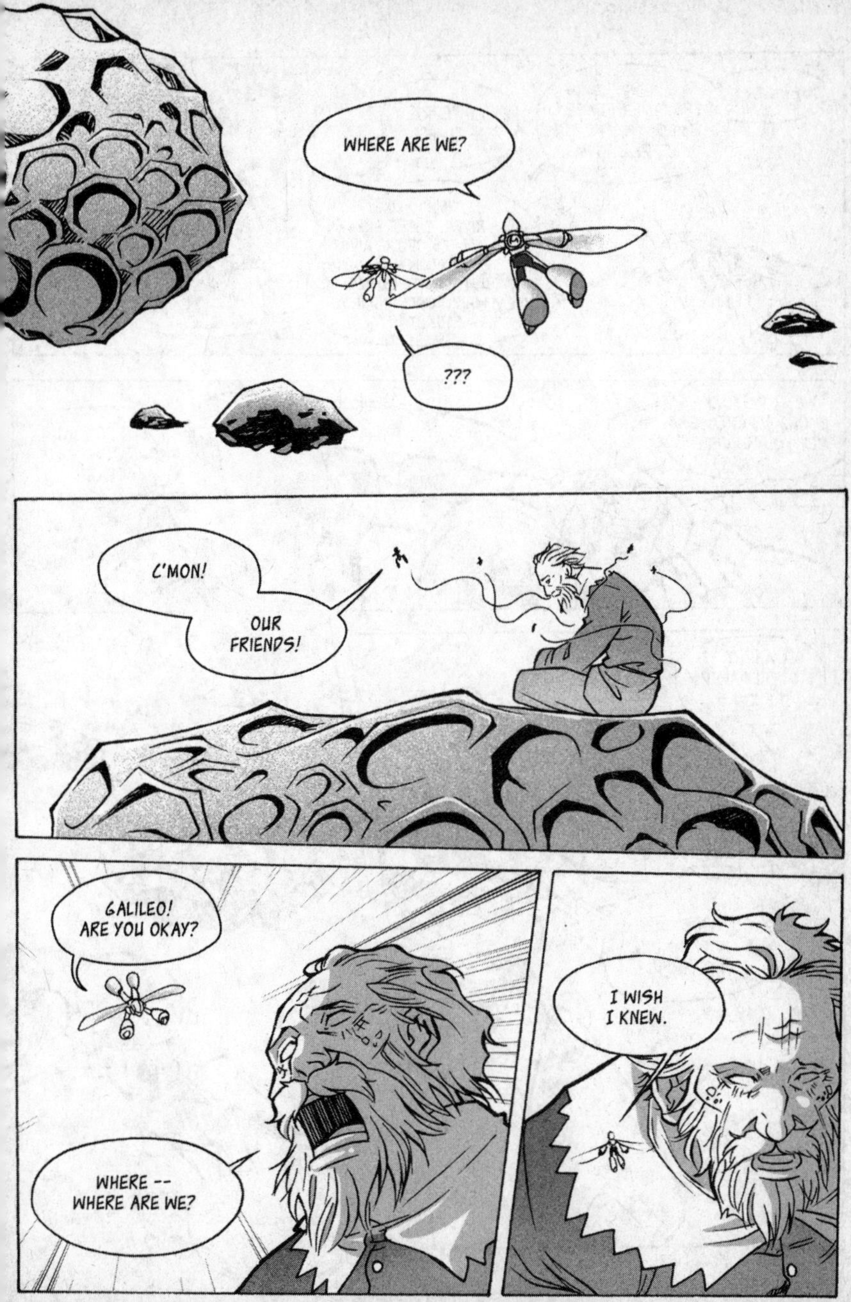
WHERE ARE WE?
???
C'MON!
OUR FRIENDS!
GALILEO! ARE YOU OKAY?
WHERE -- WHERE ARE WE?
I WISH I KNEW.

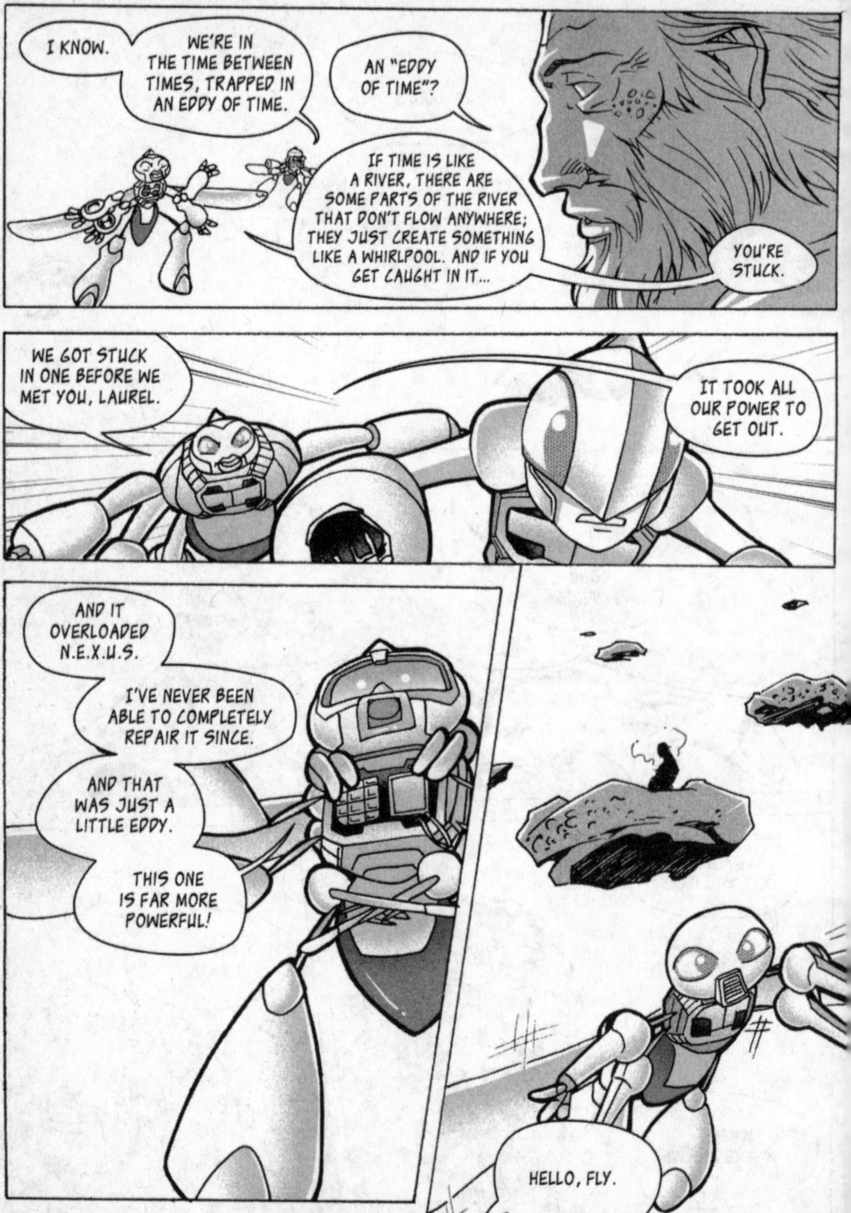
I KNOW.
WE'RE IN THE TIME BETWEEN TIMES, TRAPPED IN AN EDDY OF TIME.
AN "EDDY OF TIME"?
IF TIME IS LIKE A RIVER, THERE ARE SOME PARTS OF THE RIVER THAT DON'T FLOW ANYWHERE; THEY JUST CREATE SOMETHING LIKE A WHIRLPOOL. AND IF YOU GET CAUGHT IN IT...
YOU'RE STUCK.
WE GOT STUCK IN ONE BEFORE WE MET YOU, LAUREL.
IT TOOK ALL OUR POWER TO GET OUT.
AND IT OVERLOADED N.E.X.U.S.
I'VE NEVER BEEN ABLE TO COMPLETELY REPAIR IT SINCE.
AND THAT WAS JUST A LITTLE EDDY.
THIS ONE IS FAR MORE POWERFUL!
HELLO, FLY.

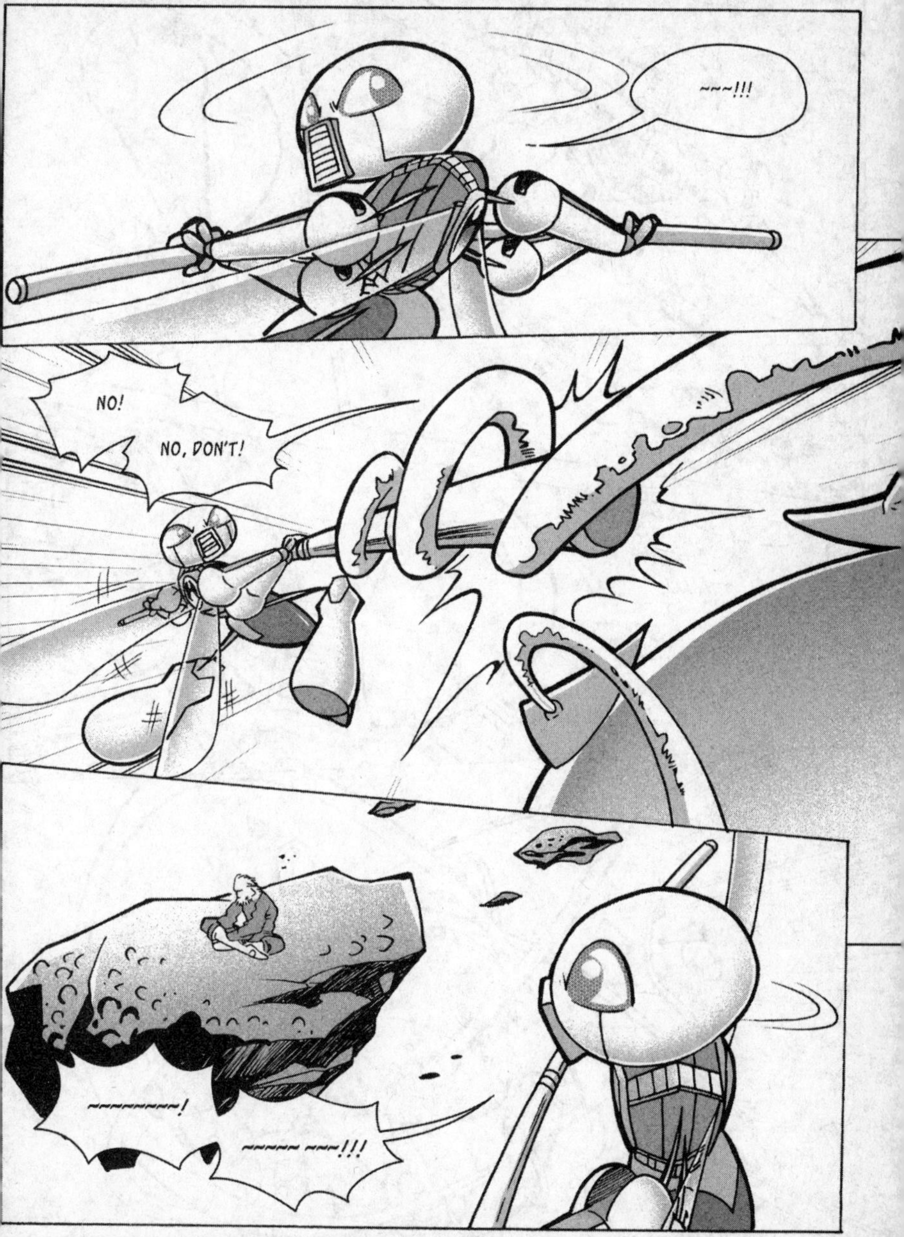
~~~!!!
NO!
NO, DON'T!
~~~~~~~~~!
~~~~~ ~~~!!!
~~~~~

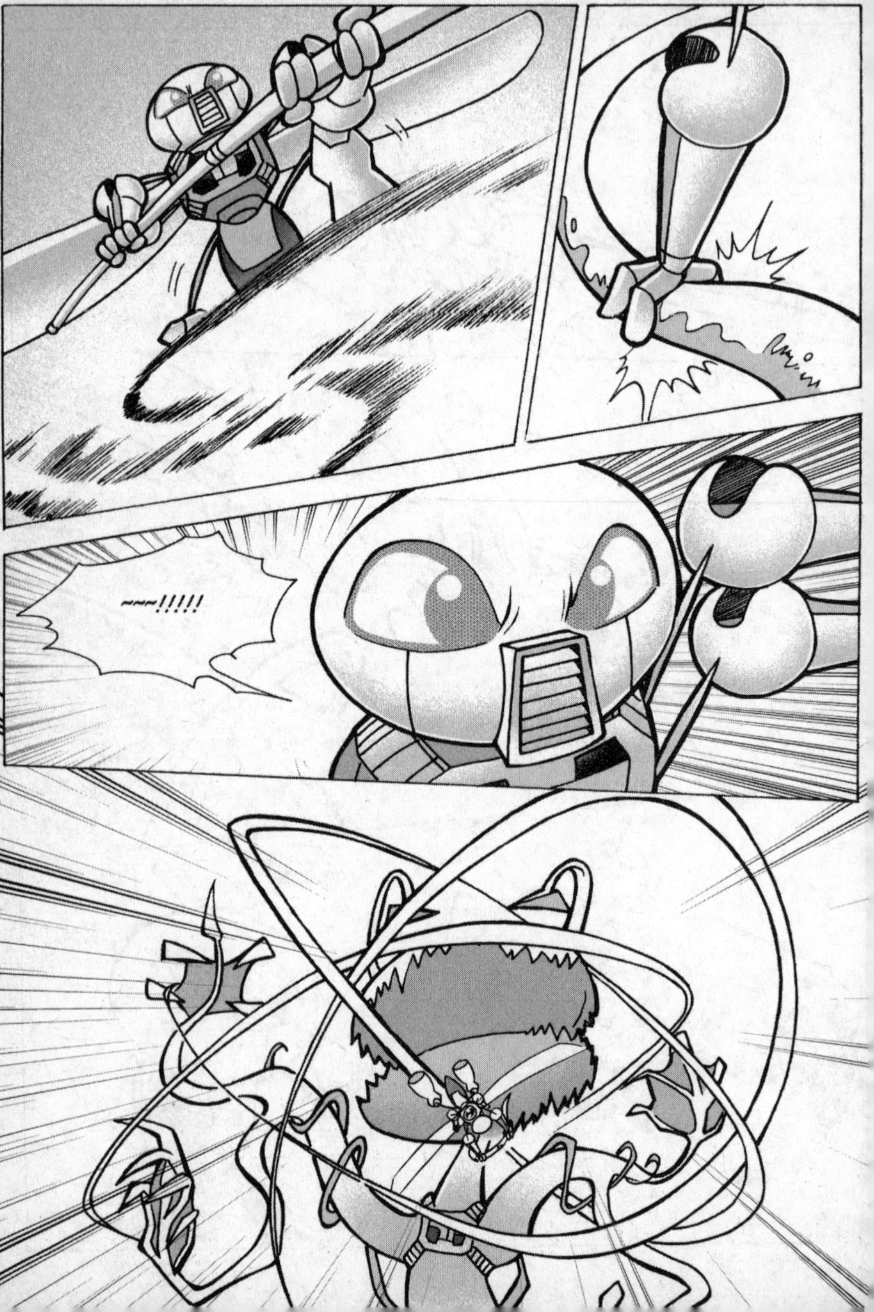
——!!!!!

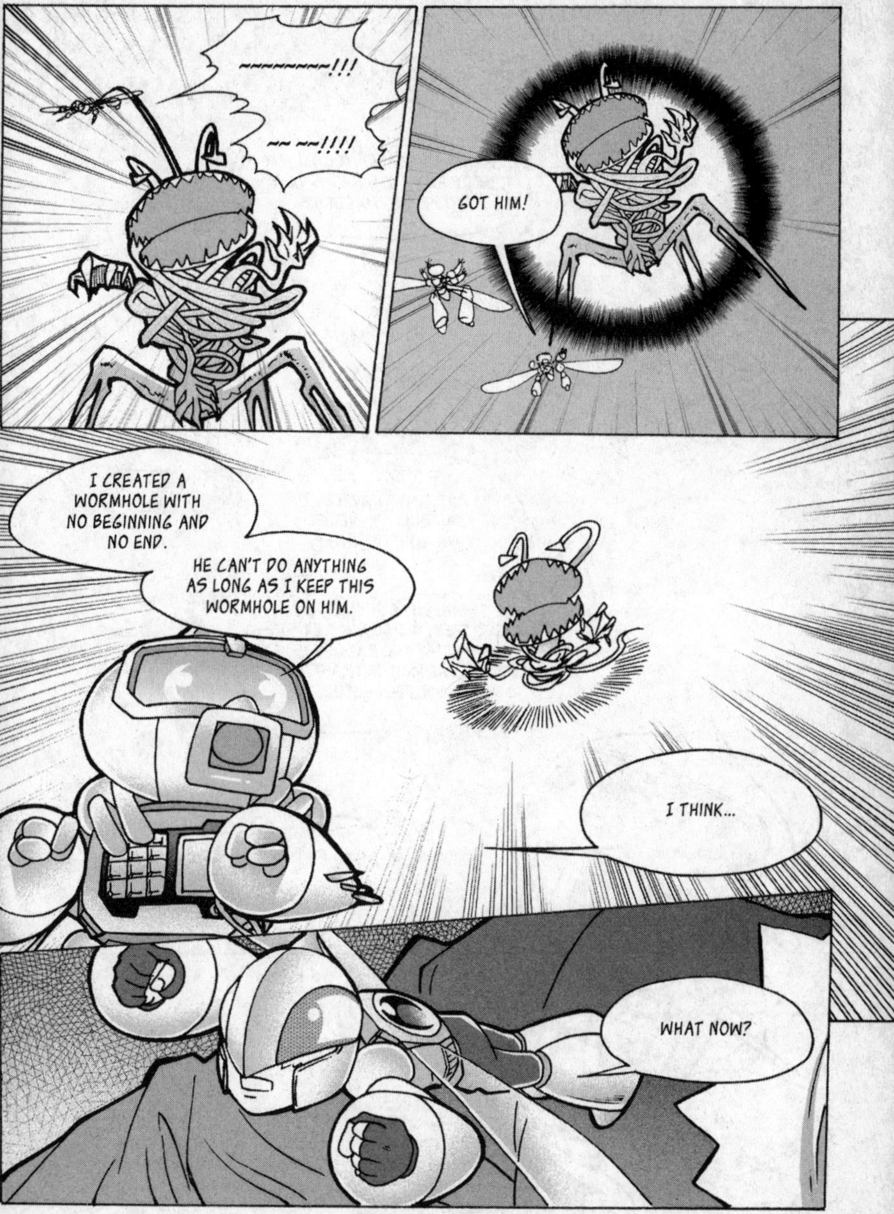

~~ ~~!!!!
GOT HIM!
I CREATED A WORMHOLE WITH NO BEGINNING AND NO END.
HE CAN'T DO ANYTHING AS LONG AS I KEEP THIS WORMHOLE ON HIM.
I THINK...
WHAT NOW?

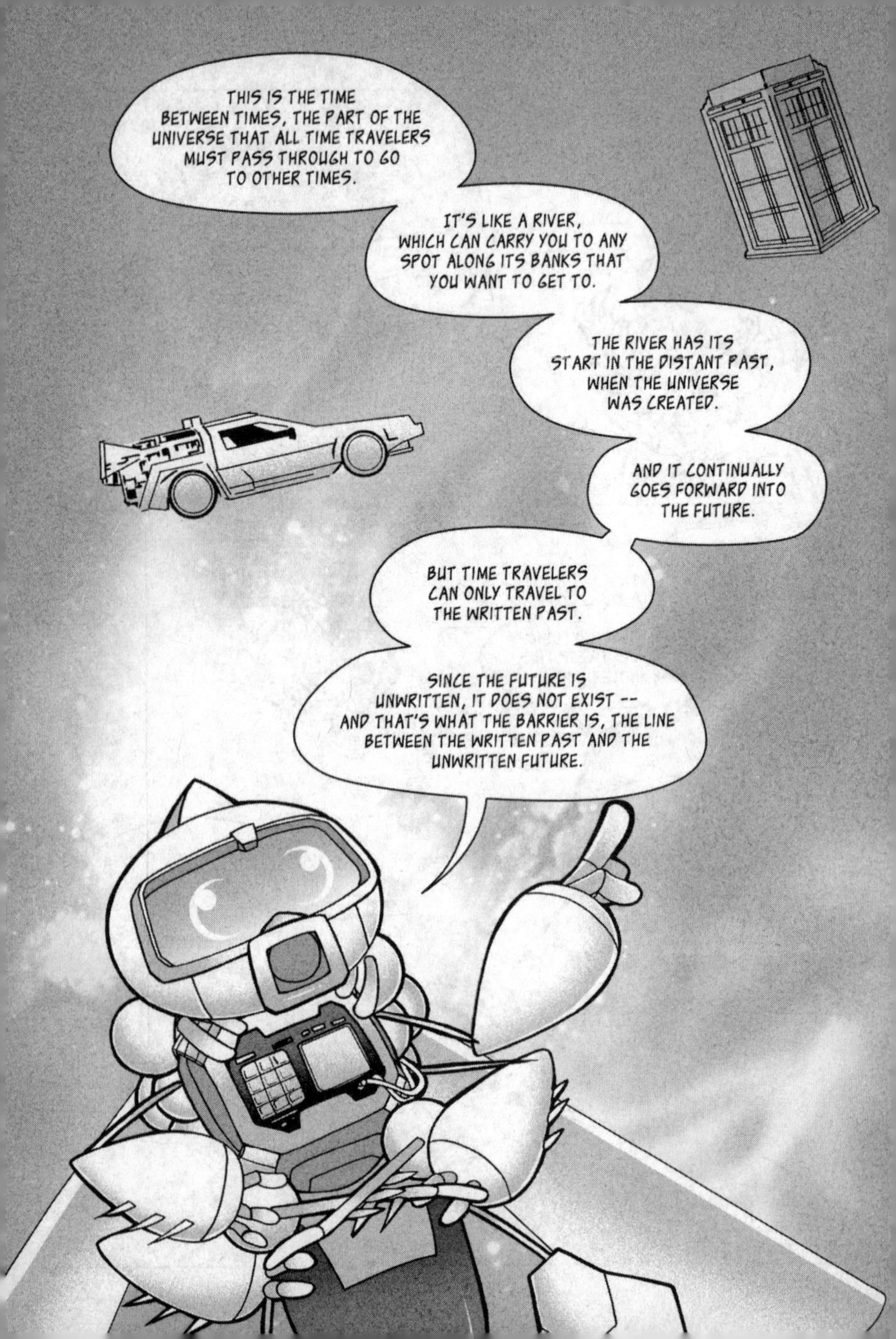
THIS IS THE TIME BETWEEN TIMES, THE PART OF THE UNIVERSE THAT ALL TIME TRAVELERS MUST PASS THROUGH TO GO TO OTHER TIMES.
IT'S LIKE A RIVER, WHICH CAN CARRY YOU TO ANY SPOT ALONG ITS BANKS THAT YOU WANT TO GET TO.
THE RIVER HAS ITS START IN THE DISTANT PAST, WHEN THE UNIVERSE WAS CREATED.
AND IT CONTINUALLY GOES FORWARD INTO THE FUTURE.
BUT TIME TRAVELERS CAN ONLY TRAVEL TO THE WRITTEN PAST.
SINCE THE FUTURE IS UNWRITTEN, IT DOES NOT EXIST -- AND THAT'S WHAT THE BARRIER IS, THE LINE BETWEEN THE WRITTEN PAST AND THE UNWRITTEN FUTURE.

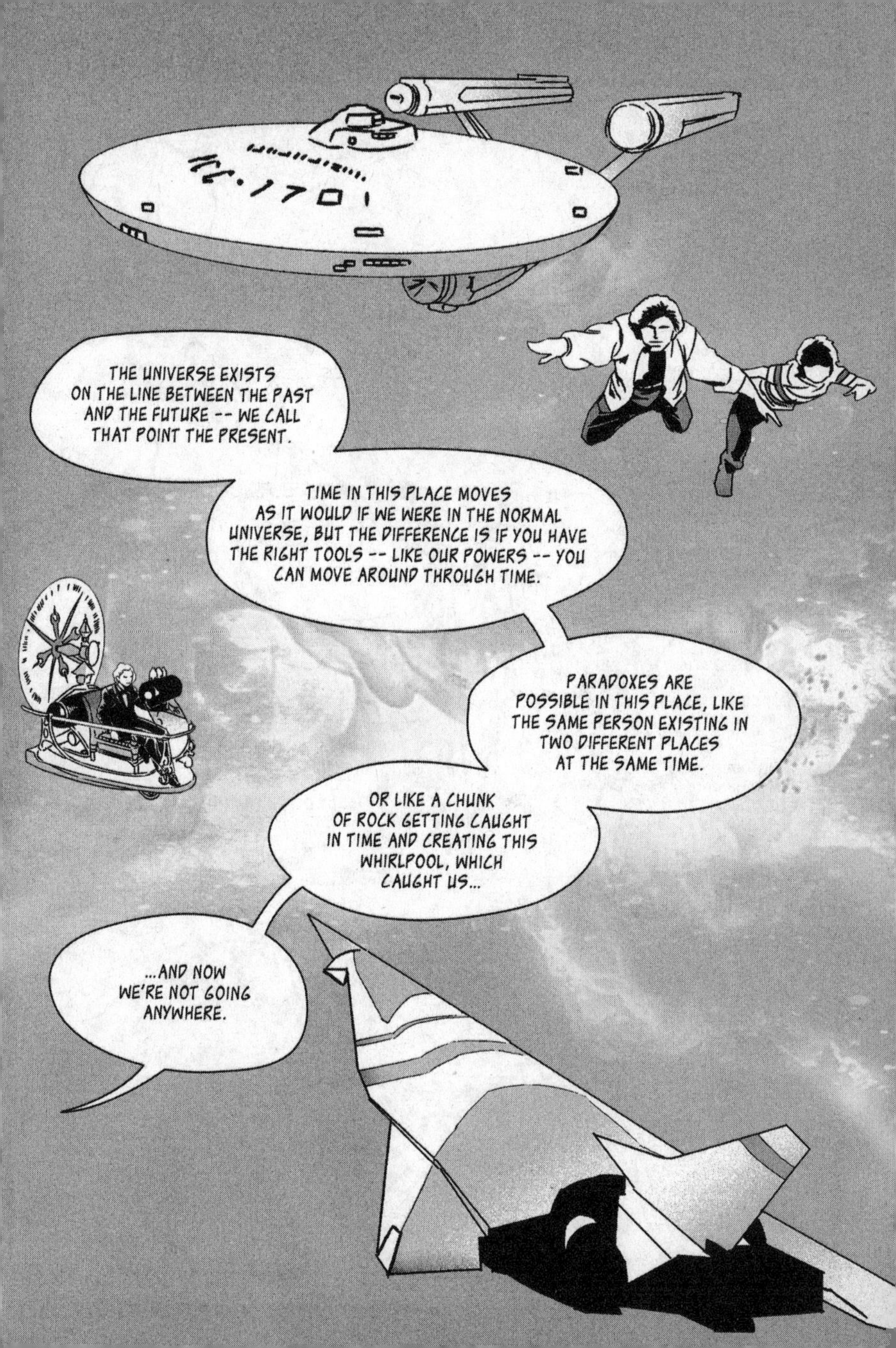
THE UNIVERSE EXISTS ON THE LINE BETWEEN THE PAST AND THE FUTURE -- WE CALL THAT POINT THE PRESENT.
TIME IN THIS PLACE MOVES AS IT WOULD IF WE WERE IN THE NORMAL UNIVERSE, BUT THE DIFFERENCE IS IF YOU HAVE THE RIGHT TOOLS -- LIKE OUR POWERS -- YOU CAN MOVE AROUND THROUGH TIME.
PARADOXES ARE POSSIBLE IN THIS PLACE, LIKE THE SAME PERSON EXISTING IN TWO DIFFERENT PLACES AT THE SAME TIME.
OR LIKE A CHUNK OF ROCK GETTING CAUGHT IN TIME AND CREATING THIS WHIRLPOOL, WHICH CAUGHT US...
...AND NOW WE'RE NOT GOING ANYWHERE.

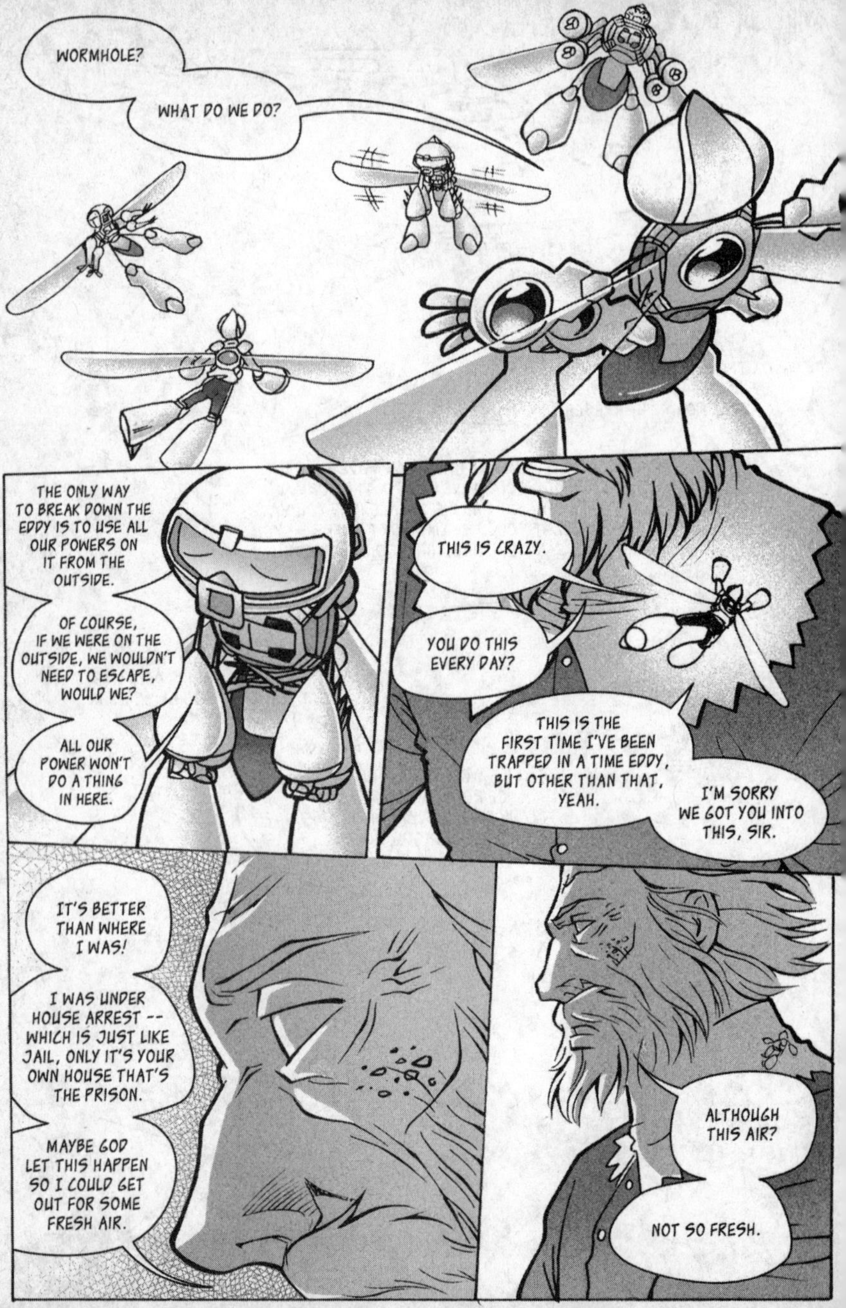
WORMHOLE?
WHAT DO WE DO?
THE ONLY WAY TO BREAK DOWN THE EDDY IS TO USE ALL OUR POWERS ON IT FROM THE OUTSIDE.
OF COURSE, IF WE WERE ON THE OUTSIDE, WE WOULDN'T NEED TO ESCAPE, WOULD WE?
ALL OUR POWER WON'T DO A THING IN HERE.
THIS IS CRAZY.
YOU DO THIS EVERY DAY?
THIS IS THE FIRST TIME I'VE BEEN TRAPPED IN A TIME EDDY, BUT OTHER THAN THAT, YEAH.
I'M SORRY WE GOT YOU INTO THIS, SIR.
IT'S BETTER THAN WHERE I WAS!
I WAS UNDER HOUSE ARREST -- WHICH IS JUST LIKE JAIL, ONLY IT'S YOUR OWN HOUSE THAT'S THE PRISON.
MAYBE GOD LET THIS HAPPEN SO I COULD GET OUT FOR SOME FRESH AIR.
ALTHOUGH THIS AIR?
NOT SO FRESH.

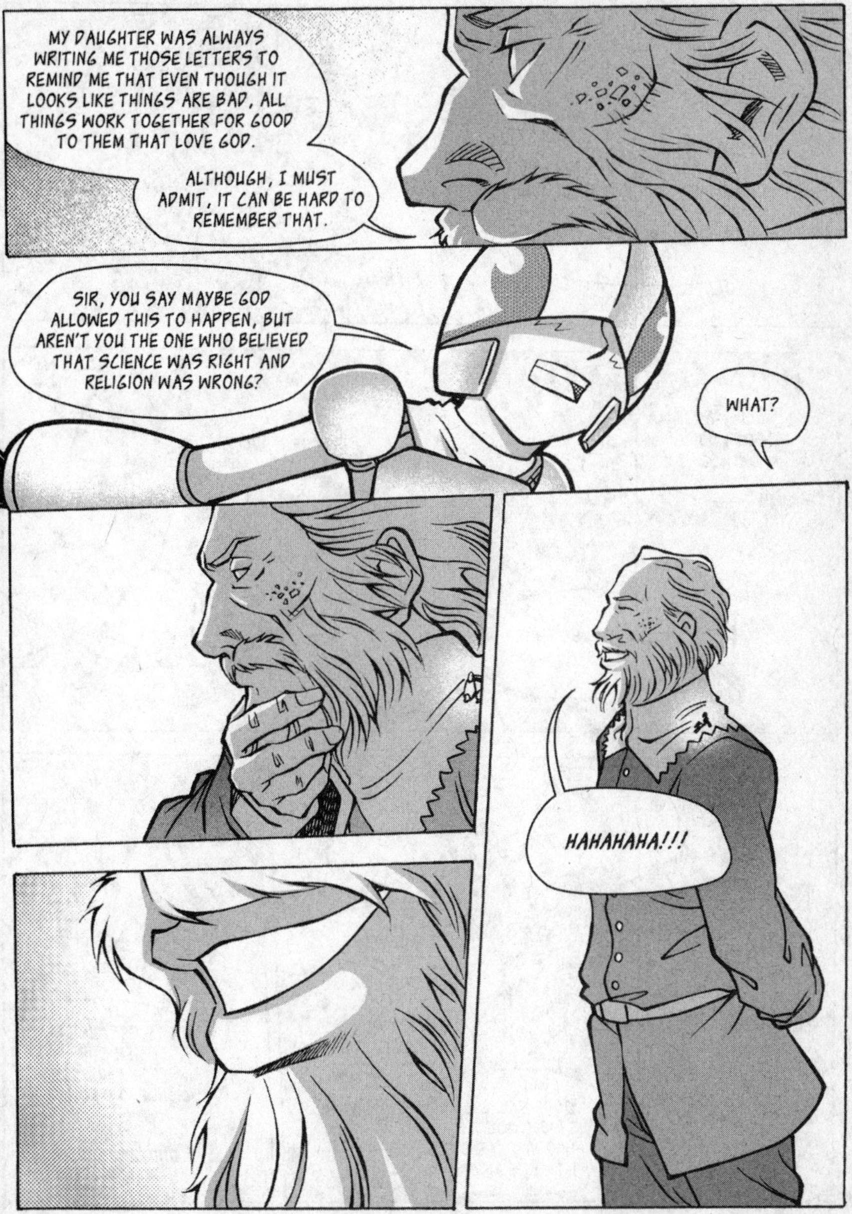
MY DAUGHTER WAS ALWAYS WRITING ME THOSE LETTERS TO REMIND ME THAT EVEN THOUGH IT LOOKS LIKE THINGS ARE BAD, ALL THINGS WORK TOGETHER FOR GOOD TO THEM THAT LOVE GOD.
ALTHOUGH, I MUST ADMIT, IT CAN BE HARD TO REMEMBER THAT.
SIR, YOU SAY MAYBE GOD ALLOWED THIS TO HAPPEN, BUT AREN'T YOU THE ONE WHO BELIEVED THAT SCIENCE WAS RIGHT AND RELIGION WAS WRONG?
WHAT?
HAHAHAHA!!!

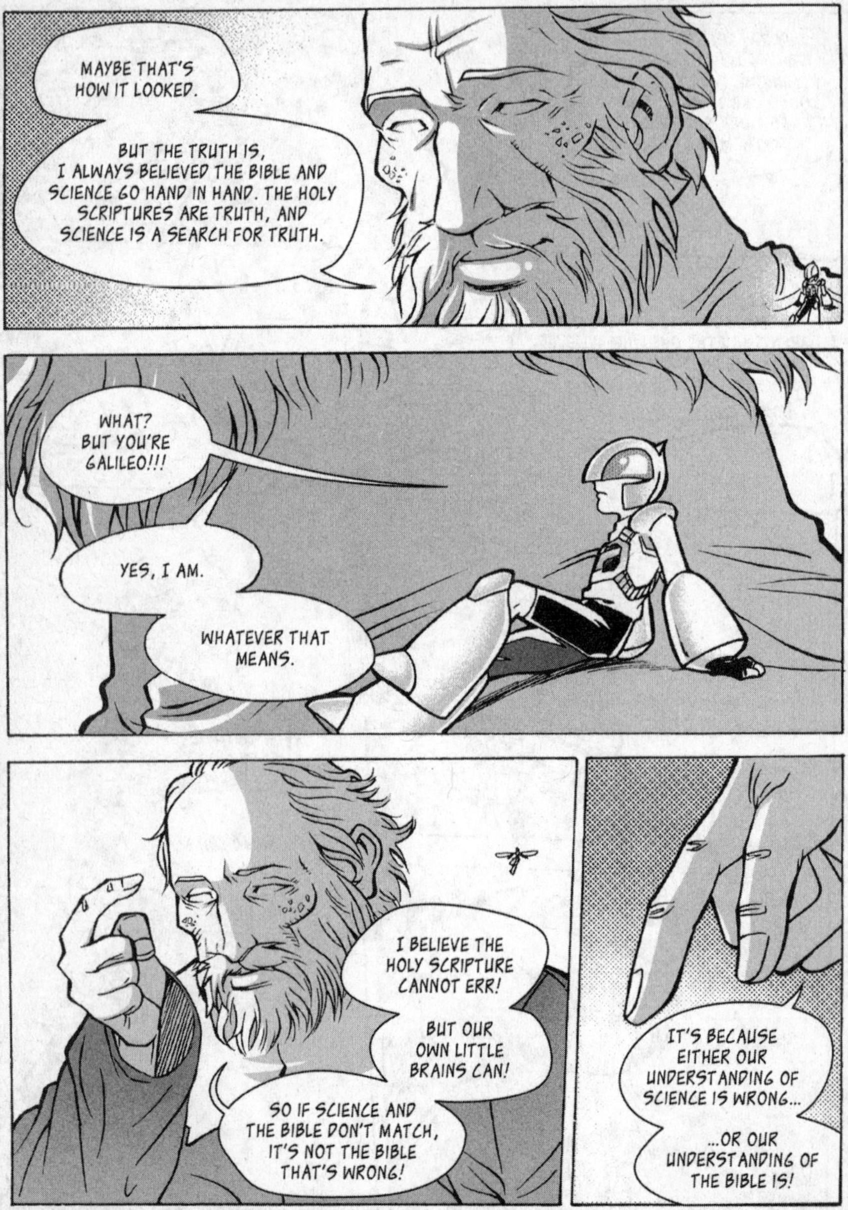
MAYBE THAT'S HOW IT LOOKED.
BUT THE TRUTH IS, I ALWAYS BELIEVED THE BIBLE AND SCIENCE GO HAND IN HAND. THE HOLY SCRIPTURES ARE TRUTH, AND SCIENCE IS A SEARCH FOR TRUTH.
WHAT? BUT YOU'RE GALILEO!!!
YES, I AM.
WHATEVER THAT MEANS.
I BELIEVE THE HOLY SCRIPTURE CANNOT ERR!
BUT OUR OWN LITTLE BRAINS CAN!
SO IF SCIENCE AND THE BIBLE DON'T MATCH, IT'S NOT THE BIBLE THAT'S WRONG!
IT'S BECAUSE EITHER OUR UNDERSTANDING OF SCIENCE IS WRONG...
...OR OUR UNDERSTANDING OF THE BIBLE IS!

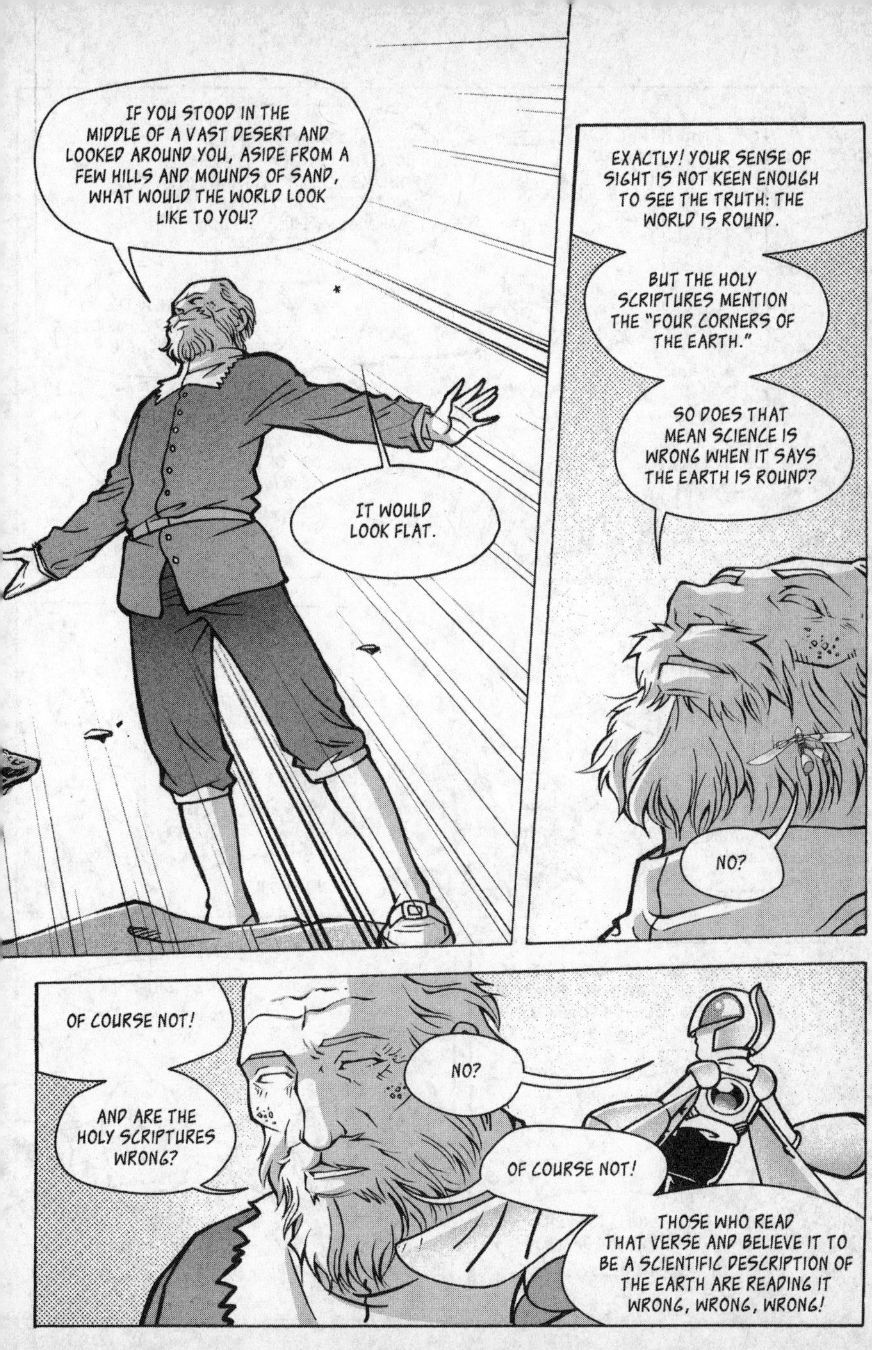
IF YOU STOOD IN THE MIDDLE OF A VAST DESERT AND LOOKED AROUND YOU, ASIDE FROM A FEW HILLS AND MOUNDS OF SAND, WHAT WOULD THE WORLD LOOK LIKE TO YOU?
IT WOULD LOOK FLAT.
EXACTLY! YOUR SENSE OF SIGHT IS NOT KEEN ENOUGH TO SEE THE TRUTH: THE WORLD IS ROUND.
BUT THE HOLY SCRIPTURES MENTION THE "FOUR CORNERS OF THE EARTH."
SO DOES THAT MEAN SCIENCE IS WRONG WHEN IT SAYS THE EARTH IS ROUND?
NO?
OF COURSE NOT!
NO?
AND ARE THE HOLY SCRIPTURES WRONG?
OF COURSE NOT!
THOSE WHO READ THAT VERSE AND BELIEVE IT TO BE A SCIENTIFIC DESCRIPTION OF THE EARTH ARE READING IT WRONG, WRONG, WRONG!

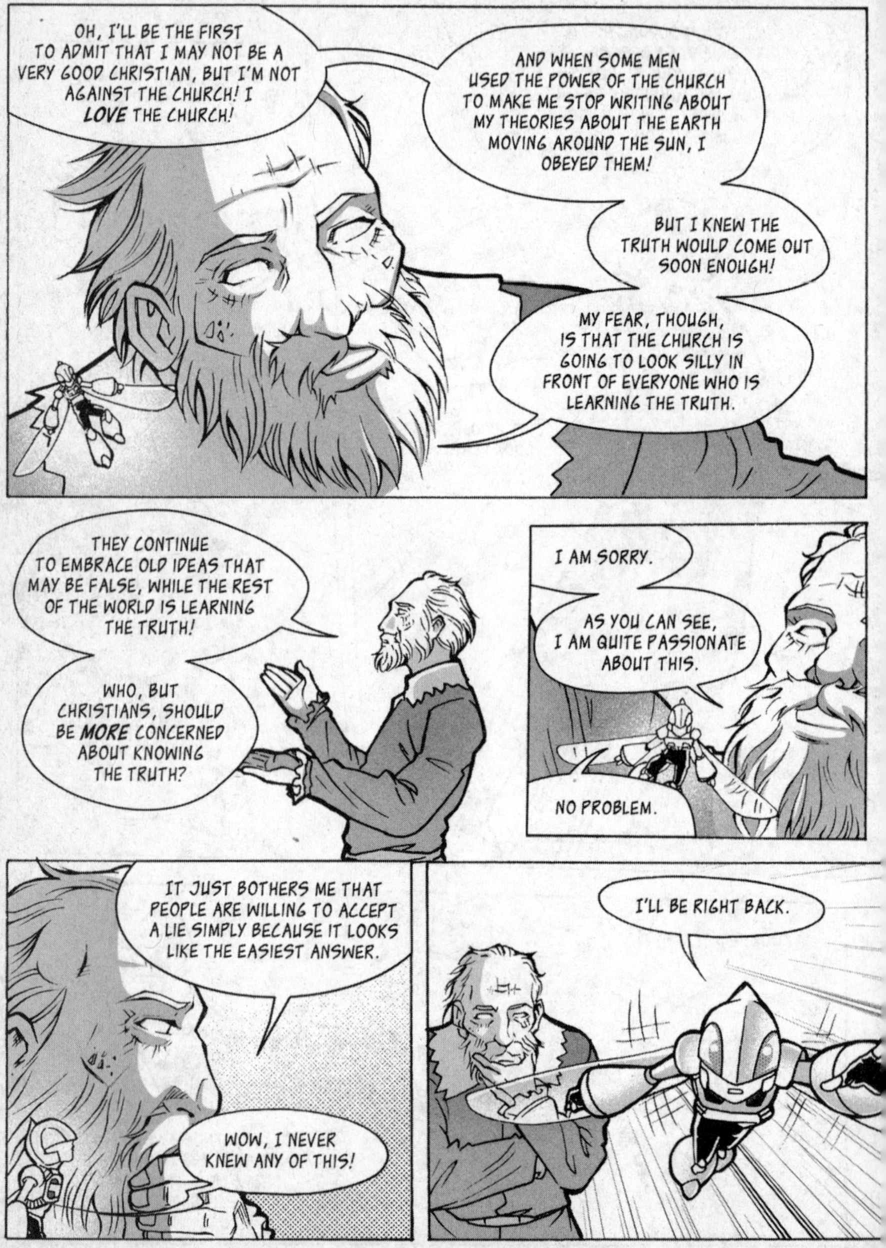
OH, I'LL BE THE FIRST TO ADMIT THAT I MAY NOT BE A VERY GOOD CHRISTIAN, BUT I'M NOT AGAINST THE CHURCH! I *LOVE* THE CHURCH!
AND WHEN SOME MEN USED THE POWER OF THE CHURCH TO MAKE ME STOP WRITING ABOUT MY THEORIES ABOUT THE EARTH MOVING AROUND THE SUN, I OBEYED THEM!
BUT I KNEW THE TRUTH WOULD COME OUT SOON ENOUGH!
MY FEAR, THOUGH, IS THAT THE CHURCH IS GOING TO LOOK SILLY IN FRONT OF EVERYONE WHO IS LEARNING THE TRUTH.
THEY CONTINUE TO EMBRACE OLD IDEAS THAT MAY BE FALSE, WHILE THE REST OF THE WORLD IS LEARNING THE TRUTH!
WHO, BUT CHRISTIANS, SHOULD BE *MORE* CONCERNED ABOUT KNOWING THE TRUTH?
I AM SORRY.
AS YOU CAN SEE, I AM QUITE PASSIONATE ABOUT THIS.
NO PROBLEM.
IT JUST BOTHERS ME THAT PEOPLE ARE WILLING TO ACCEPT A LIE SIMPLY BECAUSE IT LOOKS LIKE THE EASIEST ANSWER.
WOW, I NEVER KNEW ANY OF THIS!
I'LL BE RIGHT BACK.

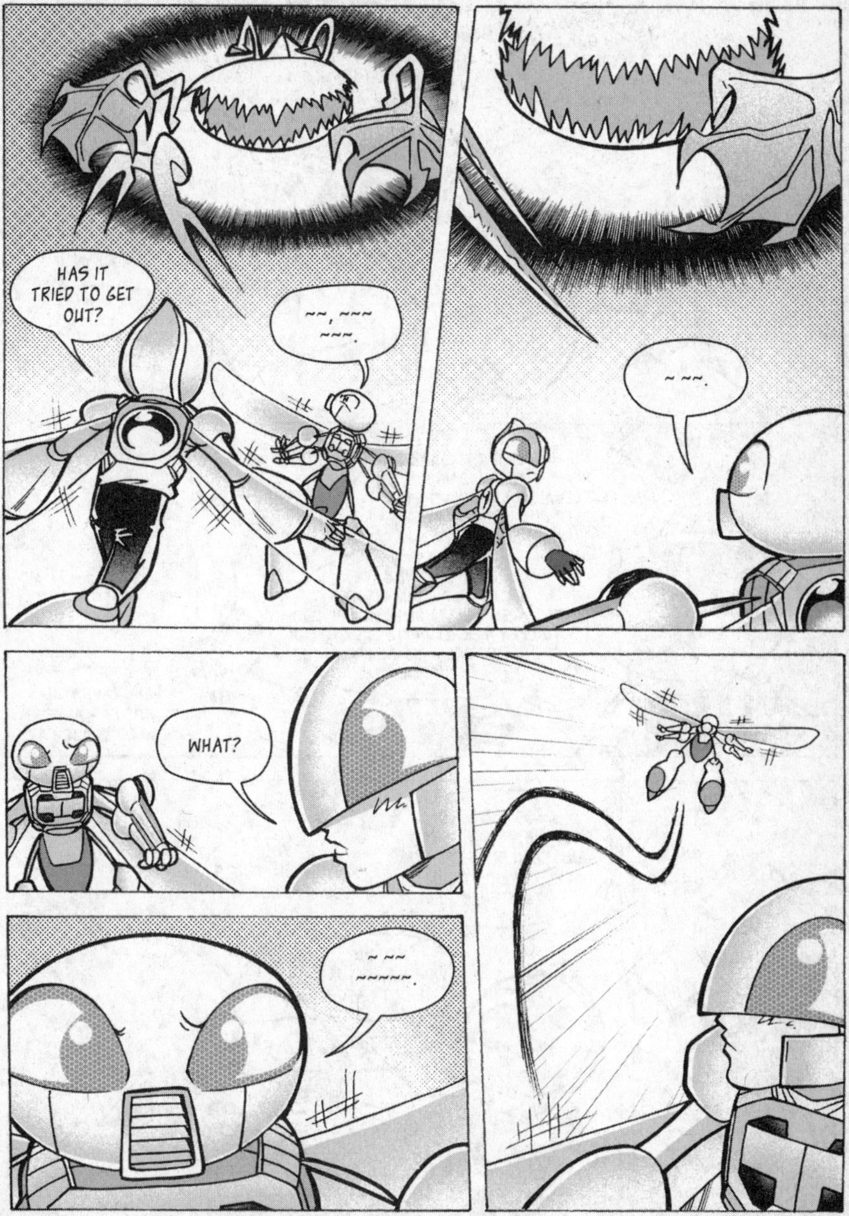
HAS IT TRIED TO GET OUT?
~~, ~~~ ~~~.
~ ~~.
WHAT?
~ ~~ ~~~~~.

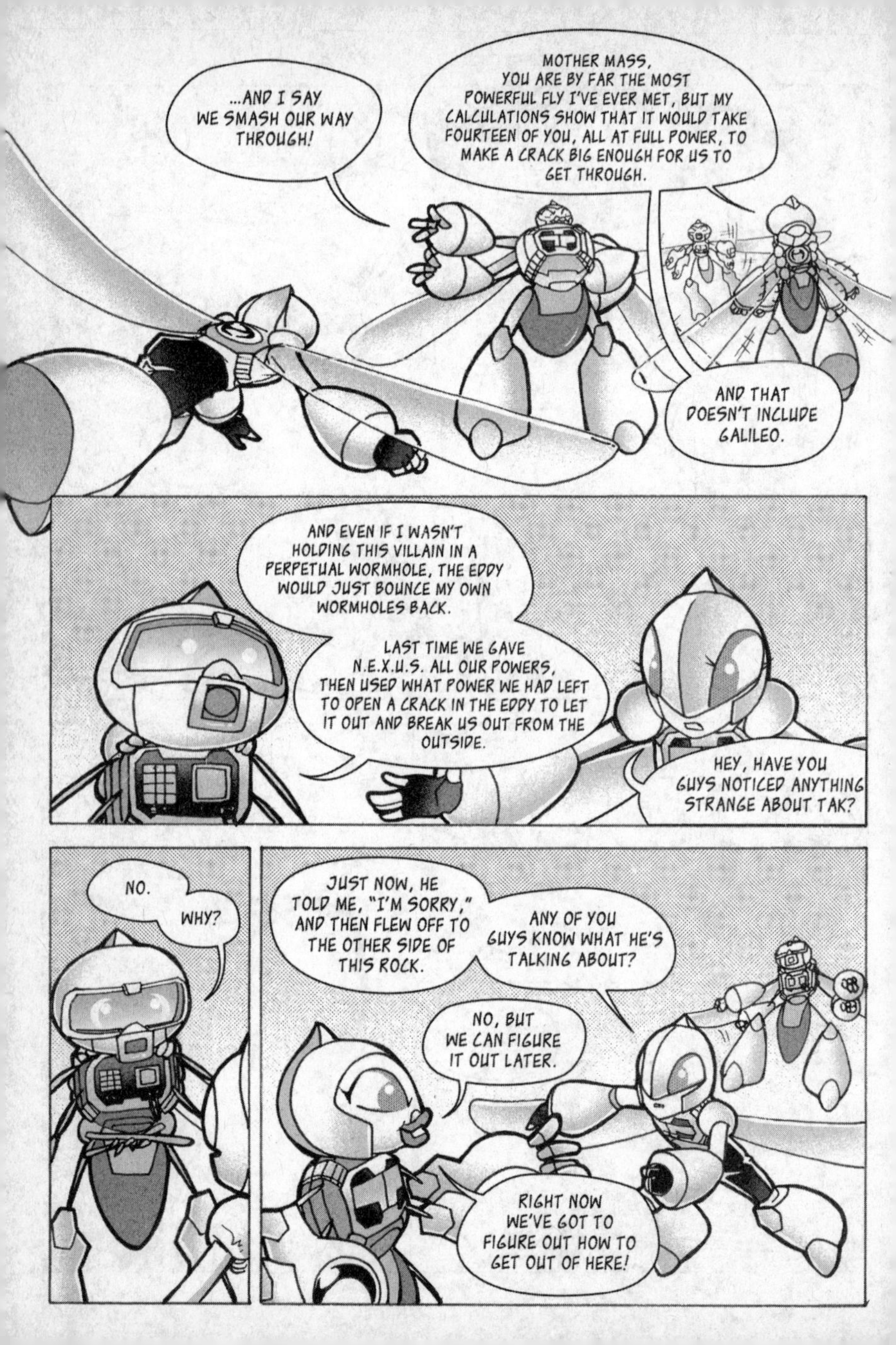
...AND I SAY WE SMASH OUR WAY THROUGH!
MOTHER MASS, YOU ARE BY FAR THE MOST POWERFUL FLY I'VE EVER MET, BUT MY CALCULATIONS SHOW THAT IT WOULD TAKE FOURTEEN OF YOU, ALL AT FULL POWER, TO MAKE A CRACK BIG ENOUGH FOR US TO GET THROUGH.
AND THAT DOESN'T INCLUDE GALILEO.
AND EVEN IF I WASN'T HOLDING THIS VILLAIN IN A PERPETUAL WORMHOLE, THE EDDY WOULD JUST BOUNCE MY OWN WORMHOLES BACK.
LAST TIME WE GAVE N.E.X.U.S. ALL OUR POWERS, THEN USED WHAT POWER WE HAD LEFT TO OPEN A CRACK IN THE EDDY TO LET IT OUT AND BREAK US OUT FROM THE OUTSIDE.
HEY, HAVE YOU GUYS NOTICED ANYTHING STRANGE ABOUT TAK?
NO.
WHY?
JUST NOW, HE TOLD ME, "I'M SORRY," AND THEN FLEW OFF TO THE OTHER SIDE OF THIS ROCK.
ANY OF YOU GUYS KNOW WHAT HE'S TALKING ABOUT?
NO, BUT WE CAN FIGURE IT OUT LATER.
RIGHT NOW WE'VE GOT TO FIGURE OUT HOW TO GET OUT OF HERE!

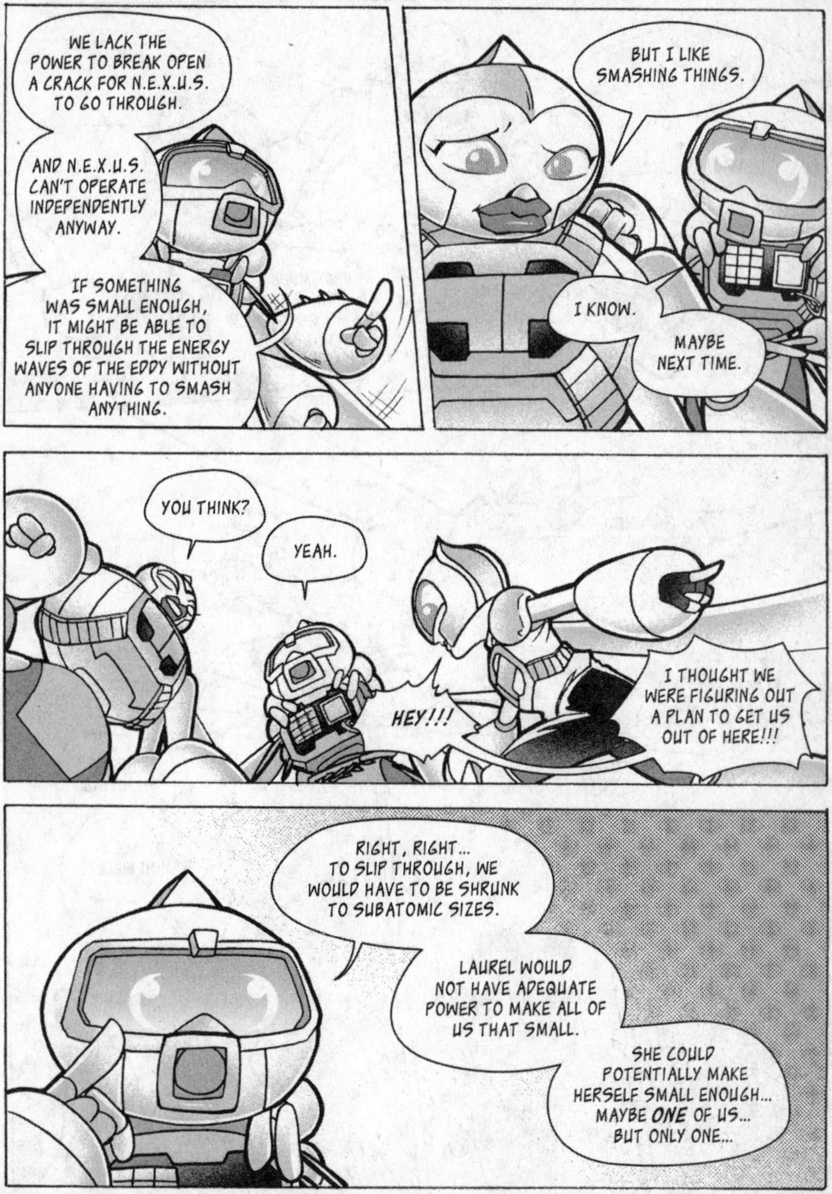
WE LACK THE POWER TO BREAK OPEN A CRACK FOR N.E.X.U.S. TO GO THROUGH.
AND N.E.X.U.S. CAN'T OPERATE INDEPENDENTLY ANYWAY.
IF SOMETHING WAS SMALL ENOUGH, IT MIGHT BE ABLE TO SLIP THROUGH THE ENERGY WAVES OF THE EDDY WITHOUT ANYONE HAVING TO SMASH ANYTHING.
BUT I LIKE SMASHING THINGS.
I KNOW.
MAYBE NEXT TIME.
YOU THINK?
YEAH.
HEY!!!
I THOUGHT WE WERE FIGURING OUT A PLAN TO GET US OUT OF HERE!!!
RIGHT, RIGHT... TO SLIP THROUGH, WE WOULD HAVE TO BE SHRUNK TO SUBATOMIC SIZES.
LAUREL WOULD NOT HAVE ADEQUATE POWER TO MAKE ALL OF US THAT SMALL.
SHE COULD POTENTIALLY MAKE HERSELF SMALL ENOUGH... MAYBE *ONE* OF US... BUT ONLY ONE...

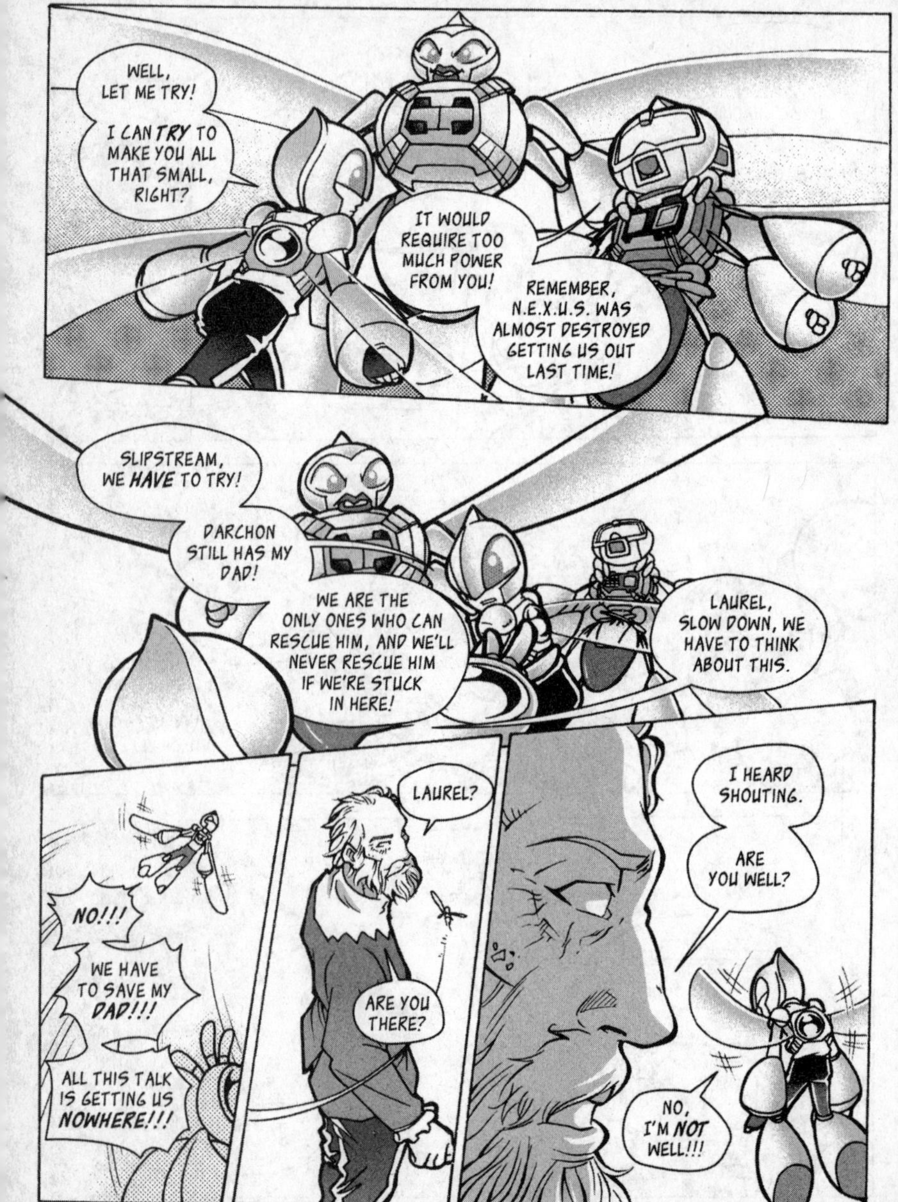
WELL, LET ME TRY!
I CAN TRY TO MAKE YOU ALL THAT SMALL, RIGHT?
IT WOULD REQUIRE TOO MUCH POWER FROM YOU!
REMEMBER, N.E.X.U.S. WAS ALMOST DESTROYED GETTING US OUT LAST TIME!
SLIPSTREAM, WE HAVE TO TRY!
DARCHON STILL HAS MY DAD!
WE ARE THE ONLY ONES WHO CAN RESCUE HIM, AND WE'LL NEVER RESCUE HIM IF WE'RE STUCK IN HERE!
LAUREL, SLOW DOWN, WE HAVE TO THINK ABOUT THIS.
NO!!!
WE HAVE TO SAVE MY DAD!!!
ALL THIS TALK IS GETTING US NOWHERE!!!
LAUREL?
ARE YOU THERE?
I HEARD SHOUTING.
ARE YOU WELL?
NO, I'M NOT WELL!!!

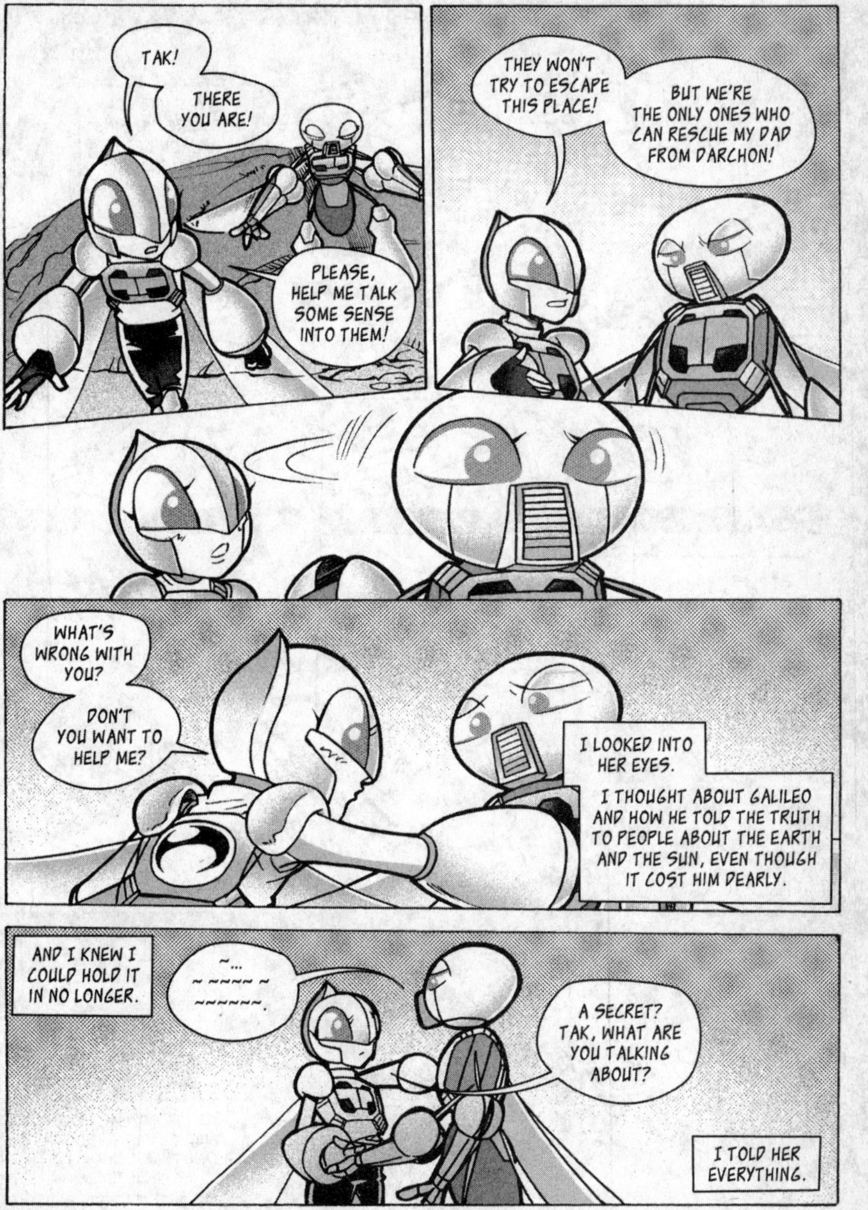
TAK!
THERE YOU ARE!
PLEASE, HELP ME TALK SOME SENSE INTO THEM!
THEY WON'T TRY TO ESCAPE THIS PLACE!
BUT WE'RE THE ONLY ONES WHO CAN RESCUE MY DAD FROM DARCHON!
WHAT'S WRONG WITH YOU?
DON'T YOU WANT TO HELP ME?
I LOOKED INTO HER EYES.
I THOUGHT ABOUT GALILEO AND HOW HE TOLD THE TRUTH TO PEOPLE ABOUT THE EARTH AND THE SUN, EVEN THOUGH IT COST HIM DEARLY.
AND I KNEW I COULD HOLD IT IN NO LONGER.
~... ~ ~~~~~ ~ ~~~~~~.
A SECRET? TAK, WHAT ARE YOU TALKING ABOUT?
I TOLD HER EVERYTHING.

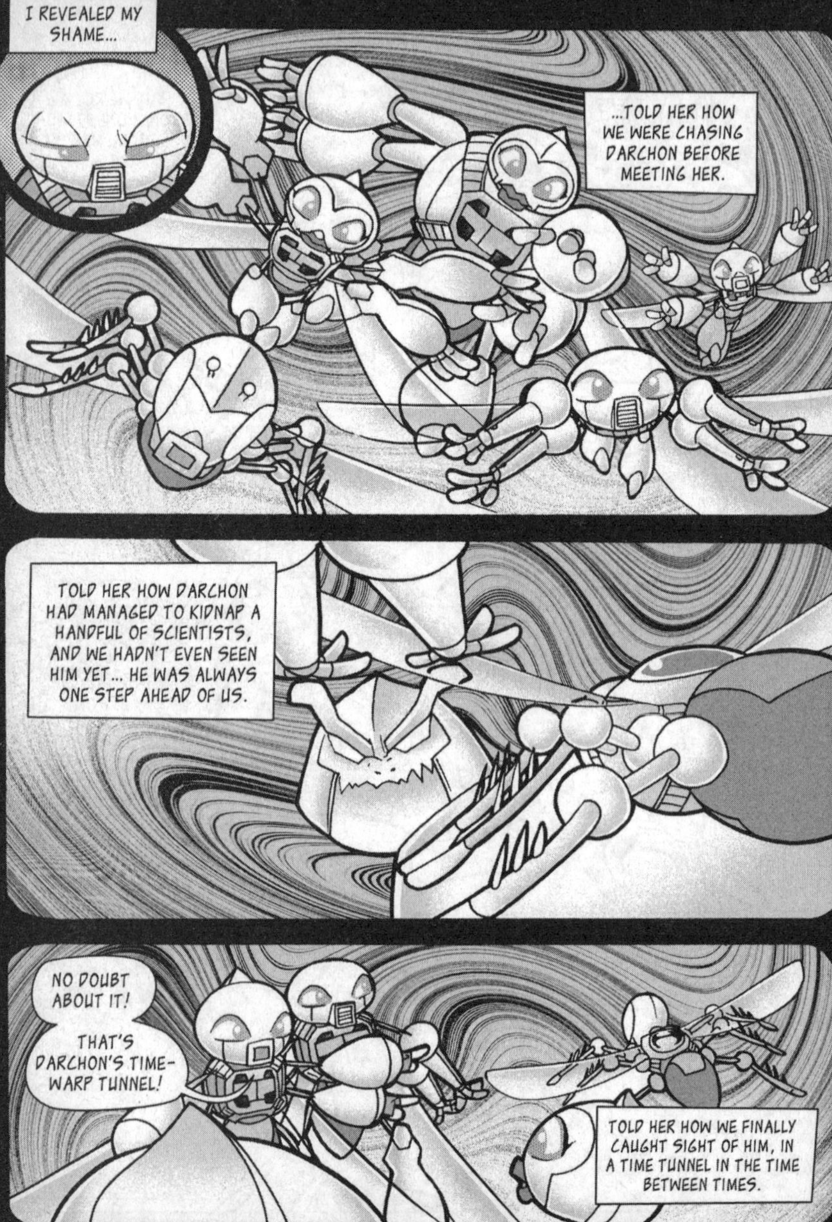
I REVEALED MY SHAME...
...TOLD HER HOW WE WERE CHASING DARCHON BEFORE MEETING HER.
TOLD HER HOW DARCHON HAD MANAGED TO KIDNAP A HANDFUL OF SCIENTISTS, AND WE HADN'T EVEN SEEN HIM YET... HE WAS ALWAYS ONE STEP AHEAD OF US.
NO DOUBT ABOUT IT!
THAT'S DARCHON'S TIME-WARP TUNNEL!
TOLD HER HOW WE FINALLY CAUGHT SIGHT OF HIM, IN A TIME TUNNEL IN THE TIME BETWEEN TIMES.

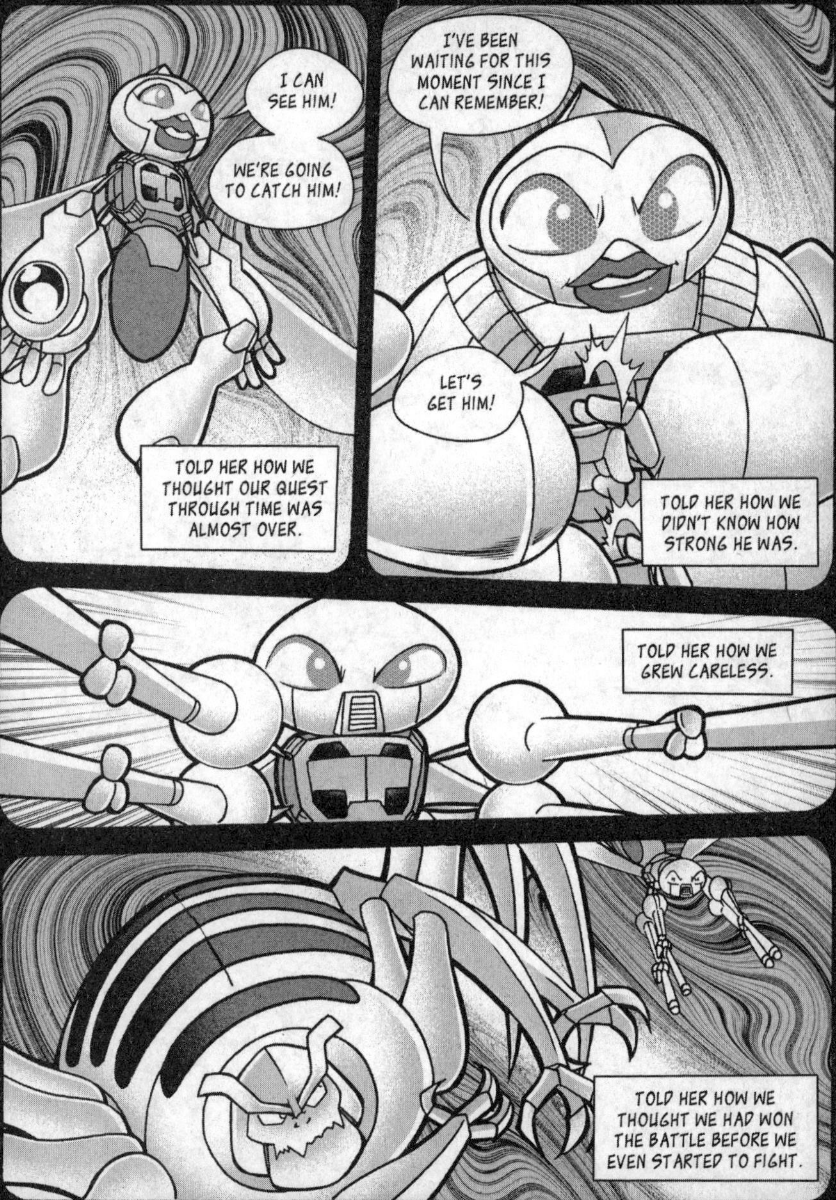
I CAN SEE HIM!
WE'RE GOING TO CATCH HIM!
TOLD HER HOW WE THOUGHT OUR QUEST THROUGH TIME WAS ALMOST OVER.
I'VE BEEN WAITING FOR THIS MOMENT SINCE I CAN REMEMBER!
LET'S GET HIM!
TOLD HER HOW WE DIDN'T KNOW HOW STRONG HE WAS.
TOLD HER HOW WE GREW CARELESS.
TOLD HER HOW WE THOUGHT WE HAD WON THE BATTLE BEFORE WE EVEN STARTED TO FIGHT.

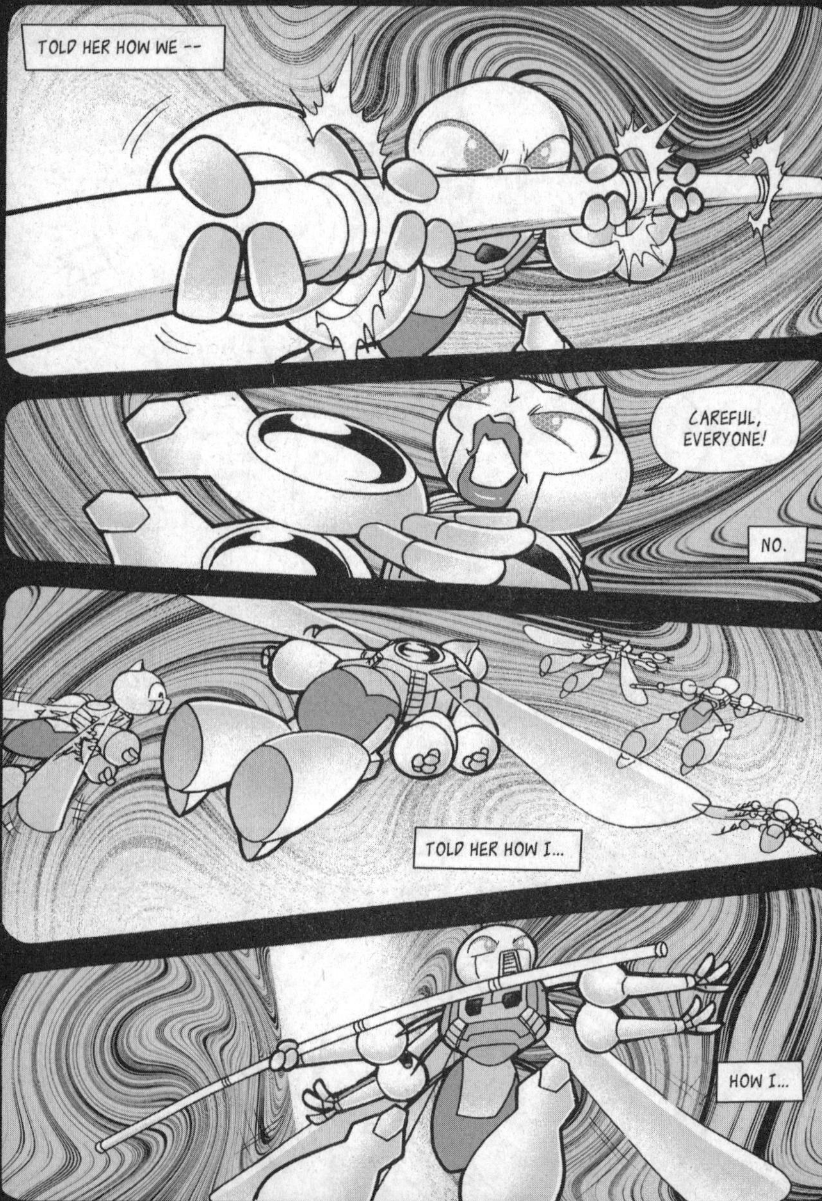
TOLD HER HOW WE --
CAREFUL, EVERYONE!
NO.
TOLD HER HOW I...
HOW I...

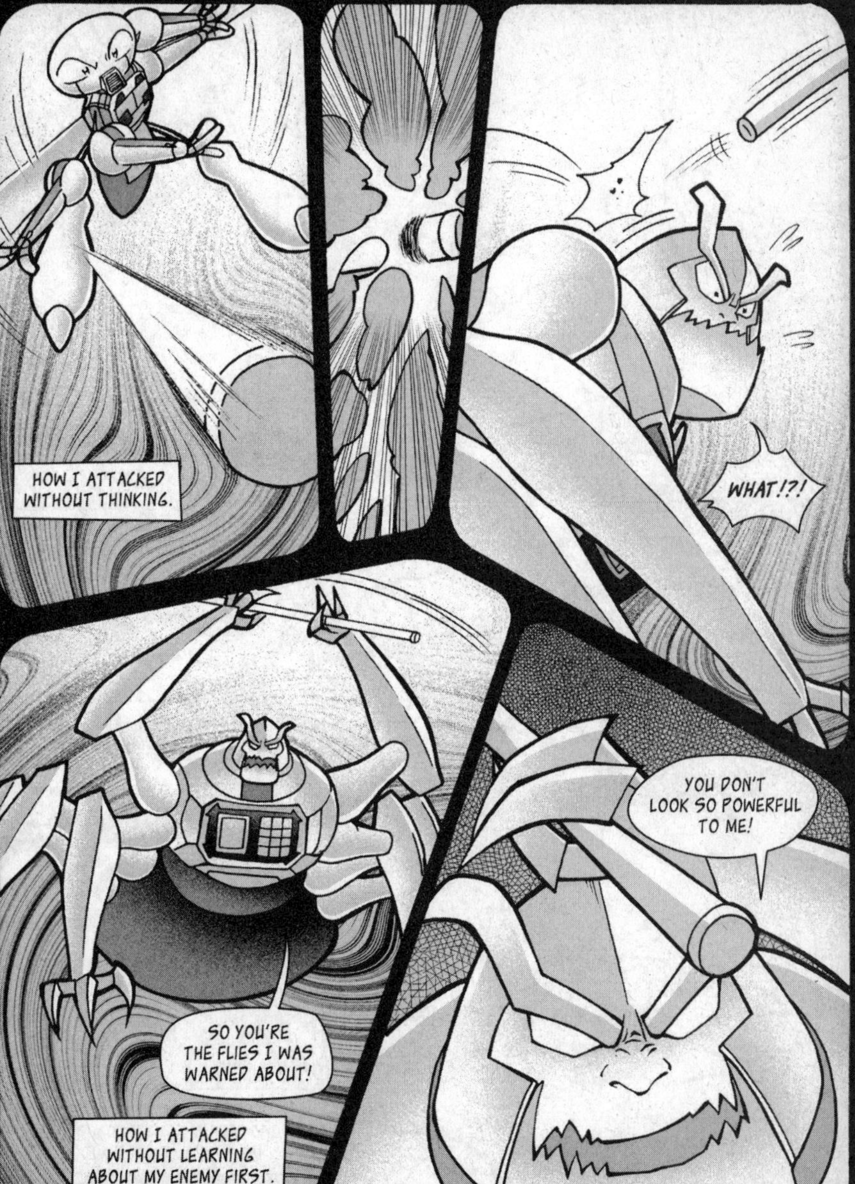
HOW I ATTACKED WITHOUT THINKING.
WHAT!?!
SO YOU'RE THE FLIES I WAS WARNED ABOUT!
HOW I ATTACKED WITHOUT LEARNING ABOUT MY ENEMY FIRST.
YOU DON'T LOOK SO POWERFUL TO ME!

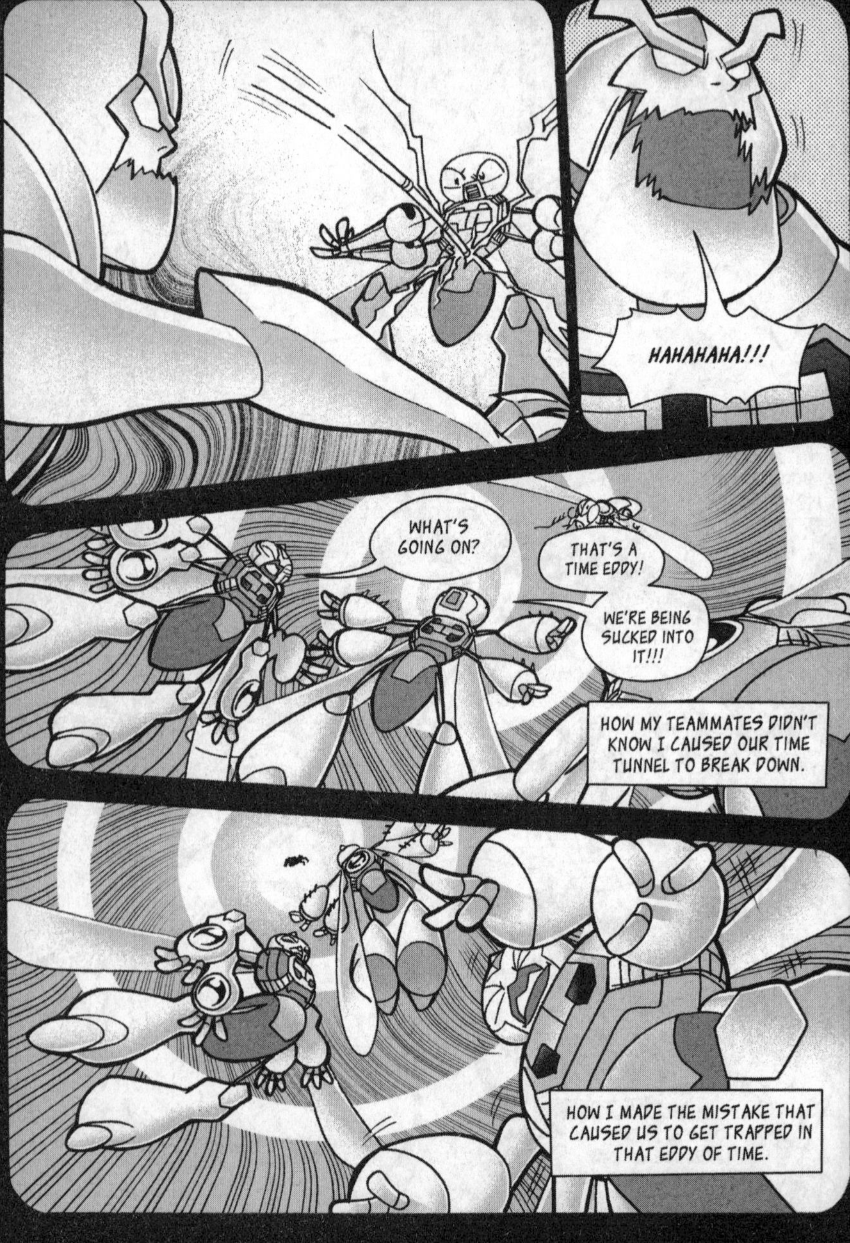
HAHAHAHA!!!
WHAT'S GOING ON?
THAT'S A TIME EDDY!
WE'RE BEING SUCKED INTO IT!!!
HOW MY TEAMMATES DIDN'T KNOW I CAUSED OUR TIME TUNNEL TO BREAK DOWN.
HOW I MADE THE MISTAKE THAT CAUSED US TO GET TRAPPED IN THAT EDDY OF TIME.

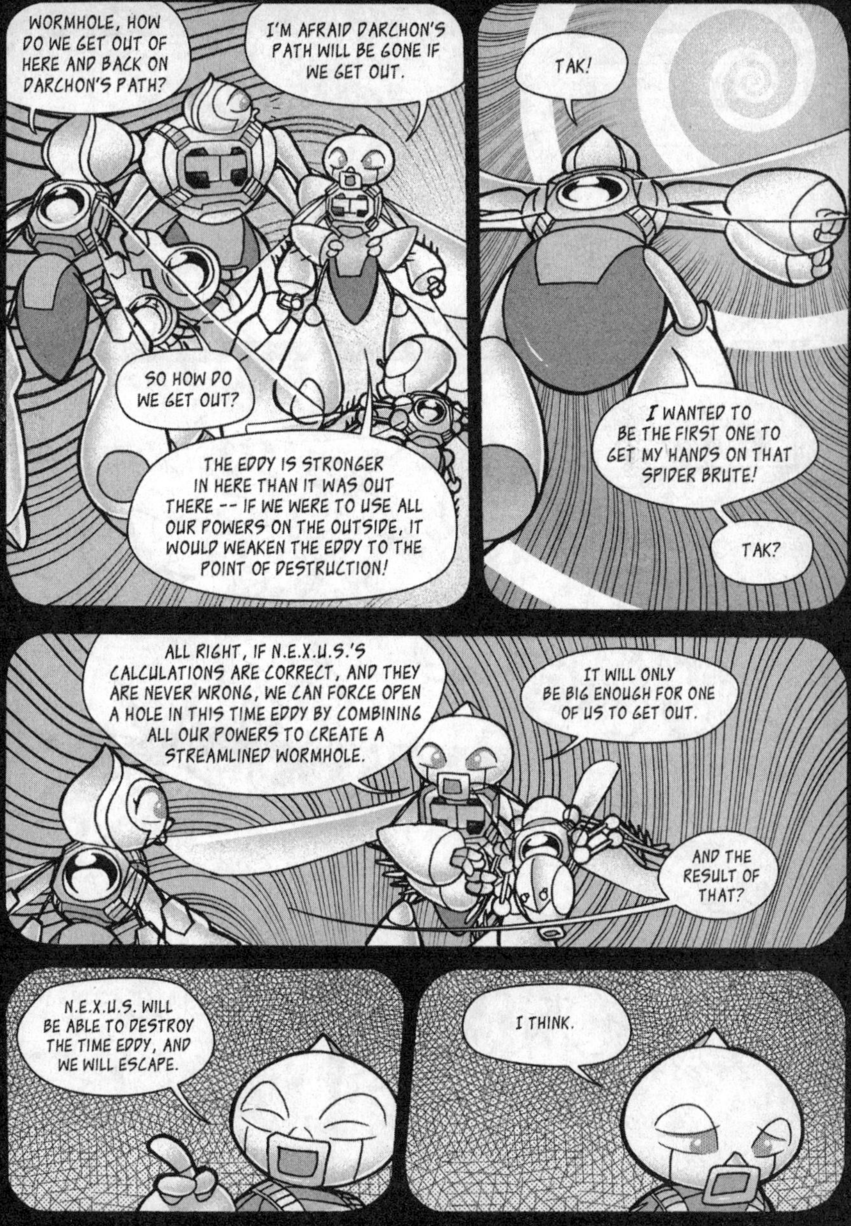
WORMHOLE, HOW DO WE GET OUT OF HERE AND BACK ON DARCHON'S PATH?
I'M AFRAID DARCHON'S PATH WILL BE GONE IF WE GET OUT.
SO HOW DO WE GET OUT?
THE EDDY IS STRONGER IN HERE THAN IT WAS OUT THERE -- IF WE WERE TO USE ALL OUR POWERS ON THE OUTSIDE, IT WOULD WEAKEN THE EDDY TO THE POINT OF DESTRUCTION!
TAK!
I WANTED TO BE THE FIRST ONE TO GET MY HANDS ON THAT SPIDER BRUTE!
TAK?
ALL RIGHT, IF N.E.X.U.S.'S CALCULATIONS ARE CORRECT, AND THEY ARE NEVER WRONG, WE CAN FORCE OPEN A HOLE IN THIS TIME EDDY BY COMBINING ALL OUR POWERS TO CREATE A STREAMLINED WORMHOLE.
IT WILL ONLY BE BIG ENOUGH FOR ONE OF US TO GET OUT.
AND THE RESULT OF THAT?
N.E.X.U.S. WILL BE ABLE TO DESTROY THE TIME EDDY, AND WE WILL ESCAPE.
I THINK.

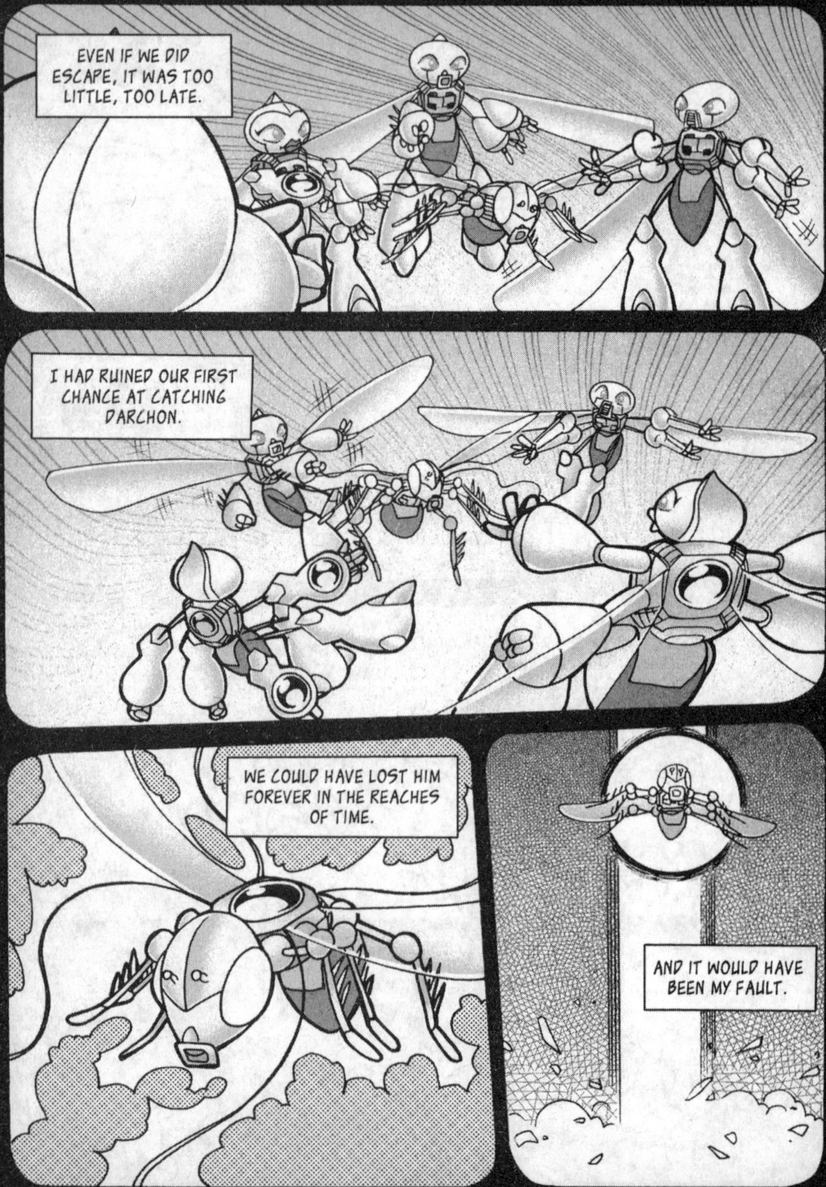
EVEN IF WE DID ESCAPE, IT WAS TOO LITTLE, TOO LATE.
I HAD RUINED OUR FIRST CHANCE AT CATCHING DARCHON.
WE COULD HAVE LOST HIM FOREVER IN THE REACHES OF TIME.
AND IT WOULD HAVE BEEN MY FAULT.

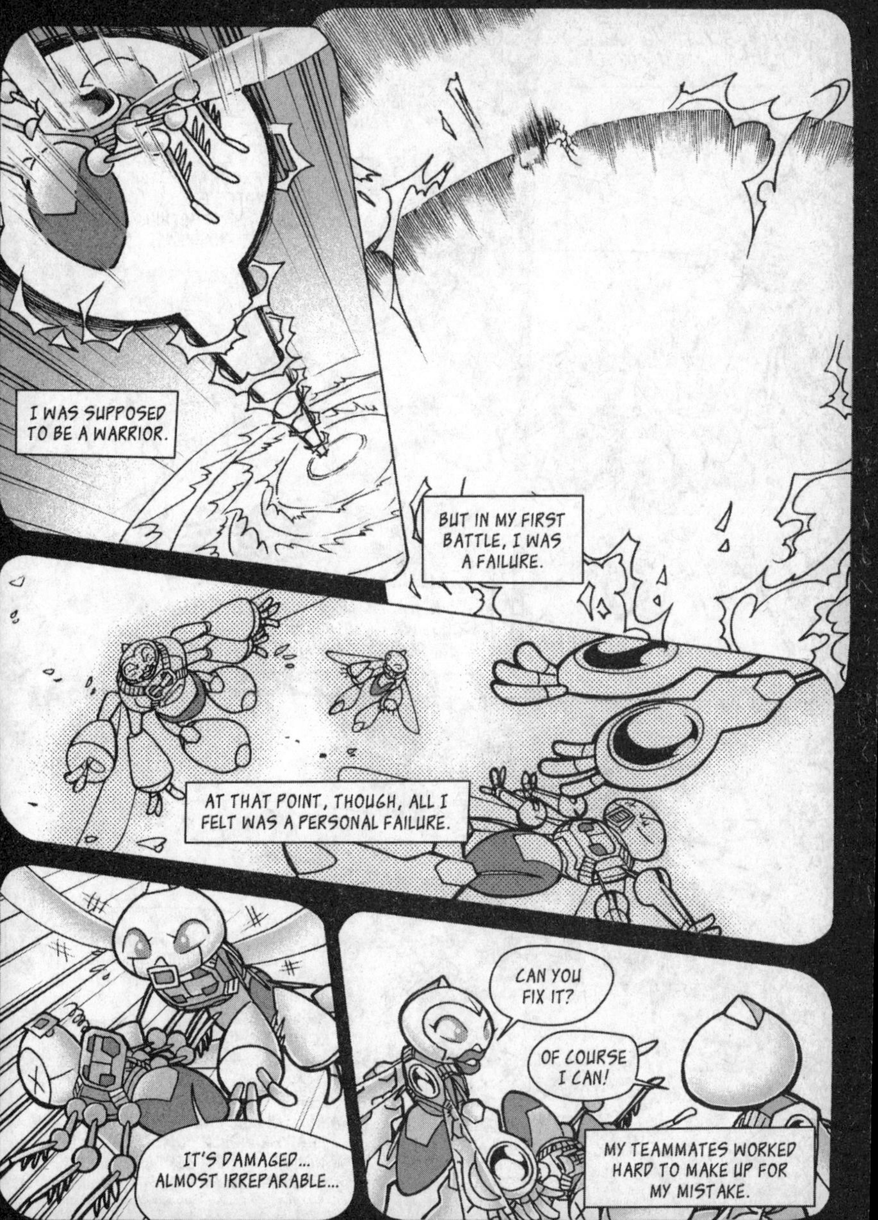
I WAS SUPPOSED TO BE A WARRIOR.
BUT IN MY FIRST BATTLE, I WAS A FAILURE.
AT THAT POINT, THOUGH, ALL I FELT WAS A PERSONAL FAILURE.
IT'S DAMAGED... ALMOST IRREPARABLE...
CAN YOU FIX IT?
OF COURSE I CAN!
MY TEAMMATES WORKED HARD TO MAKE UP FOR MY MISTAKE.

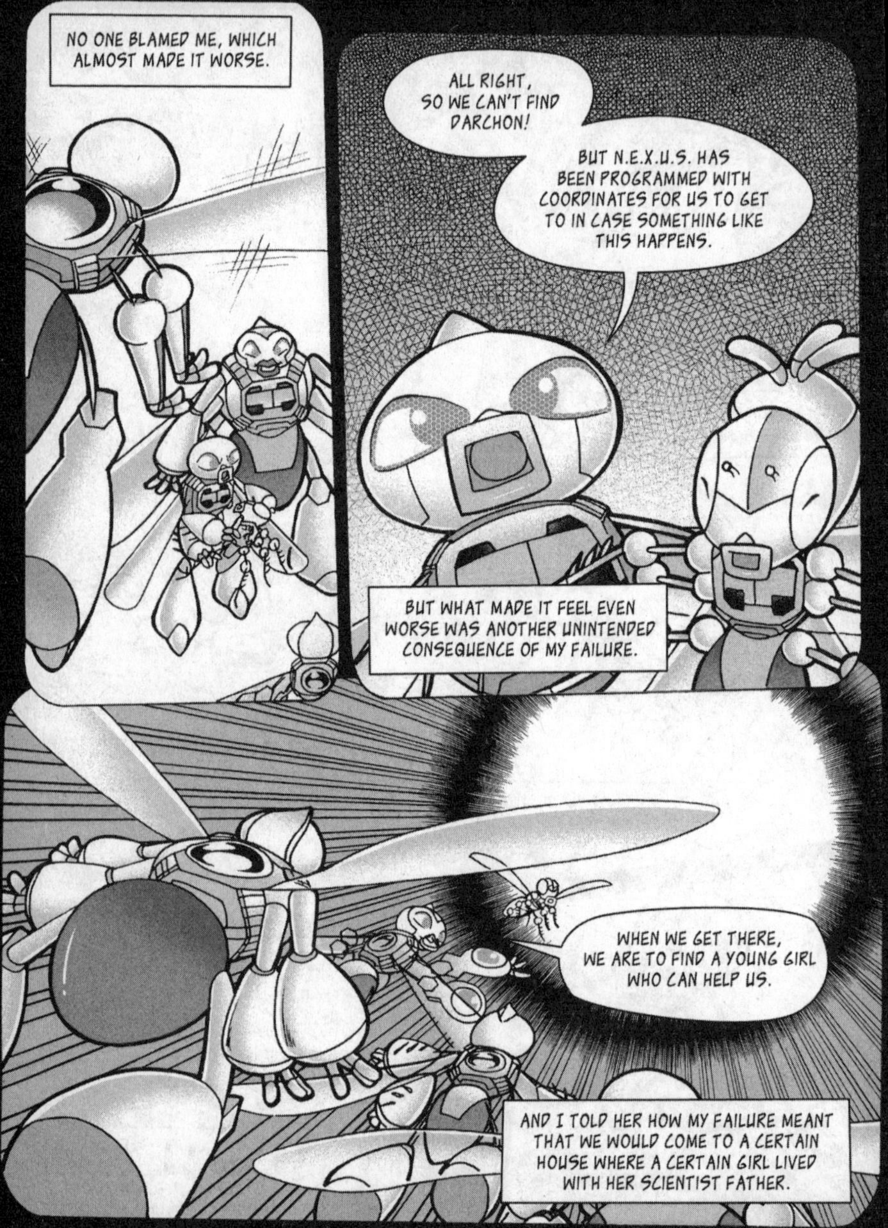
NO ONE BLAMED ME, WHICH ALMOST MADE IT WORSE.
ALL RIGHT, SO WE CAN'T FIND DARCHON!
BUT N.E.X.U.S. HAS BEEN PROGRAMMED WITH COORDINATES FOR US TO GET TO IN CASE SOMETHING LIKE THIS HAPPENS.
BUT WHAT MADE IT FEEL EVEN WORSE WAS ANOTHER UNINTENDED CONSEQUENCE OF MY FAILURE.
WHEN WE GET THERE, WE ARE TO FIND A YOUNG GIRL WHO CAN HELP US.
AND I TOLD HER HOW MY FAILURE MEANT THAT WE WOULD COME TO A CERTAIN HOUSE WHERE A CERTAIN GIRL LIVED WITH HER SCIENTIST FATHER.

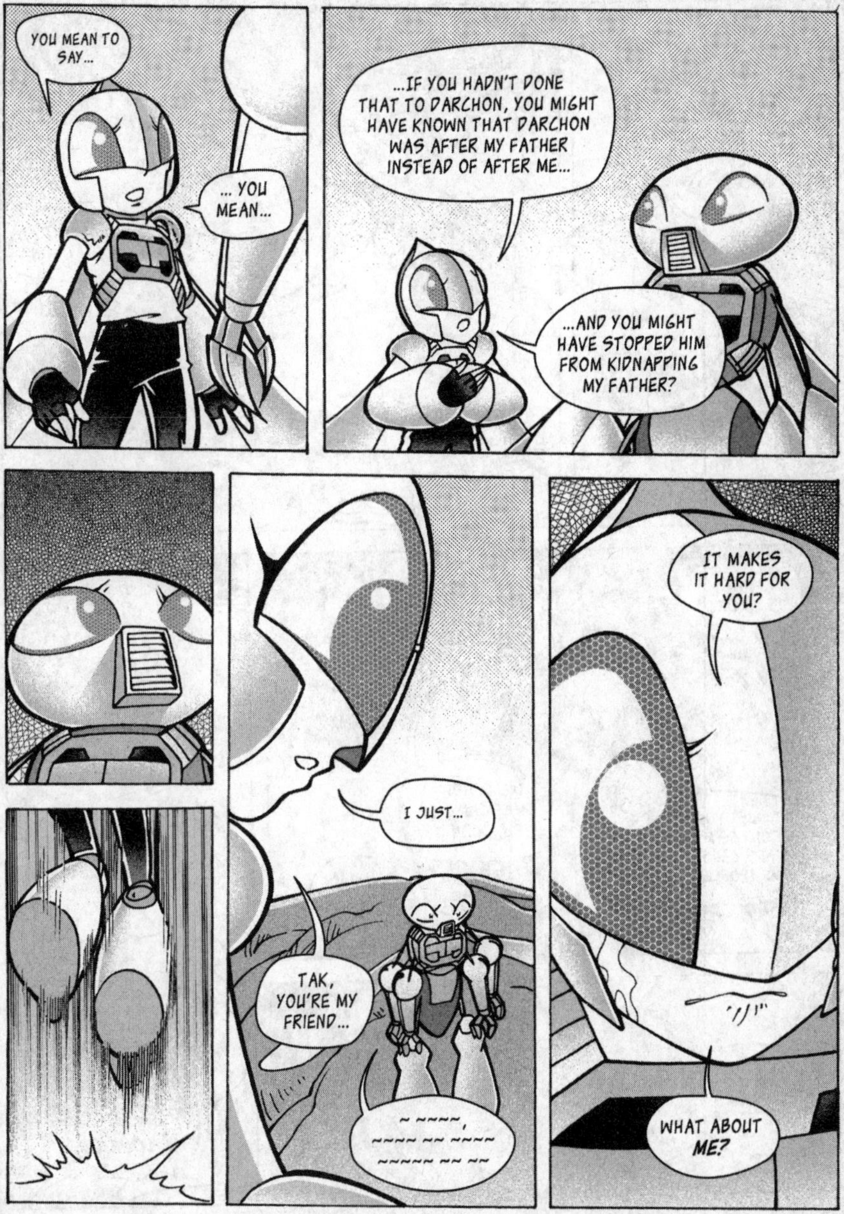
YOU MEAN TO SAY...
... YOU MEAN...
...IF YOU HADN'T DONE THAT TO DARCHON, YOU MIGHT HAVE KNOWN THAT DARCHON WAS AFTER MY FATHER INSTEAD OF AFTER ME...
...AND YOU MIGHT HAVE STOPPED HIM FROM KIDNAPPING MY FATHER?
I JUST...
TAK, YOU'RE MY FRIEND...
~ ~~~~, ~~~~ ~~ ~~~~ ~~~~~ ~~ ~~
IT MAKES IT HARD FOR YOU?
WHAT ABOUT ***ME?***

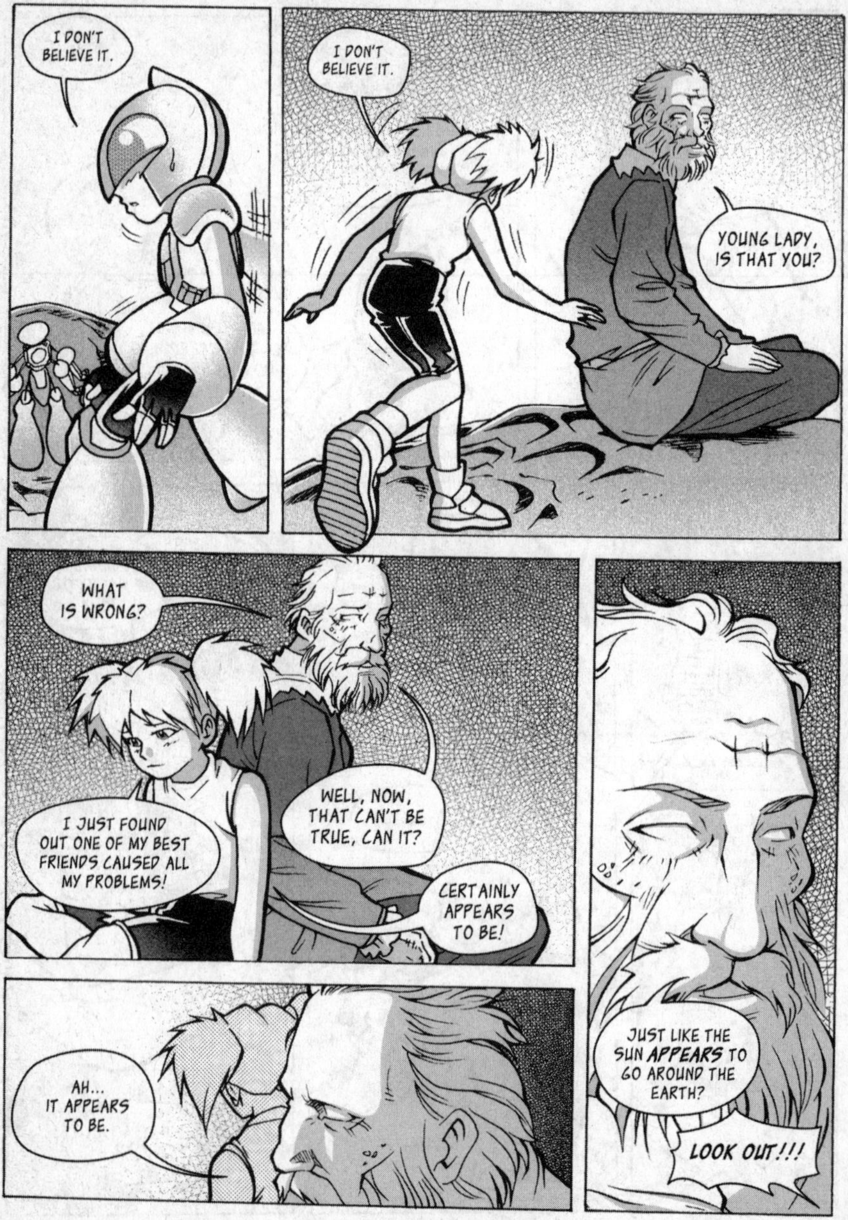
I DON'T BELIEVE IT.
I DON'T BELIEVE IT.
YOUNG LADY, IS THAT YOU?
WHAT IS WRONG?
I JUST FOUND OUT ONE OF MY BEST FRIENDS CAUSED ALL MY PROBLEMS!
WELL, NOW, THAT CAN'T BE TRUE, CAN IT?
CERTAINLY APPEARS TO BE!
JUST LIKE THE SUN *APPEARS* TO GO AROUND THE EARTH?
LOOK OUT!!!
AH... IT APPEARS TO BE.

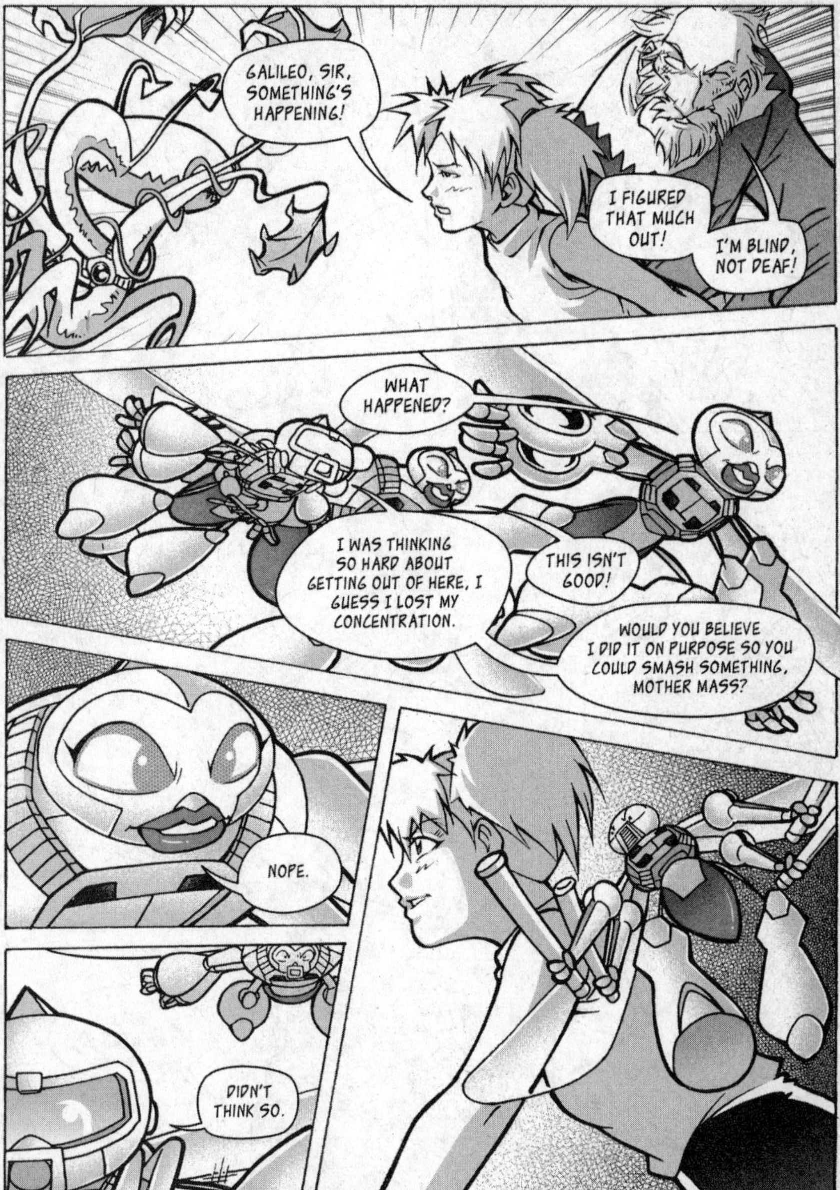
GALILEO, SIR, SOMETHING'S HAPPENING!
I FIGURED THAT MUCH OUT!
I'M BLIND, NOT DEAF!
WHAT HAPPENED?
I WAS THINKING SO HARD ABOUT GETTING OUT OF HERE, I GUESS I LOST MY CONCENTRATION.
THIS ISN'T GOOD!
WOULD YOU BELIEVE I DID IT ON PURPOSE SO YOU COULD SMASH SOMETHING, MOTHER MASS?
NOPE.
DIDN'T THINK SO.

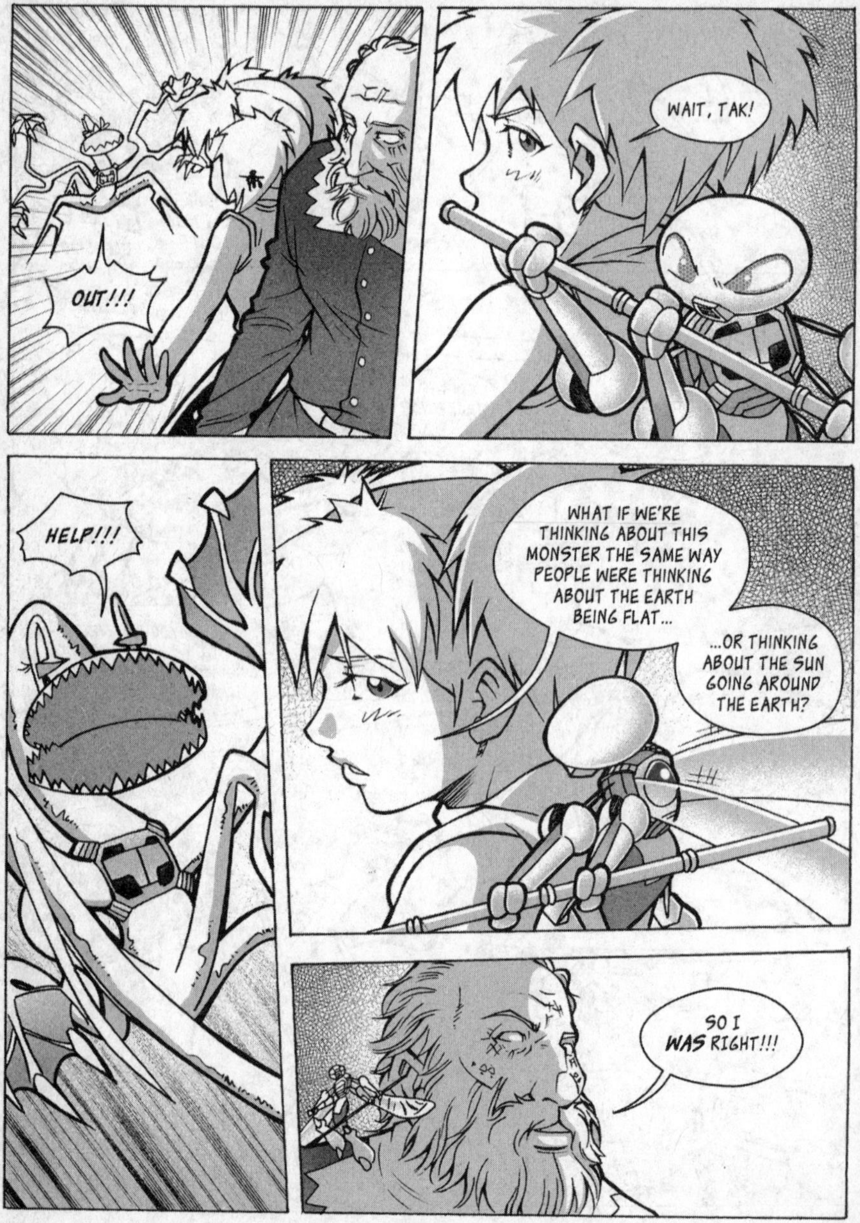
OUT!!!
WAIT, TAK!
HELP!!!
WHAT IF WE'RE THINKING ABOUT THIS MONSTER THE SAME WAY PEOPLE WERE THINKING ABOUT THE EARTH BEING FLAT...
...OR THINKING ABOUT THE SUN GOING AROUND THE EARTH?
SO I **WAS** RIGHT!!!

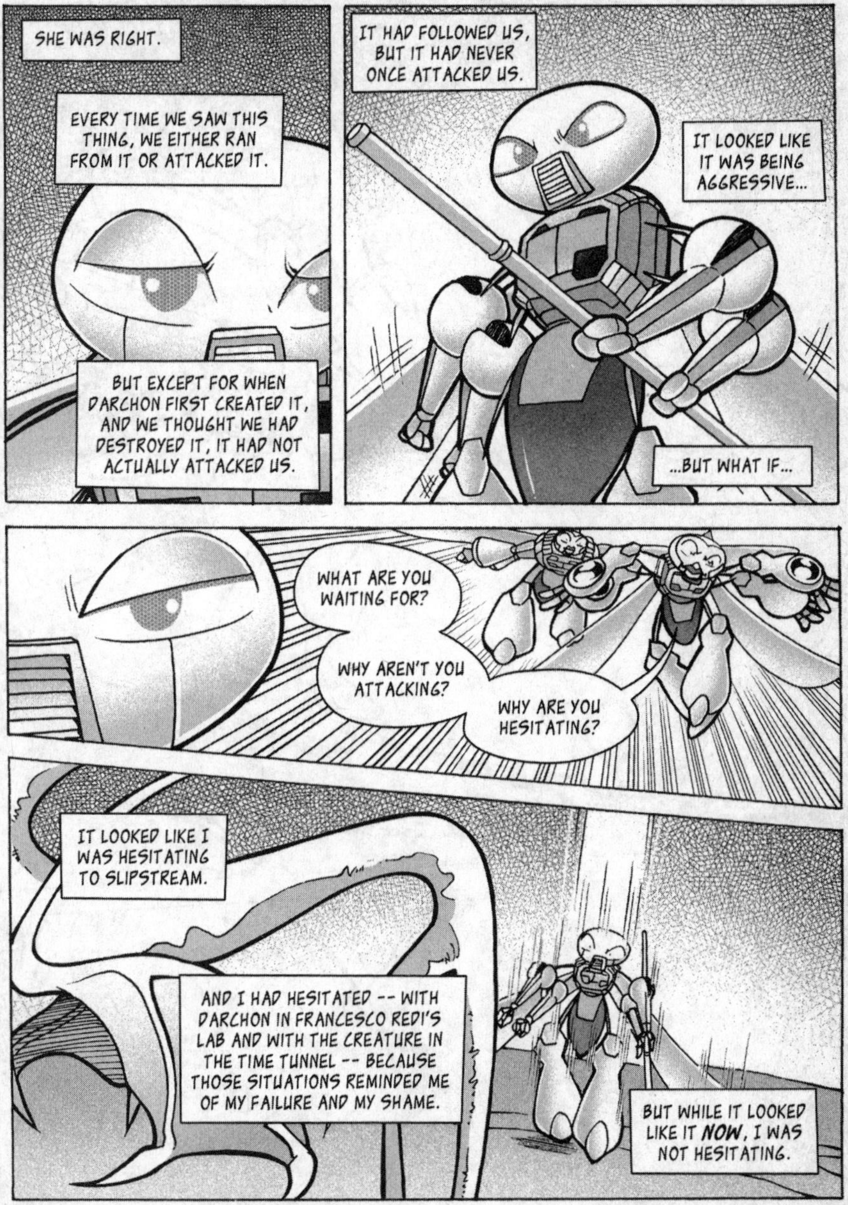
SHE WAS RIGHT.
EVERY TIME WE SAW THIS THING, WE EITHER RAN FROM IT OR ATTACKED IT.
BUT EXCEPT FOR WHEN DARCHON FIRST CREATED IT, AND WE THOUGHT WE HAD DESTROYED IT, IT HAD NOT ACTUALLY ATTACKED US.
IT HAD FOLLOWED US, BUT IT HAD NEVER ONCE ATTACKED US.
IT LOOKED LIKE IT WAS BEING AGGRESSIVE...
...BUT WHAT IF...
WHAT ARE YOU WAITING FOR?
WHY AREN'T YOU ATTACKING?
WHY ARE YOU HESITATING?
IT LOOKED LIKE I WAS HESITATING TO SLIPSTREAM.
AND I HAD HESITATED -- WITH DARCHON IN FRANCESCO REDI'S LAB AND WITH THE CREATURE IN THE TIME TUNNEL -- BECAUSE THOSE SITUATIONS REMINDED ME OF MY FAILURE AND MY SHAME.
BUT WHILE IT LOOKED LIKE IT *NOW*, I WAS NOT HESITATING.

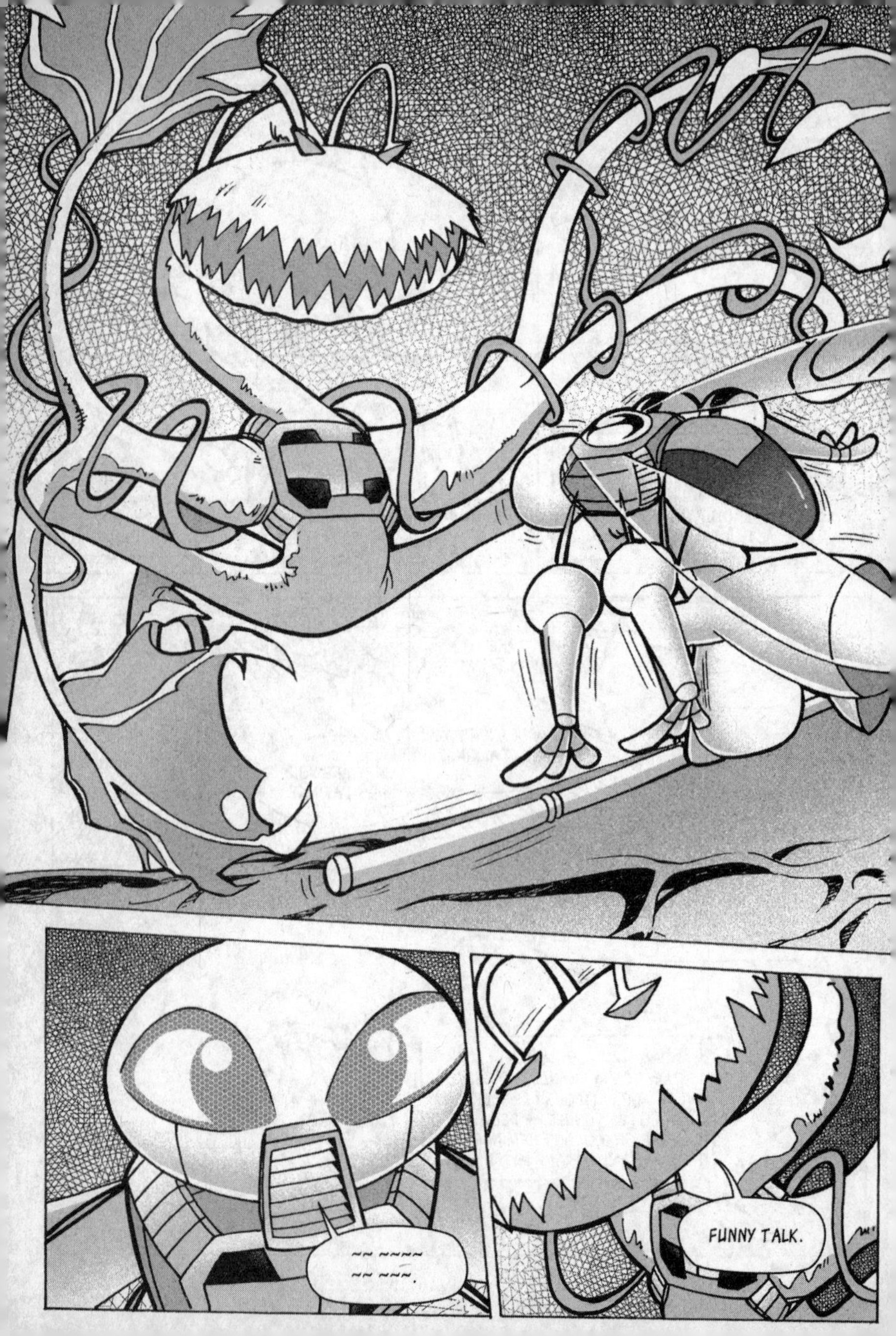
~~ ~~~~ ~~ ~~~.
FUNNY TALK.

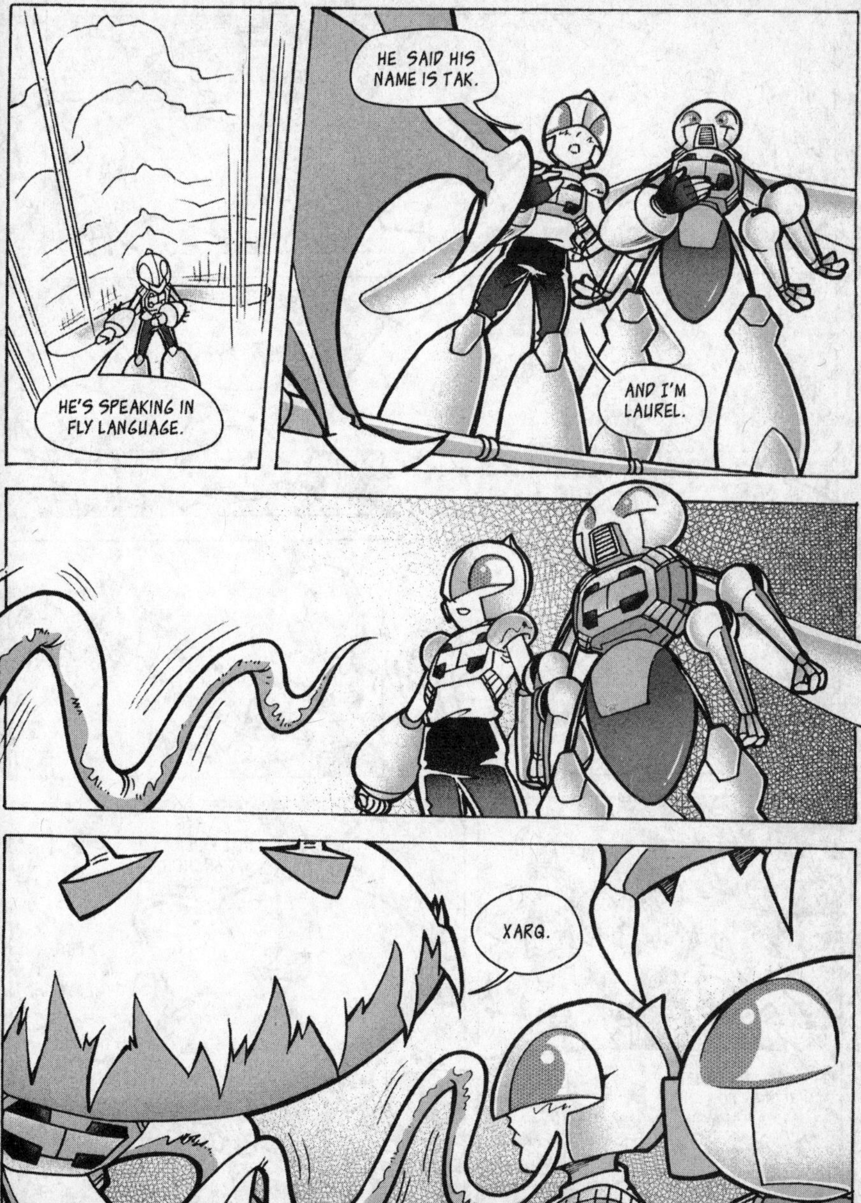
HE'S SPEAKING IN FLY LANGUAGE.
HE SAID HIS NAME IS TAK.
AND I'M LAUREL.
XARQ.

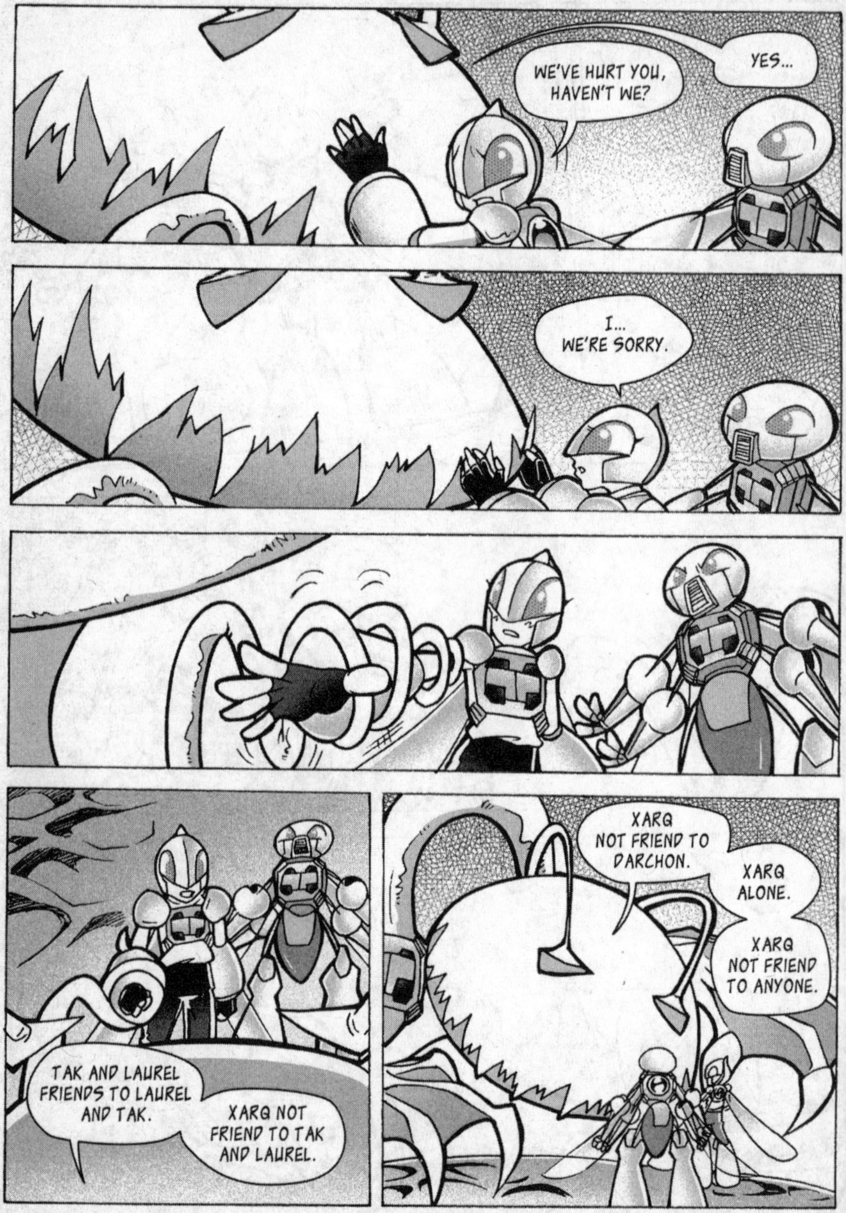
WE'VE HURT YOU, HAVEN'T WE?
YES...
I... WE'RE SORRY.
TAK AND LAUREL FRIENDS TO LAUREL AND TAK.
XARQ NOT FRIEND TO TAK AND LAUREL.
XARQ NOT FRIEND TO DARCHON.
XARQ ALONE.
XARQ NOT FRIEND TO ANYONE.

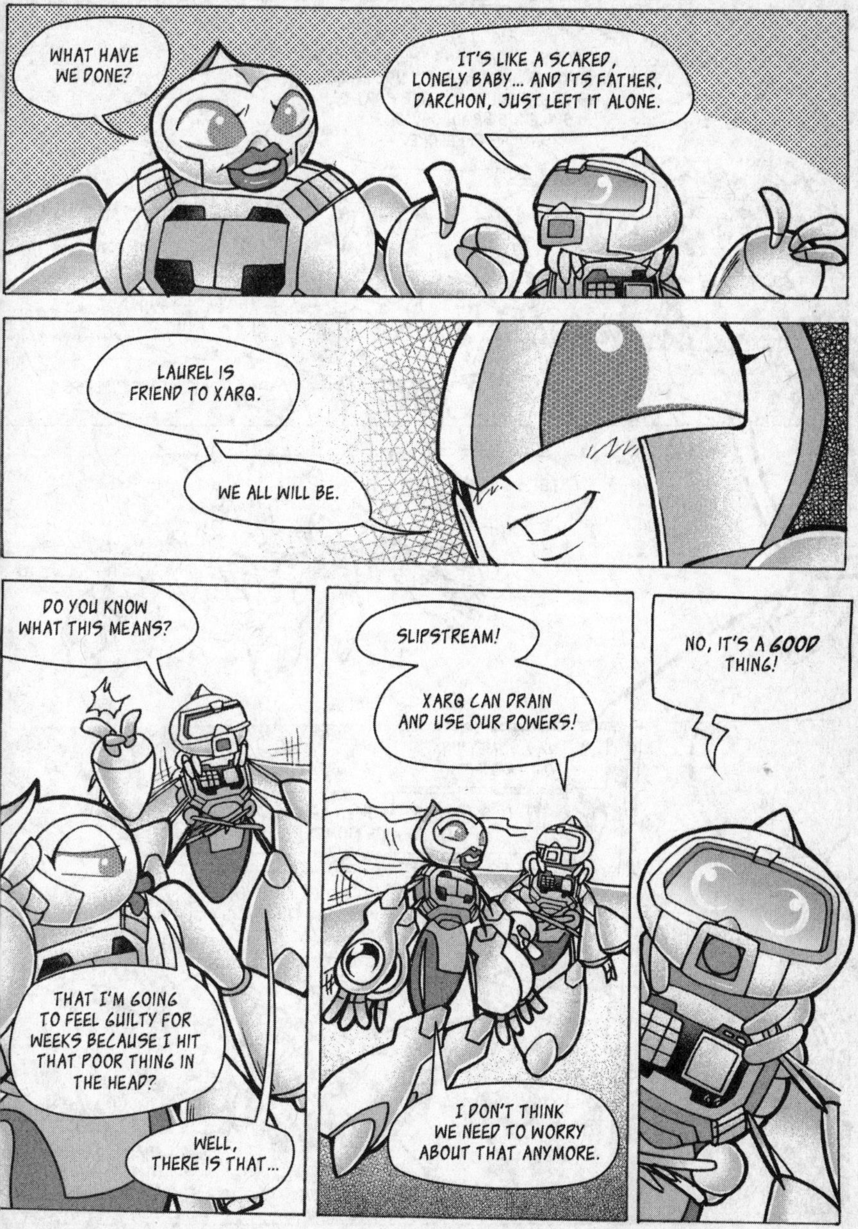

WHAT HAVE WE DONE?
IT'S LIKE A SCARED, LONELY BABY... AND ITS FATHER, DARCHON, JUST LEFT IT ALONE.
LAUREL IS FRIEND TO XARQ.
WE ALL WILL BE.
DO YOU KNOW WHAT THIS MEANS?
THAT I'M GOING TO FEEL GUILTY FOR WEEKS BECAUSE I HIT THAT POOR THING IN THE HEAD?
WELL, THERE IS THAT...
SLIPSTREAM!
XARQ CAN DRAIN AND USE OUR POWERS!
I DON'T THINK WE NEED TO WORRY ABOUT THAT ANYMORE.
NO, IT'S A GOOD THING!

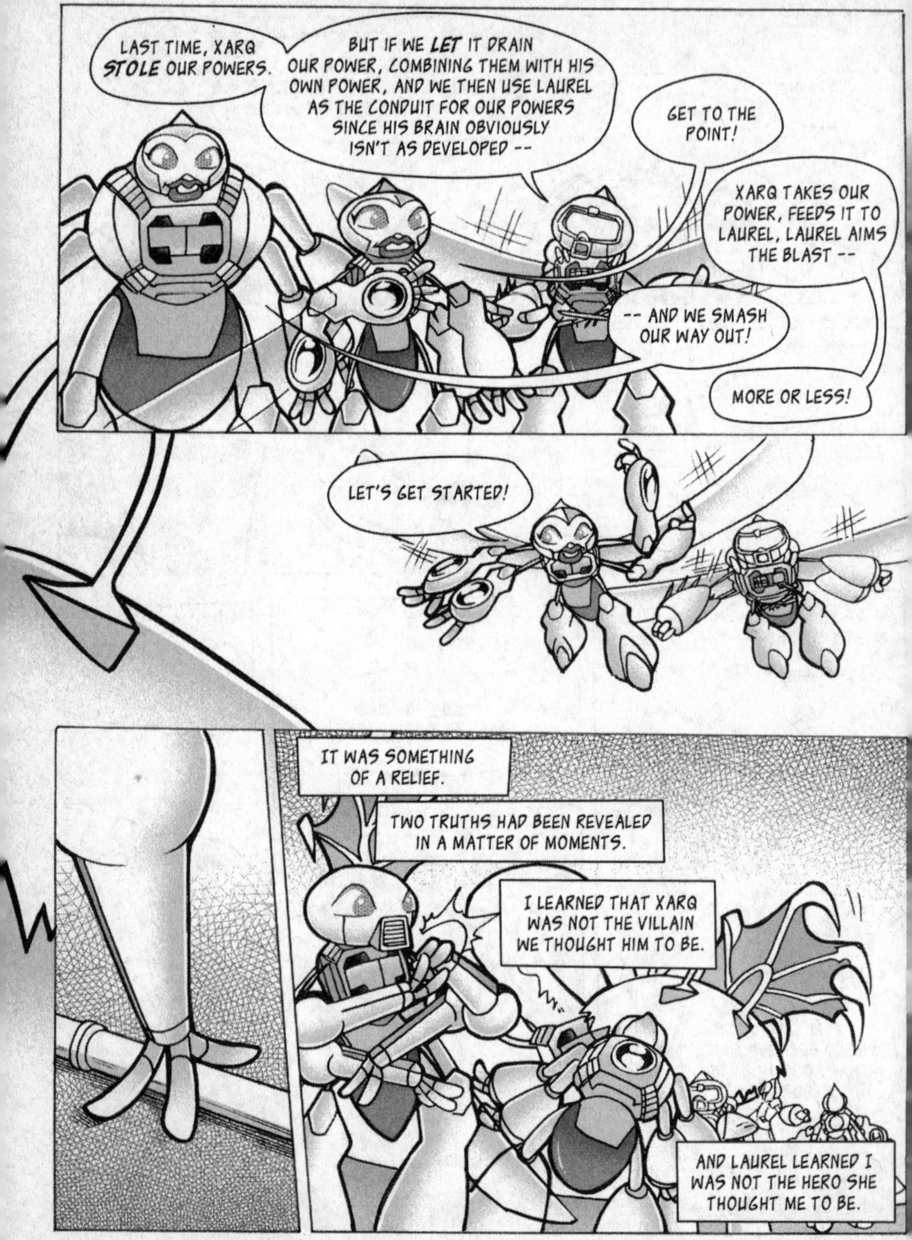
LAST TIME, XARQ STOLE OUR POWERS.
BUT IF WE LET IT DRAIN OUR POWER, COMBINING THEM WITH HIS OWN POWER, AND WE THEN USE LAUREL AS THE CONDUIT FOR OUR POWERS SINCE HIS BRAIN OBVIOUSLY ISN'T AS DEVELOPED --
GET TO THE POINT!
XARQ TAKES OUR POWER, FEEDS IT TO LAUREL, LAUREL AIMS THE BLAST --
-- AND WE SMASH OUR WAY OUT!
MORE OR LESS!
LET'S GET STARTED!
IT WAS SOMETHING OF A RELIEF.
TWO TRUTHS HAD BEEN REVEALED IN A MATTER OF MOMENTS.
I LEARNED THAT XARQ WAS NOT THE VILLAIN WE THOUGHT HIM TO BE.
AND LAUREL LEARNED I WAS NOT THE HERO SHE THOUGHT ME TO BE.

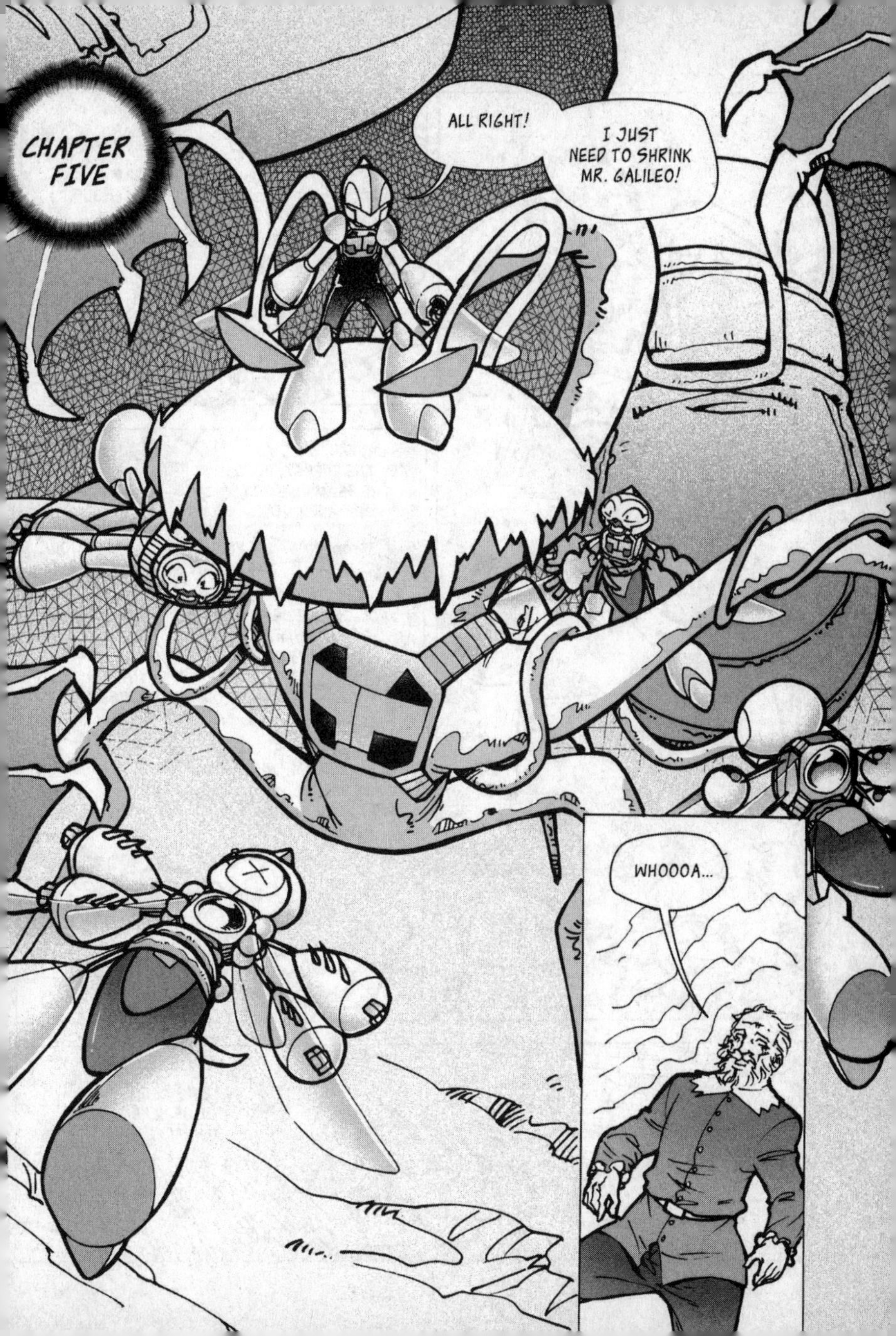
CHAPTER FIVE
ALL RIGHT!
I JUST NEED TO SHRINK MR. GALILEO!
WHOOOA...

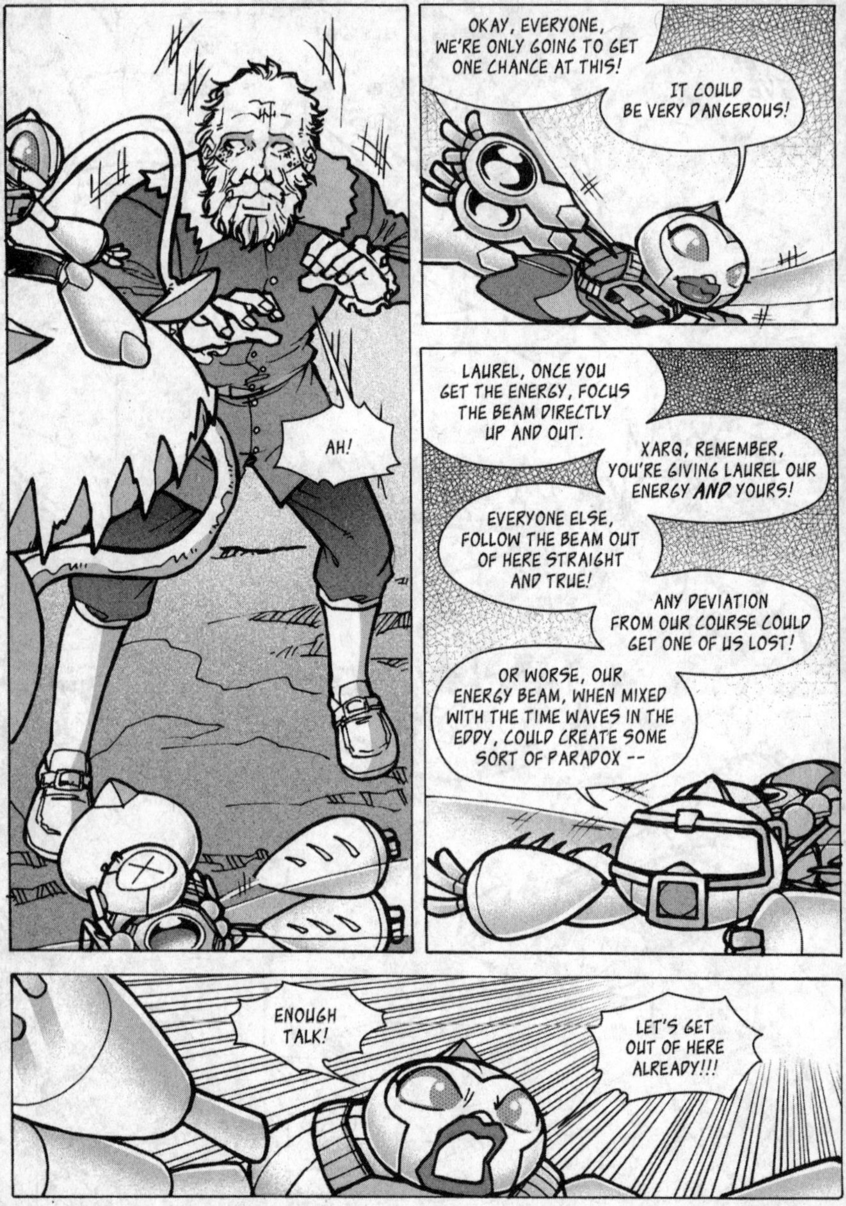
AH!
OKAY, EVERYONE, WE'RE ONLY GOING TO GET ONE CHANCE AT THIS!
IT COULD BE VERY DANGEROUS!
LAUREL, ONCE YOU GET THE ENERGY, FOCUS THE BEAM DIRECTLY UP AND OUT.
XARQ, REMEMBER, YOU'RE GIVING LAUREL OUR ENERGY *AND* YOURS!
EVERYONE ELSE, FOLLOW THE BEAM OUT OF HERE STRAIGHT AND TRUE!
ANY DEVIATION FROM OUR COURSE COULD GET ONE OF US LOST!
OR WORSE, OUR ENERGY BEAM, WHEN MIXED WITH THE TIME WAVES IN THE EDDY, COULD CREATE SOME SORT OF PARADOX --
ENOUGH TALK!
LET'S GET OUT OF HERE ALREADY!!!

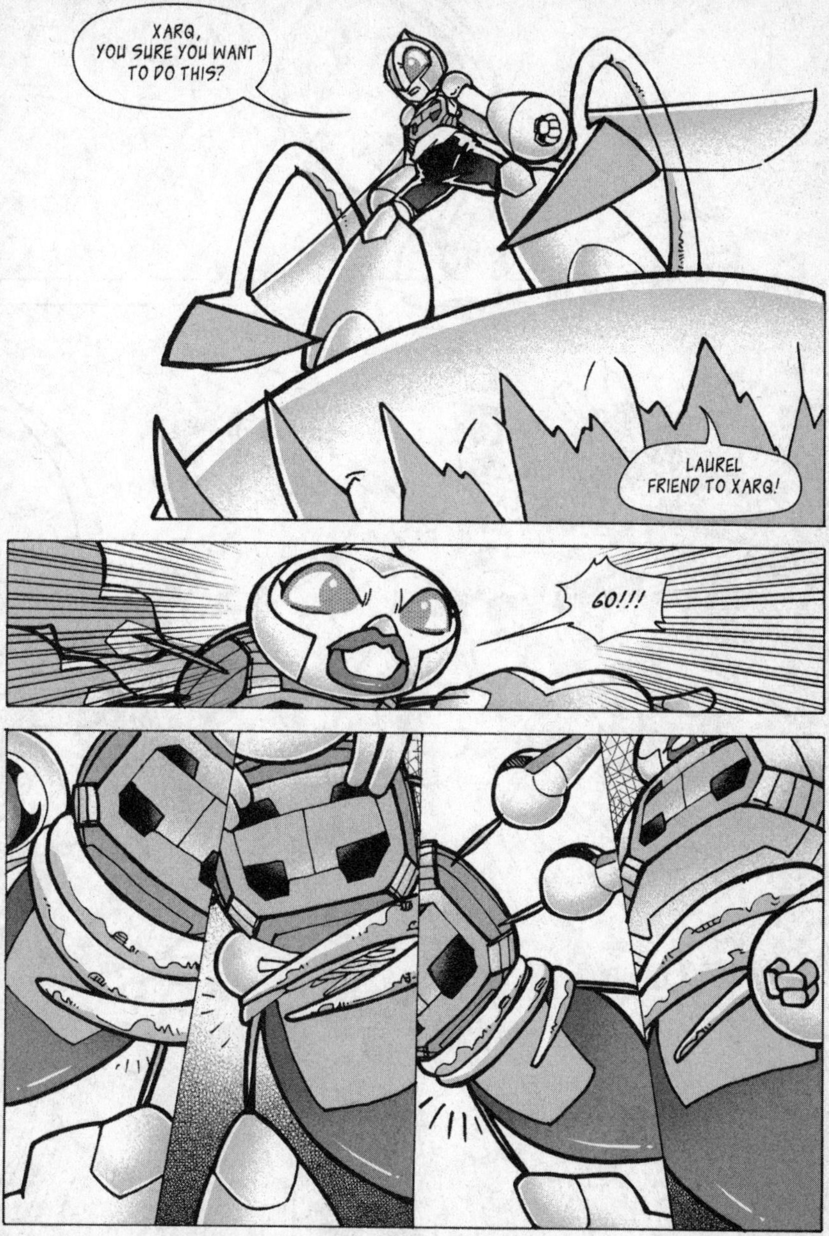
XARQ, YOU SURE YOU WANT TO DO THIS?
LAUREL FRIEND TO XARQ!
GO!!!

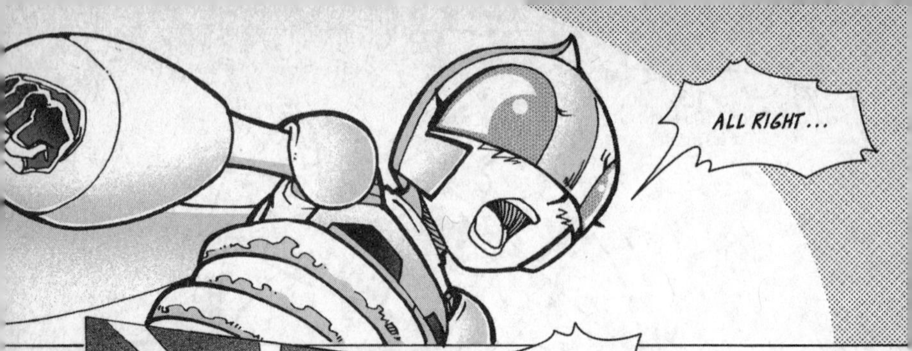
ALL RIGHT...
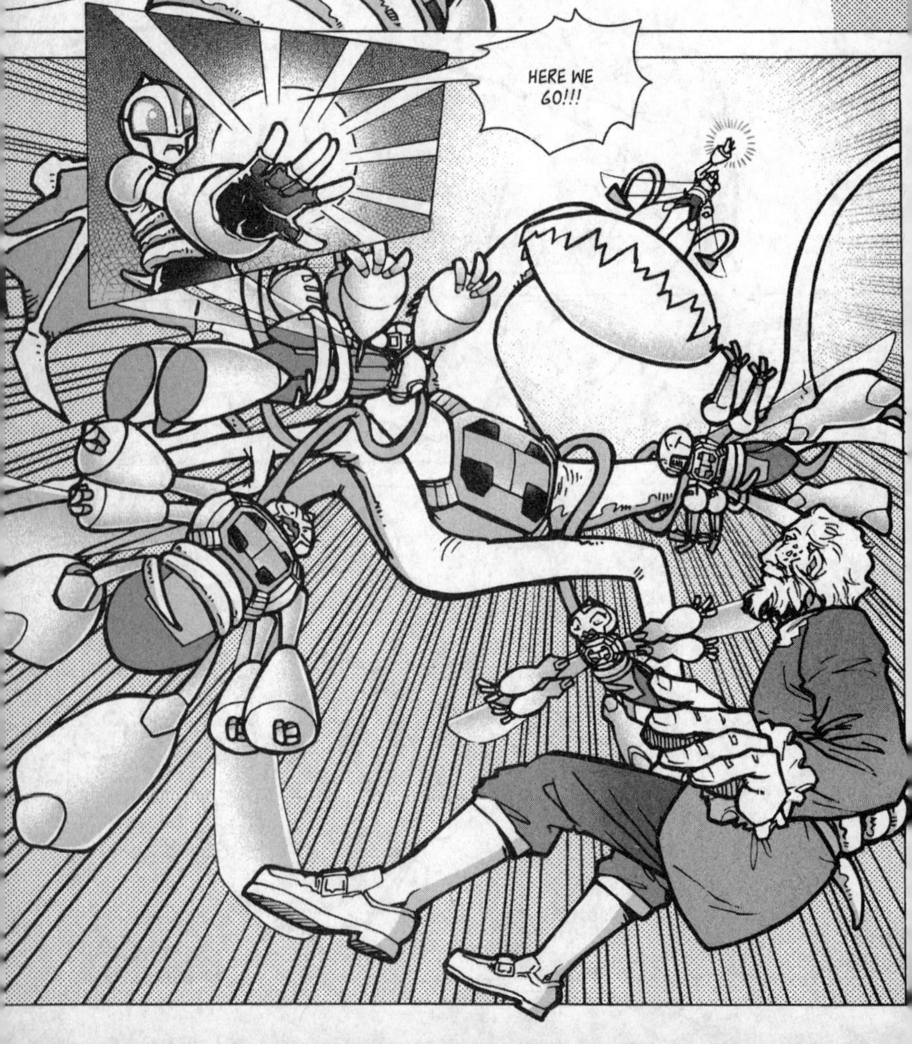
HERE WE GO!!!

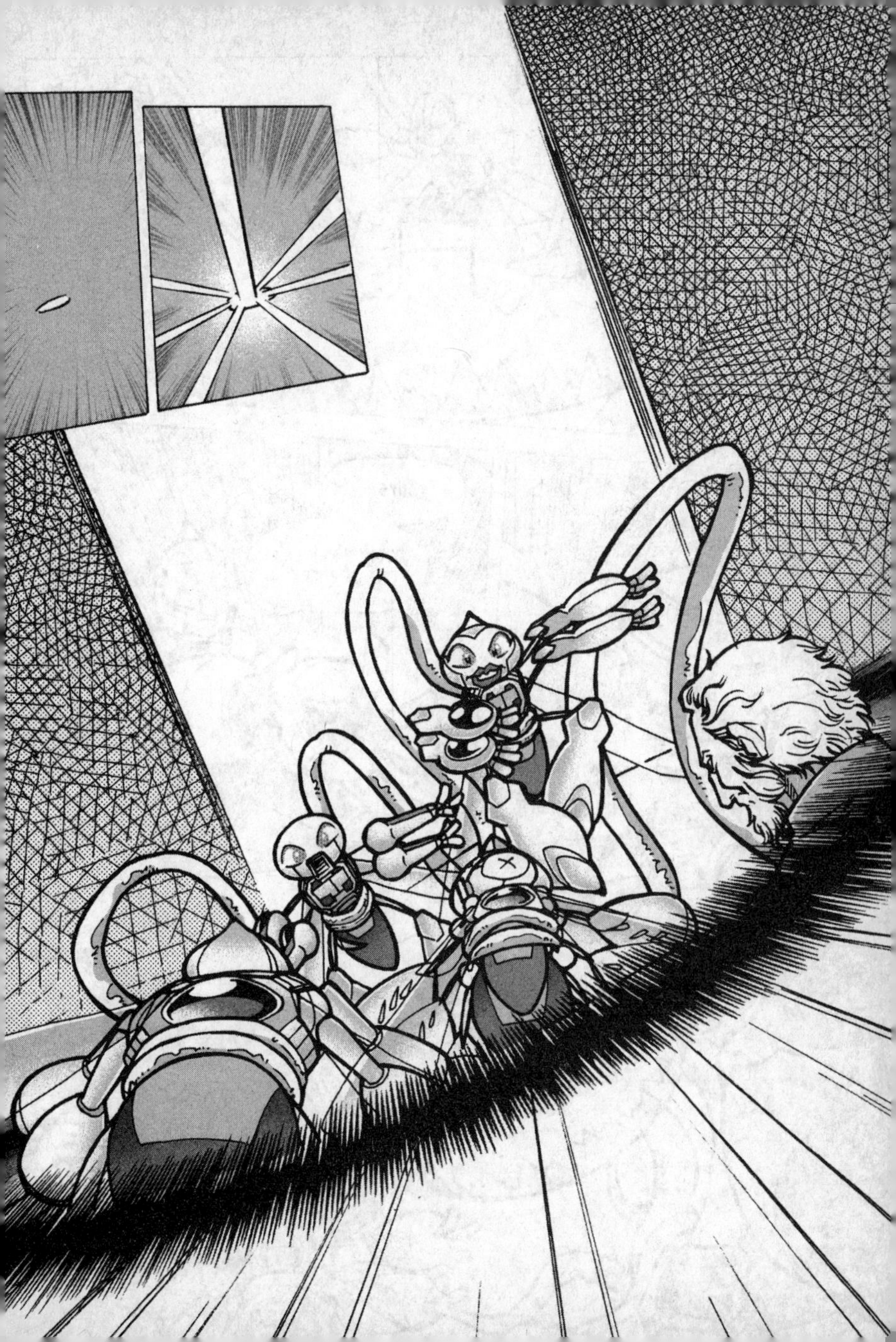

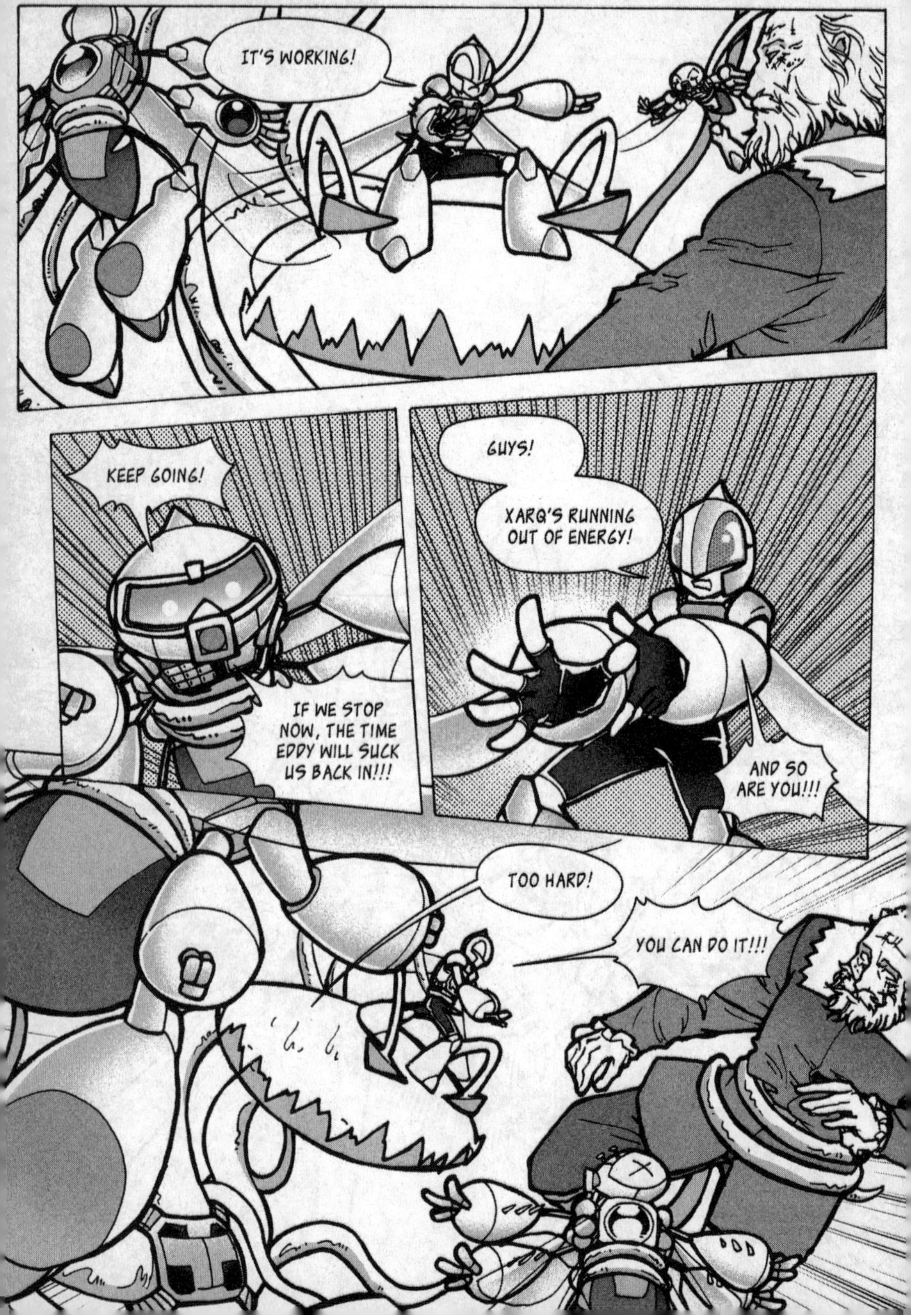
IT'S WORKING!
KEEP GOING!
IF WE STOP NOW, THE TIME EDDY WILL SUCK US BACK IN!!!
GUYS!
XARQ'S RUNNING OUT OF ENERGY!
AND SO ARE YOU!!!
TOO HARD!
YOU CAN DO IT!!!

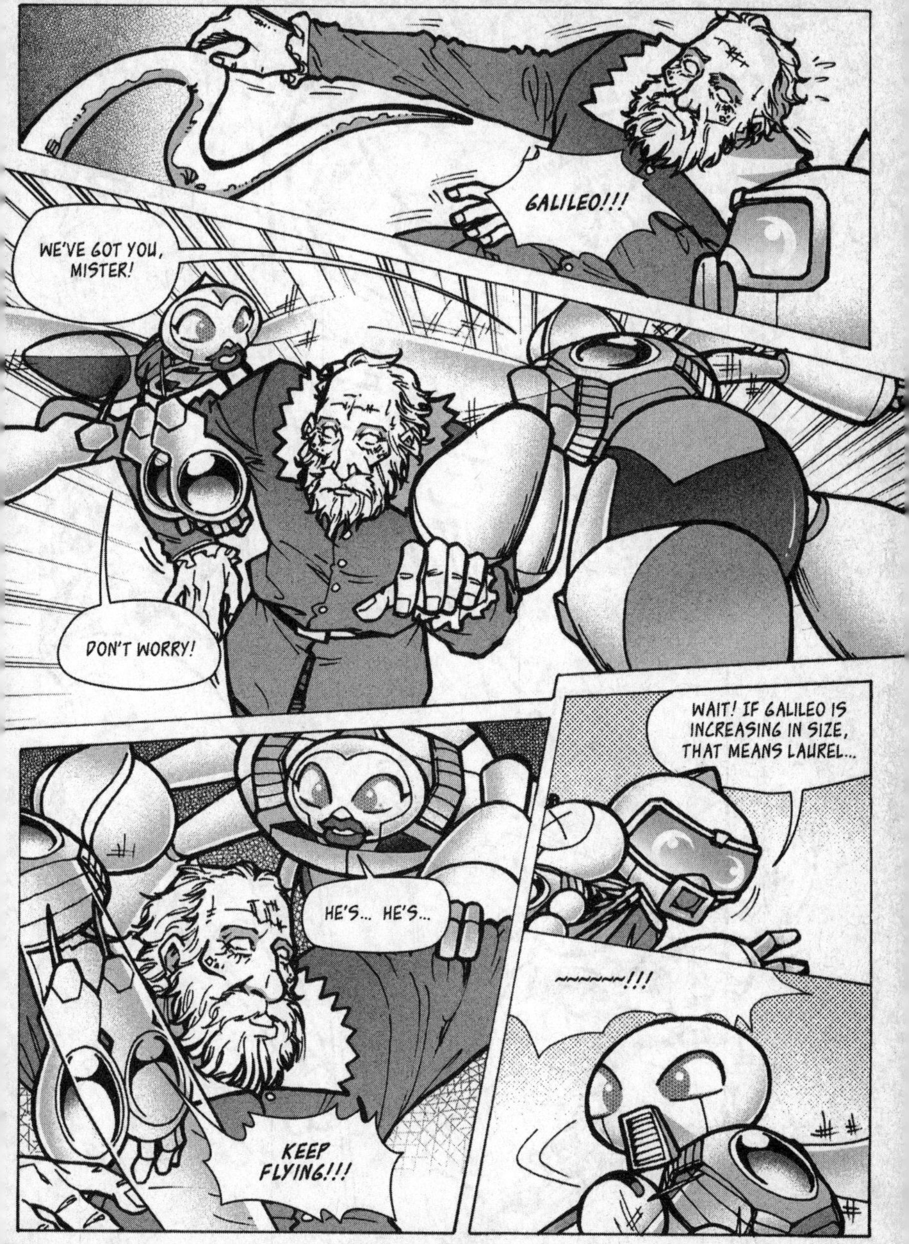
GALILEO!!!
WE'VE GOT YOU, MISTER!
DON'T WORRY!
HE'S... HE'S...
KEEP FLYING!!!
WAIT! IF GALILEO IS INCREASING IN SIZE, THAT MEANS LAUREL...
~~~~~~!!!
~~~~~~

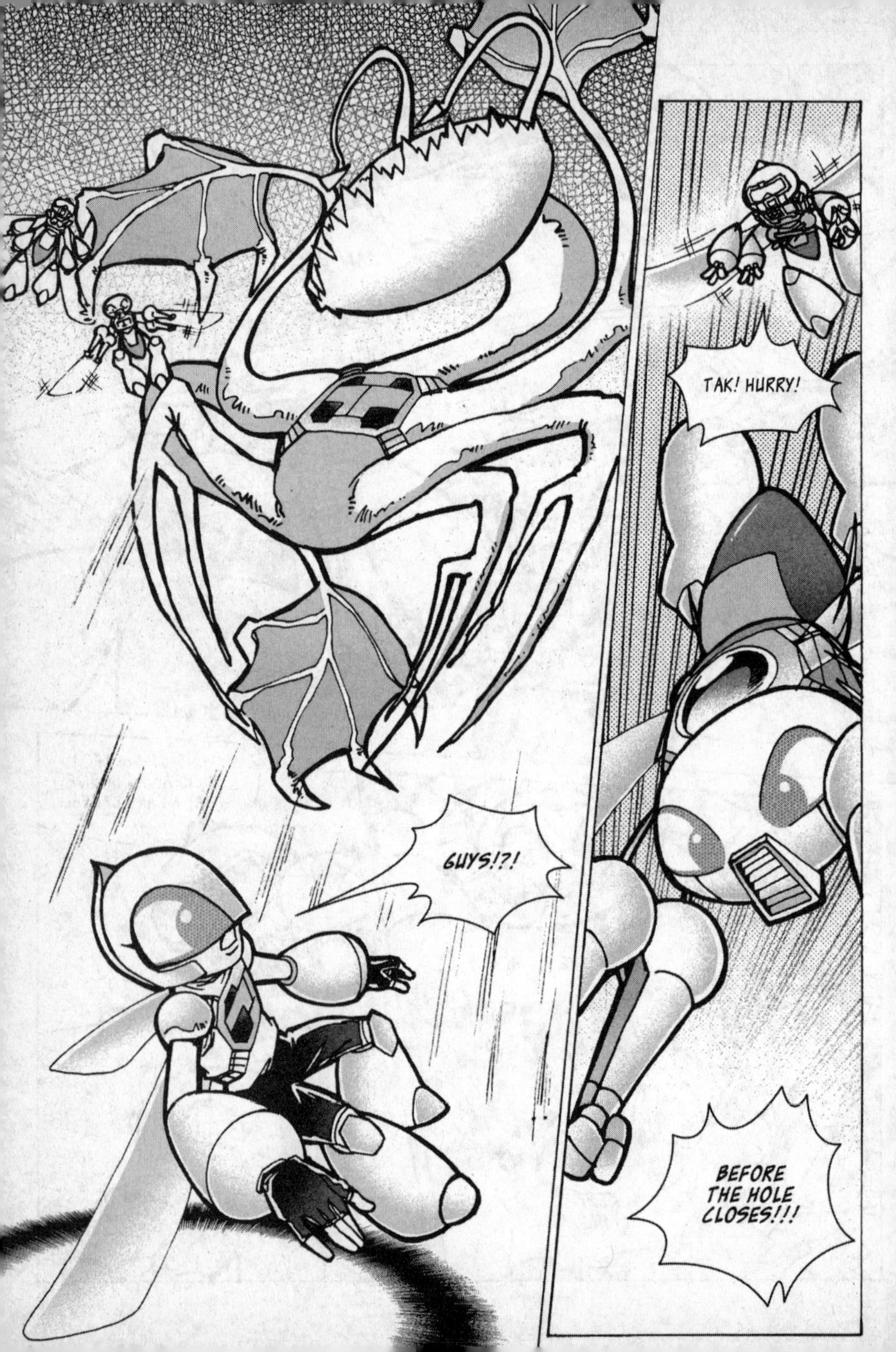
GUYS!?!
TAK! HURRY!
BEFORE THE HOLE CLOSES!!!

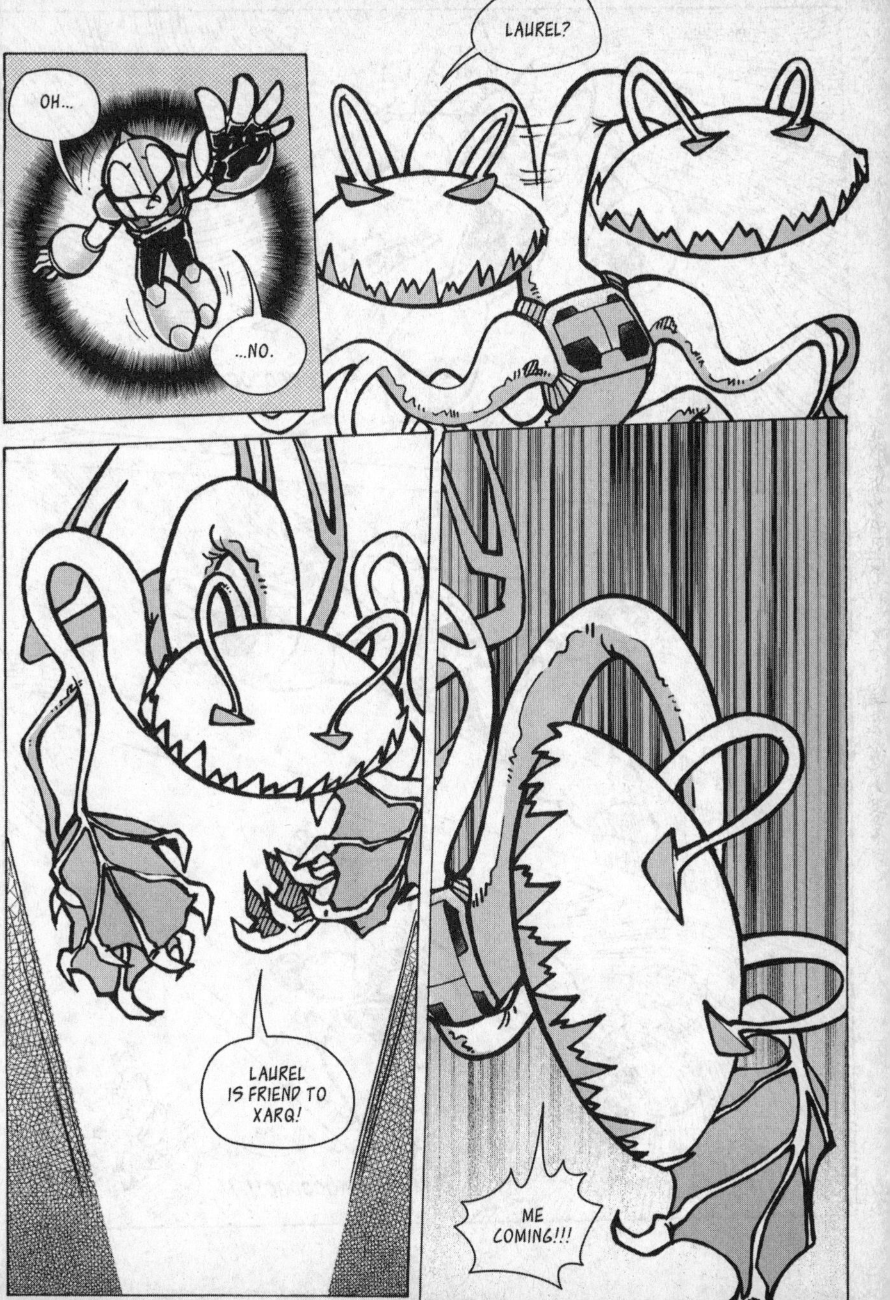
OH...
...NO.
LAUREL?
LAUREL IS FRIEND TO XARQ!
ME COMING!!!

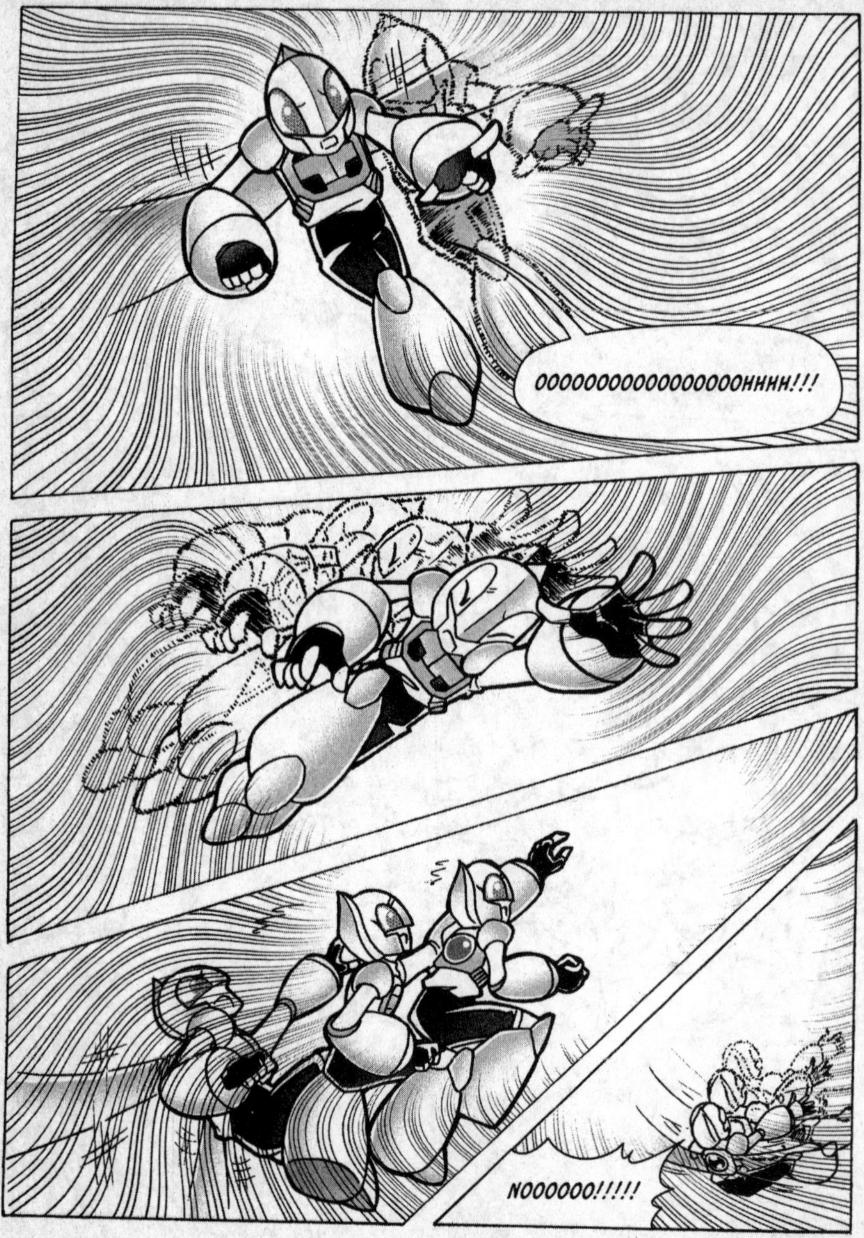
OOOOOOOOOOOOOOOOOHHHHH!!!
NOOOOOO!!!!!

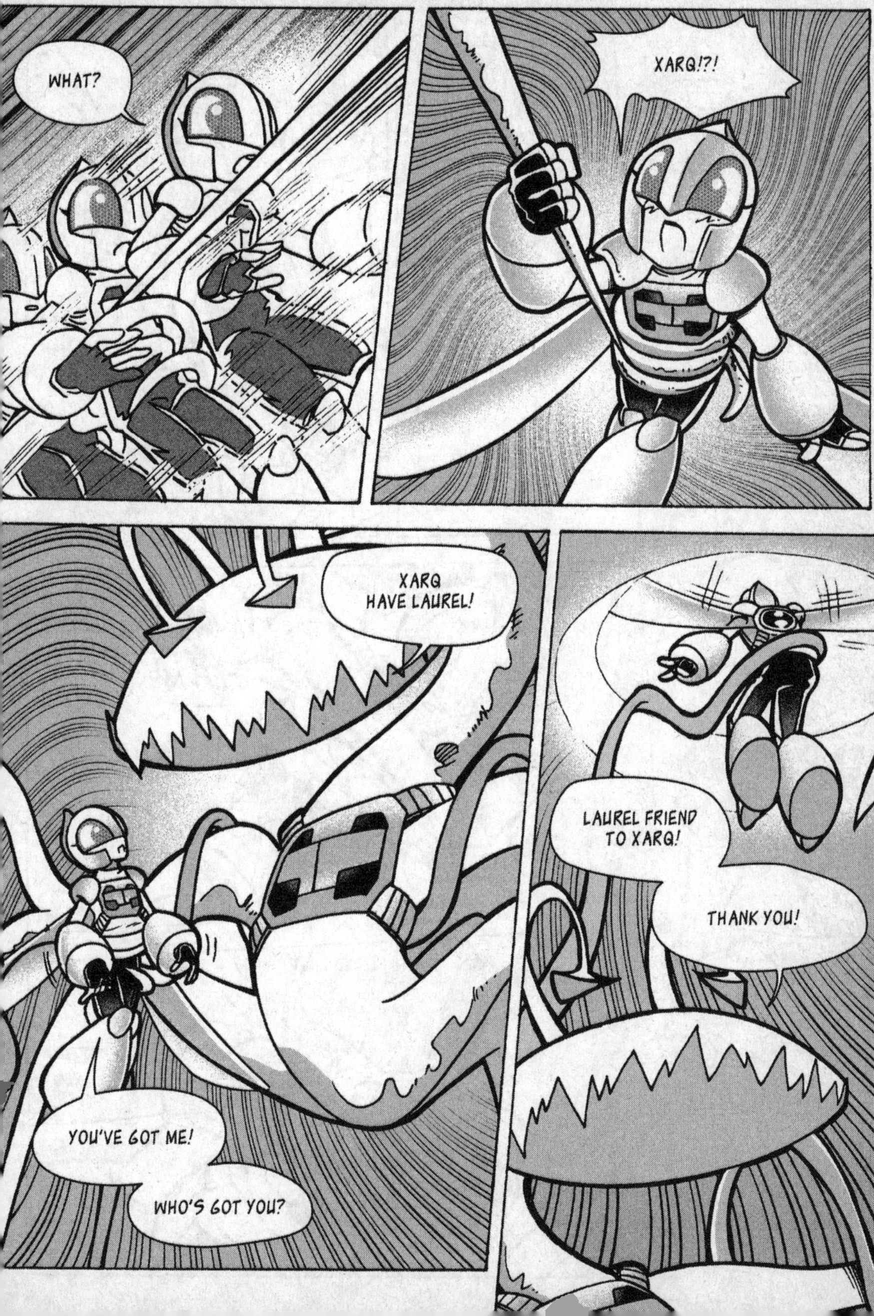
WHAT?
XARQ!?!
XARQ HAVE LAUREL!
YOU'VE GOT ME!
WHO'S GOT YOU?
LAUREL FRIEND TO XARQ!
THANK YOU!

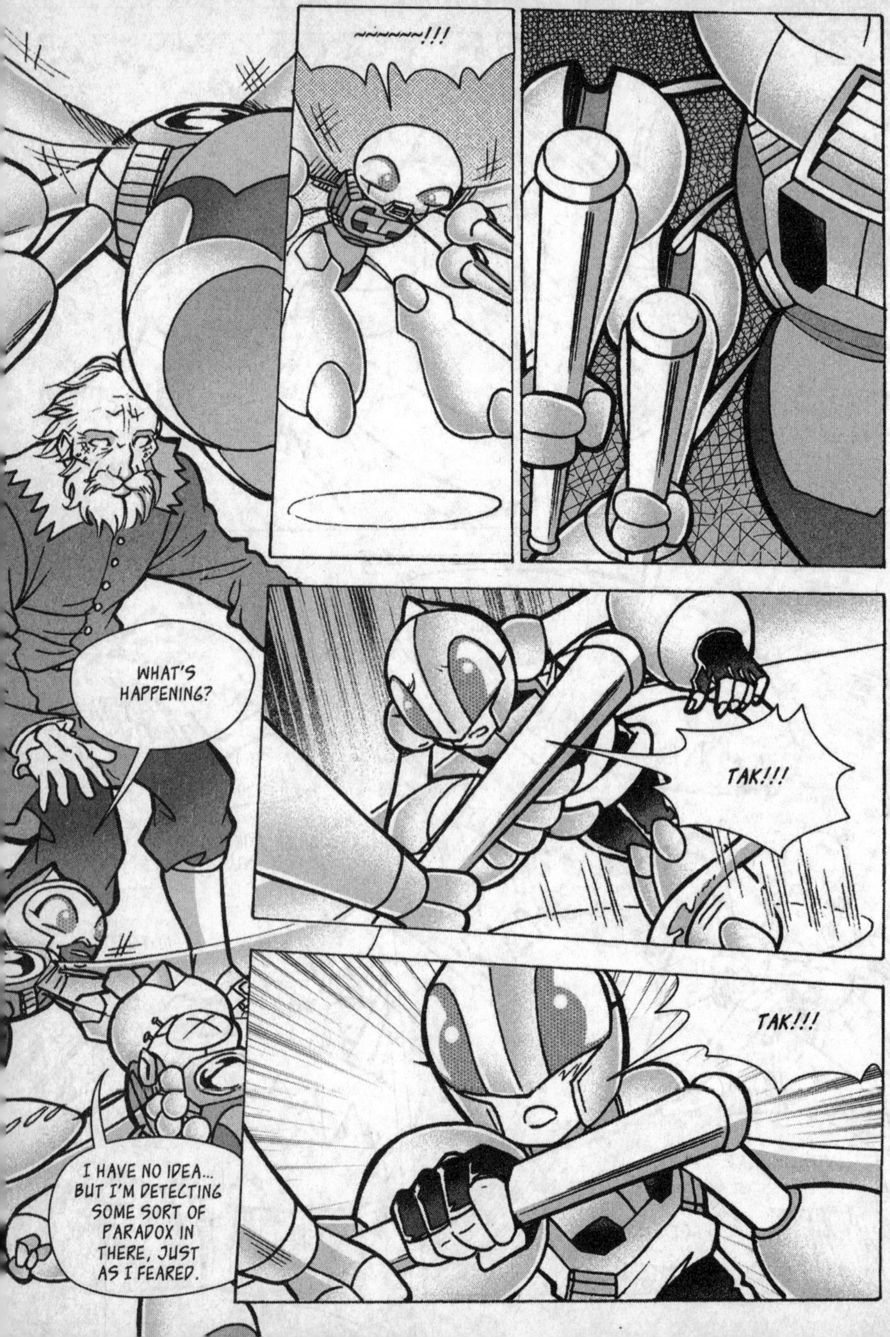
WHAT'S HAPPENING?
I HAVE NO IDEA... BUT I'M DETECTING SOME SORT OF PARADOX IN THERE, JUST AS I FEARED.
~~~~~~~!!!
TAK!!!
TAK!!!
~~~~~~~

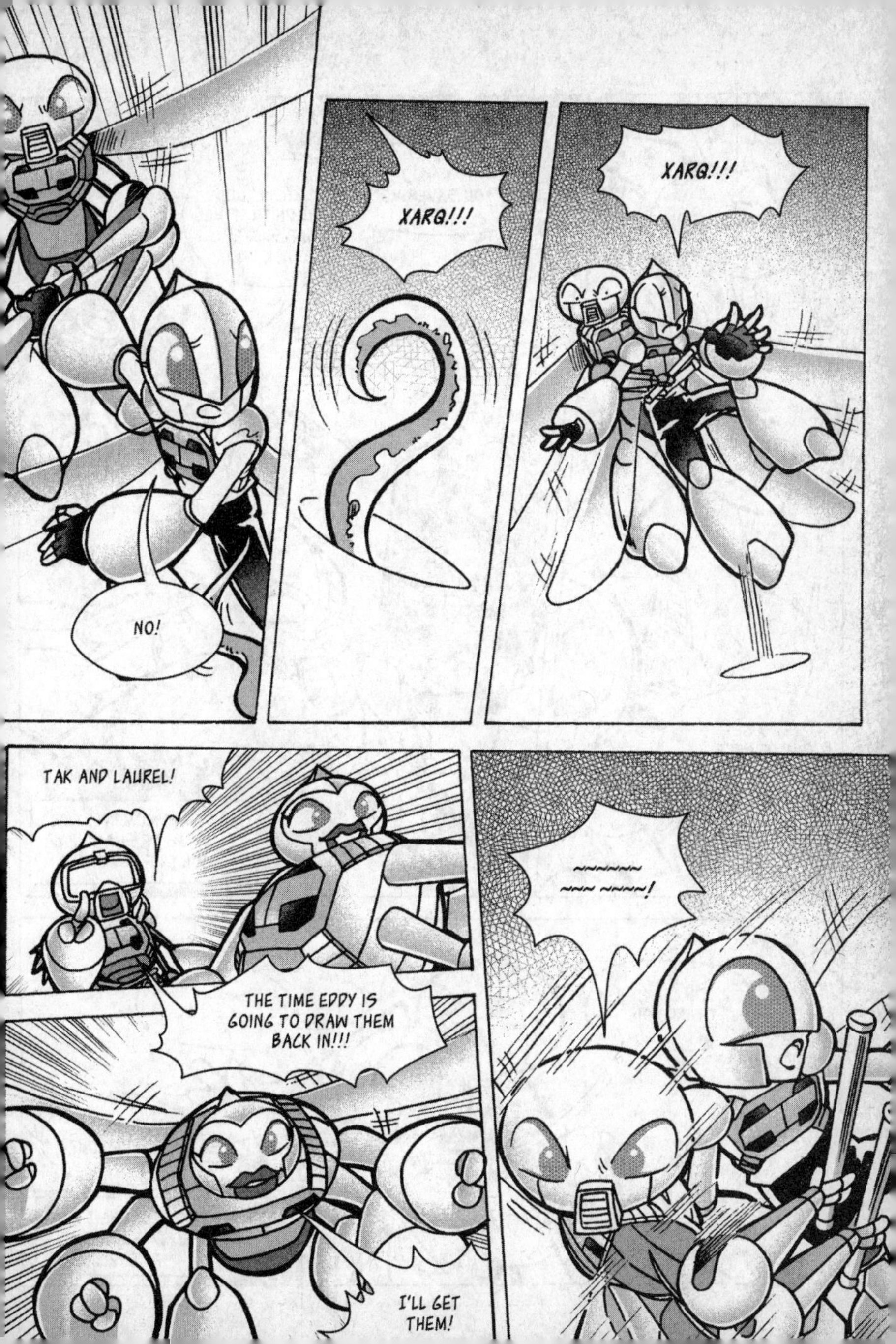
NO!
XARQ!!!
XARQ!!!
TAK AND LAUREL!
THE TIME EDDY IS GOING TO DRAW THEM BACK IN!!!
I'LL GET THEM!
~~~~~~ ~~~ ~~~~!
~~~~~~

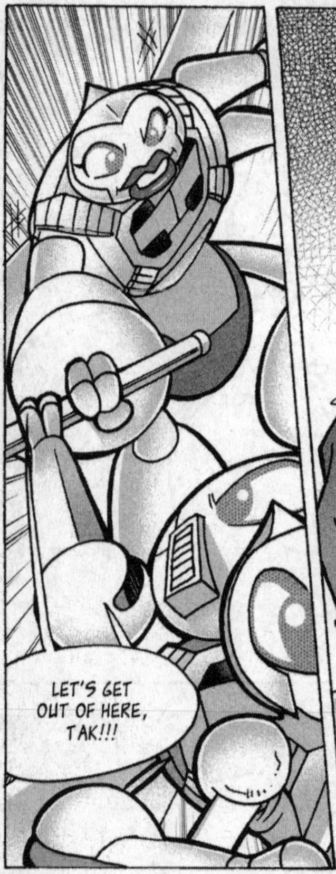
LET'S GET OUT OF HERE, TAK!!!

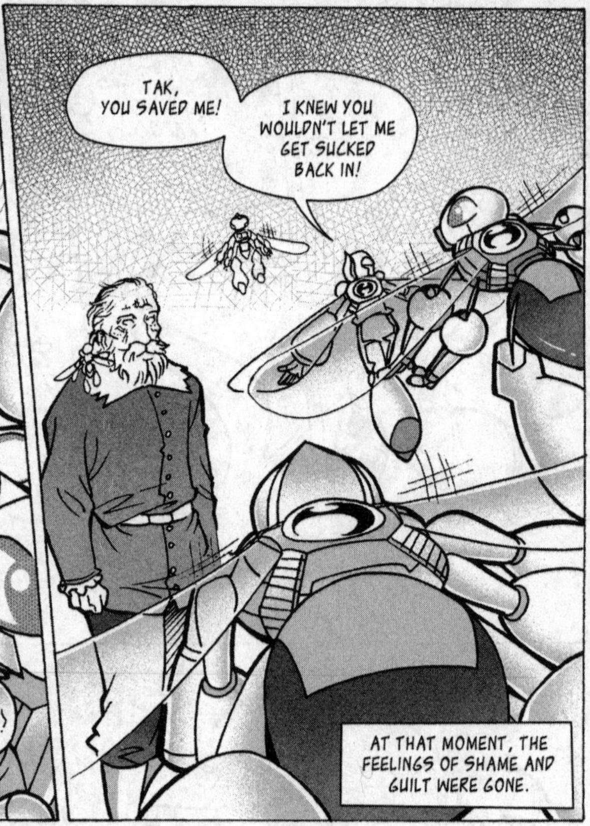
TAK, YOU SAVED ME!
I KNEW YOU WOULDN'T LET ME GET SUCKED BACK IN!
AT THAT MOMENT, THE FEELINGS OF SHAME AND GUILT WERE GONE.

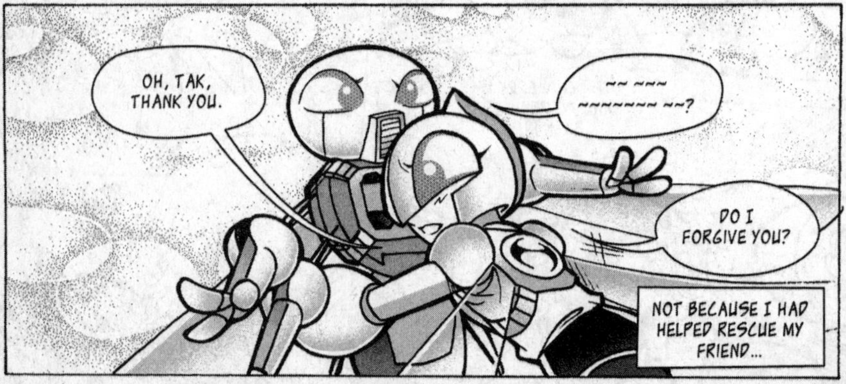
OH, TAK, THANK YOU.
~~ ~~~ ~~~~~~~ ~~?
DO I FORGIVE YOU?
NOT BECAUSE I HAD HELPED RESCUE MY FRIEND...

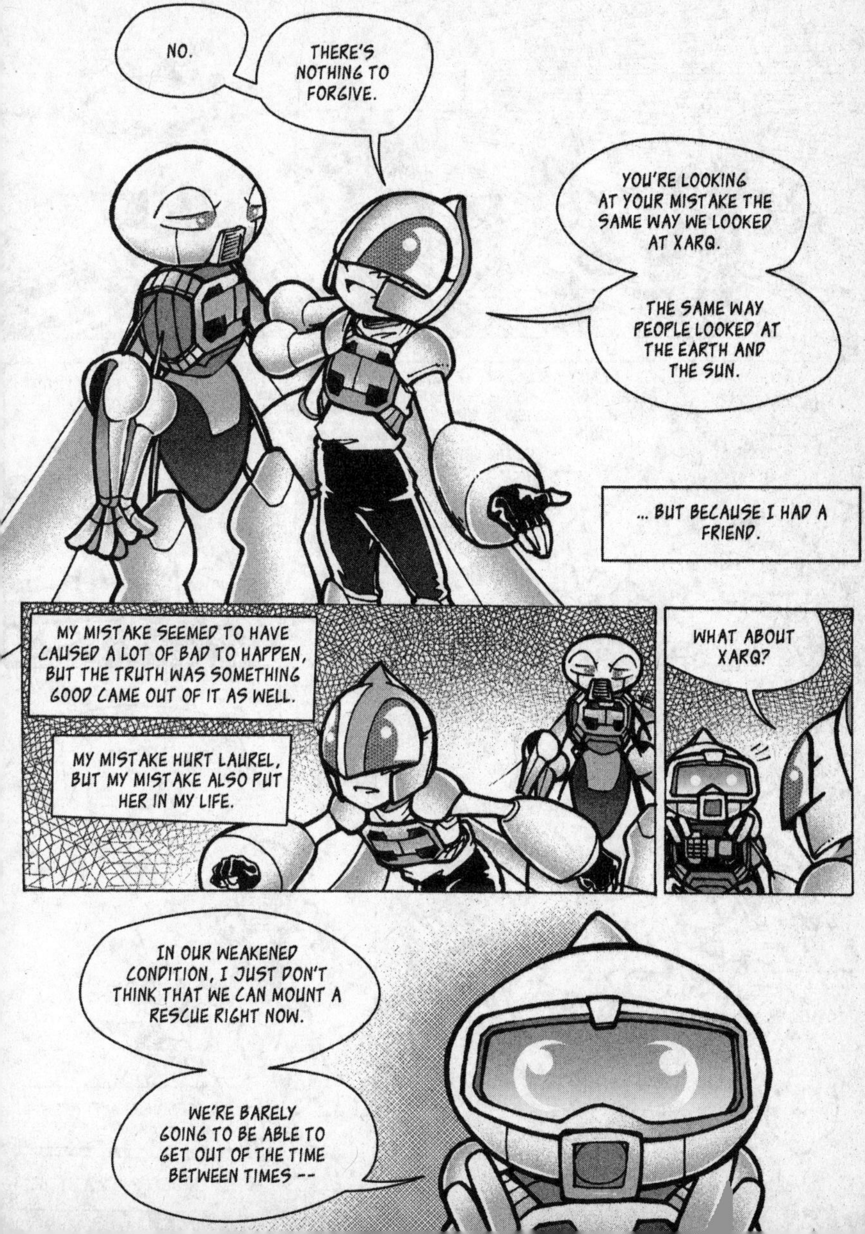
NO.
THERE'S NOTHING TO FORGIVE.
YOU'RE LOOKING AT YOUR MISTAKE THE SAME WAY WE LOOKED AT XARQ.
THE SAME WAY PEOPLE LOOKED AT THE EARTH AND THE SUN.
... BUT BECAUSE I HAD A FRIEND.
MY MISTAKE SEEMED TO HAVE CAUSED A LOT OF BAD TO HAPPEN, BUT THE TRUTH WAS SOMETHING GOOD CAME OUT OF IT AS WELL.
MY MISTAKE HURT LAUREL, BUT MY MISTAKE ALSO PUT HER IN MY LIFE.
WHAT ABOUT XARQ?
IN OUR WEAKENED CONDITION, I JUST DON'T THINK THAT WE CAN MOUNT A RESCUE RIGHT NOW.
WE'RE BARELY GOING TO BE ABLE TO GET OUT OF THE TIME BETWEEN TIMES --

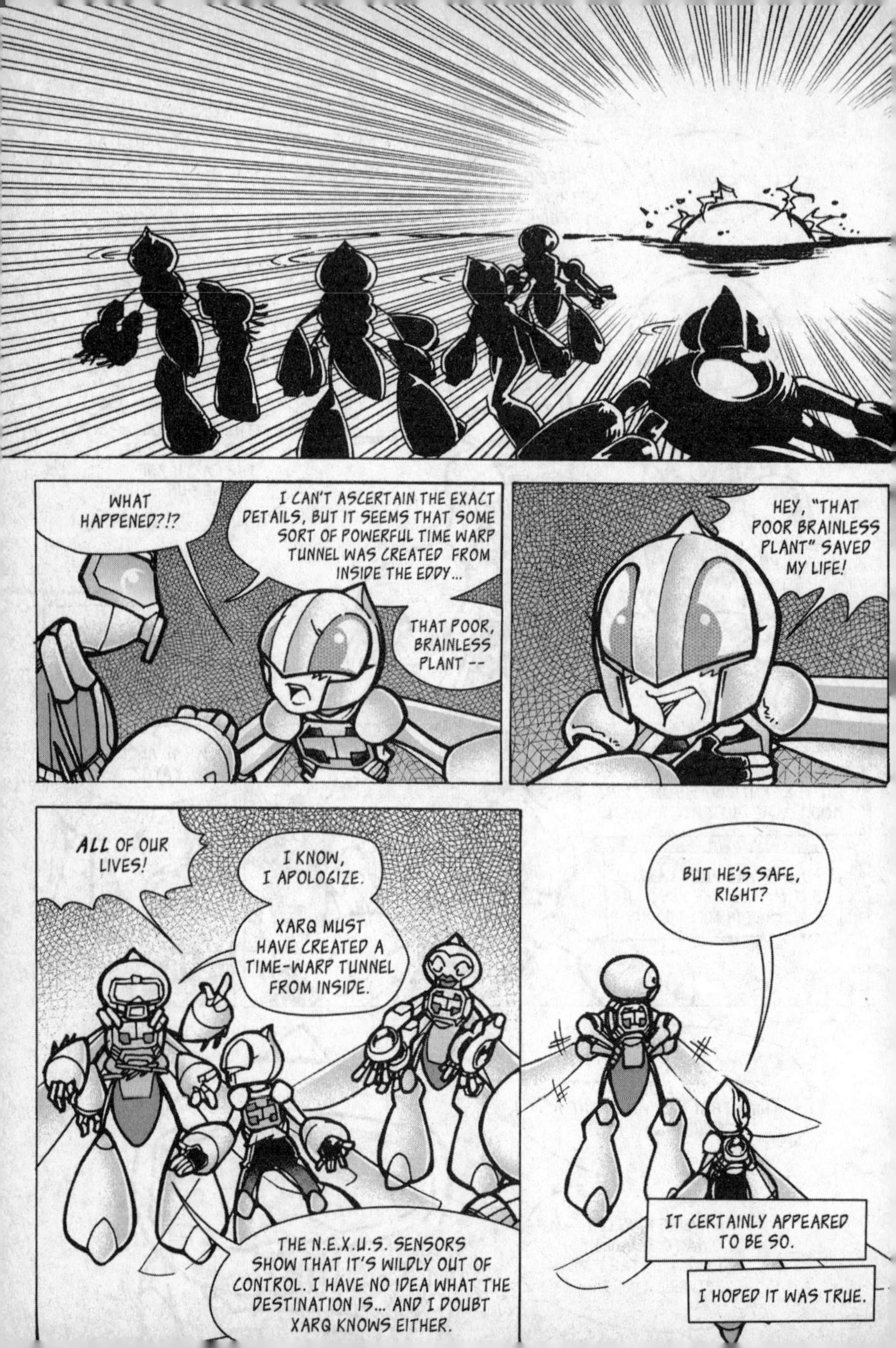
WHAT HAPPENED?!?
I CAN'T ASCERTAIN THE EXACT DETAILS, BUT IT SEEMS THAT SOME SORT OF POWERFUL TIME WARP TUNNEL WAS CREATED FROM INSIDE THE EDDY...
THAT POOR, BRAINLESS PLANT --
HEY, "THAT POOR BRAINLESS PLANT" SAVED MY LIFE!
ALL OF OUR LIVES!
I KNOW, I APOLOGIZE.
XARQ MUST HAVE CREATED A TIME-WARP TUNNEL FROM INSIDE.
THE N.E.X.U.S. SENSORS SHOW THAT IT'S WILDLY OUT OF CONTROL. I HAVE NO IDEA WHAT THE DESTINATION IS... AND I DOUBT XARQ KNOWS EITHER.
BUT HE'S SAFE, RIGHT?
IT CERTAINLY APPEARED TO BE SO.
I HOPED IT WAS TRUE.

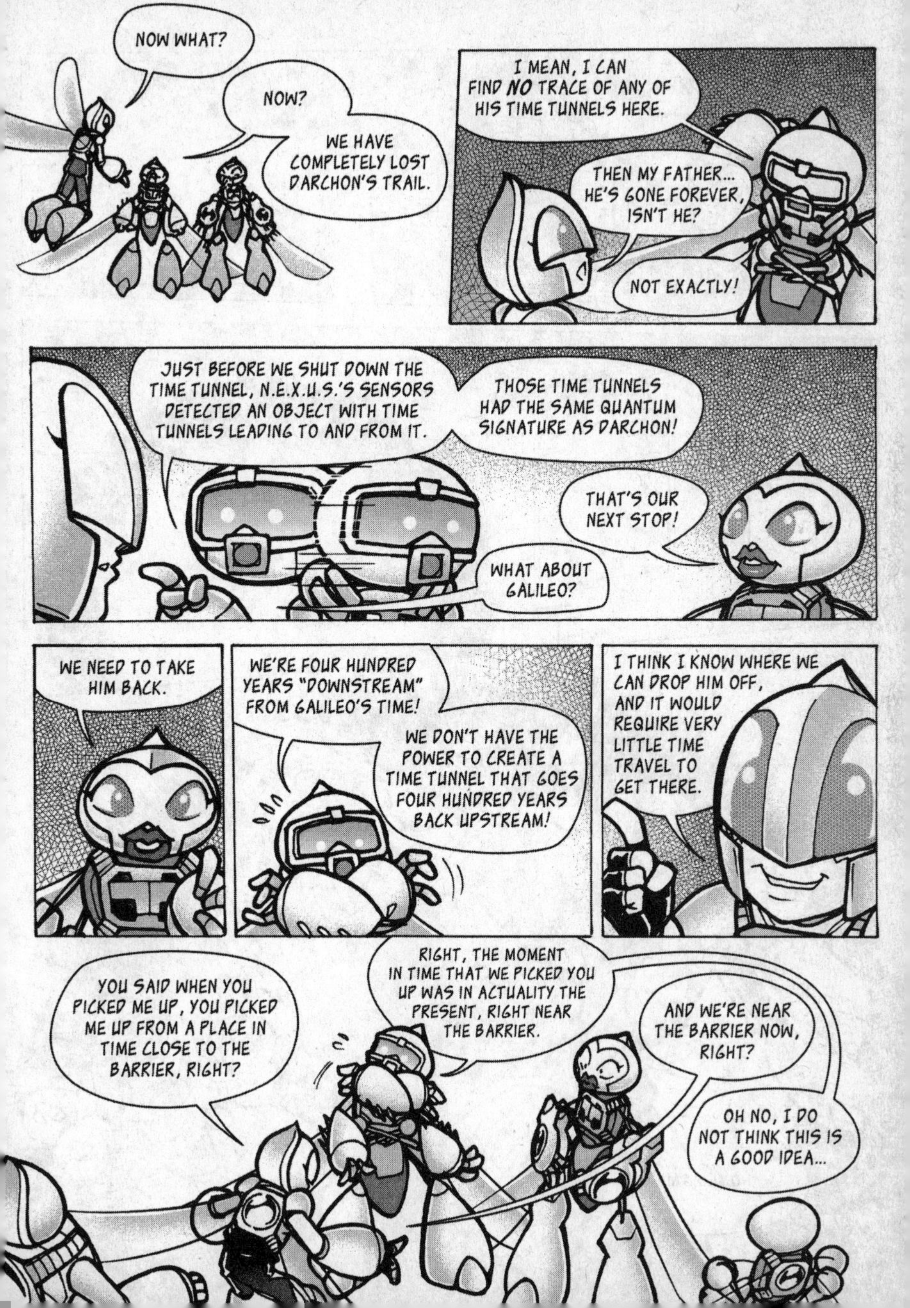
NOW WHAT?
NOW?
WE HAVE COMPLETELY LOST DARCHON'S TRAIL.
I MEAN, I CAN FIND NO TRACE OF ANY OF HIS TIME TUNNELS HERE.
THEN MY FATHER... HE'S GONE FOREVER, ISN'T HE?
NOT EXACTLY!
JUST BEFORE WE SHUT DOWN THE TIME TUNNEL, N.E.X.U.S.'S SENSORS DETECTED AN OBJECT WITH TIME TUNNELS LEADING TO AND FROM IT.
THOSE TIME TUNNELS HAD THE SAME QUANTUM SIGNATURE AS DARCHON!
THAT'S OUR NEXT STOP!
WHAT ABOUT GALILEO?
WE NEED TO TAKE HIM BACK.
WE'RE FOUR HUNDRED YEARS "DOWNSTREAM" FROM GALILEO'S TIME!
WE DON'T HAVE THE POWER TO CREATE A TIME TUNNEL THAT GOES FOUR HUNDRED YEARS BACK UPSTREAM!
I THINK I KNOW WHERE WE CAN DROP HIM OFF, AND IT WOULD REQUIRE VERY LITTLE TIME TRAVEL TO GET THERE.
YOU SAID WHEN YOU PICKED ME UP, YOU PICKED ME UP FROM A PLACE IN TIME CLOSE TO THE BARRIER, RIGHT?
RIGHT, THE MOMENT IN TIME THAT WE PICKED YOU UP WAS IN ACTUALITY THE PRESENT, RIGHT NEAR THE BARRIER.
AND WE'RE NEAR THE BARRIER NOW, RIGHT?
OH NO, I DO NOT THINK THIS IS A GOOD IDEA...

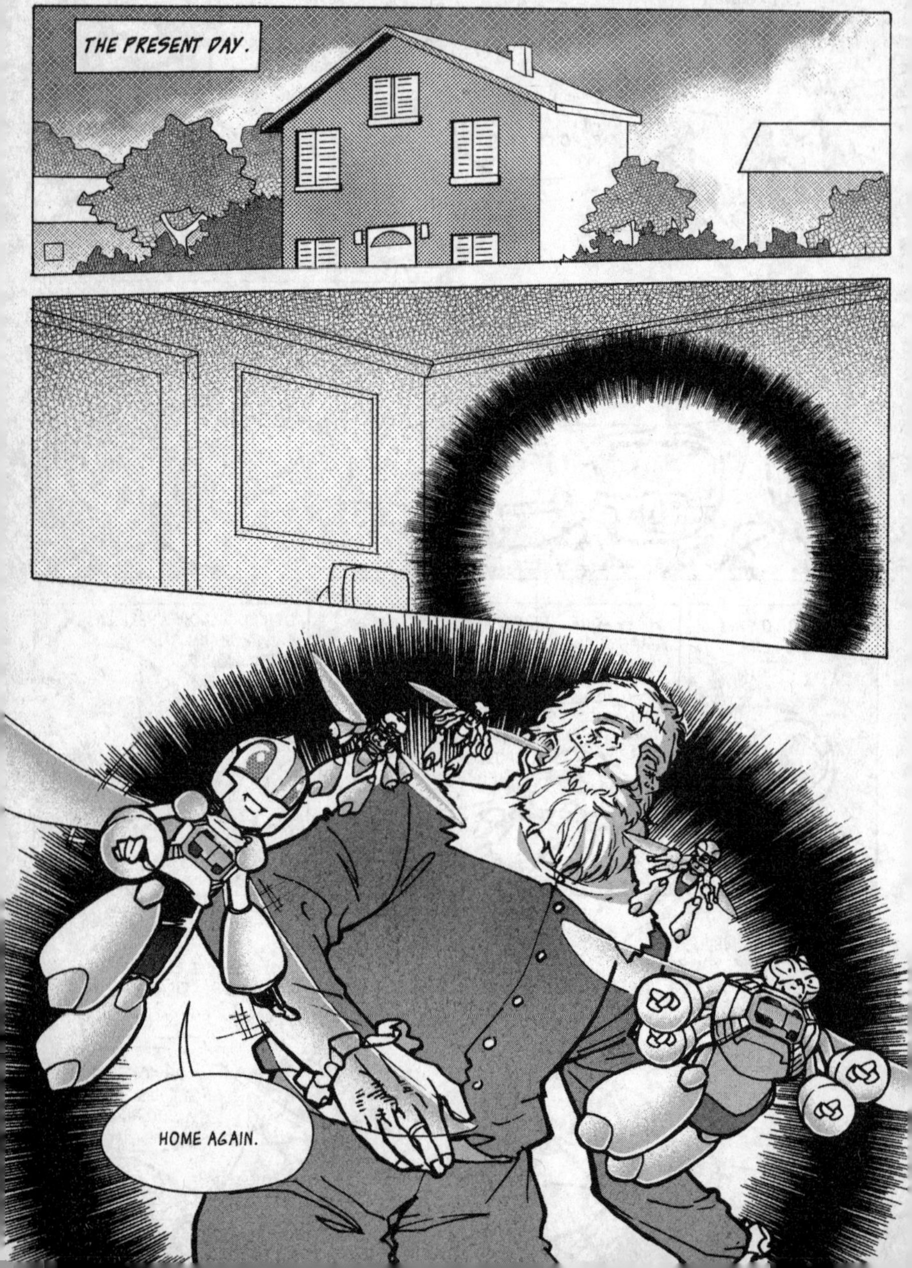
THE PRESENT DAY.
HOME AGAIN.

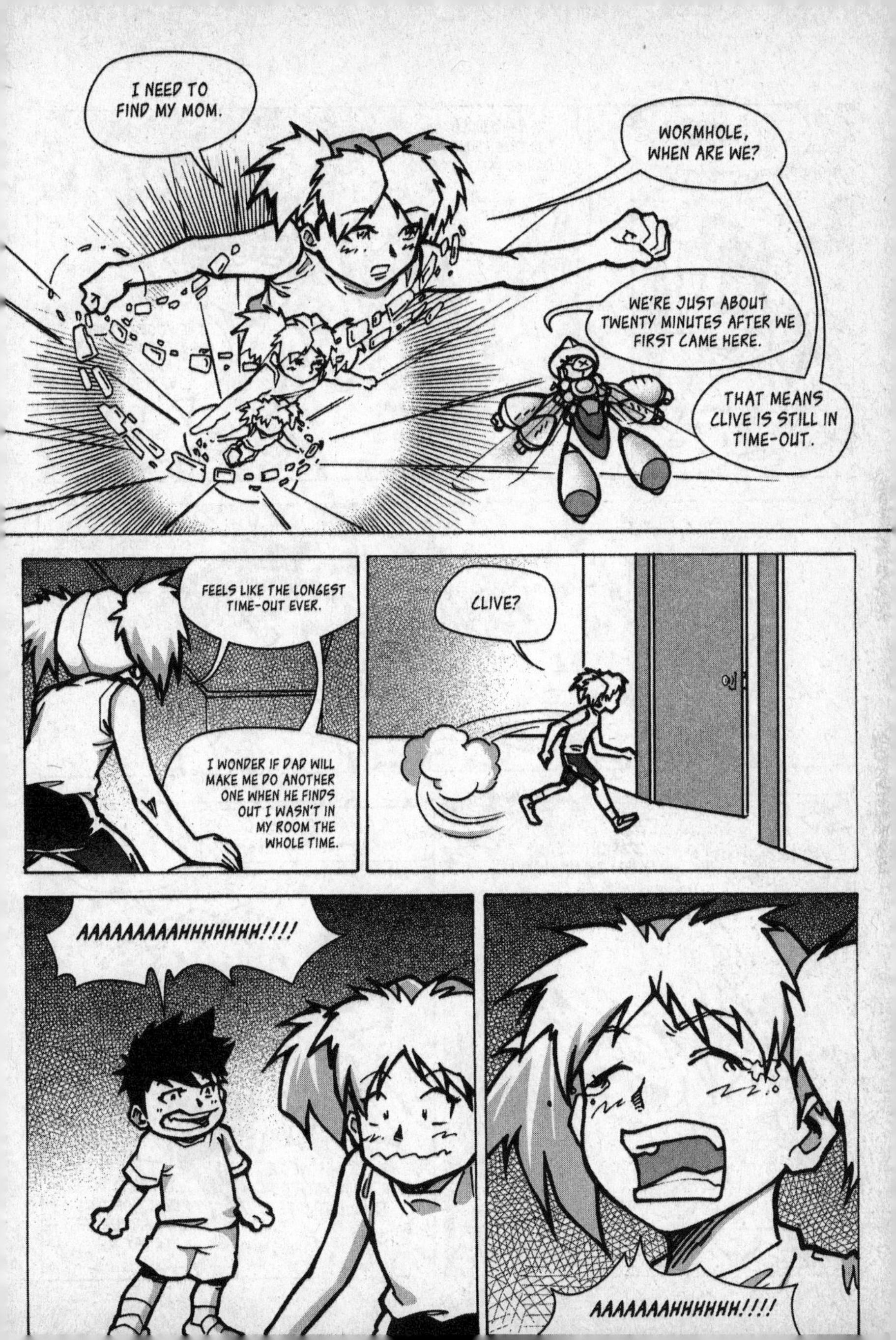
I NEED TO FIND MY MOM.
WORMHOLE, WHEN ARE WE?
WE'RE JUST ABOUT TWENTY MINUTES AFTER WE FIRST CAME HERE.
THAT MEANS CLIVE IS STILL IN TIME-OUT.
FEELS LIKE THE LONGEST TIME-OUT EVER.
I WONDER IF DAD WILL MAKE ME DO ANOTHER ONE WHEN HE FINDS OUT I WASN'T IN MY ROOM THE WHOLE TIME.
CLIVE?
AAAAAAAAAHHHHHHHH!!!!
AAAAAAAHHHHHH!!!!

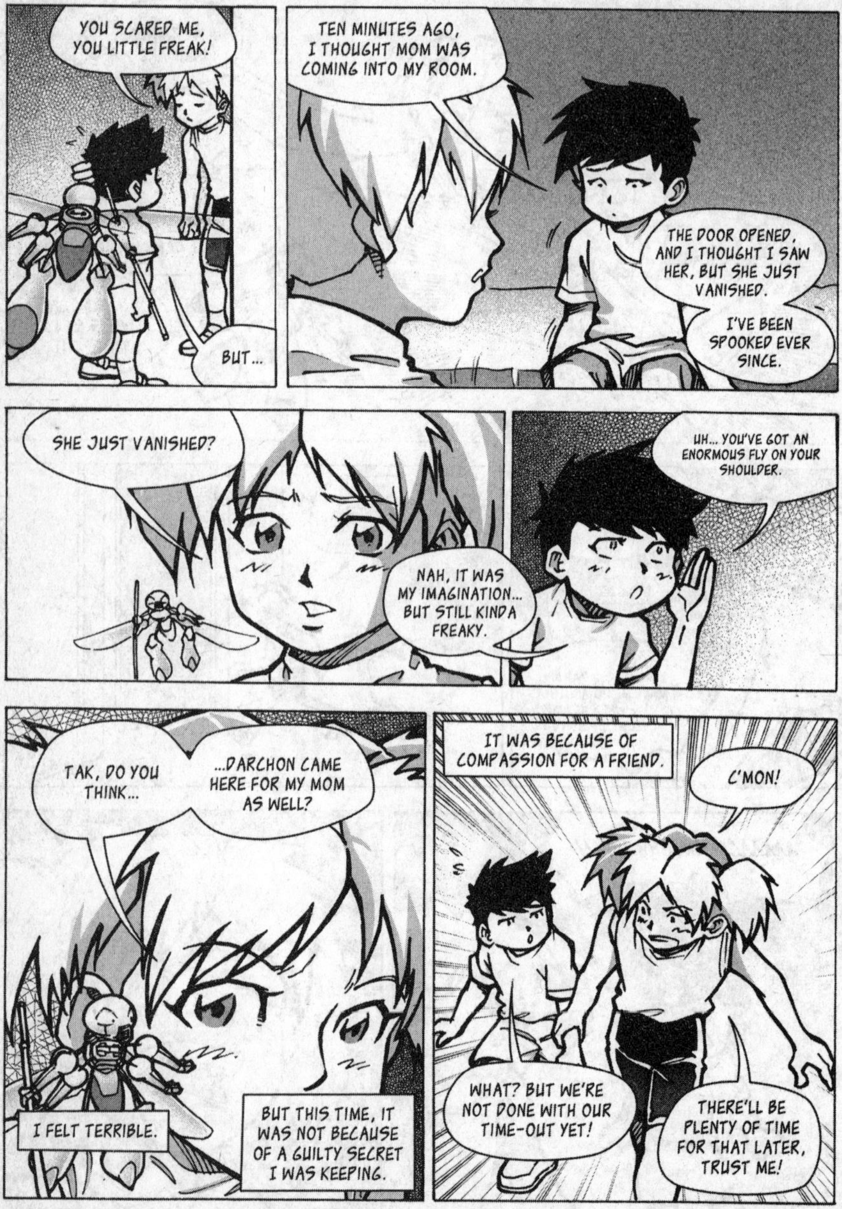
YOU SCARED ME, YOU LITTLE FREAK!
BUT...
TEN MINUTES AGO, I THOUGHT MOM WAS COMING INTO MY ROOM.
THE DOOR OPENED, AND I THOUGHT I SAW HER, BUT SHE JUST VANISHED.
I'VE BEEN SPOOKED EVER SINCE.
SHE JUST VANISHED?
NAH, IT WAS MY IMAGINATION... BUT STILL KINDA FREAKY.
UH... YOU'VE GOT AN ENORMOUS FLY ON YOUR SHOULDER.
TAK, DO YOU THINK...
...DARCHON CAME HERE FOR MY MOM AS WELL?
I FELT TERRIBLE.
BUT THIS TIME, IT WAS NOT BECAUSE OF A GUILTY SECRET I WAS KEEPING.
IT WAS BECAUSE OF COMPASSION FOR A FRIEND.
C'MON!
WHAT? BUT WE'RE NOT DONE WITH OUR TIME-OUT YET!
THERE'LL BE PLENTY OF TIME FOR THAT LATER, TRUST ME!

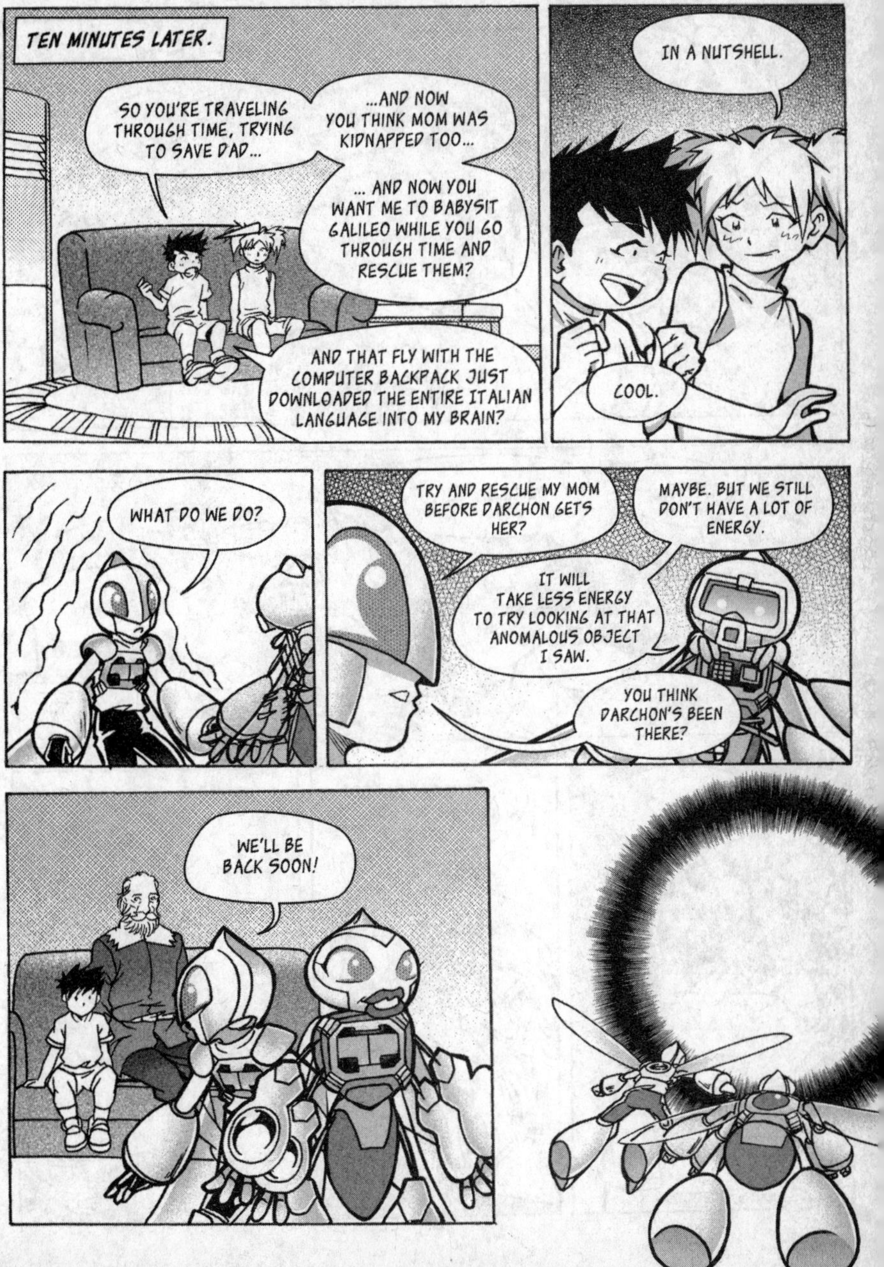

TEN MINUTES LATER.
SO YOU'RE TRAVELING THROUGH TIME, TRYING TO SAVE DAD...
...AND NOW YOU THINK MOM WAS KIDNAPPED TOO...
... AND NOW YOU WANT ME TO BABYSIT GALILEO WHILE YOU GO THROUGH TIME AND RESCUE THEM?
AND THAT FLY WITH THE COMPUTER BACKPACK JUST DOWNLOADED THE ENTIRE ITALIAN LANGUAGE INTO MY BRAIN?
IN A NUTSHELL.
COOL.
WHAT DO WE DO?
TRY AND RESCUE MY MOM BEFORE DARCHON GETS HER?
MAYBE. BUT WE STILL DON'T HAVE A LOT OF ENERGY.
IT WILL TAKE LESS ENERGY TO TRY LOOKING AT THAT ANOMALOUS OBJECT I SAW.
YOU THINK DARCHON'S BEEN THERE?
WE'LL BE BACK SOON!

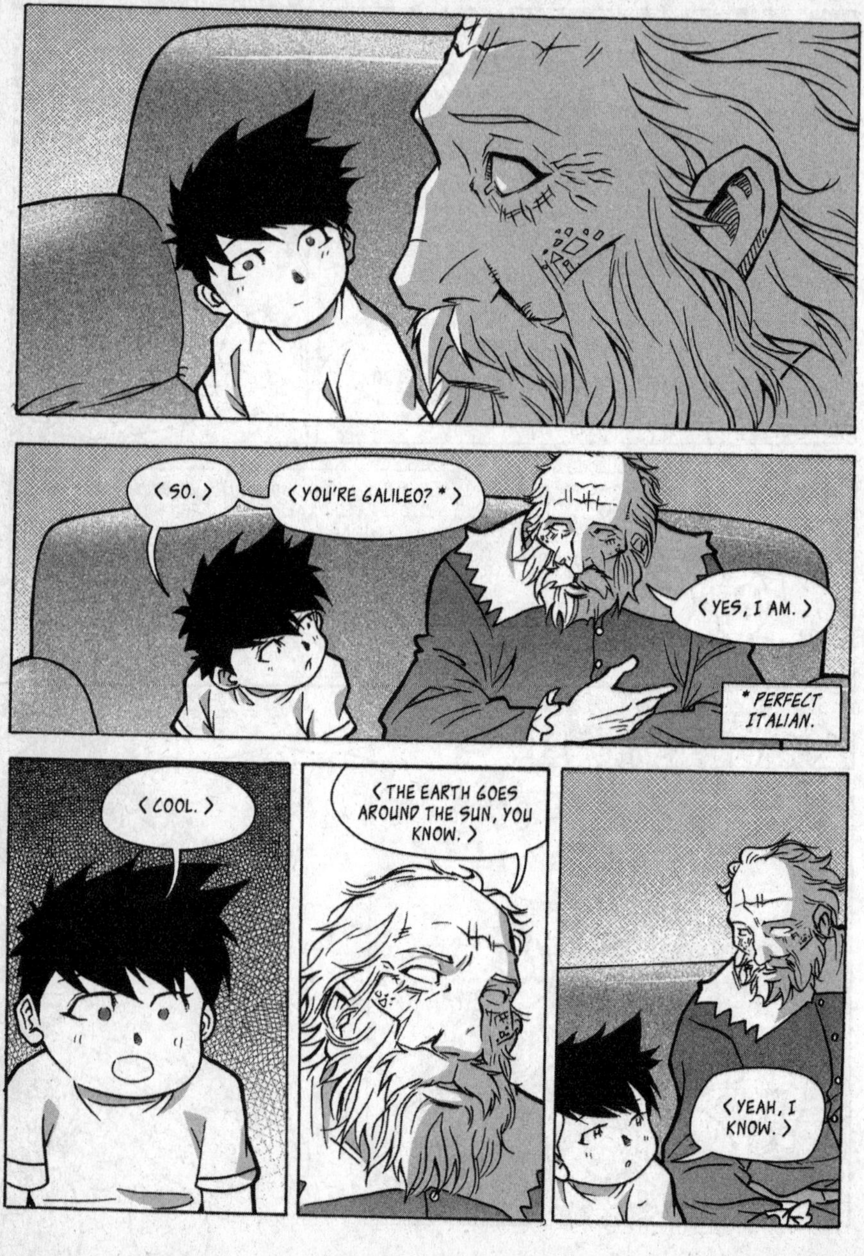

〈 SO. 〉
〈 YOU'RE GALILEO? * 〉
〈 YES, I AM. 〉
* PERFECT ITALIAN.
〈 COOL. 〉
〈 THE EARTH GOES AROUND THE SUN, YOU KNOW. 〉
〈 YEAH, I KNOW. 〉

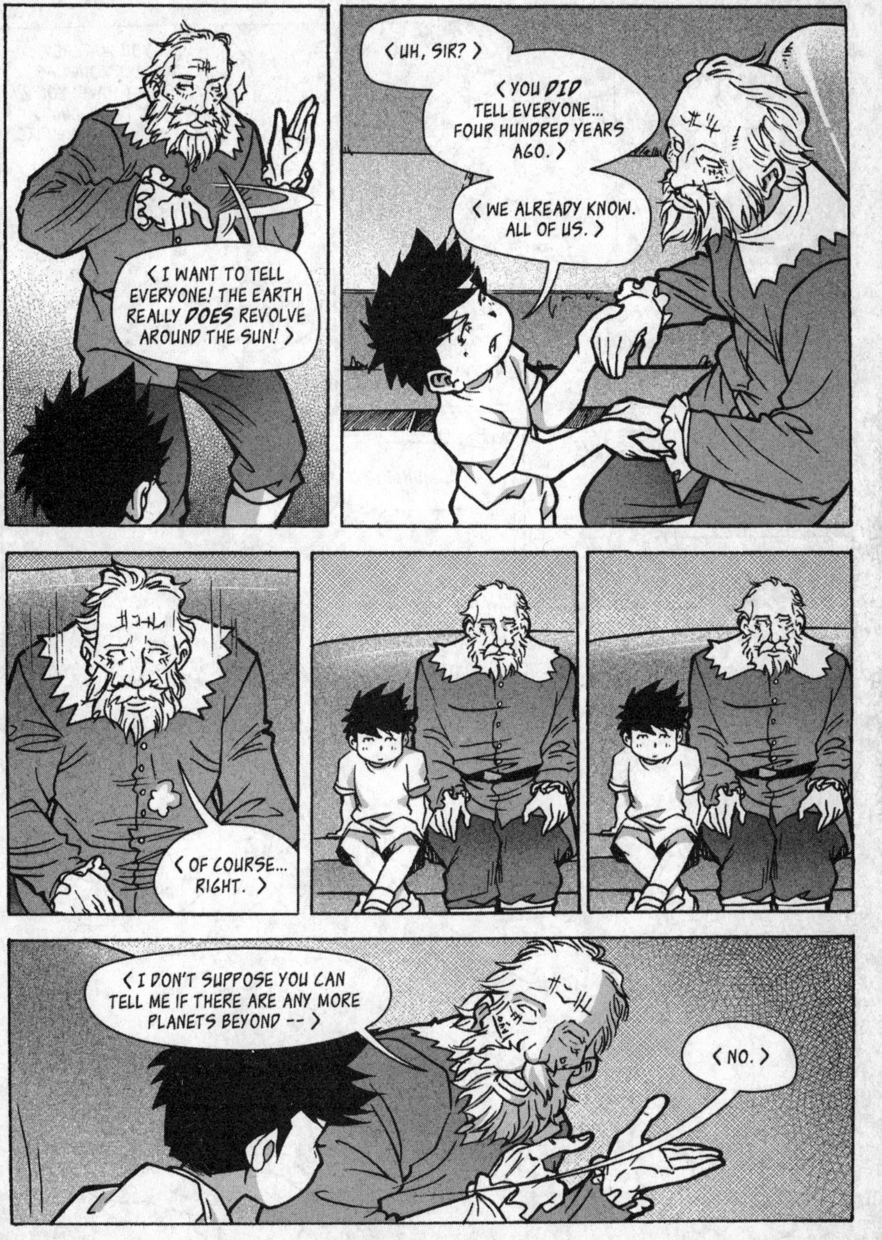
< I WANT TO TELL EVERYONE! THE EARTH REALLY DOES REVOLVE AROUND THE SUN! >
< UH, SIR? >
< YOU DID TELL EVERYONE... FOUR HUNDRED YEARS AGO. >
< WE ALREADY KNOW. ALL OF US. >
< OF COURSE... RIGHT. >
< I DON'T SUPPOSE YOU CAN TELL ME IF THERE ARE ANY MORE PLANETS BEYOND -- >
< NO. >

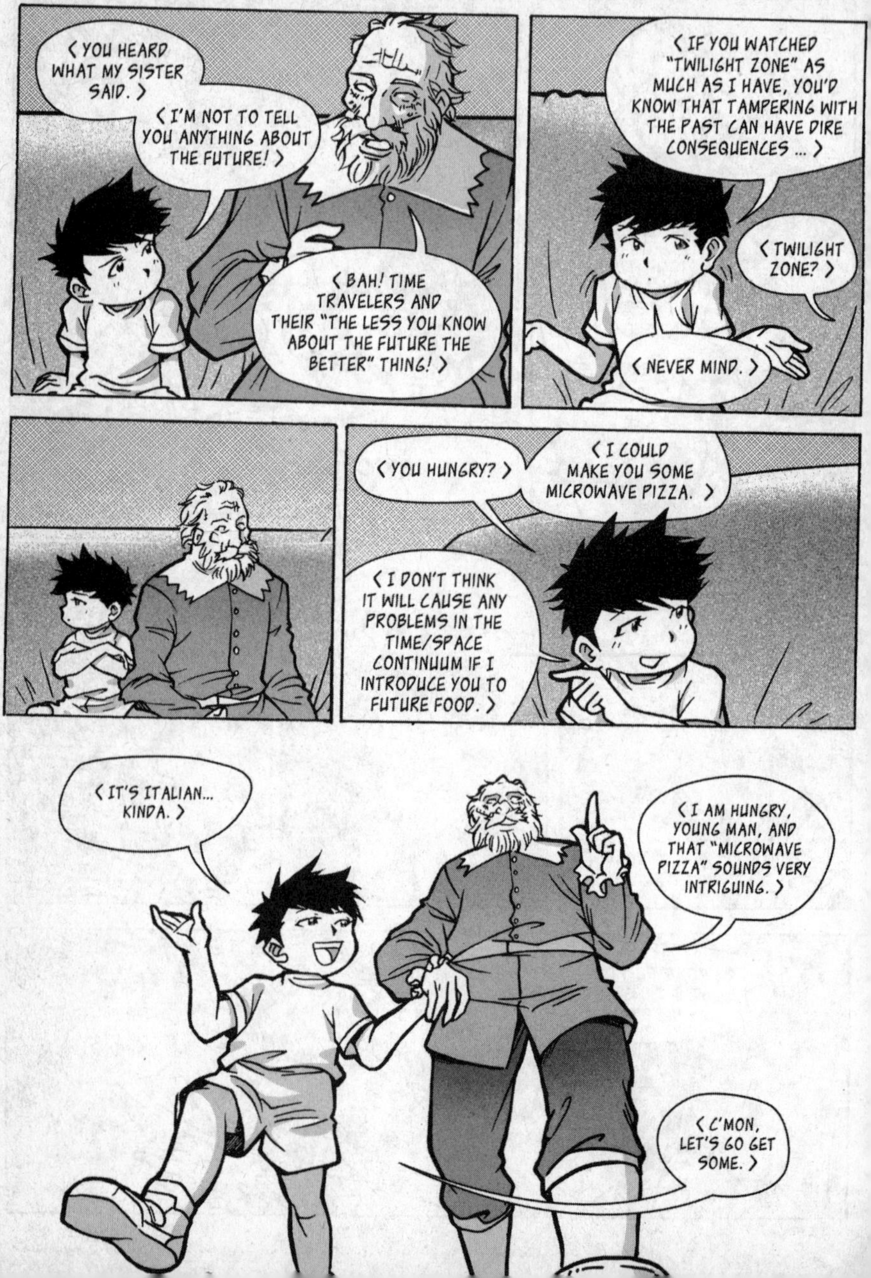

< YOU HEARD WHAT MY SISTER SAID. >
< I'M NOT TO TELL YOU ANYTHING ABOUT THE FUTURE! >
< BAH! TIME TRAVELERS AND THEIR "THE LESS YOU KNOW ABOUT THE FUTURE THE BETTER" THING! >
< IF YOU WATCHED "TWILIGHT ZONE" AS MUCH AS I HAVE, YOU'D KNOW THAT TAMPERING WITH THE PAST CAN HAVE DIRE CONSEQUENCES ... >
< TWILIGHT ZONE? >
< NEVER MIND. >
< YOU HUNGRY? >
< I COULD MAKE YOU SOME MICROWAVE PIZZA. >
< I DON'T THINK IT WILL CAUSE ANY PROBLEMS IN THE TIME/SPACE CONTINUUM IF I INTRODUCE YOU TO FUTURE FOOD. >
< IT'S ITALIAN... KINDA. >
< I AM HUNGRY, YOUNG MAN, AND THAT "MICROWAVE PIZZA" SOUNDS VERY INTRIGUING. >
< C'MON, LET'S GO GET SOME. >

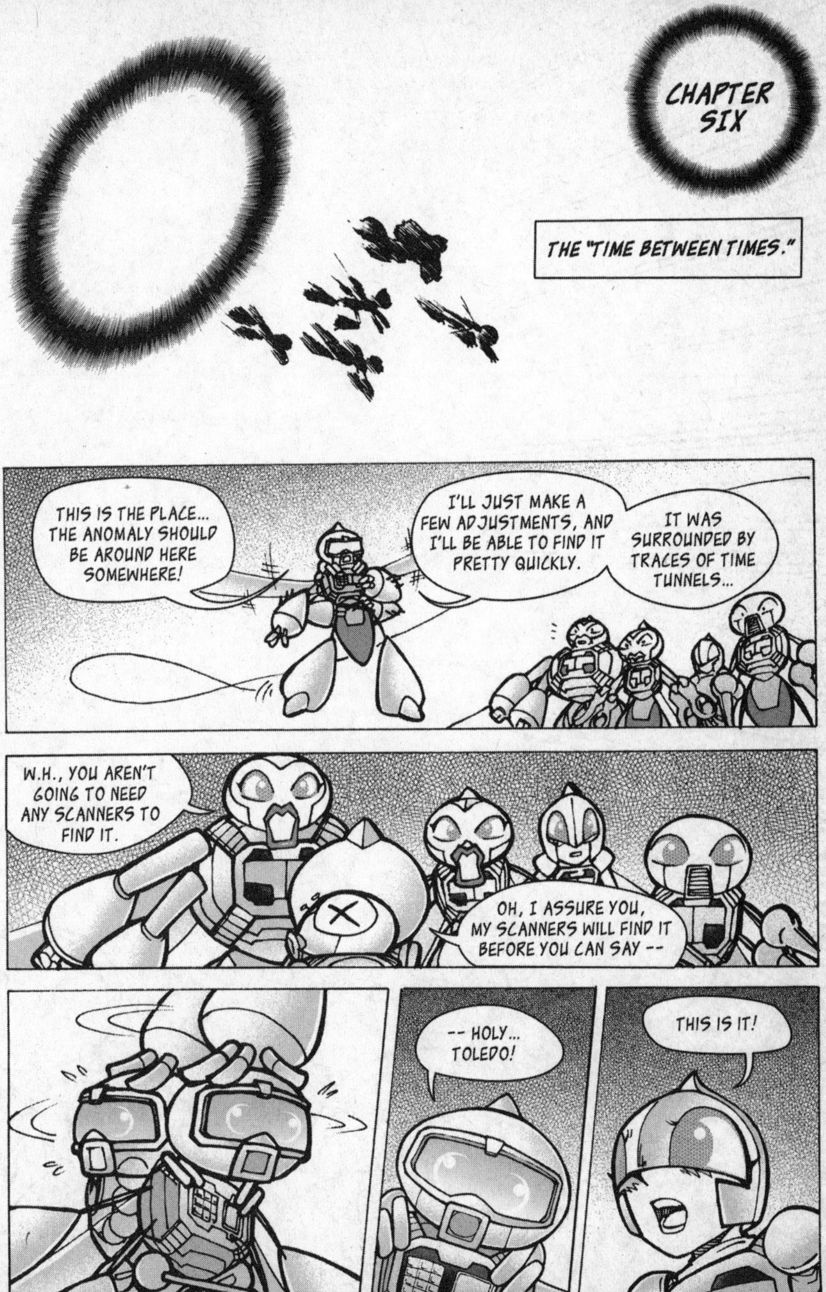
CHAPTER SIX
THE "TIME BETWEEN TIMES."
THIS IS THE PLACE... THE ANOMALY SHOULD BE AROUND HERE SOMEWHERE!
I'LL JUST MAKE A FEW ADJUSTMENTS, AND I'LL BE ABLE TO FIND IT PRETTY QUICKLY.
IT WAS SURROUNDED BY TRACES OF TIME TUNNELS...
W.H., YOU AREN'T GOING TO NEED ANY SCANNERS TO FIND IT.
OH, I ASSURE YOU, MY SCANNERS WILL FIND IT BEFORE YOU CAN SAY --
-- HOLY... TOLEDO!
THIS IS IT!

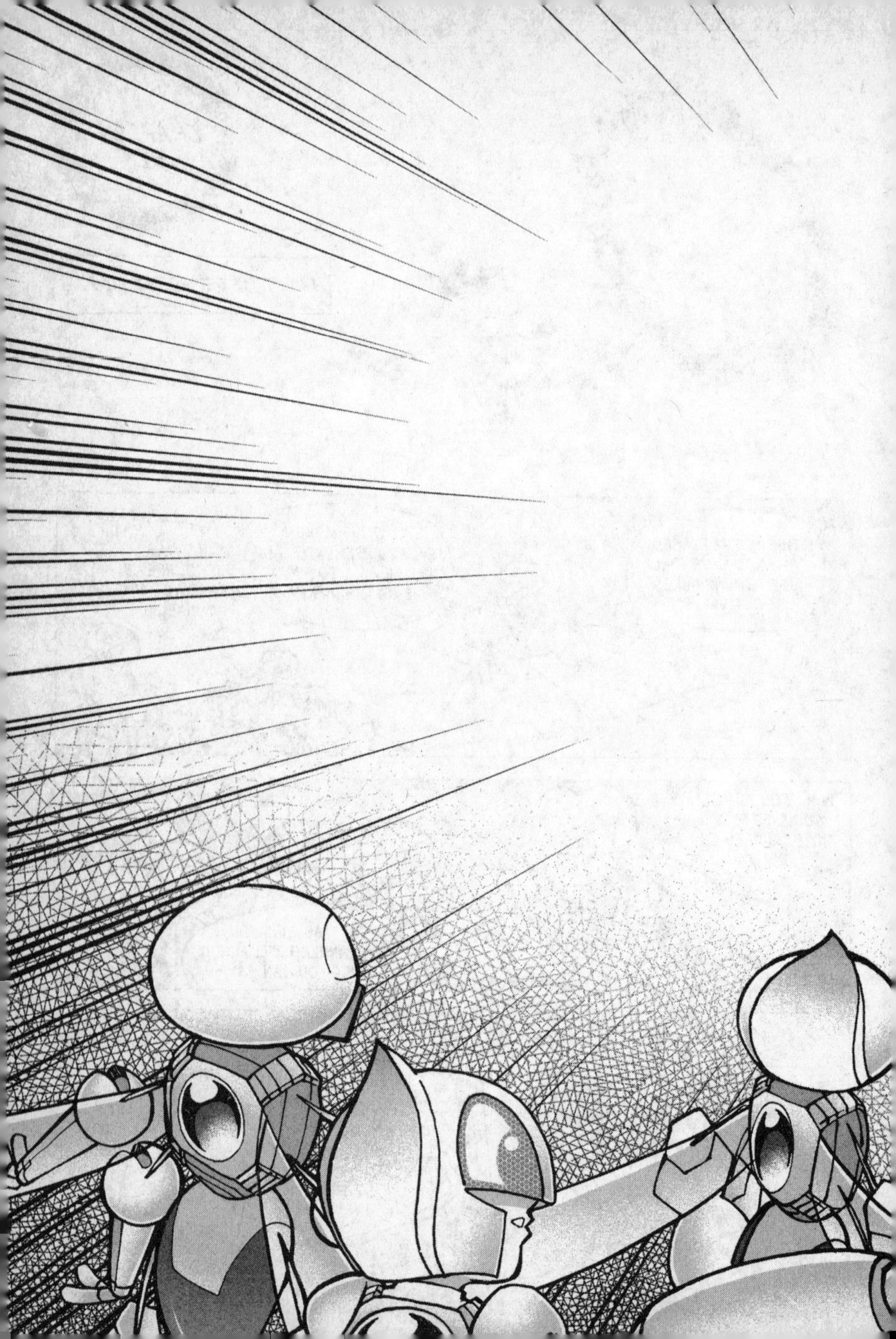

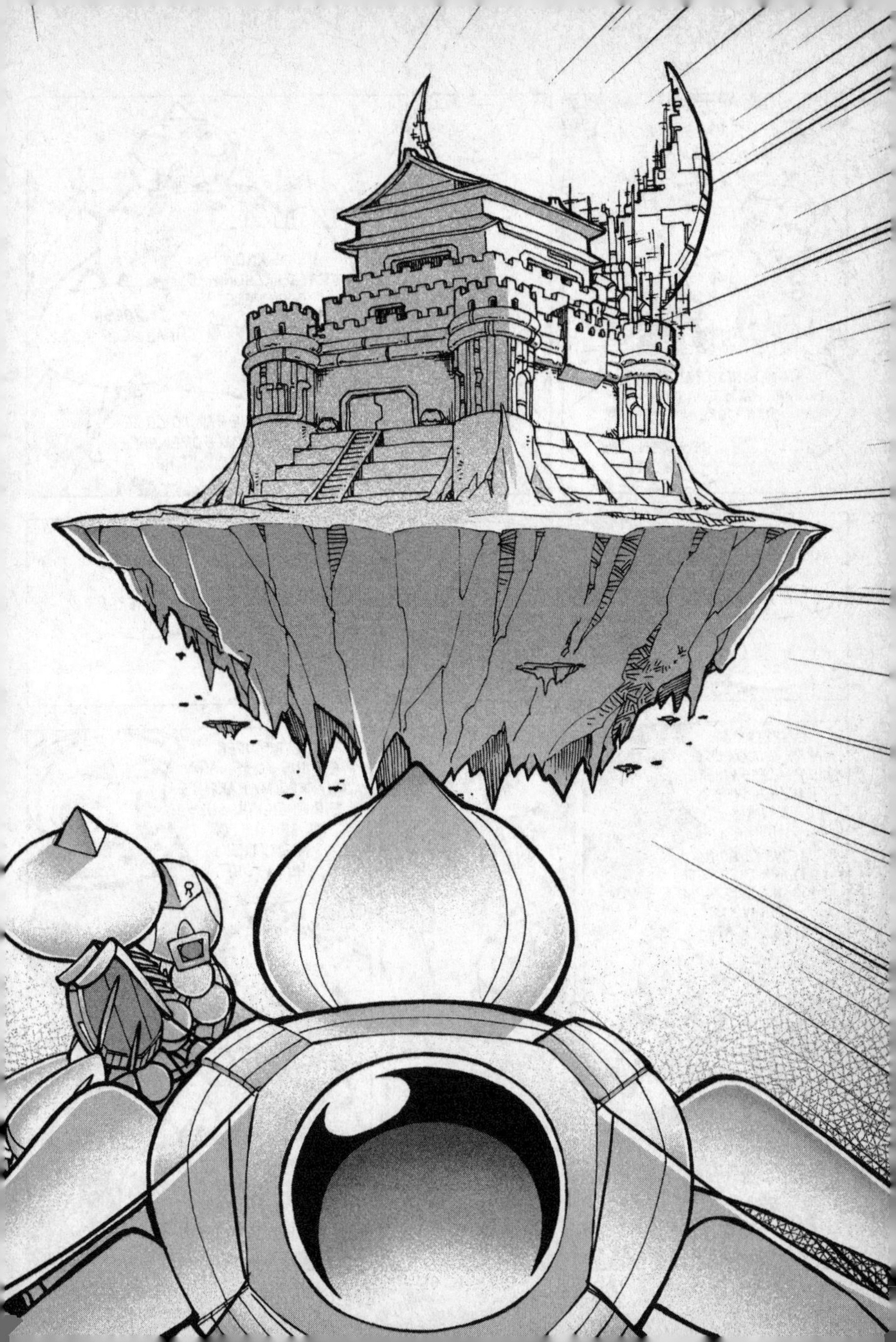

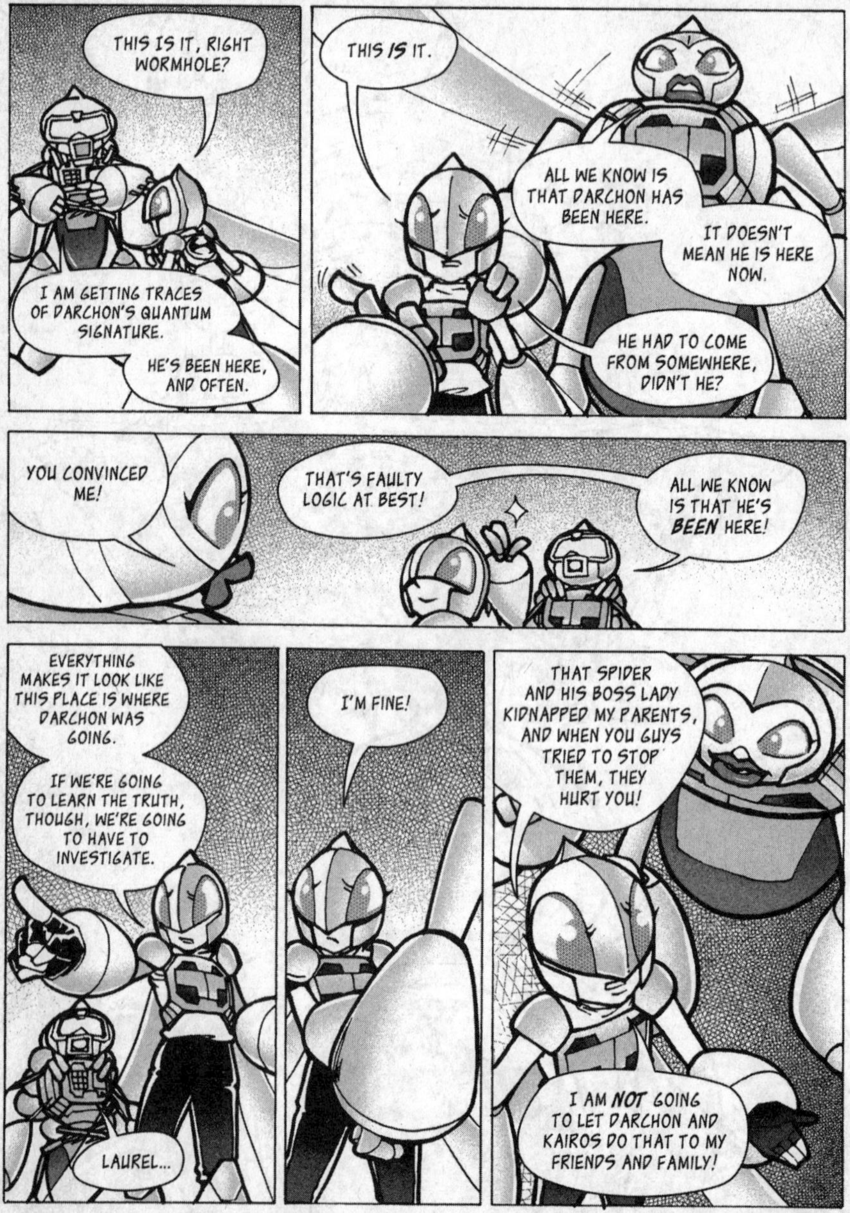
THIS IS IT, RIGHT WORMHOLE?
I AM GETTING TRACES OF DARCHON'S QUANTUM SIGNATURE.
HE'S BEEN HERE, AND OFTEN.
THIS *IS* IT.
ALL WE KNOW IS THAT DARCHON HAS BEEN HERE.
IT DOESN'T MEAN HE IS HERE NOW.
HE HAD TO COME FROM SOMEWHERE, DIDN'T HE?
YOU CONVINCED ME!
THAT'S FAULTY LOGIC AT BEST!
ALL WE KNOW IS THAT HE'S ***BEEN*** HERE!
EVERYTHING MAKES IT LOOK LIKE THIS PLACE IS WHERE DARCHON WAS GOING.
IF WE'RE GOING TO LEARN THE TRUTH, THOUGH, WE'RE GOING TO HAVE TO INVESTIGATE.
LAUREL...
I'M FINE!
THAT SPIDER AND HIS BOSS LADY KIDNAPPED MY PARENTS, AND WHEN YOU GUYS TRIED TO STOP THEM, THEY HURT YOU!
I AM ***NOT*** GOING TO LET DARCHON AND KAIROS DO THAT TO MY FRIENDS AND FAMILY!

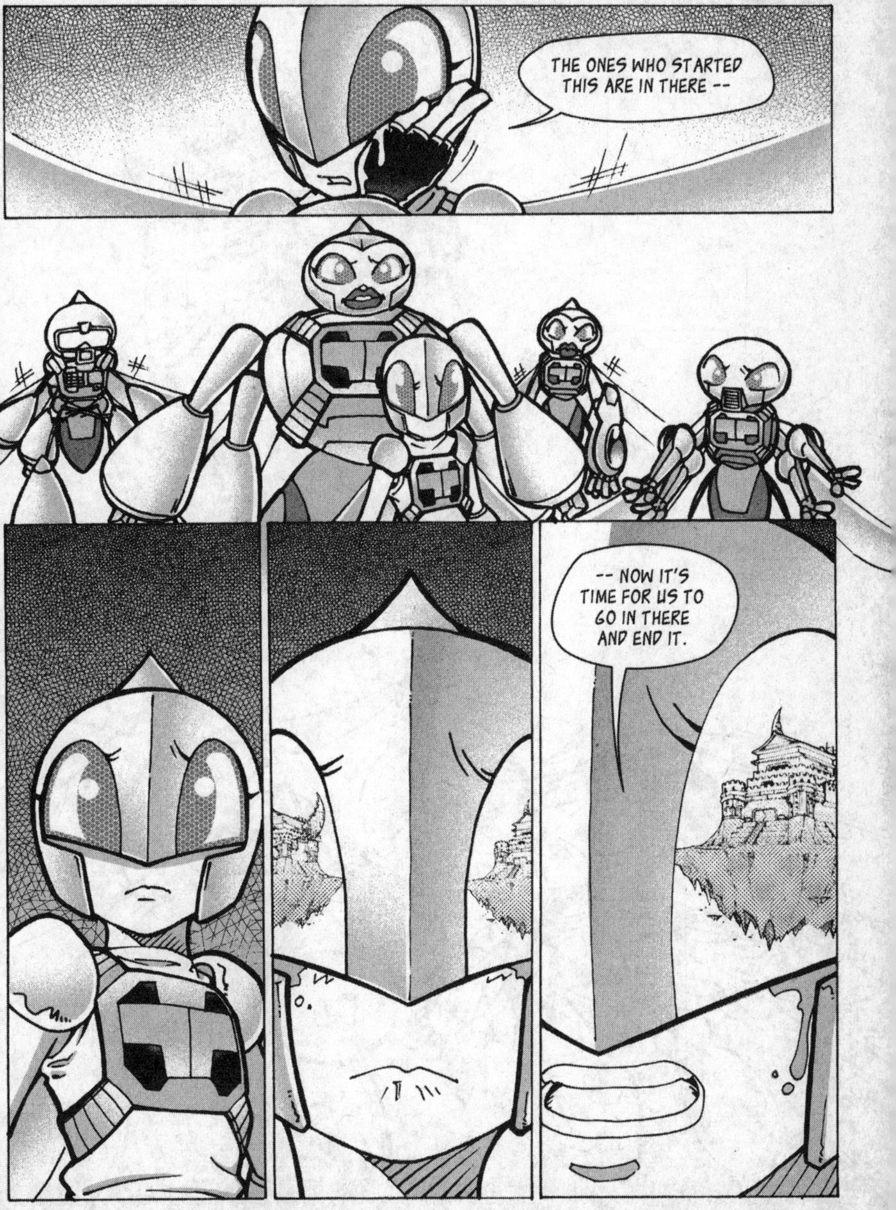
THE ONES WHO STARTED THIS ARE IN THERE --
-- NOW IT'S TIME FOR US TO GO IN THERE AND END IT.

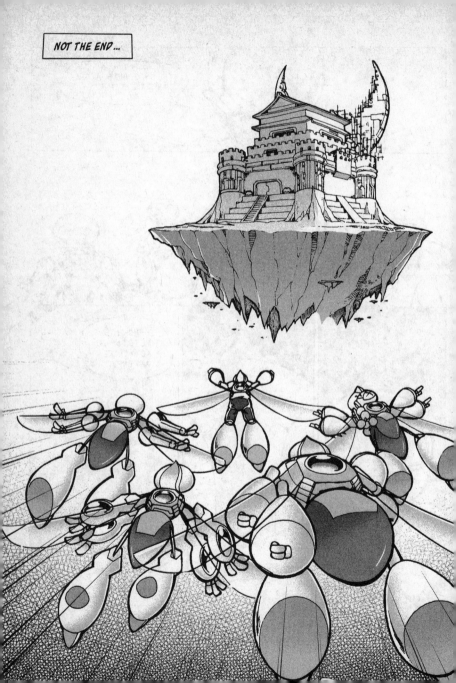

NOT THE END...